A Dream of Italy

Nicky Pellegrino

ORION

An Orion paperback

First published in Great Britain in 2019
by Orion Fiction
This paperback edition published in 2019
by Orion Fiction,
an imprint of The Orion Publishing Group Ltd,
Carmelite House, 50 Victoria Embankment
London EC4Y 0DZ

An Hachette UK company

1 3 5 7 9 10 8 6 4 2

A CIP catalogue record for this book
is available from the British Library.

ISBN 978 1 4091 7898 9

Typeset by Deltatype Ltd, Birkenhead, Merseyside

Printed in Great Britain Clays Ltd, Elcograf S.p.A.

www.orionbooks.co.uk

'Don't live a little, live a lot.'

Alice Hoffman, *The Rules Of Magic*

Montenello

Every morning Salvio Valentini walked the same way. Zigzagging up steep steps, past shuttered buildings with faded 'For Sale' and 'To Rent' signs, not stopping to rest until he reached the small piazza high in the town. There he said his first '*buongiorno*' of the morning to old Francesco Rossi, who spent his days sitting beside the long-dry fountain, trying to sell his few wrinkled apples.

Salvio always bought one and, biting into its soft, sweet flesh, turned and walked the final few metres across the piazza to the Town Hall where he would sit at his desk and work until it was time to eat lunch.

He loved this dilapidated medieval town with its narrow streets, fresh mountain air and views across the valley below. When he had stood as Montenello's mayor he promised to restore the place to its former glory. He would make sure the abandoned buildings didn't crumble to ruins and do his best to see that this didn't become yet another Italian ghost town. Salvio had meant every word but six months later still had no idea how to make it happen. In the meantime, even more of its residents had died or turned their backs on the town.

Clinging to a mountain, Montenello looked impressive from a distance. People passing by often paused to take pictures. But few bothered to drive the final stretch of road to pay a visit and those who did, never stayed for long.

This town didn't have any of the things tourists look for. It wasn't beside the sea; there were no smart shops, fancy bars or historically significant monuments. It was just another hilltop village. And yet it was beautiful and Salvio couldn't bear to see it fade away. Somehow he would save it. He just needed to dream up a clever idea.

At first he thought the wisest plan was to track down those who had left. Hours of sifting through dusty files yielded the names of several owners of abandoned properties and Salvio spent days delving further into the records to find out where some of them had gone. Many had headed for the cities, mostly Rome or Milan. Others had travelled further to places overseas. All were lured away when times were hard, dreaming of a better life. Now Salvio sent out letters and emails trying to tempt them to return.

He crafted those notes with so much hope and care. You still have a home in Montenello and will be welcomed with open arms whenever you return, he wrote, reminding them of the slow pace of life, the fresh breezes and bright sunshine, the food, the wine, the traditions, all the things that made this part of Italy worth coming back to. 'Our quality of life is second to none,' he promised.

Some didn't bother to reply. If they did write it was to say they weren't interested, they had finished with Montenello and weren't going to pay any property taxes they might owe either. A few were brusque, others composed lengthy emails, but the message was the same. We don't want the house any more. It is nothing but a burden. As far as we're concerned the *comune* can keep it.

'This is crazy. Imagine giving up a house,' Salvio said to his assistant Augusto who had shuffled across and was peering over his shoulder at the latest email.

Augusto was so ancient that if ever he didn't appear at work in the morning everyone feared the worst. He was a frail, bony man but his mind was sharp and he remembered so much about Montenello's past.

'These people feel as if they escaped, they don't want to be reminded of what they used to be when they were poor,' he told Salvio. 'What we need here now is new blood, foreigners

2

who think a crumbling Italian building is romantic. Find them and Montenello's problems are solved.'

'You are suggesting we should rent out the empty houses to tourists?'

'Absolutely no.' Augusto looked horrified. 'Then they would be the *comune*'s responsibility and there aren't the funds to restore them properly. If the owners don't want these places then we must sell them to people who do.'

Salvio considered the idea. More than anything he wanted to be the one to halt this town's decline. If he could help it flourish again, fill it with people and life, he would feel as if he had achieved something truly worthwhile. Glancing out of the window down at the windswept piazza empty aside from the old apple seller, he thought anything was worth a try.

'OK,' he agreed. 'If we get these some of these families to legally sign their houses over to us then I suppose we have every right to sell them on to whoever we like.'

'Of course,' said Augusto, dusting his hands together as if all was decided. 'Foreigners with money will come, they will renovate Montenello for us, and our problems will be solved, just like I said.'

'How much will people pay for these properties?' Salvio was dubious. 'Some are close to being ruins. They are worth almost nothing.'

'Almost nothing is what we should ask for them,' said Augusto, crisply.

'And where will we find potential buyers?' Salvio ran a restless hand through his thick, dark hair; he could see so many problems. 'How will we reach them?'

Augusto shuffled back across the room and sat down at the desk that housed the shiny new computer he had taught himself to use with only a minimum of frustrated muttering beneath his breath.

'That is very easy, we will use my Internet.' He threw his

arms wide and beamed as if he had invented the whole thing himself. 'We will make an advertisement.'

Live your dream of Italy.
Here is your chance to buy your own home in south-ern Italy for less than the price of a cup of coffee. The picturesque mountain town of Montenello is selling off some of its historic buildings for just ONE EURO each. The only conditions are that purchasers must renovate their new home within the next three years and that they plan to contribute in a meaningful way to this small and friendly community.

To be considered as a future resident of Montenello contact the town's mayor, Salvio Valentini. Live your dream of Italy for just one euro.

Mimi

The Silver Divorcees met on the second Wednesday of every month. There were times Mimi felt as if the only thing keeping her going was the prospect of gathering in some cheap and cheerful restaurant and drinking too much wine as all of them talked at once. The few occasions over the past couple of years that she could recall laughing properly were her Silver Divorcee evenings.

Despite the name not one of them had silver hair. All were tended to regularly by skilful colourists, a couple were Botoxed, and at least one was keeping a cosmetic surgeon busy. Still, they were a social phenomenon, apparently, part of a rising tide of middle-aged couples deciding to divorce after decades of putting up with one another.

'These are the new freedom years,' Mimi's closest friend Sinead declared. 'The kids have left home, we're financially secure and we don't have to deal with anyone's dropped socks. This is our time and we're not going to spend it cleaning up after other people.'

Mimi wasn't especially buoyed by those remarks. Her friend's situation was entirely different to hers. Sinead was the one who had walked away from her marriage, striking out for freedom and independence, determined she wasn't going to spend another minute with the nice but dull man who had been by her side for the past thirty years.

'Fuck that,' Sinead said (she swore more now she was divorced). 'Perhaps the two of us had something in common once but we don't any more. I want my life back.'

Mimi, on the other hand, had been happily married; at

5

least, she had thought so. With their two sons gone to university, she and Glenn had been making plans to move out of London and build their dream house somewhere leafy and green. Glenn had seemed as enthusiastic about the idea as she was. They used to sit together watching *Grand Designs* and talk about how they might manage something similar. So when Glenn told her he had rented an apartment because their relationship had run its course and it was time for a fresh start, Mimi had been rocked.

He refused couple's counselling and only offered her clichés. He still loved Mimi but he wasn't in love with her. He needed some space. He wanted a new life.

And so her husband moved out, and Mimi was left behind in their old life, alone in the family house surrounded by all their shared stuff. She spent a lot of time rearranging things, trying to make the place seem more her own. Buying a new bed, shifting the sofas, painting a feature wall and filling the living room with plants – none of it helped much.

'Just sell the house, settle up with him and move on,' Sinead urged her.

Mimi could see the sense in this advice but not how to follow it. 'Move on where?'

'Your work isn't keeping you in London, is it? You could go absolutely anywhere.'

'That's the problem,' Mimi said.

Sinead was an incurable solver of other people's problems. 'Go and live in a little village somewhere just like you were planning to before the break-up,' she advised.

'Which village, though? I can't just stick a pin into a map.'

'I don't see why not. It doesn't really matter which place you choose. You need to make a move. You're stuck.'

'I am aware of that.' Mimi squinted in the bright light of the ladies' toilets as she reapplied her perfect pinky-brown lipstick. She was sure Sinead had followed her in on purpose, determined to have this conversation. She was standing right beside Mimi now, talking at her reflection in the mirror.

'Un-stick yourself,' she counselled, 'and do it sooner rather later. You've never been this indecisive before, have you?'

'No, but I always had a vision of what I wanted in life.' Mimi slipped the lipstick back in her bag and gave her short, fair hair a quick fluff with her fingers. 'I saw myself being married, having a family, working as an illustrator. I saw Glenn and me going on long walks and eating Sunday lunch in country pubs. All of a sudden the vision has disappeared completely, it's like the screen's gone blank. I can't see a way forward any more.'

Sinead stared at her, bereft of advice, temporarily at least.

'Another glass of wine and some food, that's as far ahead as I want to look right now,' said Mimi, quickly. 'Come on, or the others will think we've abandoned them.'

They were at an Italian restaurant favoured by the Silver Divorcees mainly for its bring-your-own-booze Tuesdays. Mimi enjoyed the food, always ordering the pizza with burrata because she loved to slice into the soft cheese and watch its creamy centre oozing over the crisp, charred dough. She was the only one among the Silver Divorcees still eating carbs and saturated fat, but then all the others were dating; they were on Tinder or signed up with elite matchmaking agencies.

That was what they were discussing when Mimi and Sinead made it back to the table, shrieking with laughter at stories of Tinder encounters gone wrong.

'So when I woke in the night, I thought he was stroking my shoulder,' Jayne was saying now. 'Then I turned over and it was actually this huge, hairy dog which had wriggled into bed between us and was drooling on my pillow. I could not make the thing move. In the end I got up, left a note to say I was a cat person, and went home.'

Sinead jumped into the conversation. 'The dog wasn't actually in the room when you were ...'

7

'Yes! It was lying on the rug, staring at us and panting. I kept catching its eye. It was really off-putting.'

'Oh my God, that reminds me of the time I was dating the guy who had these Burmese cats ...'

Mimi listened to their voices growing louder. She never had similar stories to share. She had been with Glenn for thirty years. It was impossible to imagine herself with anyone else.

'Men ... I really don't know why we bother.' Someone trotted out that line almost every time the Silver Divorcees met up; tonight it was Jayne, shaking her head in dismay. 'All of us should buy a big house, move in together, and give up on them altogether.'

'You're right, we probably should,' agreed Sinead.

'Count me in,' said Mimi. 'It sounds like a great idea.'

'Me too,' added Dottie.

'Why don't we stop talking about this and actually do it?' said Sinead, leaning forward, arms crossed. The Silver Divorcees had been her idea in the first place and she thought of herself as the group's leader. 'Let's pitch in and buy a holiday villa, the four of us. Seriously, I mean it.'

'Nice idea but I can't afford it,' said Jayne.

'What if it hardly costs us anything? Hang on a minute, I saw this ad on Facebook.' Sinead rummaged for her phone and started jabbing at the screen. 'Here we go, this is it: Live Your Dream of Italy.'

She read the advertisement aloud with extra emphasis on the words, 'just one euro'.

'Sounds too good to be true; there must be a catch,' said Jayne.

'Not necessarily,' Dottie countered. 'I'm pretty sure I read an article about that in the *Telegraph*. The ad's gone viral and they interviewed the mayor of the town..'

'Salvio Valentini,' said Sinead, reading from the screen again.

and things left unsaid. This time Gino was hurt and Edward sorry, but it didn't change the way he felt, like he was buried alive in his own existence.

For a while they carried on as if nothing had been said. Edward spent his days in the spare room they had turned into his office, writing articles for newspapers and magazines, and dull content for company websites. Gino went to his studio where he worked long hours custom-making furniture from recycled timber. On Saturdays they walked the coastal trail from Bondi to Coogee or had friends over for a barbecue. On Sundays they swam lengths in the ocean pool. They visited the same places, and saw the same people. Edward tried, he really did, until he couldn't try any longer.

They were having Sunday lunch with Gino's family. Edward always enjoyed these occasions. They were chaotic and noisy, with too much food and too many children. This time they were gathered for a picnic in the Botanic Gardens and Gino's father was being querulous. It was too cold in the shade and too hot in the sunshine. The peperonata was overcooked, the pasta al forno too dry, the meatballs needed oregano. It had been over fifty years since he had immigrated to Australia but his accent was so thickly Italian and his chatter so rapid that often Edward struggled to understand him.

'He does that on purpose. The old man hates you,' Gino said, darkly.

'No, he doesn't.'

'Yeah, really he does.'

It was true it had been tricky for a while when they first got together. Gino hadn't even come out to his family at that point, although Edward thought his older sisters must have guessed. So there was this big drama, with his father declaring his only son dead to him, and his mother crying a lot. Edward had known they would come round eventually. They were old-fashioned people and very devout Catholics, so of course they needed time to adjust to the idea. He was OK with that.

It was fine now, although they were still careful when Gino's parents were around. They kept their distance from each other, no kissing, no touching at all, nothing that gave them away as a couple. Edward had never really resented that. It was only for Sunday lunches and the odd dinner, so it wasn't going to kill them.

Gino struggled though. Even on this sunny day, with the harbour glittering and the Prosecco chilling, Edward could sense he was slightly on edge.

They had spread picnic rugs on the grass and the kids played a rowdy game of football before being defeated by the heat and flopping down beside them demanding lemonade. Edward was sitting surrounded by Gino's sisters. There were four of them, all dark-eyed, dark-haired and so meticulously groomed that hanging out with them felt like being in a Dolce & Gabbana advert.

Tia was the youngest, the only sister not to have married or had children yet, and Edward's best friend. At least once a week they met for a cocktail or a walk on the beach without Gino, who had always been slightly mystified by the close relationship between them.

Often strangers thought they were a couple, which Edward found amusing and liked to play up to. He would rest an arm round across her shoulders or brush her dark curls from her face. 'We'd have beautiful babies,' he would tease as Tia shook her head and laughed.

She was the person he had come closest to confiding in, but he held back, out of loyalty to Gino, perhaps, or because he was still struggling to put his feelings into words. Edward had so much – great friends, a beautiful home, enough money – everything he needed. He was ashamed of wanting more.

Still, Tia must have noticed there was something off-kilter.

12

'You're very quiet today,' she remarked, as he was finishing his pasta. 'Is everything OK?'

He looked up from his plate. 'Yeah, of course.'

'Are you sure?'

'Oh, I'm feeling a bit over everything right now,' he admitted. 'Probably could do with a holiday.'

'You guys haven't been on one of your,' she lowered her voice, 'gay cruises for ages, have you?'

For a while they had taken lots of those cruises and it seemed the perfect holiday: Gino loved making their stateroom a home away from home; Edward liked waking up somewhere new each day; both of them enjoyed the non-stop partying.

'You can only do so many of them and I've reached my limit,' he told Tia.

'Time for something different then?'

'I think so, but ...' He looked towards Gino and widened his eyes.

'No so keen?'

Edward shook his head. 'Sydney's a beautiful city so why do we have to keep leaving it?' he said, flatly.

'Ah right, I see.'

He stared at the iconic view: the Opera House, the arch of the bridge beyond it and the ferries ploughing through the wide harbour. Dropping his voice to an almost-whisper, Edward let the words come out.

'I don't know if he and I have got anything in common any more.'

The expression on Tia's face flickered from dismay to something else – determination? As her mother murmured about dishing out the tiramisu, she patted her taut stomach and complained about being much too full to manage another thing.

'I need a walk to digest all that pasta,' Tia declared. 'Edward, stop eating and come with me.'

They headed towards Mrs Macquarie's Chair at a stroll because the afternoon heat was building and there was a lot they needed to say.

'What's wrong with me?' Edward asked her. 'I have a good life so why am I feeling like this?'

She took his hand and squeezed it. 'You still care for Gino, though?'

'Yes, of course, he's my family ... you're my family. I can't imagine life without either of you. But then I think about the future – the same routines, the same life, nothing changing except us all getting older – and I start to panic.'

'Have you said all that to Gino? How does he feel?'

'It's not a conversation we can have. He gets upset; he thinks I'm criticising him. And perhaps I am, indirectly at least. Should it be such a huge surprise if we're growing apart? We were so young when we got together, almost kids, really. I still had all my hair, for God's sake. That's how long ago it was.'

Tia smiled. 'I remember – such a pretty blond boy and the two of you ridiculously in love while my parents were freaking out.'

'You were a child back then. I'm surprised it made such an impression on you.'

'I could tell what you had together was special. It still is; I'm sure of that.'

'I love him, but ...' Edward shrugged, miserably. 'I'm not so certain that's enough any more.'

Tia pulled him to a stop beside the sandstone rocks. 'Don't give up what you've got. I'd give anything to have that kind of love, really I would. It's not easy to find.'

Edward was surprised. She had never said anything like that to him before. He knew there were guys in Tia's life; she often went out on dates, but no one seemed to hold her interest for long and Edward always assumed she wasn't in any hurry to settle down.

'Tia, do you want—?'

She tugged at his arm again, sharply this time. 'Listen to me. You can shake Gino out of his rut. Do something crazy and impulsive. Book a trip, make him go skydiving, sell your apartment: I don't know exactly, just make sure you give yourselves the best chance you can. Promise me that.'

Tia was so beautiful, with her dark hair drifting over her shoulders and her skin gilded by sunshine. Surely she could have any guy she wanted?

'There aren't many men like Gino around, I can promise you that,' she said, softly.

'OK then,' Edward agreed. 'There's no way I'll get him to jump out of a plane but maybe we can take a trip somewhere. I'll think about it.'

'Thank you.' Linking her arm through his, Tia leaned against him. 'For a moment there I thought you were going to break all our hearts.'

They turned and started walking back. The tiramisu would be waiting and Gino's father growing fractious again. As they drew closer, Edward saw the old man, sitting on a fold-out chair, holding forth about something. Some day Gino would look exactly like that. His jaw would soften and his hair grow snowy, and his manner become more imperious. Edward couldn't help wondering if he would still be around to see it.

Do something crazy; shake him out of his rut. It was easy to say but harder to make happen. Edward would have to think about it.

Weekday life went on as usual, Edward at his desk trying not to distract himself by checking into social media or reading long articles in the *New York Times*. From time to time he thought of Tia's advice but didn't make a move to do anything about it.

He began seeing the advertisement everywhere he looked.

Three friends shared it on Facebook, it cropped up on Twitter, there was even an article about it in a newspaper he glanced at in a cafe where he was grabbing a coffee.

'*Live your dream of Italy*,' it kept nagging him. Apparently, in some town called Montenello they were giving away houses. The name seemed very familiar and Edward tried to recall if this was the place that Gino's parents had come from originally. Yes, he thought it might be.

Edward found himself entertaining wild ideas. Spend one euro on a house and go to Montenello to visit it, maybe even do the place up. He gave the fantasy free rein. Then he started considering the idea seriously. Perhaps this was the 'something crazy' he was looking for. After all, they enjoyed renovating and Gino had grown up speaking Italian at home, so it wasn't beyond the bounds of possibility. And what if this actually was his parents' home town? If it didn't work out, what had they lost? Nothing at all, really.

He sent off the email without mentioning it to Gino. Almost certainly there would be thousands of applications and his wasn't in with a chance. But Edward thought it was worth a go. Besides, he had to try something.

Elise

It had got to the point where Elise almost ran past estate agents' windows. She skipped over property pages in newspapers and never picked up interiors magazines because she couldn't handle how envious she felt of all those people who had their own homes and filled them with beautiful things.

It didn't matter how hard she and Richard saved, she was sure they would never have enough money for a deposit on a place. Prices in Bristol kept climbing and just day-to-day life was so expensive. All that money Richard had needed to spend on his car recently, and Elise still paying off her student loan. No wonder they couldn't get ahead.

The flat they lived in was tiny and always smelled of curry. There were two Indian restaurants below and Elise often noticed people standing outside, peering at the menus and trying to decide between them. She knew it didn't matter which choice they made. Looking down from the window of their flat, she could see how the two places shared one huge kitchen. All those vats of butter chicken and dhal, bubbling away, filling their rooms with the scent of spices, which had seemed exotic when they first moved in and everything was new and exciting but now, almost three years later, just made Elise feel faintly nauseous all the time.

'We've got to get out of here,' said Richard, who hadn't liked curry much in the first place. 'What if we get evening jobs in a bar or something?'

'How much do you think that would pay?' asked Elise, willing to crunch more numbers even though she was sure they would never add up to what was needed.

They had stopped buying takeaway coffees, shopped for groceries at Aldi and almost never went to the pub any more. Richard was already working weekends, helping his dad who was a builder. During the week he taught at a primary school in Hotwells. He had been lucky to get that position. Elise was doing maternity cover at a private girls' school and wasn't sure where she would go once it was over.

'Maybe we should give up and spend what we've managed to save on an amazing holiday,' she suggested.

'It's not a completely stupid idea,' Richard conceded. 'So where would we go?'

This was a favourite fantasy. They would huddle round Elise's laptop looking at tropical islands in the Pacific, walking trails in South America and adventures on the Mongolian steppe.

'What's the food like there?' Richard would ask. 'Do they have much of a problem with mosquitoes?'

Elise always got tired of the game before he did. She would start to wonder where the people who took all these holidays got their money from and how she had gone so wrong. She had worked hard, got good A levels and outstanding grades at college, done charity work, played sport and developed creative hobbies (because everyone said to succeed you had to be a well-rounded person). And where was the reward? There was no sign their life would ever stop being such a struggle.

'Let's go out for a few drinks tonight,' she said to Richard as they were rushing to get ready for work one Wednesday morning.

'To the local for happy hour?' he asked.

'I'd rather go to that pub down by the river, the one that does the expensive gin and tonics and the Maris Piper chunky fries with mayonnaise.'

'The Pump House.' He raised his eyebrows. 'Really?'

'Yes, let's splash out for once.' Without some sort of treat to look forward to, she might not get through the day. 'I like that place. We can walk there and save on the taxi fare.'

It was an especially challenging day at school with the unruly girls louder than usual and even the quieter ones not paying attention. By the time she got home, worn out and discouraged, all Elise wanted was to pull on her baggiest, fleeciest track pants, lie on the sofa and dial in a pizza. But she was twenty-five, for God's sake, and these were the years she was meant to be having fun. So she changed into her jeans and her newest top from Zara, tonged a few curls into her long blonde hair, and put on some eyeliner.

'We're still going out then,' said Richard when he saw her. He looked tired and didn't sound enthusiastic.

'Yes, come on. We'll perk up when we've had gin.'

The walk to the Pump House was enough to revive them, a brisk half hour with a chill wind biting through their Puffa jackets. Richard ordered the drinks and Elise found a table beside the window with a view over the river.

'Don't even ask what this lot cost,' he said, appearing with two tall tumblers. 'There's foraged nasturtium pods in here, a twist of Sicilian orange peel and something else too ... it's not just a gin, it's an experience.'

Elise screwed up her face. 'Perhaps we should have gone to the local for a half-price sauvignon blanc.'

'Nah, a couple of fancy cocktails isn't going to make any difference to things in the long run. We may as well enjoy them.'

They took slow, small sips, making the drinks last and Elise looked out the window at the river where on summer mornings she and Richard used to go rowing. That was how they had met, when they were members of a boat club, and they loved being on the Avon. But then Richard started working most weekends and it didn't seem worth paying the membership fees, so they had let the hobby slide away.

'I miss it too,' said Richard, managing to read her thoughts.

'This summer we should try to get out there again.'

'Yeah, that would be nice,' agreed Elise. 'We should plan some day trips in the holidays too. Let's go to the beach at Weston-super-Mare and the Portishead Lido. Or we could borrow a tent and go camping.'

'Maybe ... depends if Dad's got much work for me. Last summer things were pretty busy, remember.'

Elise shrugged and looked away. The tables near them were crowded with people laughing, drinking and eating. Everyone seemed to be having a better time than they were.

'This isn't working out for us, is it?' she said suddenly.

'What isn't?' Richard's face registered alarm.

'Plodding along, being sensible, working hard and saving up. It isn't getting us anywhere. It's pointless.'

'Do you have a better idea?'

'Not really.'

'Because I'm doing the best I can, you know. I'm not sure what else you expect.'

'I'm not getting at you, Richard,' she said, knowing how much he hated criticism. 'All I'm saying is maybe we need to change things.'

'How?' He still sounded defensive.

'Shake things up, be daring, take risks.'

'You mean put everything on a horse in the Grand National?'

'Of course not.' Elise stared down at her half-empty gin glass. 'I think we need to be more dynamic, look for opportunities ... oh, I don't know. Ignore me, I had a crappy day.'

'It's true that we're plodding along,' Richard acknowledged. 'But I don't see what other option we have.'

She shrugged. 'Me neither. I'm just feeling as if we have to do something.'

'I'll take some time off this summer, OK? We'll go on that camping trip. And what if we rejoin the rowing club? Would you feel better about things then?'

Richard was such a good guy. With his broad, freckled face and stocky build, at first glance Elise hadn't thought he was her type at all. But then she got to know him and it was so easy to be charmed. She discovered he had a quirky sense of humour and a tendency for small kindnesses. No one made her laugh like Richard did, no one made her feel so cared for. In her better moods Elise thought meeting him had been like winning the lottery.

'Let's definitely get back into our rowing,' she agreed, because Richard sounded so hopeful, and she didn't have the heart to tell him she was pretty sure it was going to take much more than that to keep her happy in the long run.

She was in the staffroom drinking tea and trying to get some marking done when she eavesdropped on the conversation. The head of languages had been reading the *Guardian* and the physics teacher stopped to look at an article with him.

'They're selling houses in Italy for one euro each? Seriously? That has to be some made-up rubbish doesn't it?'

'It might well be for real. Some of those small towns are struggling to keep their populations up and falling into disrepair.'

'Why don't you buy one? Could be an interesting little project.'

'Nice idea ... if I was twenty years younger and had some DIY skills I might consider it. But I don't think I'm the right guy to restore an ancient ruin.' The head of languages put aside the newspaper. 'It's an opportunity for someone, but on balance I reckon I'm better off trying to teach French to the fifth form.'

Elise waited till they had gone before she got up to fetch the newspaper. It was lying open at the article they had been discussing.

'*Live your dream of Italy ...*' it began. She scanned it fast, then went back and read more carefully, noting down the email address, before putting the newspaper back where she had found it and heading off to her next class.

In her head the words kept playing like a song: '*Live your dream of Italy*'.

Montenello

Salvio was beginning to wonder if it had all been a mistake. At first when the emails started trickling in he had been caught up in the excitement. He and Augusto began in an organised manner, creating files headed 'yes', 'no' and 'maybe'. But very quickly they were overwhelmed and when their advertisement went viral and was picked up by the media they lost control entirely. Phone lines were jammed, computers crashed, people became hysterical. Only Augusto seemed serene. He bought himself a smartphone so he could access emails at home in the evenings, and continued to work his way through them slowly, not seeming to care that hundreds more were flooding in as he did so.

The atmosphere in the Town Hall remained fraught and Salvio could sense the blame falling on him. He kept reminding everyone to keep calm, to let the phones ring, ignore the emails and get on with their usual work.

'When all this fuss dies down we will make a decision. But we can't hope to consider every single application,' he told Augusto.

'Of course not,' his assistant agreed. 'I will keep reading until I have found exactly the right people then I will stop.'

'How will you know they're the right people?'

Augusto looked puzzled. 'Because it will be obvious.'

'Do you really think so?'

'Of course,' he said, with certainty.

To Salvio all those emails were starting to seem the same. Everyone loved Italy, adored the food, the climate, the people, was looking for a project or a challenge, needed an escape from a tough job or a stressful situation or couldn't afford the price of a house back home. He didn't think he could stand to read another; at least not today.

Shutting down his computer, he slipped on his coat 'I'm heading out. I have some appointments this afternoon,' he told Augusto.

'You will be coming back later?'

'Probably not. I'll see you in the morning.'

Augusto gave a small salute. 'Very good. I will stay here and keep reading through these applications.'

'You should head home early,' suggested Salvio, concerned the old man was overdoing it.

'No, no, I have a feeling this could be the day we find our first future citizen of Montenello. If so I will be in touch.'

It felt so good to escape his desk. With a wave at Francesco Rossi, stationed beside the mossy old fountain selling his apples as usual, Salvio hurried down the steep streets to the garage where he kept his car, a classic Alfa Romeo Spider, left to him by his father. Its white paint was polished to a high shine and on weekends he liked to drive it too fast with no real destination in mind. Today, though, he knew exactly where he was going. There were no appointments, as he had claimed. What Salvio needed was to see his mamma, to taste her cooking and listen to her talk, the way he always did when he had a problem.

His mother was the reason he had returned home to the south in the first place. When his father died he was certain she would struggle living alone in the *trullo* house the pair of them had spent so long trying to restore together. Salvio was living in Milan at the time and working in sales. He gave up his job, ended things with his girlfriend (in truth he had been looking for an excuse to do that for quite some time), and moved back to care for his mamma.

While happy enough to have him there, she had made it

very clear that she could look after herself. Within a few months the restoration of the *trullo* was complete and she was putting in a swimming pool. Salvio still had no idea what she had said to the workmen to hurry them along but by the time she registered the place as a holiday rental he thought he was beyond being surprised by her.

'If there are tourists staying in the *trullo*, then where will you and I live?' he had asked.

'You have a life in Milan, *caro*, and I have a future with Giovanni. I will live with him,' his mother said, crisply.

'Giovanni?' Surely he must have misunderstood. 'You mean the farmer who lives next door?'

'Yes.'

Salvio was astounded. He pictured the small, sun-browned man who nodded at him every time he drove past on his rusty tractor, heading off to tend the olive groves and cherry orchards.

'Have you been ...' he began hesitantly.

'When your papa was sick, Giovanni helped us in so many ways. We grew close.'

'But when did you—' Salvio was still in shock.

'Papa was aware he was dying, Salvio. Knowing I wouldn't be alone was a comfort to him in those final months. None of us expected you to move home for good. You had a career and we thought you would be settling down in Milan, marrying your girlfriend, having children. And it is time for that, Salvio. You are a thirty-year-old man, what are you waiting for? Am I never to be a nonna, never to know the joy of holding your son or daughter in my arms ...?'

'Mamma, stop,' Salvio interrupted. 'We were talking about you and Giovanni, not me.'

'We had finished talking about that.'

'No, we hadn't.'

'What more is there to say?'

'Are you going to marry him?'

His mother considered the question. 'Eventually, perhaps, but we are in no hurry.'

'So you'll live together? No other plans I haven't heard about yet?'

'Well, perhaps just one plan.'

'Mamma?'

'We are going to convert Giovanni's barn into a restaurant. I have always wanted to have more people to cook for and this will be my chance.'

'At your age, really?'

She winced at that. 'I am in my fifties, *caro*, and it is not so old. Besides, Giovanni's niece Martina will help me and we will make simple, local dishes our customers will enjoy out on the terrace surrounded by olive trees and ... you know, Martina is a lovely young woman. You must meet her very soon. The two of you would be perfect together. Why didn't I think of that sooner? Perhaps a little lunch or dinner at the weekend, very casual, I'm not matchmaking, *caro*, just seeing if you get on. Because you aren't so young yourself my darling and it is time to grow up and take on some responsibilities ...'

Salvio leaned back in his chair, stared up at the conical roof of the *trullo*, and tried not to sigh. His mother meant well. She didn't realise thirty wasn't considered old any more, that most people were leaving it until much later to settle down and start their families. He had a plenty of living left to do before he wanted any of that.

All the same he wasn't going back to Milan and leaving his mother behind with some man he hardly knew. He needed to stay close by. So he began looking for a job and, with a lack of sales positions to apply for, ended up standing as Montenello's mayor. It had been an impulsive move and in the small town there was a great deal of mumbling that he was far too young for the job but at least he was keen and energetic and, in truth, no one else was interested. So

26

now here he was, living only a forty-minute drive away from his mother, a drive with an interesting mix of winding hill roads and straight highways, a drive he made very regularly in his beautiful car, although she claimed she would entirely understand if he was too busy to visit quite so often.

His mamma was such a beautiful woman with soft curves and long glossy hair like silk shot through with silver. No wonder that nuggetty little Giovanni had made a move the moment he sensed Salvio's father was failing. Time had passed and the pair of them were married now but there was still some awkwardness there. Whenever he paid a visit, Giovanni would shake his hand, exchange a few polite words then make himself scarce, rattling away in his old tractor. That suited Salvio, who preferred having his mother to himself; he was an only child, after all, and they had always been close.

As he sped away from Montenello, over-taking other cars, one hand on his horn, Salvio hoped she would have some time to stop and chat. Over summer the restaurant was so busy that a conversation with her was always a brief or disjointed thing. But it was chilly today with the sky threatening drizzle so surely there would be no people wanting to eat surrounded by the olive trees and for once they might talk without her being distracted.

Salvio turned off the main roads and headed down dusty lanes that crosshatched past fields of red earth and old trees, farmlets guarded by barking dogs and *trullo* houses with their distinctive conical roofs. At intervals there were signs pointing the way to the Ristorante di Donna Carmela. It always amazed Salvio that so many tourists persisted in following them and somehow managed to find the place.

He eased the car through a narrow gateway, parking next to a small farmhouse cheered with a fresh coat of white paint. The old stone barn beside it had been made more picturesque when it was converted into a restaurant. Bougainvillea climbed its walls now and a garden was planted with prickly pears.

He found his mother in the kitchen, leafing through a folder of recipes. Looking up at the sound of his footsteps, she smiled. 'Salvio, what a surprise! But shouldn't you be at work? Is anything wrong?'

He kissed her on both cheeks, catching her clean soapy scent, and for a moment longed to lean in and hold on to her like he had as a boy. 'Everything is fine. I just decided to leave work early and come to see you.'

'Are you hungry?'

'For your cooking, Mamma? Always.'

He loved to watch her in the kitchen. She cooked like she did most things, with an easy confidence. There was no show or fuss, in fact, she appeared to be making very little effort at all, but somehow artichokes were trimmed, steamed and drenched in garlicky olive oil, fava beans became an earthy purée, tender slices of eggplant were wrapped around an oozing centre of mozzarella cheese, sweet red peppers were gently roasted, a table was filled with dishes and Salvio was being urged to eat, eat, eat.

She laid out a linen napkin, filled a glass with wine poured from a dusty unlabelled bottle then took a seat beside him and, as Salvio picked up his fork, began telling him her news. He heard how he had missed his chance with Giovanni's niece who had fallen for a local boy and was surely going to marry him. How there were plans this summer to put extra tables in the dining area, hire more wait staff and find another couple of kitchen hands. She shared gossip about people he didn't know and described in detail the plot of a movie she and Giovanni had recently watched. For Salvio, it didn't matter what his mother talked about, just the sound of her voice soothed him.

'And what about you?' she asked, finally. 'Are things good?'

'Not so great,' he admitted. 'I think I've screwed up.'

Salvio knew his mother wouldn't have heard about the advertisement. She refused to waste time reading newspapers or looking at the Internet, insisting there was no space in her brain for all that information, and if there was anything she needed to know then someone would tell her. So she was intrigued now to learn about the plan to save Montenello and bombarded him with questions. Was it going to be a lottery and would they pick names out of a hat? Would he interview the successful applicants? Were there any special requirements – age limits, language skills, financial situation? What would happen if these people didn't renovate the houses as they had agreed to? And what if they decided to sell?

'Those are all points we ought to have considered but instead we rushed in and now we have chaos,' Salvio told her, using a crust of bread to scoop up the remains of the fava bean purée.

'You aren't enjoying this job?'

'Some days I do, but this wasn't one of them.'

'Maybe it's not for you? All those years working in sales and making good contacts ... it seems a shame to waste them.'

'But there are no jobs here.'

'Then you must go back to the city. I will miss you, but I will understand.'

'That is exactly the problem in the south, Mamma. So many ambitious young people have left to look for better jobs. Some of us need to come back and have our families here, or what will happen?'

His mother's eyes widened.

'Not that I'm ready for a family yet,' Salvio hastened to add. 'But some day I want my children to grow up here, surrounded by countryside and forests, just like I did, not in some grim little apartment.'

'How many children do you think you will want, *caro mio*?'

'I haven't thought that far ahead.'

She sighed. 'I always planned to have a large family but it was impossible for me.'

Salvio knew about the miscarriages and stillbirths his mother had suffered. She had told him many times. Still he listened again as she repeated her sad story.

'My poor Salvio, you should have had lots of brothers and sisters; instead only ghosts,' she finished as always.

'You would have been such a wonderful mamma to all of them.'

'Some day soon I hope to be a wonderful nonna.' She managed a smile. 'You must have at least two children, preferably more. Find a girl who is younger than you, a strong and healthy one. She should be clever and attractive, of course, but don't forget the importance of temperament.'

Salvio felt his phone vibrating in his pocket and pulled it out to check who was calling. 'Mamma, I have to take this. It is Augusto, he is FaceTiming me.'

'FaceTiming? What? I don't know about this.'

'I didn't realise Augusto knew either. But look,' Salvio held up his phone and his mother peered at it, moving her face closer to the screen.

'Augusto? It is Donna Carmela. Can you see me?'

'I think so.' The old man's face brightened with a smile. 'Ah yes, there you are, signora. Are you looking at me?'

'Yes, yes, I am.'

'Then I have made a success.' He sounded thrilled. 'Do you have a smartphone yet, Donna Carmela? No? Then you must get one. It is incredible. Truly it does almost everything. My life is changed.'

Either Augusto had the phone at an unfortunate angle or the lighting was bad because his face seemed to be made up entirely of dark shadows and pouchy folds of skin.

'I am calling with important, confidential news,' he announced.

'How exciting!' Salvio's mother replied.

'Confidential news,' Augusto repeated.

'Yes,' she said, expectantly.

Salvio intervened. 'Mamma, aren't you busy? Surely there is something you should be getting on with in the kitchen?'

'No, nothing at all, not right now.'

'Augusto and I need to talk privately,' Salvio said, firmly.

She gave him a disappointed look. '*Va bene*, I will go, if you insist. But Augusto, if this is about the applications to buy a house in Montenello then what you want is younger women, not old ones. Single women who are strong and healthy, attractive and clever.'

'Mamma, please.'

As she stood and began to move away, she continued talking, her voice growing louder. 'A good nature is essential, generosity, calmness, oh and honesty. But most important of all is that she is *young*!'

Once his mother was too far away to eavesdrop, Salvio turned back to Augusto. 'Yes, what is it?'

'I have found her,' he announced. 'A woman that I know is completely right for us. I have put her in the "Yes" pile and I absolutely refuse to remove her.'

'OK, tell me all about her.'

'Well, she ... she ...' Augusto paused for a moment then lowered his voice. 'I am afraid Donna Carmela isn't going to approve.'

Mimi

It had been the wine talking, of course. That was often the way with the Silver Divorcees, as Mimi had discovered. They would be wildly enthusiastic about something – heading away for a mini-break or an adventure holiday – then the next day everyone would find an excuse for why they couldn't possibly do it.

Still it had been fun composing the email and coming up with a list of reasons why a bunch of middle-aged Englishwomen needed a place in southern Italy. Because we can't find love in London, was Jayne's contribution. Because a real tan looks better than a fake one, came from Dottie. And so it went on.

There was a lot of laughter as Mimi sent off the email, then they opened another bottle of wine and started talking about something else entirely, a difficulty with someone's job or a problem with one of their children; Mimi couldn't quite remember. But the next morning, waking with a dry mouth and an ache in her head, she checked her messages and found an automatic response from the community of Montenello.

Thank you for your inquiry about buying a home in our beautiful town. We have received many replies to our advertisement and are currently assessing all the applications. We will be in touch with the successful candidates as soon as possible. Kind regards, Salvio Valentini, mayor.

It all came rushing back then and Mimi really hoped the town had been deluged with emails and no one got round to reading the silly nonsense they had come up with after drinking far more than they should have.

Settling at her desk, she tried to get on with the illustrations for a children's book she was working on, but couldn't help doing a Google search for Montenello to see what it looked like. Aside from the recent news stories there wasn't much to be found: some pictures that showed a cluster of ancient buildings perched on a mountaintop and a few paragraphs describing the place as a small town, untouched by tourism, where the population had dwindled in recent years.

Mimi wondered what sort of state the houses they were giving away might be in. It would be satisfying to renovate a piece of history that otherwise would go to rack and ruin, and she let herself dream about a simple dwelling made of old stone and filled with her favourite possessions – not the clutter her husband had left behind. She gave the house a pretty garden and a swimming pool. Wouldn't it be amazing to have a place like that where she could feel far away from the unhappiness of the past couple of years, and be restored just like her new home?

That weekend she met Sinead for a coffee. 'Do you remember our plan to buy a house in Italy for one euro?' she asked her.

'Oh yes, that was a funny night. I can't believe we actually sent that crazy email.'

'I know.' Mimi laughed with her.

'Nice idea for us to have a holiday home, though,' said Sinead. 'Shame it'll never happen.'

That was not the way Mimi had been thinking. 'But maybe we could get somewhere in Italy if we all pooled our resources,' she suggested, tentatively. 'Not one of those places, obviously, but a small apartment near the sea. Why don't we think about it?'

Sinead dismissed the idea with a quick shake of her head.

'You were up for it the other night,' Mimi pointed out. 'It was your plan in the first place.'

'I was overexcited. Those shared arrangements never work out. Can you imagine us even agreeing on a place? The squabbles over bills – Jayne's always broke, which wouldn't help. We'd have to furnish it and decorate; everyone would have an opinion. Then living together? Dottie has that obsession with tidiness that would drive a normal person insane.'

'OK, you've made your point. Forget I said anything.'

Sinead sipped her coffee and said thoughtfully. 'You could do it, though.'

'By myself?'

'Yeah, why not? You need to make a change right now, so go for a big one. Sell up and move to Italy.'

Mimi shook her head. 'I think I'd like to keep some sort of base here and can't afford both.'

'You could if you only paid one euro for a house in that ghost town. Why don't you give it a go? You may have to compose another email, though. I don't think the one we sent is going to do the trick.'

Mimi assumed her friend had been kidding but when she got back to the empty house that had once been filled with her family, it occurred to her there was no reason not to try. Going solo in Italy couldn't feel any lonelier than living here.

What if she sent another message to the mayor of Montenello, this one carefully crafted and designed to catch his eye? She mulled it over for a while then hit on a plan that started to enthuse her. Instead of writing her application, she would draw it; she was an illustrator, after all.

The remainder of the weekend was spent working on ideas. Mimi sketched pictures of herself and the life she imagined she might lead in Montenello: whitewashing the walls of her new home, shopping for fruit in the market, drinking wine in a bar among a group of locals, skipping down the uneven steps of a steep and narrow street, wandering through an olive grove with her sons Otis and Ben beside her. She composed a few words to accompany the images and found a translation service to turn them into Italian. And finally, when she ought to have been getting on with her real work, she turned the whole thing into a sort of picture book.

By the time she sent it off, Mimi felt almost as if the scenes she had portrayed actually could happen.

Edward

Edward knew few things made Gino unhappier than the prospect of going to church. With such a devout family, his younger years had been punctuated by Mass and Vespers, confessions and confirmations, and now very little could entice him through the doors of any place of worship.

'I'm spiritual, not religious,' he said whenever his parents tried to pressure him into joining them in the pews of the church they had attended pretty much since stepping off the boat from Italy.

Still, even Gino couldn't refuse to go to his cousin's wedding. Not when it was being held at St Mary's Cathedral with the full Nuptial Mass, twelve bell-ringers and a choir to sing 'Ave Maria'. Not when the entire family would be there and his mother had cried because she was so worried he wouldn't be too.

'So we'll put on our good suits, sit through the Mass and enjoy the party afterwards,' said Edward. 'How bad can it be?'

'I don't want you to come,' Gino said, gruffly.

'I'm sorry?'

'It'll be awkward.'

'Don't be ridiculous. I'm not exactly new on the scene, am I? And I've been to all the other weddings.'

'Yes, but this will be different.'

'I don't see why.'

'Just trust me, OK? It will be.'

Gino was moody for the rest of the week and Edward did his best to avoid him, staying longer at his desk and training later at the gym. Usually any invitations they received from friends and family were stuck to the fridge with a magnet, this one had been hidden away somewhere. It wasn't that Edward cared one way or another about going to a wedding, it just seemed odd that suddenly he was to be excluded from the occasion. He could find no explanation for it.

Early on Saturday morning he went for a walk with Tia along Bondi Beach. It was set to be a hot day and later the sands would be crowded with bodies toasting themselves in the sun but for now there were only joggers, walkers and surfers. Later they would share a plate of triple stack pancakes at Speedos Cafe and then Tia had plans to go shopping for a wedding outfit. Edward thought she seemed unenthused by the prospect.

'I'll come with you, if you like,' he offered. 'I've got nothing else on.'

'Are you sure?'

'Yeah, Gino's working. He's running late with an order for a dining table and he'll be at his studio most of the day, I expect.'

'You might need to treat yourself to a new outfit too,' Tia suggested. 'It's pretty fancy at St Mary's, you know.'

'I'm not going to the wedding,' Edward told her.

'What? But Laura and Tom invited you, didn't they?'

'I assume they did, but Gino doesn't want me there. I've no idea why. He's being weird about it for some reason.'

Tia stared at him. 'Oh.'

'Do you know something I don't?'

'No, not really.'

A huge wave crashed onto the beach and raced towards them, the water lapping round their ankles. Edward squeaked at its unexpected chill and Tia laughed, splashing more towards him with her feet.

'If you get me soaking wet we won't be able to go for breakfast,' Edward warned. 'No pancakes.'

'Now that's a serious threat,' said Tia. 'I'll behave, I promise.'

They walked a little further along the wide crescent of golden sand and then she turned to him and said, 'I might be able to guess what's going on with Gino.'

'Do me a favour and enlighten me.'

'I suspect it may have something to do with the same-sex marriage thing.'

Edward was taken aback. 'What has that got to do with anything?'

'Ever since it was legalised the family keep expecting you to announce your engagement,' explained Tia. 'They've all been dropping heavy hints, even my mother.'

'They want us to get married?'

'Apparently.'

'But why?' he asked, still astonished. 'Do they feel like it will make us more acceptable or something?'

'Not exactly.' Tia said, hesitantly. 'I think it's more that marriage is what they understand. It's what we're all expected to do; the way we're meant to lead our lives. So now the law has changed and Gino is getting pressured to fit in.'

'Even by your father?'

'Papa hasn't said anything but I don't think he'd object to it.'

'It's great that it's been legalised but that doesn't need to change anything for us,' Edward told her. 'Gino feels the same way.'

'Does he?' Tia wondered. 'Have the two of you talked about it recently?'

'No, I didn't think we needed to.'

'All I'm saying is that going to a family wedding together and having everyone asking if you'll be next ... he'd hate it, especially as the two of you have been going through such a rough patch.'

Edward stopped walking. 'Tia, do you actually think he wants us to get married?'

Tia looked at him, tilting her head as she thought about it. 'You know what Gino's like, he's happiest when things are done properly. In his own way he's as traditional as our parents. So yeah, actually I think he might.'

'Shit. I had no idea.'

Digging his toes into the soft sand, he stared out at the sea. Edward hardly ever swam these days but suddenly he had the urge to escape the land and be out there buffeted by the waves.

'You know what, forget about the pancakes,' he told Tia. 'Let's get wet.'

Tossing his keys and phone into her tote bag, Edward turned and ran into the shallows. He dived beneath a wave, wanting the shock of the cold now, swimming further out from the shoreline, as behind Tia him shouted something and her words were drowned out by the sound of the surf.

When he'd swum deep enough, Edward trod water and looked back towards the beach. Out here that sense of being trapped inside his own life didn't feel quite so intense. He watched Tia waving at him from the water's edge and thought about this new reality. So Gino might want a wedding. There was a time when Edward would have gone through with it, purely to keep him happy. Now the idea left him feeling panicked. While he wasn't ready to break up, he definitely didn't want to commit himself further.

Body-surfing back towards the shore, the panic turned to dread. Edward couldn't ignore this any longer. Neither he nor Gino was getting what they wanted from this relationship. No one was happy.

'Look at you,' Tia shook her head at the sight of him dripping wet in shorts and T-shirt. 'Crazy man.'

'It was refreshing,' Edward told her.

'You don't even have a towel.'

The sun was warming up already. Edward held his arms wide and tilted his head to the sky. 'I'll be dry in no time; it's fine.'

'Is it?' Tia sounded worried. 'Are you going to talk to Gino about all this?'

'Yeah probably.' He didn't want to discuss it right now.

'Looks like I'll be eating breakfast and shopping on my own this morning then?'

He grinned at her. 'Sorry about that.'

Kissing Tia goodbye, Edward walked slowly back to the apartment, trying to sort through his thoughts. All these years together and now he and Gino had come to a point they never imagined reaching. It looked very like a crisis. Clearly something needed to happen, but what?

Edward remembered the email he had sent to the mayor of the small Italian town where they were giving away abandoned houses. Montenello. He must find out if it was the town Gino's parents had emigrated from more than half a century ago. Wouldn't it be perfect if he could distract him with a trip there, a project, even a different sort of life altogether? It might give them a chance to find their way back to the way they used to be.

Nothing ever worked out like that though, did it? Things didn't slot together so conveniently.

Reaching home, Edward took a shower to rinse the salt from his skin, then towelling himself dry, went and grabbed his phone to quickly check his emails.

Elise

Elise had a new philosophy. It had developed shortly after she and Richard had sent off an application to buy a house in Italy for just one euro. Obviously, they didn't have a hope in hell of that coming off but it seemed to symbolise a step in the right direction. She decided to dedicate the rest of the year to looking for opportunities, taking risks and making things happen.

'It's the only way our lives will change,' she said to Richard. 'I'm sure of it.'

Richard embraced the idea – he pretty much always went along with her enthusiasms. They started buying Lotto tickets again, even though it was a waste of money. She found a website that listed hundreds of competitions to enter and they spent their evenings trying to win the bigger ticket items. And Richard read a book about affirmations and goal-setting.

'We have to focus more on our aims,' he explained and so an entire Sunday afternoon was devoted to writing out colour-coded lists and making up dream boards of the things they longed for – a house, a garden, an outdoor fireplace, a couple of loungers beneath a sun umbrella, a kitten.

'It's not like we want anything outrageous, just the stuff other people have,' said Richard, as they cut out photos from old magazines bought in a charity shop and stuck them on a large piece of card they were going to hang up in their poky kitchen.

'If we throw enough balls in the air one of them has to land somewhere useful,' said Elise. 'And even if it doesn't, at least we feel like we're doing something.'

It became a game, with both of them on the lookout for new ideas. They practised positive thinking, started meditating and invested in trying new things that scared them – starting with a high ropes challenge that involved swinging through the trees.

'If nothing else this is exhilarating,' Elise decided.

'Do you feel better than you did?' asked Richard.

'Better about what?'

'Everything, really.'

'I feel like we've taken back some control, like we're in the driving seat, or sort of closer to it anyway. Isn't it funny how things work out? Seeing that advert in the paper was what changed everything for me but now, if I did get the chance to buy a house in Italy for one euro, I think I might turn it down. It would be a nightmare, wouldn't it?'

'I'd be keen on renovating a place of my own some day,' mused Richard. 'Perhaps not in Italy, though, because of not speaking the language; I bet you'd get really ripped off by the local tradesmen.'

'Maybe that advert was just what we needed to jog us out of our apathy and improve our attitude,' suggested Elise.

'Yeah,' agreed Richard. 'We were in a downward spiral of negative thinking and it helped us break the chain.'

Elise couldn't help smiling. He was in the habit now of quoting from that book he had read and she found it quite endearing. 'But what if the mayor writes back and begs us to buy one of his houses?'

'He won't,' Richard said. 'We've had that automated response and we'll probably never hear from them again.'

Changing their attitude didn't really make much difference. There were no prizes from any of the competitions they entered and they certainly didn't win Lotto. The only significant change had been to her mood, realised Elise. When she woke in the morning, she didn't want to sink beneath the duvet and hide from the world. At school the pupils seemed less maddening and at the end of the day she still had some energy left. She was altogether more hopeful.

'Something good is going to happen soon,' she took to saying. 'I'm sure of it.'

The call from her parents came on a Sunday evening. They had some news. Elise braced herself, fearing one of them was sick, but then realised they sounded excited. They were downsizing, they told her. The house was much too big so they were going to sell up and buy an apartment, which would free up some funds for them to take a few foreign holidays.

'And we want to give you some money,' her dad told her. 'It won't be a huge amount, but you can put it towards a place of your own.'

Elise started jumping up and down in the middle of the kitchen. This seemed the answer to their problems.

'We're going to be able to buy a house,' she shrieked to Richard, after she had put down the phone. 'It's all coming together at last.'

He was too cautious to get overexcited. They needed at least a 10 per cent deposit plus would have to pay for legal fees and a survey on whichever property they found, and then there was the stamp duty. Even adding in the savings they already had, it might not be enough.

Elise felt crushed. 'You're right. It probably won't work.'

'It's a start though,' Richard added, hurriedly. 'And it's a fantastic thing for your parents to do. Maybe I can get my dad to lend me some cash. It's not like he's short of it, but last time I asked he said he believed in his kids fending for themselves.'

'What if he kept a share in any house we buy?' asked Elise. 'It could be a long-term investment.'

'I'll talk to him and see what he thinks.'

'Shall we look at some places for sale then? Just for an

43

hour. If we find one we really love we could print off the pictures and stick them on our dream board.'

They spent far longer than an hour going through the all the property websites. There was one house in Hotwells they liked and Elise considered ringing the estate agent and making an appointment to view it. A two-storey terrace with a tiny backyard, it was fairly drab but she could imagine turning it into a home. There was space outside for a small table and chairs where they could eat on summer evenings, and a fireplace to make the living room cosy in winter. Elise wanted that house so much she ached for it.

She called her father back. 'It's probably too early to say, but do you have any idea how much you might be able to give me?' she asked. 'Only we've seen a house we quite like the look of.'

'We've done a few sums based around what we're likely to get for our place and how much we'll need for an apartment and our savings. It's only an estimate though, a ballpark figure,' he warned her, before naming an amount so low that Elise felt all the hope drain out of her. 'Will that help enough, love?'

'It'll be a big help,' she managed to say in a normal-enough voice while shaking her head at Richard. 'Thanks, Dad, it's so generous of you guys.'

Elise couldn't wait to get off the phone and have a cry. She listened to her father chatting for a few minutes longer before telling him she had to go but would call again soon.

Richard was ready with a hug, a prolonged and reassuring squeeze of his thick, muscled arms. When he let her go, Elise went to the dream board and started peeling off the shots of the house they had only just stuck on.

'Don't do that. There's still my dad to talk to, remember,' said Richard.

'What are the chances of him helping? He's so stingy he doesn't even pay you a fair rate when you work for him.'

'We've got to be resilient and stay positive,' insisted Richard.

'You're quoting from that book about goal-setting again, aren't you?' For once she didn't find it so appealing.

'Yes, but I mean it. Whatever your parents manage to give us will be a bonus, money that yesterday we didn't know we were going to get. You kept saying something good was going to happen and it did. Who knows what else is in store? Stay hopeful, Elise. It's going to be fine, I know it is.'

Montenello

It was a beautiful day in Montenello. The spires of the town's three churches and the old tower at its highest point soared towards a clear blue sky, the air felt clean and cold, and Salvio made the walk from his home up the steep streets to the Town Hall with a new sense of purpose.

It had been such a good idea to visit his mother. Salvio had needed a reminder that this move south was the right thing, even if it had been made for an unhappy reason. He wondered what his father would think about the changes his death had brought about and hoped it might make him proud to see his son running this town and fighting to turn around its fortunes.

The place seemed to be coming back to life a little already. Most mornings when he made this walk he hardly saw a soul but today there were two women standing by a door-step chatting. He couldn't remember their names but greeted them and was rewarded with a *buongiorno*. Further on an old man was sweeping up fallen leaves. He was wearing a peaked hat and some sort of faded blue uniform. Salvio had never seen him before and was fairly sure the council didn't employ a street cleaner. He made a mental note to check while smiling encouragingly at the man who nodded and wished him good morning before continuing with his work.

When he reached his office, Augusto was waiting and also in high spirits. He shut the door and hushed his voice. 'I have found more candidates,' he whispered.

'Do we really need to be so secretive about this?' Salvio whispered back.

'Yes, the gossip in this place … if we are not careful the whole town will know everything we have discussed. We don't want anyone questioning our decisions. When we are ready we'll make an official announcement.'

'Augusto, did you never think of standing for mayor?' Salvio had wondered about this before, but never voiced the question.

'No, I'm much too old.'

'What about when you were a younger man?'

'In those days I was too irresponsible.' There was the hint of a smile on Augusto's face.

'But you know absolutely everything about the way Montenello works.'

'And that makes me a very good assistant to the mayor who is young and full of energy, and is doing a fine job.'

'Do you think so? Thank you.' Salvio was pleased.

'Of course, of course,' Augusto reassured him. 'Now, first of all let me show you the woman we have chosen to come and live in Montenello.'

His fingers flew over the keys of his computer and he opened a file that was strikingly different to any of the others. It was rather like one of the graphic novels that Salvio had gone through a stage of reading. Beautifully composed illustrations and a few spare lines of prose told the story of a woman living in a town very much like this one. She had a slender figure and fair hair, and there was something about the way she had portrayed herself that suggested she was middle-aged.

'How old is she?' he asked Augusto.

'In her fifties maybe, she doesn't actually say. Not young enough to please Donna Carmela though, I'm certain.'

'Her application stands out. It's very well done.'

'She has a feel for the place already,' said Augusto, excitedly. 'See here she is buying fruit from a man who looks very like Francesco Rossi. That bar she has drawn could be ours and the piazza is similar.'

'Maybe Montenello is like some other Italian town she's visited,' suggested Salvio. 'She may even have come here at some point.'

'She speaks Italian,' Augusto continued.

'Or she used a translation service.'

'You don't like her?' Augusto sounded disappointed. 'What a shame because I have already composed an email that says how excited we will be to welcome her to our town. I saved it in my draft folder.' He began clicking on things and muttering. 'It should be right here. That's strange. I can't have ... oh dear, I have. How unfortunate it seems I have pressed the send button. I am so sorry but I am still getting used to this computer. Is there any way we can get the email back before she reads it?'

'You signed it with my name?' Salvio remarked, his eyes scanning the email Augusto had sent, apparently inadvertently.

'Of course,' the old man said, blithely. 'It wouldn't be official otherwise.'

Salvio knew when he had been out-manoeuvred. 'It seems that this Mimi Wilson will be coming to Montenello then.'

'Evidently it was meant to be.' Augusto still sounded upbeat. 'Now let me show you our next selection. I think you will like them.'

'Have you emailed these people already too?'

'Of course not, I have only just read their application so there hasn't been time.'

This was a more conventional approach: a one-page letter and several photographs that showed two men with their arms around each other and their heads held close. One had a smoothly shaved scalp and the other was dark-haired; both were tanned and looked as if they went to the gym a lot.

'Why them?' Salvio asked. 'Edward Roberts and Gino Mancuso.'

'Diversity,' replied Augusto.

'You think they would bring us something we're missing?'

'Of course.'

'I guess that makes sense. Anything else?' asked Salvio

'This man Gino Mancuso,' he pointed to the dark one, 'is Italian. The letter says his father left for Sydney, Australia on a ship over fifty years ago. So it would be like a homecoming, a return to his roots.'

'Send them one of your acceptance emails then.' It was a random way to make a decision but then things had been haphazard from the outset. And even if they spent weeks deliberating, there was no guarantee they would end up making better choices.

'Very good! And I will sign it with your name, yes?'

'Of course.' Salvio had the feeling he would have done it anyway.

'You should pick the next one personally,' said Augusto, magnanimously. 'Sit down at my desk and have a look through. I have changed a few things about the way it is organised. No more maybes. This is the small file for those we like and this is the large one for those we have rejected.'

He fumbled as he clicked and a photo opened on his screen. It showed a couple; probably in their mid-twenties. He had a well-scrubbed look about him and a pleasant smile. She was completely dazzling and Salvio couldn't stop staring.

'Sorry, this is the wrong folder,' Augusto sounded flustered.

'Did you reject them?'

The old man nodded. 'They have nothing special. Unfortunately, so many of the young people gave us the same story – they are working hard, saving up, but can't afford to buy a home in the cities they live in. I feel sorry for them all but how do I choose one above the others?'

The girl's hair was a soft buttery blonde and framed her face with spirals of messy curls, her deep blue eyes were slightly too large and her chin a little pointed. Salvio was enchanted.

'Elise Hartman and Richard Lynch,' Salvio said, reading the screen over Augusto's shoulder. 'Put them in the yes folder. They're my pick.'

The old man was startled. 'Are you certain? You don't usually make such a quick decision.'

'Yes, I'm quite sure.' Salvio felt intrigued by this girl; he would like to meet her. 'They seem right to me.'

'*Va bene.*' Augusto shrugged. 'But Donna Carmela is going to be disappointed in us. Very disappointed.'

'We still have another empty house left to sell,' Salvio reminded him

'That is true,' said Augusto. 'This time I will look for a buyer your mamma will approve of. Leave it to me, signore.'

Mimi

Mimi had called an impromptu gathering of the Silver Divorcees. They met at a Malaysian place and, over plates of sambal eggplant and coconut chicken curry, she broke her big news. 'I'm buying a house in southern Italy.'

'Whoa, back up a bit,' said Jayne. 'How did this happen?'

Sinead was wide-eyed. 'You didn't ... OMG, you did!'

'What? Somebody explain,' demanded Dottie

Mimi was enjoying the effect the announcement was having. She teased it out a little further. 'We were all together when we talked about it.'

'Really?' Dottie seemed confused.

'In that Italian place,' Sinead reminded her.

Dottie shook her head. 'Still nothing.'

'And it's costing me less than the price of a cup of coffee,' Mimi said.

It was beginning to dawn on Jayne. 'Oh, I'm remembering now. We were completely smashed and sent off an email to the mayor of some awful town. Did you actually hear back from him? Oh hell, do we have to buy one of his old houses?'

'You don't, but it seems I might.'

Mimi explained about the second email she had sent. 'I heard back from the mayor this morning. Fortunately he's written in English. I'll read you what he said.'

Dear Mimi Wilson,

We are delighted to inform you that your application to

buy a house in Montenello has been successful and we look forward to welcoming you to our beautiful town.

Your new home is waiting for you. It has three bedrooms, a terraced garden and a view over the valley, and is full of potential. Of course you may wish to visit before you commit yourself to the purchase. We would be happy to assist with your arrangements, help you find a place to stay, etc. It will also be a pleasure to put you in contact with local craftspeople that can help you achieve your vision for this special place.

Congratulations on having secured a house here for just one euro. Please get in touch and let us know how you wish to proceed. We hope to meet you very soon and help you live your dream of Italy.

Kind regards,

Salvio Valentini, Mayor of Montenello

When she had finished there was a moment's silence then everyone started talking at once. Sinead was particularly loud, Dottie astonished and Jayne seemed to find the whole thing hilarious.

'You've bought a ruin,' she hooted.

'Not yet,' Mimi pointed out, 'but it may be on the cards. And who knows, it might not be that bad, although the phrase "full of potential" strikes me as ominous.'

'That and the fact that they've offered to help you find a place to stay,' said Jayne. 'Your one-euro house most likely doesn't have a roof.'

'Is it a bit odd that they haven't sent any photographs?' asked Sinead. 'You should email and ask for one. Oh, and what about hidden costs – property taxes, legal fees etc. We should do some googling and find out about the process of buying a property in Italy because it's bound to be quite different there.'

There she went, issuing advice again. Sinead was lovely

but she could be overbearing at times and Mimi didn't want her to ruin the fun of this fantasy for now.

'The plan is to go over and check all that out,' she said. 'My book project is almost finished and I could do with a break. So who's coming?'

They were tempted but there were so many reasons it was impossible. No money (Jayne), other trips planned (Dottie), in the middle of an intensive course of laser treatment to even out her complexion (Sinead, which explained why her skin had been looking flaky).

'So it seems like I'll be visiting Montenello on my own then.' Mimi was disappointed as she would have preferred some company. 'Unless I can talk another friend into it.'

'What are the chances of you going ahead and actually buying the place, do you think?' asked Sinead.

'Who knows,' replied Mimi nonchalantly, although in truth she thought they were pretty slim. 'I'm going to have a few days in Italy – good food, local wine, hopefully some sunshine. Plus I'll meet this guy Salvio Valentini and take a look at the house he's offering because I'm curious ... and it can't do any harm, right?'

'It might be fabulous,' said Sinead. 'Then how envious will we be?'

'You'll invite us to stay, right?' said Jayne. 'Once it's all done up and lovely.'

'Will you put in a swimming pool?' Dottie wanted to know.

Mimi listened to their chatter. What she hadn't mentioned was that time was running out. It was coming up to two years since the separation from Glenn and soon he would be pushing for a divorce. There was no point in her contesting it and dragging things out further. The house would be sold and their assets divided. He would come and pick up some of the clutter she had never much liked – goodbye mid-century antiques and Swiss modular furniture – she would pack what she loved into boxes. Mimi was sure she would feel relieved once it was all over but for now it was a black cloud waiting on the horizon.

That was why it felt so good to have something to look forward to, not only the trip but the possibilities it held. Most likely the house in Montenello would be unsuitable but there was a tiny chance things might work out and in the meantime Mimi was enjoying herself more than she had in ages.

She had already forwarded the mayor's email to her sons and asked what they thought about her buying a place in Italy. The boys would be sure to mention it to Glenn since they were still close and told him almost everything. Her ex-husband would think it was a terrible investment but Mimi didn't care. She felt almost mischievous.

It was such a relief not to need anyone's permission or approval. Otis and Ben were grown up, her husband had another woman (at least according to mutual friends). Mimi had felt hurt to be so quickly replaced but now was comforted to realise it meant she was freer than in years. If she wanted to chase some crazy dream to Italy, well that was her business wasn't it?

'I would love a swimming pool,' she told Dottie. 'I think the summers get very hot and it's quite a drive to the nearest beach. But they say the garden is terraced so it may be very steep. I guess I won't know till I get there.'

Edward

Edward experienced a few moments of elation. Hearing back from the mayor of Montenello just when he had been feeling so suffocated by his life had been such a huge surprise and seemed an incredible stroke of luck. There was a house in Italy waiting for them. Quite small, only two bedrooms and very simple apparently, but there was plenty of scope for improvement, according to the email.

This would not be news to thrill Gino. Italy had never been on the list of places he wanted to visit. When they were younger they had travelled together through south-east Asia and from one coast of America to the other. They had been on cruises down the Rhine and around the Caribbean. But for some reason, any suggestion they fly to Rome and drive south to where Gino's family had once lived was met with a total lack of enthusiasm.

'Don't you want to discover your heritage?' Edward had asked a few times.

'Not particularly, no,' Gino always replied.

His parents never went back either. To begin with, life was hard and they cared more about settling down in Sydney, working and getting ahead. When the children came along it was too difficult and later, when they might have done it, so many of the family had followed them to Australia or moved away to other places, that it hardly seemed worth it. At least that was what Tia told Edward.

He couldn't understand their attitude. To him, Gino's background seemed so exotic compared to his own. Edward's parents were true blue Aussies. They never slipped into speaking a foreign language or covered the kitchen table with freshly made pasta. There were no sauces simmering for six hours while Pavarotti sang Neapolitan love songs. It was Edward who loved all that, not Gino. Edward was the one who had always wanted to go to Italy.

So the first rush of elation was quickly replaced by a hum of worry. How was he going to dig Gino out of the rut their lives were in and make him take a trip there? Edward had no idea.

He turned to Tia for advice. She was still a little huffy with him for skipping out on their breakfast plans at the weekend. But when Edward told her he had some big news and promised to take her to the Chiswick for lunch, she relented.

They met on a rainy Friday and sat at a table with a view of the kitchen garden. Edward ordered crisp zucchini flowers stuffed with lemony goat curd, a salad of sliced yellow peaches with rocket and Spanish ham, and a tartare of swordfish with an acidic kick of green tomato and lime. This was the way he loved to eat, small tastes of flavours, everything light and nourishing.

'So what's your big news?' Tia asked. 'Have you booked a trip somewhere fabulous?'

'Better than that, I've bought a holiday house.'

'You've what?'

'In Italy,' Edward finished.

Tia dropped her fork and stared at him. 'Are you serious? Does Gino know?'

'Yeah, no, that's the problem. It's in some place called Montenello.'

'You mean my parents' town?'

Edward had thought so. 'That's right, unless there are two of them.'

The plates of food remained untouched as he explained what he had done. A waiter brought Tia the pasta dish she had chosen, a mound of linguine tossed through with shellfish, freshly podded peas and peppery olive oil, but she didn't pick up her fork.

'For God's sake why?' she asked Edward, when he had finished. 'What were you thinking?'

'Do something crazy and impulsive, you said.'

'Right, so it's my fault.' Tia sounded stunned. 'You're not actually dreaming of relocating to Italy?'

'Well, I don't know.' He hesitated. 'I mean, I could do my job from there – most of it anyway. And Gino has been talking about cutting down on the amount of work he takes on. We're at a stage in our lives when we have more freedom so we could spend time in Italy if we really wanted to. Whether it's the right place ... whether I can even get Gino there ... but it's only one euro and worth taking the risk.'

'OK, so go to Italy.' Tia picked up her fork and twirled it though the linguine. 'But definitely don't tell him about the house, not till the very last minute.'

'No? Then what will I say? There needs to be a pretty good reason for us to be going or I'll never be able to persuade him.'

'Let's eat and I'll think about it.'

Tia had discovered her appetite. She finished her pasta, grazed from his plates then ordered a dessert of fig and honey tart.

'Right, I've got it,' she announced once she had put down her spoon. 'This is going to be all about the timing. You need to plan a trip to Italy and make sure the dates clash with Laura and Tom's wedding. Because Gino would be thrilled to have an excuse not to go.'

'He's doing it to please your parents,' said Edward. 'They'll be disappointed if he's not there.'

'Yes, but it's their home town in Italy and that will make a difference. They're both so nostalgic these days, wistful even. They talk about it much more than they used to. I think they regret not going back and now they feel like it's too late.'

'So they'll be pleased if Gino does?'

'I hope so. You should say you've found bargain flights and are locked into those dates.'

'Gino will suspect I'm lying.'

'Probably. But he won't know that you've committed to buying some derelict house for one euro, will he? Once you're there, take him to see it. Surprise him. I can't imagine that going too well but you never know.'

'You're a genius.'

'I'm cunning. When you're the youngest in a family like mine you have to be.'

Tia wanted to see a photograph of the house. She laughed when Edward admitted he hadn't been sent one.

'It's probably just burned-out rubble covered in graffiti.'

'No, I'm pretty sure it's an actual house.' Edward pulled out his phone to show her the email. 'It's going to need some restoring but that might be fun.'

Tia read the mayor's letter, then laughed again and said, 'Two bedrooms, eh? Well, let me know what mine is like.'

Edward felt cheered by their conversation. For the first time in ages it seemed as if life was opening up. Travelling to a country he had never visited before, eating and living differently, spending time with Gino without all the usual distractions. And maybe the house would turn out to be a project that excited them both. After lunch was over, walking through Woollahra and browsing in the windows of expensive boutiques and antique shops, Edward couldn't help hoping he had found a way to fix things.

Elise

The horse-riding lesson had been Elise's idea, part of an ongoing programme of activities designed to push them out of their comfort zone. She had found a riding centre in north Somerset and booked without telling Richard.

It was obvious right away he wasn't at all comfortable on horseback. His body was hunched and the instructor kept encouraging him to sit taller and lengthen his legs. Even from the other side of the sand arena, Elise could see he was wearing his most determined expression

In contrast she had loved everything about the experience from the moment they arrived at the stables and set eyes on the horses. She patted their necks and breathed in the smell of them – honey mixed with hay, leather and dust. Mounting up there were a few nerves but aboard the chestnut mare, she felt her body relax into the rhythm of its walk.

'Are you ready to try a trot?' the instructor called.

'Yes, definitely,' she responded.

'No!' Richard sounded panicked.

It all seemed to flow for Elise: rising to the trot, keeping her hands low and her legs relaxed against the flanks of the horse. Even the short canter round the arena at the very end of the lesson was more thrilling than scary.

'You're a natural,' Richard called, looking on. 'Either that or you've been secretly practising.'

She was sorry when the instructor told her it was time to take both feet out of the stirrups and swing down to the ground.

'I'd love to try that again,' she said, landing on the sand and handing back the reins.

'Take a course of lessons,' suggested the instructor. 'There's a discount if you book in for ten.'

Elise screwed up her face. 'Too expensive, sadly.'

'Think about it,' he urged. 'I think you'd progress very quickly.'

In the days that followed Elise held onto that feeling of being carried forward by the horse, not quite in control but almost. It had been so freeing and she wondered what it might be like to go over a jump or gallop down a beach.

'Go back for another lesson,' Richard encouraged her. 'I'll come.'

'But you hated it.'

'I didn't love it,' he admitted. 'But I'll come and watch you.'

'There's no point. It costs an absolute fortune so it's not a thing I'm ever going to be able to pursue properly. Let's choose something else we can do together.'

'What about the mountain bike park at Ashton Court? We can hire the bikes and that shouldn't be too expensive.'

'Sure,' said Elise and with the tiniest of sighs she packed away the memory of riding the horse, just as she had her dream of owning that little terraced house in Hotwells. Why think too much about all the things she couldn't have?

It was Richard who opened the email from the mayor of Montenello. He was sitting on the sofa with his laptop on his knee, fiddling with his phone and watching an action film on television.

Elise was staring at him, wondering in a semi-irritated way why he couldn't focus on one screen at a time, when she saw a series of expressions flit across his face. First confusion, then a dawning of surprise, followed by a tentative smile.

'Is this for real?' he said. 'It can't be. No wait, I actually think it is.'

'Is what for real?'

Richard turned the laptop towards her. 'It's an email from those people in that Italian town. They want us to buy one of their houses.'

'Are you serious?'

'Come and see.'

She sat beside him on the sofa and grasped the laptop. 'A spacious five-bedroom home with a large terrace,' she read aloud, 'just waiting for you to bring your vision and energy to it. There is so much potential to create the home of your dreams in Italy. We look forward to welcoming you.'

For a few moments they sat together in silence, both re-reading the email, quietened by disbelief.

Then Elise let out a whoop. 'We've got a house. Can you believe it? A place of our own in Italy.'

'But we're not going to buy it.'

'Yes we are.'

'It's almost certainly a shithole,' Richard pointed out.

'So what? It would be ours and that's the important thing.'

'Didn't you tell me you wouldn't really want it? That it would be a nightmare?'

'Maybe I did,' Elise conceded. 'But now I think this is our best chance of owning a place so we should email straight back with a confirmation.'

'They're suggesting we go and take a look at it first. Surely that's the best idea. I mean it's a risk if—'

'No,' Elise interrupted. 'The biggest risk is losing out. It's only going to cost us one euro, isn't it?'

'Plus taxes and legal fees ... I think we should be a bit more cautious.'

'We're seizing opportunities remember? We're making stuff happen. And this could be it, the good thing we've been

61

waiting for. This may change the rest of our lives.' Elise was all fired up. 'I really want it, Richard.'

'If you want it then so do I.' He laughed, nervously. 'Let's buy a house then, shall we?'

Montenello

When the weather was cold, Montenello could be bleak. Even the houses looked unfriendly, with their windows shuttered and doors firmly closed. Some days the buildings on the higher slopes were half-hidden in a misty swirl of cloud and the people on the streets so swathed in hats and scarves you could hardly see their faces.

Still there were rituals of life nearly everyone kept to, no matter what. In the mornings coffee was drunk, standing at the counter of the small bar. If anything had happened this was the place to talk about it. From his post behind the bar its patron, Renzo, heard about their aches, pains and doctors' visits, quietly watching and listening, rarely speaking up himself although he was surely a font of local knowledge.

Once they had drunk their coffee, the women drifted away to buy food either at the local shop – which was filled with dried pasta and bottled tomatoes, and hung with salami and stretched curd cheeses – or at one of the vans that appeared daily in the piazza – selling vegetables on a Monday, fresh meat on a Wednesday, fish on a Friday. The women filled baskets and trolleys, while the men stood beside the fountain and the statue of Garibaldi at the centre of the piazza, or sat out on benches if the day wasn't too cold.

Lunch was often eaten in a low-ceilinged *trattoria*, its roughly plastered walls covered with bright ceramics and tables topped with oilcloth covers. At midday, Assunta opened its doors, put out baskets of still-warm crusty bread and carafes of fruity wine and offered her customers whatever she had cooked. At this time of year that meant hearty

63

soups of pasta and beans or sauces simmered until even the toughest cuts of meat surrendered and served atop thick ribbons of handmade pasta.

Assunta's kitchen opened to a cramped dining area that grew overcrowded, steamy and warm. There were shouted conversations from one table to the next as she ladled out food and ferried plates. And then abruptly the place would empty as with full bellies everyone returned to work or went home to snooze away the afternoon.

In summer they might come together later to sit in the piazza or play another game of cards in the bar. But during winter Montenello closed early. Fires were lit and people gathered round them; the streets stayed empty. Only Renzo's bar remained open, and often Salvio was the only customer in there.

Tonight it was raining hard, and he ran across the piazza with his coat over his head, towards its lighted windows. The door opened with a dull ring but there was no sign of Renzo so, after a few moments, he grabbed a beer, left some cash beside the till and took his usual stool at the counter.

Salvio was mulling over a problem – several, actually. There was always some issue with the rubbish collection, people complaining about holes in roads that wanted filling or street lamps that needed repairing. But the issue most concerning Salvio on this particular evening was Augusto. He was behaving strangely.

For some reason he had gone completely cold on their project to reinvigorate Montenello. There was still one house left to sell but no progress at all had been made finding someone to buy it. Salvio wasn't sure if he was even reading the applications any more.

Whenever Salvio asked about it and offered to take over, he only shrugged and said, 'Surely there is no need to rush?'

Why lose interest after being so eager at first? Augusto's health seemed fine; he hadn't caught any of the coughs and colds going around. His mood was upbeat and he was performing his duties otherwise as efficiently as ever.

Sipping his beer, Salvio was deep in his thoughts and barely noticed Renzo appear and start filling a bowl with potato crisps.

'That rain is coming down harder, signore,' Renzio remarked. 'I hope you have an umbrella.'

Salvio startled. 'I'm sorry? What did you say?'

'I was talking about the weather.' Renzo uncorked a bottle of red wine and poured himself a decent measure.

'I'll take one of those too,' Salvio told him, draining his beer.

Despite all the talk he overheard each day Renzo was remarkably discreet. But on long, dark winter evenings, as they finished a bottle of wine, sometimes he shared small confidences with Salvio that often proved useful. It was a matter of coaxing out the information because Renzo shied away from direct questions. Once the first glass had been drunk and they were well into the second, he became a little easier to draw out.

'I hope Augusto made it home all right in this heavy rain,' Salvio remarked, as Renzo buried his nose in his glass. 'At that age you worry they're going to have falls.'

'True, signore,' Renzo agreed.

'I was asking him the other day why he never stood for mayor. He claims he was too irresponsible, at least when he was younger.'

'Ah, yes.'

'Of course, some people don't want responsibility, and I can understand that.'

Renzo only nodded.

'And he's a valuable assistant. I dread to think how I'd cope without him. He knows everything about this place.'

Renzo topped up the wine glasses. 'Augusto loves his job,' he said.

'I hope so.'

'He is a man who likes to stay busy in his brain.'

This is how it usually started, with an observation. Then Renzo might go further and let slip some small nugget, but not always.

Salvio waited patiently, watching as Renzo busied himself behind the bar. He was a wiry man with thick grey hair, keen eyes and a rare smile. Now, though, it spread across his face.

'Augusto as mayor, there never was any chance of that. In small towns like this one people have long memories.'

Salvio's eyes widened but he managed not to respond with a question.

Renzo sipped his wine, and added, 'He will be safe this evening. Assunta will make sure of that. No need for you to worry.'

'Assunta?' Salvio was taken aback. Surely nothing was going on there. There had to be twenty years at least between them. As soon as her name came out of his mouth he could tell Renzo was about to dodge away from the hint of a question.

'She is an excellent cook that woman,' Salvio said quickly. 'Pasta and cauliflower today, almost as good as my mother makes it.'

Renzo nodded. 'Ah yes, she sent over a bowl for me. My mother never used anchovies, just a lot of chilli and bread-crumbs. But Assunta's way is fine too.'

Salvio wanted to know more about Augusto. What had he done that the whole town still remembered? Was there more than a friendship between him and Assunta? But he knew from experience there was no point in asking Renzo.

'Assunta's trattoria is good but Montenello needs more than one restaurant,' Salvio said, instead.

'Your tourists would like that,' replied Renzo. 'This town will be very quiet for them, I think. Especially if they have come from a city.'

It was one of Salvio's big worries too. What if he had oversold this place to all these people and they were disappointed? The whole scheme could so easily flounder if the buyers they had chosen didn't fall in love with Montenello.

'One of them is planning to visit quite soon, a British woman, travelling alone,' he confided. 'That's another thing I must do – find her a place to stay.'

Renzo tipped the wine bottle so Salvio's glass received the last few drops. 'We need the hotel to reopen.'

'Or at least some rooms to rent, that would be helpful.'

'Didn't you tell me your mother has a *trullo* she keeps for holiday accommodation?'

'It's forty minutes away in the valley.'

'That's an easy enough drive. Your mother has a nice restaurant too, yes? A good place for your tourists to stay then.'

It could be the perfect solution, realised Salvio. The *trullo* was fitted with underfloor heating. It was an example of how an old building could be restored so it looked authentic but still had modern conveniences.

'That's a great piece of advice, thank you. I'll talk to Augusto about it in the morning.'

Finishing his wine, Salvio shrugged on his damp overcoat and borrowed an umbrella someone had left behind. As he opened the door and stepped into the heavy curtain of rain, he heard Renzo chuckling to himself.

'Augusto mayor of Montenello? Hah, what an idea!'

Mimi

Mimi had never travelled alone before now. It only dawned on her as she was carefully folding clothes into a suitcase. There had been years of family holidays, camping in Cornwall and villas in Spain as her sons were growing up. Glenn had taken her on some interesting trips and in the early days she had backpacked around Europe with a friend. But closing the door on an empty house, catching a taxi, standing in a queue at the check-in counter and browsing round the airport shops entirely by herself was a new experience.

When the mayor of Montenello had emailed photographs of the *trullo* house he had found for her to rent, Mimi had been charmed. A drystone hut with a conical roof, she could imagine sketching something similar for a children's fairy tale. Goblins might live there, or kindly witches. And the cost had been so reasonable Mimi had booked it for a seven-day stretch without really thinking through how it might be, on her own in the middle of nowhere.

She hoped there was someone nearby who spoke decent English. And that driving a rental car on Italian roads wouldn't be too hair-raising. Mimi told herself this had been a great idea, that she was a good driver and could do it. She tried to feel excited rather than anxious, but wasn't really successful.

The journey involved only the most perfunctory exchanges with strangers. Her drive from Bari airport was easier than anticipated, with only one real hair-raising moment, but still Mimi found herself biting her fingernails nervously. It was dusky and darkening by the time she saw the first of the

68

signposts she had been told to look out for. She pulled onto a narrow back road and the car's satnav instructed her to turn around as soon as it was safe but Mimi had been primed to ignore it and stick to following a series of rustic signs.

The final turn through a set of iron gates was so tight she was thankful to have rented the smallest vehicle available. Mimi sighed with the relief of arriving, then parked the car and climbed out to stretch her legs.

The moon was rising and pricks of starlight beginning to appear. It was chilly and the air smelled of woodsmoke. Ahead of her was the *trullo*, a fairy tale made real. Mimi stood beside the car for a few moments staring at the quaint house surrounded by olive trees and drystone walls and wondering what lay in the darkness beyond it. Suddenly she wanted to be indoors with all the lights on. Grabbing her suitcase, she made her way down the stone-flagged pathway, retrieved the key from beneath a potted geranium beside the door as instructed and let herself in.

The *trullo* had a living room with whitewashed walls, a kitchenette to one side and an archway that led to a bedroom. Its conical ceilings gave the illusion of space, although the house was actually tiny.

Mimi did all the things she always did on arrival – bounced on the bed (rather hard, as suspected), unpacked and hung up her clothes, put her books in a neat pile. She texted Otis and Ben to let them know she had arrived safely, then went to get a glass of water and check if any supplies had been left.

On the dining table she found a note propped against a heavy, old-fashioned torch. 'Please join me for dinner in Ristorante di Donna Carmela – I will wait up!'

Mimi wasn't especially keen on going back out into the night. She would rather wait till morning and orient herself then. But she didn't want to seem unfriendly.

Locking the door behind her and slipping the key back

beneath the pot plant, she aimed the flickering beam of the torch around the garden. She could see a glint of water from the swimming pool, and beside it a pergola. Further away was a cluster of lights that might be a restaurant but Mimi wasn't certain how she was supposed to reach it.

The gap in the drystone wall would have been easy to miss had she not been looking so carefully. There was no proper path beyond it, just the tilled red earth of the olive grove, but Mimi could hear music now and the lights seemed brighter so she kept going. By the time she reached the barn she could smell food cooking, something delicious that had been simmered for a long time, and she felt her stomach rumble.

Pushing open the heavy wooden door of the barn to find an empty dining room, Mimi faltered.

'Signora, come in, come in.' The voice was deep and strong, and Mimi found it belonged to a small, round woman. She had glossy hair that curled to her waist and was lightly sprinkled with grey, dark eyes and olive skin, gold hoops in her ears and a red apron fastened round her waist.

'Donna Carmela?'

The woman smiled and beckoned her to sit at a table set up with linen, cutlery and glassware. 'Such a long journey, you are hungry, yes, you need a good meal and some wine. Fortunately, you are in the right place.'

'Are you open?' Mimi asked, looking round at the other tables, all vacant and bare.

'This time of year we are only half open. If people want to eat then I want to cook. In the height of summer it is different, very lively, so many customers but now I get to take my time and there is no menu. I serve what I have made and hope you enjoy it.'

'I'm sure I will. It smells wonderful,' sighed Mimi as a napkin was placed in her lap, glasses were filled with sparkling water and red wine, a basket was heaped with bread.

'You must excuse my husband; he has eaten already and gone to bed. Giovanni is a farmer and he keeps early hours. You will meet him in the morning.'

'He looks after the olive trees?'

'We grow olives, cherries and almonds. Giovanni works on our land and many other properties in the area, he is a busy man.'

Mimi felt a rush of envy for Donna Carmela, whose life was rooted in this lovely place, who had a husband and most likely children living nearby. The loneliness of her world seemed starker and sadder in comparison.

'I was planning to join you for dinner,' Donna Carmela announced. 'Unless you would prefer ...'

'Oh yes, that would be lovely,' said Mimi. 'I'd love you to tell me all about the area. I'm considering buying a place not far away, you see.'

Donna Carmela nodded, evidently unsurprised. Mimi supposed she must meet lots of English people with dreams of owning a house here. She wondered how the locals felt at the invasion of people who didn't speak their language or understand their way of life.

The first course was a pasta dish, pappardelle in a silky meaty sauce. It wasn't until she took her first taste that Mimi truly felt she had arrived in Italy. Her mouth filled with the flavours, and the comfort of eating chased the tensions of the journey from her mind.

'Not bad?' said Donna Carmela, seated opposite her.

'Fabulous,' Mimi told her. 'Why does Italian food never, ever taste this good when you eat it in other places?'

'I think it has some to do with the land itself. The tomatoes were grown here and bottled last summer, the herbs are from my garden, the lamb was raised nearby, the olive oil is from our trees. What you are tasting is the sunshine, the blue skies and the pure air, the atmosphere of this place.'

'Have you and Giovanni always lived here?' asked Mimi.

71

'Giovanni, yes; I had another life before this one.' With a one-shouldered shrug, Donna Carmela tore a crust of bread to soak up some of the sauce. 'What about you, signora? Tell me about yourself.'

Mimi described her life working as an illustrator and living alone in her too-big North London house. 'Everybody left – my sons went to university, and not long afterwards my husband moved out too,' she explained.

'You miss them,' said Donna Carmela, sympathetically.

'Oh, I miss my sons. They're pretty good at keeping in touch but I miss seeing them, smelling them, hearing them. It's been difficult to let go.' Mimi wasn't sure why it seemed so easy to confide in this woman. 'Do you have children?'

'Just one son. He lives not far away so I can see him often.'

'You are lucky then.'

'Yes, and he is a good son. But your children want you always to be their mamma; they don't understand you are a person without them. So at our age, signora, it is good to have a little space to lead your own life, yes?'

'I guess,' said Mimi, dubiously.

'And now you have left home too,' pointed out Donna Carmela. 'You are here in Italy to look at places to buy.'

'In a town called Montenello. Do you know it?'

Donna Carmela gave a small nod.

'Is it not very nice?' asked Mimi, anxiously.

'There are towns like that all over Italy, old houses clinging to the side of a mountain, with the ruined tower of a castle at the very top. Perhaps you will find it nice.'

'I hope so.'

'Or perhaps you might prefer to settle in a valley or closer to a beach. The choice is entirely yours.'

'It is,' said Mimi, wondering when choosing things had become such a fraught and challenging business.

Donna Carmela fetched the second course, swordfish in a buttery sauce of capers on a bed of wilted chicory with a mineral tang. Then there was pistachio cake and tiny cups of strong sweet coffee that held the threat of a sleepless night for Mimi but smelled too wonderful not to sip.

'You said you led another life before this one?' she ventured as Donna Carmela poured the coffee.

'My first husband died,' she replied, matter-of-factly. 'He was sick for many years, a difficult time. Afterwards I remade my life just as you are doing now. And here I am.'

She made it sound easy. But Donna Carmela seemed formidable, one of those women who coped no matter what.

'I never expected this,' Mimi admitted. 'All those years when I was so busy with my career and the boys, keeping the house running smoothly, making sure everything got done. I never imagined this would be how it ended, with me on my own.'

Donna Carmela scooped up the last of the cake and dropped it on Mimi's plate, dusting her fingers clean on her apron.

Mimi attempted to sound more cheery. 'Of course, it's not an ending, really. It's a new beginning – that's what my friends keep telling me.'

'You don't always feel the way other people say you should,' Donna Carmela said lightly. 'And right now you are on holiday. So eat more cake, drink more wine, have a good time.'

Edward

The way Gino liked to relax was to cook. If Edward arrived home to find the kitchen full of bags overflowing with produce, and every burner on the stove lit beneath pots bubbling with sauces and roiling with water, then he always knew it had been a tricky day.

Some of their friends scoffed at the idea that designing furniture could ever be stressful. It was Gino's passion, wasn't it, his craft? But he had fussy customers, late bill payers, issues sourcing materials like any other business. And there were times a piece he was making didn't meet his expectations. It could be a tiny flaw, something about the wood grain or the finish that no one else's eye would ever pick up, but for Gino it was disheartening. So then he would try to cook himself into a better mood.

Edward had come to dread those meals. There was always more to eat than he could comfortably stomach, at least three courses of rich food. And if he pushed aside a still-full plate, Gino would assume he hadn't enjoyed it.

This evening he smelled whatever was cooking when he was still halfway down the path. Opening the front door he began picking out individual ingredients. The earthiness of fermented shrimp paste, the fragrance of coriander and sesame oil, spices being toasted and garlic softened. Asian fusion then, most likely from the cookbook Gino had requested for Christmas. Edward braced himself. Both his mood and the food were likely to be complicated.

'Hey.' Gino greeted him without looking up from what he was doing. 'I thought we'd eat outside. Could you set the table? Chopsticks please, and lots of serving spoons.'

He held still for a moment while Edward kissed him, then sprang into motion again, stirring and chopping, his face a frown of concentration. At least it wasn't French food, which meant Gino constantly leaving the table to finesse the next dish and barely a relaxed moment. Or even worse some sort of elaborate degustation. An Asian banquet meant a couple of hours sitting over a table covered in plates before the big clean-up began.

Gino's food was nearly always delicious. Tonight he served a light fish curry, sweetened with tomato and soured with tamarind. There was a mahogany-skinned chicken that had been simmered in masterstock and meltingly tender pork in a sauce of caramelised palm sugar. And vegetables, of course: Chinese broccoli and stir-fried cabbage.

'You must have been cooking for most of the day,' said Edward, valiantly trying to make inroads into each dish.

'Yeah, pretty much,' agreed Gino. 'I went to work this morning, unlocked the door then changed my mind, locked up again and left. I spent the morning shopping then came back here, expecting you to be home.'

'I had a couple of interviews and a yoga class. I didn't much feel like sitting round in my office today either.'

Edward often needed to escape his desk. He would take his laptop to a cafe or invent some errands to run. But it was rare for Gino to feel his studio wasn't where he wanted to be.

'What's up at work?' Edward asked, as he aimed his chopstick at a frond of broccoli soused in oyster sauce.

'Nothing,' said Gino, stirring caramelised pork through steamed rice. 'It's just getting harder, you know. Twenty years ago finishing that table wouldn't have been such an effort.'

'You weren't as skilled then,' Edward pointed out.

'No, but I had more energy. And mentally it was different

too. This morning I couldn't face starting a new piece so I took the day off.'

'You need longer than a day, Gino. You need a proper holiday.'

'I know,' he agreed to Edward's surprise. 'Actually, I thought I might take a couple of weeks before the end of summer. There are things round the house that need doing.'

'The house is fine,' Edward argued.

'I'd like to change our bedroom, strip off that wallpaper, do something a bit different. You know I can't just take time off; I need a project.'

This was probably Edward's chance. Still he hesitated, helping himself to more of the moist chicken tanned from its simmering in soy, sugar and star anise.

'The wallpaper will have to wait because I've got a surprise for you,' was how he began.

'What sort of surprise?' Gino didn't sound excited.

'I'm taking us on a trip. The plane tickets are bought, the accommodation is booked, the rental car is sorted.'

'A trip where?'

'Italy.' Edward said in a small voice, not daring to mention Montenello.

Gino rested the chopsticks on his bowl and, leaning back in his chair, crossed his arms over his chest. 'No thanks.'

'The tickets were crazy cheap, a bargain. And then I found this magical *trullo* house in Puglia that we can rent for almost nothing and a place that hires out classic cars. It'll be great, Gino. How can you not want to do this?'

'You don't understand.'

'Then explain it to me, for God's sake.'

Gino turned away and for a moment his face was shadowed. Then he looked back, extending one arm across the table, palm open. 'Take my hand,' he said.

Edward did as asked, curling his fingers around Gino's calloused palm.

'We can walk hand in hand here, kiss if we want to, we can be ourselves,' said Gino, softly. 'Southern Italy, it's very different to Sydney. If I'm on holiday I don't want to be judged, to have to hide who I am. I need to relax, not feel as if there's a part of me I can put on show and another part that has to be held back. I'm over that, Edward. I can't do it any more.'

'What makes you think Italy will be like that?'

'Just look at my father—'

'But he left the place decades ago and things have changed since then. He's stuck in the past. And even he is more accepting now, I think.'

'Remember how much he loved you when he thought we were friends? All that backslapping and the bear hugs? It stopped though, didn't it?'

'It was a shock for him,' said Edward. 'He said things he didn't mean back then. You can't hold that against him for ever.'

'He didn't get his attitude from nowhere,' Gino argued. 'He thinks of us as afflicted in some way, as suffering. He told me once he feels compassion for us.'

Edward's heart sank. He could imagine the old man saying that. 'It's better than feeling hatred, I suppose. He does love you, Gino.'

'I love him ... and I hate him too. There's so much tied up in that. Guilt, sadness, disappointment, anger – that's how Italy will feel to me, the way I feel about my father.'

'Won't you just come and see? I've paid for the tickets and the *trullo*.'

'Then get a refund.'

Edward wasn't prepared to give up. He had come this far so might as well make the final push.

'The dates I've booked clash with your cousin's wedding,' he offered. 'If you come to Italy there's no way you'll be able to go to that.'

Gino was silent for a moment then gave a hollow laugh. 'Good try. I had no idea you were so cunning.'

'I'm not,' Edward admitted. 'It was Tia's idea. She thinks your parents regret not going back, that they'll be pleased if you make the trip, and it'll make up for missing a big family wedding.'

Gino gave a weary shrug but didn't try to argue.

'We need this, you and me.' Edward was desperate to make him see. 'We need to go there, face whatever it is you're afraid of, and prove we can survive it. We were so certain back then, when your father threw us out of the house that night and told your mother she'd never see you again. We were so strong together.'

Tears had welled up in Gino's eyes and he brushed them aside with his rough work-worn hands.

'Maybe in Italy we'll find that strength again.' Still holding his hand, Edward squeezed it harder. 'Please?'

He held his breath for a second waiting for the reply, as tears continued to spill from Gino's half-closed eyes and he didn't speak only nodded.

'Yes, you'll come?'

'I don't know, Ed ... I'll think about it, OK?' Gino rubbed at his wet cheeks roughly with his fist. 'I must be crazy. Either that or I must really fucking love you.'

Elise

Elise was trying stay patient but everything seemed to be progressing so slowly. Part of that was down to Richard. He wasn't prepared to simply sign a contract and send a money order for one euro to the mayor of Montenello. And while Elise could appreciate the sense in knowing exactly what they were committing to, he was starting to seem pedantic.

'Just buy the house,' she groaned, as he checked yet another email. 'What else do we need to know?'

'I'd like some estimates of what the renovations are likely to cost,' Richard said in a tone that was infuriatingly reasonable. 'My father thinks it's a good idea. Anyway, they're still insisting we should visit first. They've sent details of a place we could rent. It looks amazing, actually.'

Elise glanced at his screen. With its cute conical roof and vivid turquoise swimming pool the holiday home did seem lovely. 'Too expensive?'

'Not too bad but still I reckon we should stay in the house we're meant to be buying. This guy Salvio doesn't seem keen on that idea. I'm going to email back and insist he sends over some photographs. Then we can make up our minds.'

'Why is he so reluctant to let us see it?'

'Because it's a shithole, like I keep telling you.'

'If that was the case then he wouldn't be suggesting we visit before we sign up,' pointed out Elise.

'All I know is he keeps sending emails about the history of Montenello and the townspeople's pride in its unique traditions but is incapable of answering a direct question.' Richard sounded impatient. 'If they are this hard to deal

79

with now then should we really be taking things further?'

Elise thought he was being unfair because they did have some information. They knew there were three years to refurbish and they could sell after five if they chose to. That there would be higher taxes to pay if they were non-residents. And that, while some of the townspeople did speak English, there were lots that couldn't. None of it sounded like a deal breaker. The taxes weren't prohibitive. They had found free online Italian classes and were already picking up a few basics. And they should be able to manage at least some of the renovation themselves.

Still, even Elise was taken aback when the photographs finally appeared in Richard's inbox. There were two of the exterior of a sizeable house showing a lot of worn stone, overgrown ivy and rotting wooden shutters. The other shots were worse. Paint peeled from walls and floors were uneven, ceilings sagged.

'We could camp out but it's not going to be comfortable,' said Richard.

'What's that pile of wood and twigs in the corner of a room?' wondered Elise.

'Firewood?'

'But isn't the south of Italy supposed to be hot?'

'In winter on top of a mountain it must get pretty chilly.'

Elise chased the doubts from her mind. 'It shouldn't be too bad by half term though surely. Let's go for a week then.'

'Are you sure?'

'Yes, absolutely.'

Until the flights were booked it wouldn't feel as if this was really happening. Nevertheless Elise started telling people – a couple of the other teachers at work, some of their friends, and eventually her parents. Several thought they were crazy, some were envious and others intrigued. Her parents surprised her the most. It turned out they always longed to buy a place in Italy, Spain or the south of France. It had been a favourite fantasy for a while but they never had enough money to take the risk. Elise hadn't thought of her parents as people with unfulfilled dreams. The discovery only made her more determined not to miss out herself.

Now Richard was starting to fret about the Mafia. Someone must have told him they controlled that part of Italy and he kept finding items online about crime families and gun battles. He fired off an email to the mayor of Montenello demanding to know how much of a problem it was in the town, and received nothing in return but an ominous silence.

'Apparently no one talks about it because of an unwritten rule called *omertà*,' he said, growing more concerned. 'Corruption is rife, people live in fear, it's a whole different world.'

'Can't you read about something else?' Elise was exasperated. 'The local wine and food, places of interest?'

'I'm just saying it might not be safe.'

'There are criminals in Bristol too, you know. We don't meet them because we're not involved with drug dealing or anything dodgy. It'll be the same in Italy. Whatever is going on doesn't have to affect us.'

The half-term holiday was weeks away and Elise feared Richard was going to fill the time between then and now with worries. It made her feel disloyal but sometimes she wondered what life would be like if she had ended up with someone less cautious.

She remembered first meeting Richard at the rowing club bar. How did they even get talking, never mind end up on a date? Elise never could remember although Richard always swore it was her who had made the first move.

She did recall the first date – beers and pies on the Grain Barge and then a walk down the riverside footpath. Afterwards, Elise had told her flatmate that Richard was sweet enough but she wouldn't bother seeing him again. Then the following Saturday they had bumped into each other at St Nicks market, had a couple of drinks in a nearby pub, then a few more and ended up in bed together. They stayed there for the rest of the weekend.

Right away things had felt so easy. Richard was funny and sweet, he loved to make her happy, and there was such goodness about him, such dependability. Before him Elise had never had a boyfriend she completely trusted with her feelings

He took to spending at least a couple of nights a week at her place and, when her flatmate moved out, it seemed obvious he should move in.

Had she ever thought this far ahead and imagined still being a couple? Elise didn't think so. Their lives had knitted together without her really noticing.

Her future lay with him now. Marriage, a home and babies all shimmered on the horizon. It would be great if he was a little more dynamic, that was all. It would be really great if Elise didn't always feel like she was the one doing the pushing.

Montenello

Salvio was exhausted. It had been a crazy few weeks with the constant to-ing and fro-ing of emails. They wanted so much information and advice, particularly the young English couple. Why couldn't they come and see the place for themselves then make up their minds? Salvio didn't understand it.

Augusto only seemed to be adding to his problems. He was evasive and vague, had made no progress finding a buyer for the final house but still wouldn't accept any help. What if the old man's mind was beginning to fray? Salvio very much hoped not because he had grown fond of his assistant. Lately he had been wondering what Augusto must have been like as a younger man. Irresponsible, he had admitted, and that night in the bar Renzo had hinted at the same. Hadn't there been a suggestion of some sort of relationship with Assunta? There had been no time to get the bottom of that. Life had been so busy.

And now the first of the buyers had arrived – the older Englishwoman – and Salvio was going to need help. So far his mother was the only one offering any. First thing that morning she had been on the phone, apparently under the impression he wanted her to act as his spy.

'I haven't mentioned our connection,' she hissed. 'She suspects nothing.'

'Mamma, there is no need for you to—' began Salvio.

'I like her,' his mother interrupted. 'She is the sort of woman I can imagine being friends with. And she is having a very difficult time. You must be kind to her.'

'Of course, Mamma.'

'This house you are selling, is it a disaster?'

'Well ...' Salvio couldn't lie to his mother. 'It needs some work.'

'Do you have nothing better?'

'They have all been abandoned. Every house has problems. That is why we need these people.'

Salvio heard his mother's disappointment in the moments of silence that followed.

'Mamma, are you still there?'

'Yes.'

'I will look after this woman, this ...' Tiredly, Salvio rubbed his forehead, hoping her name would come to him.

'She is lonely,' his mother said softly. 'She is thinking Montenello will offer her a new beginning. I hope she won't be disappointed.'

'Mimi Wilson,' said Salvio, relieved to have remembered. 'Augusto and I are meeting her later this morning and going to view the house together.'

'Take her for lunch. That little *trattoria* in the piazza is open, isn't it? Show her your town. Spend some time with her.'

'Yes, Mamma,' said Salvio.

'When she comes back I will find out what her impressions are and call you straight away.' She sounded excited again. 'I will cook something, a dish that is warm and heartening perhaps a sauce of Lucanica sausages, lots of pork, fennel and pepperoncino, she will enjoy that, I think.'

His mother was still talking about food when Salvio managed to make an excuse to break off the conversation. Yawning, he went to put on a pot of coffee, and was annoyed to find only a few beans left in the jar. The fridge was empty too and the crust of bread he unwrapped so hard he risked breaking his teeth on it.

At least the day was fine. Salvio opened his shutters to blue sky and crisp air. In the soft morning light the old stone of Montenello's houses was the colour of creamed honey. The town looked at its best today.

Salvio picked out a jacket, then changed his mind and dressed in casual clothes more suitable for visiting a dusty building. With a sense of anticipation, he made his walk to work.

He recognised the faces of most people he passed now, even if he didn't know much else about them. There were so many grey-haired women and balding men, at first it had been tricky to tell them apart. And they had been distrustful of him. Salvio recalled the sidelong glances and hushed conversations that stalled as he approached. He was a young man returned from the north, what did he know of them and their ways, their history or their secrets? If he had been voted in as mayor it was only because there were no other choices.

Salvio had worked hard to win them over. He spent time in the bar and the *trattoria*, lingered in the piazza, called a cheerful '*salve*' to everyone he passed, even went to Mass on Sundays. He never lost the sense he only heard what people wanted him to know, and he wasn't sure if they would ever fully accept him, but their stares had softened and they greeted him a little more warmly now. How would they treat this woman Mimi Wilson, though, a foreigner who might not speak a word of their language?

Stopping at Renzo's bar, Salvio ordered an espresso and a plain *cornetto*. In the mornings there was always a crush of people here and a warm fug of smouldering cigarettes. No one cared about the laws that forbade smoking in public places. Rules were rarely respected in Montenello. The townspeople took their pet dogs inside the *trattoria* and let them sleep beneath the tables; they parked their cars wherever they pleased, often on the pavements, and avoided paying taxes. How would all of that seem through this Englishwoman's eyes?

Salvio drank a second espresso, finished the last bites of his pastry and braced himself for the day ahead. He had promised his mother he would look after Mimi Wilson.

In the Town Hall there was the usual sense of no one doing anything fast. This had frustrated Salvio at first. It seemed to him that half the number of people should be getting through twice the amount of work. But he had come to accept there was no point in trying to rush anyone. Even Augusto, by far the most efficient member of the small staff, worked at his own unhurried pace.

Today he was installed at his desk by the time Salvio arrived in the office, squinting at his computer screen through smudged reading glasses.

Salvio greeted him with an energetic *buongiorno*. 'We have a big day ahead, remember? Mimi Wilson is coming to view the house we are proposing she should buy. Augusto, are you listening? Have you had someone to check the place? Give it a tidy up?'

Augusto seemed startled. 'Did I say I would do that?'

'Yes, last week; you told me it would be no problem.'

'Of course, of course, I will sort it out right away.'

'It's too late; we're meeting her in an hour.' Salvio couldn't hide his impatience. 'She'll just have to view the property in whatever state it's in.'

'I am so sorry, signore.' The old man sounded desolate.

'Is everything OK?' Salvio had asked him the same question every day for the past week and been assured all was fine.

Today, though, Augusto sat back in his chair, the furrow in his brow deepening. 'There is a small difficulty that has been on my mind lately,' he conceded.

'With what?' Salvio pressed him.

'The fourth house we are to sell. Its original owners have changed their decision at the last minute. One of the family members wants to come back and live in Montenello. I have emailed to say it is too late and they must honour our agreement but they are insisting and I am not sure what to do.'

'That's not such a problem. In fact, it's good news if people want to return,' Salvio told him.

'What about Donna Carmela? She is expecting us to find a nice young woman and I promised—'

'I don't think pleasing my mother is our first priority.'

'And besides, this family signed all the paperwork.'

'Even so, I think you should send a message to say we would be happy to welcome them.'

There was a mulish set to Augusto's face. 'They have been gone for years. Why would they suddenly want to come back?'

Salvio wondered why he was being so insistent. Surely it wasn't important who owned the house so long as it didn't lie empty and deteriorate any further.

'Do you know this family?' he asked.

The old man grunted dismissively. 'They made an agreement with us. I think they should honour it.'

'Forward their details to me,' Salvio told him. 'We will give them the opportunity to return if they wish. If no one has taken possession of the place after six months then we will go ahead and sell. *Va bene*?'

'*Va bene*,' agreed Augusto, although he didn't sound happy. 'But there is no need for you to be bothered with this – if it must be done, then I will do it.'

Salvio tried to ignore the tone in his assistant's voice. He acted as if the old man wasn't sitting at his desk, eyes half closed, fingers pinching the bridge of his nose; a picture of dejection.

There was something going on, details he wasn't confiding, yet another secret in this town that seemed so full of them. All Salvio could do was wait to be taken into his confidence and hope meanwhile it wasn't anything too important.

Mimi

From a distance Montenello appeared to have been hewn from the rock it stood on. Mimi pulled over to the side of the road so she could take in the view. The town looked like a fortress, all tightly packed houses and tall spires clinging to the high sides of a mountain. Suddenly, Mimi felt nervous.

Negotiating the town's streets sent her anxiety levels soaring. Some were so narrow she wasn't entirely confident her car would fit down them and Mimi had no idea what to do if she met someone coming the other way. A moped flew past and, catching sight of it at the last moment, she only just avoided an accident. Fortunately the Town Hall was at one end of a small piazza and there were a couple of parking spaces. Having arrived too early for her meeting, she decided to take a look around.

From the moment she climbed from the car, Mimi had the sense of being stared at. Out of the corners of their eyes, through the windows of the small bar, as they drove past in their cars – the townspeople were watching her, she wasn't imagining it. As she walked across the piazza, an old man at a stall selling nothing but a few apples turned his head and followed her progress, mouth hanging half open.

'*Buongiorno*,' she said to him, feeling unsettled. 'Could I buy an apple?'

His gaze not leaving her face, the old man offered her one, shaking his head when she reached into her bag for some cash.

'*Inglese*?' he asked.

'English, yes,' she replied.

'A gift.' The words were thickly accented. 'Eat. Very good.'

'Thank you so much.' She was touched by his kindness. Perhaps people here were friendly after all.

Polishing the wrinkled skin of the apple against the soft wool of her coat before biting into its flesh, Mimi turned back towards the Town Hall. She was still early but the mayor would have to deal with it.

The Town Hall was the grandest building in the piazza, two storeys high with several flags flying from a balcony and the word *Municipio* carved into the stone above it. Inside she found a long hallway with a lingering smell of mothballs and a lot of marble. All of the doors leading off it were closed and Mimi paused, unsure where she was meant to be. The one person she could find, a well-dressed woman, was leaning against a wall, absorbed in a long call she was making on her phone. It was a one-sided chat, with the woman nodding and interjecting every now and then, showing no sign of ending the conversation.

'Excuse me,' Mimi said, at last. 'I'm so sorry, but could you tell me where the mayor's office is?'

The woman started, as if she hadn't been aware of her hovering and waiting.

'The mayor,' Mimi repeated, remembering the Italian word she had looked up earlier. '*Il sindaco.*'

Pointing a finger towards one of the doors, the woman dismissed her with a glance and turned away to continue her conversation.

Mimi knocked on a door made of dark wood and varnished to a high shine, and heard a voice inside responding in Italian. She had no idea whether she had been invited to enter or told to go away. Turning the ornate gold handle anyway, she found herself in a large, high-ceilinged office. The man sitting at the desk furthest from her was fresh-faced, very good-looking and dressed in the type of clothes you might wear to go hiking. The other was much older with a neat moustache and a smart suit. He must be the mayor, she decided, greeting him with a smile. 'Signore Valentini?'

The old man shook his head, and instead the younger one responded, springing from his chair and striding over, a hand extended ready to shake hers. 'I am Salvio Valentini, pleased to meet you,' he said, warmly. 'Signora Wilson, we have been looking forward to your arrival.'

He introduced her to the older man who, to Mimi's embarrassment, turned out to be his assistant.

'I'm so sorry—' she began.

'I am young for such a job, yes?' said the mayor, cutting short her apology. 'And in truth it is Augusto here who knows everything. He will be your main contact.'

Still it was the mayor who did all the talking. He seemed keen to sell the place to her, holding forth about the lack of crime in the area and the healthiness of the mountain air. He shared his plans to bring the town back to life and revive its traditions, speaking of festivals and folklore, winter bonfires and summer carnivals.

And then he suggested coffee so the three of them left the Town Hall and crossed the piazza to a small bar where the conversation continued. Now and then the mayor would stop to introduce her to someone and there would be smiles, handshakes and awkward exchanges in fractured English.

'Perhaps we should go and see the house now,' he said at last, glancing at his watch. 'Although no, it is almost midday and there is a very good *trattoria* almost next door. I would be delighted to offer you lunch.'

'That's very kind but—'

'You must taste the local food. It is one of the best things about this region. And Assunta is an excellent cook, isn't she, Augusto?'

The old man nodded: 'Of course, of course.'

Lunch progressed with a notable lack of rush. Mimi didn't think she had ever eaten in a restaurant where the service was quite so slow. They waited at least thirty minutes for a small, round middle-aged woman to appear from the kitchen and run through the few dishes on the menu. Then there was another long interval before the food arrived. As they ate meatballs roasted with lemon leaves and a wintry caponata of celery and green olives it began to dawn on Mimi that perhaps the reason for this relaxed pace of life was that, aside from the mayor, everyone in this town was her age or much older.

'Where are all the young people?' she wondered.

This time it was Augusto who spoke. 'They emigrated or went to the cities searching for opportunities,' he explained. 'The same problem exists in many small Italian towns, signora. We must find ways to reinvent ourselves, or we die.'

'Is that why you are seeking foreigners like me to come here?'

'It is a beginning,' Augusto said, solemnly. 'This town has changed so much. I am old enough to remember a busy market out there, not just one old man selling apples. Montenello was lively in those days. Now ...'

'It is peaceful, an idyllic retreat from the craziness of the modern world,' the mayor quickly interrupted. 'I came here after spending several years living in Milan and the quality of life is so much better: no crowds, no traffic, no smog.'

'You're not tempted to go back north?' asked Mimi.

The mayor shook his head. 'The south is a jewel, not so smoothly polished, but it is the real Italy. And it is my home. I grew up not far from the *trullo* you are renting and I always hoped I would return some day.'

Once lunch had been eaten there was the suggestion of more coffee but this time Mimi insisted that she absolutely needed to see the house, it was why she had come here after all, and she would prefer not to wait any longer.

Augusto went and spoke to the cook. There was much gesturing and smiling, although no money seemed to change hands.

'Are you happy to go on foot?' the mayor asked as they left the *trattoria*. 'It is a little chilly, but it's not too far to walk.'

The house actually wasn't all that close. It took half an hour at Augusto's gentle shuffling pace and, although it was mostly downhill, Mimi was concerned for him. At one point she realised he had stopped and, turning to check he was OK, found the old man taking a photograph of her with a smartphone.

'For our town's Instagram page,' he told her. 'Social media is very important nowadays, signora.'

The mayor caught her eye and smiled. They were an intriguing pair, thought Mimi, walking on down the uneven stone-flagged street. Both so charming and friendly, they gave the impression they couldn't do enough for her. Things might be different if she actually bought the house. Mimi knew she couldn't count on their support, on anyone's, really. If she did this, she would be on her own.

The house lay at the far edge of the village. Even from the outside it seemed to be unloved. Its shutters were closed and barred, there was faded graffiti on the walls and the front door only yielded when the mayor put his shoulder to it.

'After you, signora,' he said, standing back so she could go inside.

'No, you first,' she told him, looking down the dingy hallway.

It was too dark to form much of a first impression but the mayor and his assistant rushed round flinging open shutters and once they had finished the place was flooded with light. Nothing it revealed seemed pleasant. Dust, cobwebs, broken sticks of furniture, cracked tiles, damaged ceilings, flaking paint and curling wallpaper. Mimi walked around the house trying to find something to like.

'I am so sorry, we had intended to have it tidied up but unfortunately there was no time.' The mayor was trailing round after her, and even he seemed taken aback at how bad a state the house was in.

'It smells very musty,' Mimi remarked. 'How long since anyone lived here?'

The mayor turned to Augusto. 'Ten years? Fifteen?'

'Longer than that, perhaps. I don't really remember.'

'But have you seen the view, signora?' The mayor gestured towards a set of rotting French doors. 'From the terrace you'll be able look out right across the valley. Don't go out there, right now – OK, but proceed very carefully, I am not sure how safe the structure is – stay back from the edge. This property has quite a bit of land attached, you see? Enough to make a nice garden.'

Perhaps even enough for a swimming pool, observed Mimi, standing as close to the edge of the crumbling terrace as she dared. The land fell away steeply down the hillside but there seemed to be a flatter area just beneath her covered in pink oleander, lots of yellow broom, old fruit trees and rambling mimosa.

All of it was overgrown and tangled with weeds, the place was near enough a shambles, and a sensible person would run a mile; Mimi knew that.

'It will take work but this could be a happy home again,' the too-young mayor said encouragingly. 'With your artistic vision, Signora Wilson, your creativity, surely you can already see how it might look some day?'

Mimi had imagined that was how it would be. She had assumed her mind would restore and refurbish, that she would easily conjure a dream home rising from the ruins. But it felt so oppressive in here, so full of the forgotten lives of strangers, of the people who had chosen those faded tiles on the kitchen walls, who once sat in the old armchair that was now leaking its stuffing. The back and forth of their feet had worn smooth the old stone floors, they had lowered their bodies into the cracked bathtub and piled wood onto the fireplace to warm a winter's day. Then they had left the place or, more likely, died. And Mimi felt as if sadness had settled over it along with all the dust.

The mayor was wrong, she realised. She couldn't imagine happiness here. All she felt was the house's past; there was no sense of its future.

Edward

Sunday lunch with Gino's family was a monthly ritual. It was always a rowdy occasion and Edward could remember feeling intimidated at first. The long wooden table, every bit of it covered in dishes of food, too many people elbow to elbow and everyone talking at once. Most conversations were shouted and there was always at least one argument going on. You were expected to pile your plate with a second helping and a third; it would be rude not to. There was lots of wine and to finish they poured small glasses of a bitter liqueur that Edward was promised would aid his digestion.

In contrast to his own family, whose polite Sunday roast was served on small plates because his mother was always watching her weight, meals here were an experience: colourful, loud and lots of fun.

It was true that he and Gino showed a different version of themselves at these lunches. There was never any outward sign of affection between them, they rarely sat next to one another, did nothing that would force the fact they were a couple onto those around them. Edward accepted that was how things had to be, although he knew that Gino chafed.

Today there was a large gathering. Most of the family had been to Mass and now they were standing in groups, spilling out onto the deck or crowding the kitchen, while Tia and her sisters finished preparing the meal under their mother's watchful eye. There were a few neighbours, a former colleague of Gino's father, a cousin and an older woman whose connection to the family no one ever seemed sure of.

Edward wondered what would happen if he put his arm

round Gino, kissed him on the cheek or lips, behaved in a way that came naturally in most places outside of this house. Would it really be such a big deal?

When lunch was ready there was a jostle to take their spots at the table. Gino's father always sat at its head, and Edward usually positioned himself closer to the other end, ideally next to Tia.

Today, however, he shadowed Gino and slid into the seat next to his. There was a prayer that neither of them joined in with, although they dipped their heads respectfully. And then the eating began. Platters and bowls were passed back and forth, one loaded with seafood in a puddle of oily tomato sauce, another with little ears of pasta tossed with salty anchovies, garlic, chilli and purple sprouting broccoli from the garden. There was a slow-cooked lamb shoulder with a surprising bite of spice and a calzone of red onions and ricotta. The noise level built with the scraping of cutlery over plates, the clinking of glasses and demands to pass the pepper or grate more of the Parmigiano.

Gino's mother had little appetite these days; it seemed to lessen as she aged. But she loved to watch others eat and always made sure Edward had a helping of whatever she considered the best dish.

As he ate, he listened to the conversation flow and eddy around him. Most of them were discussing the wedding. There was conjecture over how much it would cost, a debate about outfits and several complaints that the date clashed with other events people wanted to attend.

Finishing his food, Edward shook his head at the offer of a second helping of the pasta and leaned back from his plate.

'It was great but I can't manage another bite. No really, thanks but ...'

As usual, no one was listening. One of the sisters spooned some sweet-sour roasted peppers onto his plate and the cousin insisted he taste the twice-cooked eggplant with sheep cheese she had made from her great-grandmother's recipe.

It was always like this. The food varied from season to season, the talk veered in different directions, the guests might change, but broadly speaking this lunch had drifted on late into Sunday afternoons in much the same way for years and years.

Edward understood that tradition was important to these people; the way things were supposed to be done brought them a sense of comfort. When their mamma and papa were there everyone behaved more respectfully. Tia and her sisters never swore, the husbands hid their tattoos, the grandchildren put away their phones.

Was that why he and Gino put such an essential part of themselves to one side? No one had asked them to. It was an unspoken thing, a quiet expectation. They all remembered how it had been when Gino first came out and his parents realised exactly what was going on between him and his best friend. No one wanted to live through anything like that again. But times had changed. Even this family had to make progress. It was important they did, for him as much as Gino.

Leaving his second helping untouched on his plate, while nodding at something the cousin was saying, Edward extended an arm along the back of Gino's chair and sat with it draped lightly over his boyfriend's shoulders.

Gino's back stiffened immediately but nothing else changed. There was no lull in the conversation, the sisters didn't remark on it, the husbands appeared not to notice. Only Gino's father seemed to care. Edward met his gaze. The old man didn't look unhappy, just watchful, as if he was waiting to see what might happen next.

Edward smiled at him. 'So, Papa Mancuso, did Gino tell you that we're going to Italy?'

'We've been thinking about it,' Gino put in, quickly.

'I've rented a *trullo* house for us in Puglia,' Edward

97

continued, aware that other eyes were on him now and people were tuning in, 'and then we'll tour around a bit. We may even go and see if we can find any long-lost family members in the town you came from. It's Montenello, right?'

'That cursed place?' Gino's father frowned. 'There is no point, no one is left; you will be wasting your time to look.'

'But of course you must go to our village, to Montenello.' Gino's mother sounded excited. 'You will be so close and it is beautiful there. How strange but I have been dreaming of it lately. In my dream everything is as it was all those years ago. There are still oxen pulling carts through the steep streets and goats up on the roofs of the houses, my father is in his bakery and I am a little girl, waiting for a taste of the hot bread coming out of his oven.'

'Oh, Mamma,' said Gino.

'But it is not a sad dream, it is such a happy one. And I am pleased you are going there, even if it is different now and everyone we loved is gone.'

'The dates clash with the wedding,' Gino told her.

'The flights are booked and paid for,' added Edward.

The old woman didn't seem to have heard. 'I never saw much of my own country,' she said, wistfully. 'We didn't leave our own village very often in those days. And then Luigi and I travelled all this way and became Australians. What an adventure it was.'

Gino's father was watching her face now. There was such tenderness between the two of them, even after all those years together and so many children. 'You regret not going back,' he said, softly.

'I am happy for the young ones to go, for Gino and Edward, maybe some day our grandchildren. That would be wonderful.'

She smiled at Edward and, easing herself out of her seat, picked up one of the empty dishes carefully with both hands. Her daughters followed her lead, clearing the plates and platters, ferrying them to the kitchen, bringing back more food – figs baked with honey and walnuts, a tart with a paste of pistachios, lots of dark chocolate and a hint of cinnamon.

Later there would be coffee and liqueur, the women would wash the dishes and the men would talk about sport. That was how it always was. Now, though, Edward leaned closer to Gino, his arm still resting on his shoulders.

It was only a small change, but it was enough for today.

Elise

If it hadn't been for the promise of Italy then Elise didn't think she would have made it through the drudgery of these last wintry days. Struggling to get up in the dark every morning, the flat freezing cold, and then a long day teaching and home again as the daylight started to fade. It felt relentless. But now she smelled spring in the air and the thought of visiting Montenello, which in Elise's imagination was endlessly blessed with blue skies, was giving her something to aim for.

No flights were booked yet and Elise didn't understand why Richard kept delaying. It would be the half-term holiday so they were only going to get more expensive. Tonight she would insist they got on with it. Once they had sorted plane tickets and a rental car everything would be set for a more exciting future. At least that was what Elise kept telling herself.

Richard was late home that evening because he had stopped off at the pub for a quick beer with a couple of the other teachers. By the time she heard him at the front door she had a pot of chicken soup simmering on the stove and was into her second glass of red wine. She thought he looked tired. He kicked off his shoes, shrugged off his Puffa jacket and, leaving them where he had been standing, went and flicked on the television.

'How hungry are you?' Elise called.

'Hmm?' He wasn't listening.

'Shall I toast some bread to go with the soup?'

'Yeah, sure.'

Richard was channel-surfing now. He picked out a Netflix series they were binge-watching that involved a lot of guns, car chases and violence and they ate in front of the television, bowls of soup and plates of buttery toast on trays balanced on their knees.

'So Rich, shall we get those flights booked after dinner?' asked Elise.

He was staring at the television screen, as if spellbound.

'Richard?'

'Sorry, what?' A quick glance at her then he looked back at the television.

'I want to get on with things, make Italy happen. We can put the flights on my credit card if you're short this month but ... oh for God's sake.' Snatching the TV remote, she pushed the off button then said into the silence. 'That's better.'

'Hey, I was watching that,' objected Richard.

'You're always watching something,' snapped Elise.

'That's not true,' he said, defensively.

Actually it was, but she didn't want an argument. 'You can go back to it later. Let's finish dinner and get our Italy trip sorted first.'

Richard stirred his spoon through the remains of his soup, making a whirlpool of diced celery and shredded chicken. 'To be honest with you, I'm not sure it's such a great idea,' he said, cautiously.

'But we've talked about this. We agreed that it might be a risk, but we're going to take it.' Elise was exasperated. 'Do we have to go through the same discussion all over again?'

'I've been chatting to a few people. My dad thinks we'd be fools to go ahead. He says dealing with builders in a foreign country when you don't speak the language is a recipe for disaster.'

'Your dad is just worried he'll lose his cheap labourer if you're busy on your own project all summer,' Elise retorted.

'And anyway we'll be doing a lot of the work ourselves.'

'Perhaps, but there are other issues,' Richard was keeping his tone reasonable. 'Dad said he'd heard of other Italian towns selling off houses cheap. I googled and found one in Sicily so emailed the estate agent who was supposed to be handling things and heard back from her this morning. She told me she's given up on the whole thing because the scheme seems to have stalled. It sounds like it was a waste of time.'

'That doesn't mean the same thing will happen in our town.'

Richard's eyebrows raised. 'We've never been there, so it's hardly our town. And it all seems a bit dodgy to me, Elise. If we sign the agreement and commit to this place ... too much is unknown. That's the real problem. This guy Salvio Valentini is saying all the right things but how do we know if we can trust him? It could be some sort of scam.'

'Of course, it's not a scam. How could it be?' Elise was exasperated.

'There's loads of fraud going on out there these days. Loads of dodgy people,' he insisted.

'So we give up, that's what you're saying.'

'I think we should stick with our original plan,' Richard said, patiently. 'We keep saving a while longer and then with the money from your parents we'll have a deposit eventually, enough to buy a place in Bristol and start thinking about having a family. That's what I'd like ... it's what you want too, isn't it?'

Elise had thought so up till now. A couple of her friends already had kids and she had seen the way their lives changed. On visits she held their bundled-up babies and wondered when her turn would come. She imagined being in the same milky, dreamy haze, the same chaos of dirty nappies and strollers cluttering the hallway, half-giddy with sleeplessness and overflowing with love, and was filled with terror and longing.

'How will we afford to have a family if we're saddled with a huge mortgage and I'm still paying off my student loan?' she asked.

'We'll figure it out,' Richard promised. 'There are always options. I reckon my mum would help with the childcare when you went back to work.'

Elise didn't want to have a baby that was squeezed into the parts of her life where she wasn't busy looking after other people's kids. She knew plenty of women managed the juggle of work and family, but she wasn't sure how. Sitting on the sofa, her empty soup bowl on her knee, she tried to look into the future as Richard was describing it. How bleak it seemed, all daily grind and exhaustion. Where was the excitement, the fun and possibilities? Where was the sunshine?

'Even if it all went well, Italy would just be a distraction,' Richard told her. 'It's not what we've always worked towards is it?'

Clearing away the soup bowls and loading the dishwasher, Elise thought about that. Had she ever properly considered what sort of life she wanted? Or had she let herself be herded like a sheep, first to college because teaching was a steady career, and now towards the same path all her friends were choosing. Slamming the dishwasher door shut, Elise wished it wasn't such a rainy evening. She wanted to escape the flat, go for a walk down by the river and try to get things straight in her head.

Instead she leaned against the kitchen counter and closed her eyes. Richard had turned the television back on and she could hear the sound of gunfire and screaming. He was continuing to watch his show, assuming the conversation was over and everything had been decided. The easiest thing would be to do what he wanted. Richard was a great guy, caring and supportive. All her friends were always saying how lucky she was to have him and Elise loved him, really she did.

But she wasn't sure if she loved him enough to give up her dream of Italy.

Montenello

It was a day when nothing went quite the way Salvio had thought it would, beginning with a frantic knocking on his door early in the morning when he was still only half-dressed.

'One moment,' he called, hastily shrugging on his shirt, assuming there had been a crisis in town and someone had been sent to fetch him.

Instead it was his mother on the doorstep, eyes bright with excitement. 'I came as soon as I could,' she said, breezing past him and into the house. 'Make me an espresso.'

'Is something wrong? What's happened?' asked Salvio.

'I came to give you my report, of course,' she responded. 'I would have phoned last night but it seemed a little late. And this morning Signora Wilson wanted to return to Montenello first thing, so I thought it made sense to accompany her and take the chance to talk a little more.'

'She has come back?' Salvio wasn't expecting that. The Englishwoman hadn't seemed charmed either by Montenello or the house he had shown her.

His mother took a seat at the kitchen table. 'Aren't you supposed to be making coffee?'

As he filled the Moka pot, she began to talk. She told Salvio what he had already guessed: Montenello had failed to make a good impression. Its ageing population, the almost deserted streets, the lonely feel of the place, and the neglected house he had shown her: none of it appealed to Mimi Wilson.

'When we were chatting over dinner she talked about going to the coast or looking nearer to Alberobello or Ostuni. She has fallen for my little *trullo* and was wondering if she could afford something similar. I had the impression her mind was made up, Montenello definitely wasn't right.'

'Then why is she back?' wondered Salvio.

'This I haven't yet managed to discover. Something must have changed. I questioned her, of course, while we were in the car together, but she revealed nothing.' His mother sounded disappointed.

'Where is she now?'

'Walking around town. I told her I had an errand to run but that we would meet at the bar later and visit this disaster of a house together. She wants my advice. Don't worry, she still has no idea you are my son.'

'Mamma, it's fine to tell her,' said Salvio, impatiently.

She shrugged away the comment. 'The signora did mention you, actually. She enjoyed her lunch very much. The old man in the piazza, the one who sells apples, she spoke of him too. And Augusto, of course, but everyone adores him.'

'They do?' Salvio was finding him less adorable by the day.

The Moka pot hissed and bubbled on the stove. Donna Carmela turned off the gas, found two cups, poured a glossy stream of coffee into each and spooned in plenty of sugar. 'Is something wrong, *caro*?' she asked.

'No,' he insisted, taking the cup she offered him. 'Everything is fine.'

'This scheme is very important to you, isn't it? You are feeling anxious, I expect.'

'Maybe a little.' Salvio had hoped he was managing to hide it but his mother knew him so well.

'Talk to me then, tell me what is wrong,' she urged. 'I will help you if I can.'

It was a relief to have someone he could confide in. 'It's true that I'm anxious,' he admitted. 'If this whole thing is a disaster, it is my responsibility, I am the one who will look bad. It will shake the town's confidence in me just when I've

106

been working so hard to try and gain it. As for Augusto, he seems to be distancing himself from the project. At first I thought he was becoming forgetful but there is something else going on. He's as sharp as ever when he wants to be.'

'How intriguing,' said his mother.

'It's possible that I'm entirely wrong ... you mustn't say anything to him.'

'No, of course not,' she said, soothingly. 'But perhaps I should spend more time in Montenello and get to know the people here. My son is their mayor after all. And with business at the restaurant so slow at the moment, no one will care if I close for a few days. I could come and stay with you. Have a little holiday. Relax, take walks, make new friends.'

Salvio loved his mother but this was a small house and she seemed to fill it. 'What about Giovanni, won't he miss you?' he asked, nervously

'I expect so, but he will cope. And you need my help here, that is becoming obvious.'

His mother seemed energised by the prospect of a visit. When the coffee pot had been emptied she accompanied Salvio on his morning walk to the Town Hall. The streets were steep but for a small woman she had a long stride, and barely seemed breathless, even on the final stretch. And yet it took much longer than usual as she insisted on stopping to greet everyone they came across.

'Good morning, I am Donna Carmela, the mother of your mayor, so pleased to meet you.'

She patted a dog, admired one person's bright scarf and another's well-cut coat. It didn't seem fake, her charm, thought Salvio. There was something about the openness of her smile and the way her eyes crinkled and lit. People warmed to her.

'Already, I like this place more,' she declared, arriving in the piazza, and looking round approvingly as if she had never appreciated its space and symmetry before.

'Hopefully Signora Wilson is feeling the same way.' Salvio couldn't help sounding gloomy.

'You are counting on this woman, but she is not the only one you have chosen. Tell me about the others.'

'Do you have a moment? Come to the office and I'll show you.'

'*Va bene.*' She glanced at the clock tower. 'If I am a little late, Signora Wilson won't mind waiting.'

As always the Town Hall felt like a mausoleum. The place was so quiet you could hear if someone rustled a few papers at their desk and the temperature was generally a couple of degrees colder than outside, although the occasional clanks and groans of the radiators implied the heating system was working.

Donna Carmela kept on her coat as she sat in front of his computer. 'Show me,' she demanded.

Salvio opened the file for the young English couple, Richard and Elise. He suspected they were dreamers and had been wasting his time all along, which was disappointing. Then he showed her Edward and Gino, the Australians. They had booked a week's accommodation in the *trullo* so seemed at least to be coming to Italy, although Salvio couldn't see how it made sense for people that lived so far away to own a place here.

'And the fourth house, who knows whether someone from this family truly means to live here again? They may believe the building has some value and be reluctant to give it away.'

Augusto arrived just as they were finishing. He smoothed his moustache, patted his white hair in place and gave a winning smile.

'Donna Carmela how delightful it is to see you. What a surprise.'

Getting to her feet, she took his outstretched hand and dropped light kisses on his cheeks. 'I am learning all about your scheme to fill the town with new people,' she told him. 'How exciting.'

'Ah yes, we are making progress.' Augusto seemed half-distracted by something on his phone. 'Signora Wilson will be a welcome addition to Montenello, I am sure.'

'If she decides to take on the house,' said Salvio.

'Of course, she will, of course.'

'Isn't it time you went to meet her, Mamma? If you keep her waiting too long she may give up on you.'

His mother glanced at the clock on the wall. 'You are right, I am leaving now. I will let you know how it goes. Try not to worry too much, Salvio.' Swiftly she hugged him goodbye, squeezing her plump arms round his waist, and he thought she smelled of caramel and coffee.

It was silent in the office after she left, with only the slow clicking of Augusto's keyboard as he typed with two fingers. Salvio hoped he was sending a message to the family who wanted to reclaim their house in Montenello. He had promised to do it several times but in the sort of offhand manner that made Salvio doubt it would happen.

There were several meetings to fill the rest of the day. Long-drawn-out discussions about sewerage systems that needed fixing and recycling projects Salvio wanted to introduce. He always felt hopeful when these sessions began, entirely clear in his own head about the best course for the town to take. By the finish he would be worn down and disheartened as every issue was talked to death, and it seemed no matter how hard he tried, no change would ever be allowed to happen here.

Today, though, there was some enthusiasm for his recycling plan. Even his proposal to place a ban on plastic bags in the town was met with a chorus of approval. Afterwards he was congratulated for his vision.

What could be behind this new attitude? Salvio wondered if it was the plan to repopulate the town. Perhaps very slowly it was changing the way the *comune* was thinking, making them more open to progress and ideas.

Later sitting back at his desk, staring out of the window overlooking the piazza, Salvio kept wondering how Signora Wilson's second visit to her house had gone. The stakes were beginning to seem even higher now.

He was about to shut down his computer for the day when the email pinged through. It was from the young English couple and the word URGENT was typed in the subject line. Salvio assumed they were backing out of the purchase. All that time he had put into helpful communications, and now he would have to start again with someone new. With a sigh he opened the email and began to read.

> *Dear Mayor Valentini – I wanted to send you my one euro but apparently Italy won't accept British postal orders so what is the best way for me to get the money to you? I definitely want the house and would like to get on with buying it as quickly as possible. I'll be in Montenello in late May for a week but if you send me all the documentation, I can sign it and email everything back immediately.*
>
> *There's just one change and I hope it's not going to make any difference. My partner Richard has decided he doesn't want to be involved. So it's me buying the property, on my own. I'm really excited about heading over to see it,*
>
> *Thanks for all your help,*
> *Elise Hartman*

Mimi

Mimi had never intended to return to Montenello. She hadn't hated the place, but by no means did she love it. More importantly, a sane person would never buy a large, neglected house in an isolated Italian town, no matter how cheaply. That was what she decided on the drive back to the charming little *trullo*. With the decision made she spent a carefree afternoon walking through the olive groves, sketchbook in hand, before heading over to the restaurant next door for more of Donna Carmela's cooking.

There were a couple of other tables occupied by diners and she ate alone. But once everyone else had left, Donna Carmela brought over a dessert of little fried croquettes of rice pudding drizzled with orange blossom honey. Sitting down to share it, she chatted for a while about other areas that might be worth looking at, and by the time Mimi returned to the *trullo* she was thinking more along the lines of a small apartment near the sea. In the morning she would contact the mayor to tell him that Montenello definitely wasn't an option.

Checking her emails before going to bed, Mimi came across one from Glenn. She almost didn't open it because she knew her ex-husband was bound to have something annoying to say. Rashly, though, she double-clicked and began to read. It turned out he had caught up with the news she was looking at houses in Italy. He made no bones about how bad an idea this was in his opinion. Not only was she risking a poor investment, attempting a renovation by herself was unwise, and the timing entirely wrong for a move to a foreign country. The boys might have left home but they weren't independent enough for her to leave them yet. Glenn hoped she wasn't going to do anything that wasn't in their best interests.

Mimi was left fuming. Few things irritated her more than being told not to do something she wasn't actually planning on doing. And Glenn had no right to an opinion about the choices she made these days. Whatever made him think he might?

Later, lying in bed beneath the conical roof of the *trullo*, she tossed, turned and ruminated. While they were married, Mimi had mostly gone along with what Glenn wanted because it seemed easier. Her Silver Divorcee friends said he was the classic controlling type, but Mimi thought of him more as a natural leader. At the design company he owned there was a team of people reporting to him so she supposed it was instinctive for him to take on the role as CEO of his household too.

Now, instead of sleeping, she replayed scenes from their past together. His insistence on Otis and Ben going to schools of his choosing, the trips to destinations he wanted to visit, his influence over the meals she cooked, the wine she drank and the clothes she wore. Even her career was affected. She turned down projects Glenn thought wrong for her. She let go of an ambition to write the words for the children's books she illustrated, because he made her fear it was risky and she might not be good enough.

Now Mimi found herself increasingly mutinous. Not that she was crazy enough to buy a house simply because Glenn had forbidden it. Still, there was nothing stopping her from going back for a second look if she felt like it. Just the thought had made her feel better and she was able to drift off to sleep at last.

Waking early the next morning, the first thing Mimi had thought of was Glenn's email and she felt even more indignant. How dare he imply she was deserting their sons? If either of them needed her then she would be there in a heartbeat. They were her priority and always had been; nevertheless, Mimi had to be realistic. Otis and Ben didn't depend on her as they once had, nor would they want a clingy mother. It was time for her to start creating a life of her own, one where she wasn't trapped in the empty spaces they had left behind, where she didn't feel so bereft.

And so with Donna Carmela a chatty presence in the passenger seat, Mimi had driven back to Montenello feeling pleasantly disobedient.

Wandering alone through the hilltop village, she went where her feet took her, this time noticing more houses that seemed empty. Some of the townspeople she encountered stared at her wordlessly but a few others offered a nod or a brusque *buongiorno*.

Reaching the piazza, Mimi paused to buy a bag of the surprisingly sweet wrinkly apples sold by the old man, and then walked on. The morning sun had very little warmth in it but she noticed how its soft light was burnishing the old stone so it seemed to glow. She climbed higher, seeing the views open out beneath her, until she reached a half-ruined tower at the summit.

This place had its own kind of beauty, Mimi realised. There was a grittiness here, a sense that generations had clung to this town carved into the mountain, had weathered harsh years and led tough, determined lives. But if you looked closely there were early spring plants daring to flower in the tiny spaces between the scarred stone, there was the greenness of the valley below and the scrubby hills beyond it, there was the sheer expanse of sky with dark clouds slowly edging towards her. Mimi knew she was experiencing a part of Italy rarely found by other tourists. It was raw and real here. She was glad to have come.

Retracing her steps, she made her way towards the bar

where she had agreed to meet Donna Carmela. There was no sign of her yet so Mimi found a stool beside the counter and ordered a caffè latte. Sipping on it, she recognised the small, round woman who was sitting beside her and talking to the bartender. Wasn't she the cook from the *trattoria* next door? Catching her eye, Mimi smiled.

'*Buongiorno*,' she said, self-consciously trying out some Italian.

The woman measured her with a gaze. 'You were with the mayor yesterday. You had the meatballs and the caponata, but you didn't finish it,' she said in slow but fluent English.

'That's right.' Mimi was surprised she had noticed.

'You didn't enjoy it?'

'Oh no, it was very good. I just don't normally eat so much at lunchtime.'

'You are used to restaurants that serve scraps of food arranged in the middle of a large white plate?' She said it pityingly.

'Actually, I'm used to a piece of cheese and an apple at my desk,' Mimi told her. 'But the food here is irresistible. Everything I've eaten so far has been such a treat.'

There was the hint of a smile and the woman held out a large, capable hand. 'I am Assunta.'

'Mimi Wilson.'

Assunta had a firm grip and an enthusiastic handshake. 'You should come for lunch today. I have made a stew of lamb with pickled peppers, it is very good.'

'That sounds tempting,' said Mimi. 'I'm going to look at a property soon but perhaps I'll be hungry enough after that.'

'You are a part of this scheme of Augusto's to bring people back to Montenello?'

'That's right. He and the mayor have found me a house on the edge of the village.'

There was another smile, this one fonder. 'He is all for progress, Augusto. He has wanted this for a long time.'

'How do other people feel about it?' wondered Mimi. 'Is everyone OK with the idea of foreigners buying up property here?'

Assunta glanced over at the bar's patron. 'More customers for Renzo, more people wanting to eat at my *trattoria*. That can only be a good thing. But most of us don't believe it will ever happen. It is a nice dream for Augusto and a project for this young mayor who has so much energy. Eh, Renzo?'

The bartender shrugged as if he hadn't given it much thought then nodded towards Mimi's empty coffee up. '*Un altro?*'

Checking the time, she saw that Donna Carmela was running late. 'Just a mineral water please,' she told him.

Assunta lit a cigarette, dragging heavily on it before offering the packet to Mimi, who shook her head and tried to resist the urge to waft the tendrils of smoke away from her face.

'Do you remember this town before everyone moved away?' she asked.

'Not really, I am too young. It was after the war most people left, that is what Augusto says.'

'Escaping the poverty,' Mimi guessed. 'Life must have been such a struggle.'

Assunta flicked the ash from her cigarette into a saucer. 'Yes they were very poor back then. They say many starved during the war. And then of course there was the curse.'

The bartender Renzo gave her a sharp look but said nothing.

'What curse?' asked Mimi, curious.

'Old stories, no one talks of them any more.' Stubbing out her cigarette, Assunta finished her coffee. 'But it is time for me to get back to work. I will see you for lunch, yes? Don't be too late.'

Mimi watched her leave then turned to the bartender and repeated, 'What curse?'

He looked at her blankly, as if he hadn't understood, although she was almost certain he had been following their conversation.

Montenello felt as if it could be cursed she thought, glancing out at the nearly deserted piazza and the sky above it darkening with clouds. It had that kind of spooky atmosphere right now.

She waited another twenty minutes for Donna Carmela to hurry in, apologising. By then Mimi was beginning to wonder if she really needed to bother revisiting the house, particularly as it was starting to rain quite heavily.

But Donna Carmela seemed so interested in seeing the place and then the bartender produced an umbrella and since they had come all this way it made sense to carry on.

Hurrying across the wet flagstones, sharing the umbrella, they headed off down the narrow back streets 'It's a decent walk,' said Mimi. 'The house is at the far end of town. I hope I remember the way.'

'Don't worry. If we get lost I will just call Salvio,' Donna Carmela told her.

Mimi glanced at her. 'You mean the mayor? Do you know him well?'

'Ah, quite well … yes.' Donna Carmela sounded a little flustered. 'Actually he is my son.'

How strange of her not to mention it before now. Scanning her face again, Mimi realised there was a resemblance: something in the eyes and the evenness of their features, although the mayor was a lot taller.

'That's why I got such a good deal on the rental of the *trullo*?' she guessed.

'Yes … but I am not a part of this scheme to sell the houses in Montenello,' Donna Carmela hastened to add. 'I am not here to try and talk you into anything. I am curious to see the place, that is all.'

Mimi wondered if the mayor had asked her not to mention

their relationship, although she couldn't come up with any reason why he might want to do that. Perhaps people were secretive in small Italian towns like this. It seemed the only explanation.

'You must know Montenello well then,' said Mimi.

'Not really, this is quite a new job for Salvio and I have never had much reason to come here before now.'

'Have you ever heard anything about the town being cursed?' Mimi wondered.

'I don't think so. What makes you ask that?'

'Just something a woman in the bar said a little earlier. She thought that was why so many people left after the war.'

'I suppose everyone was more superstitious then,' said Donna Carmela. 'If you lost your baby or your husband died, you looked for a reason. Every town in southern Italy probably had a curse in those days. It was a convenient thing to blame.'

'Still, it seemed an odd thing for her to say to me.'

Donna Carmela shrugged. 'I am sure there are plenty of odd people in Montenello. In fact I would be very surprised if there aren't.'

By the time they found the house it had almost stopped raining. Its shutters had been left open so this time it didn't seem quite so unwelcoming. The door gave much more easily, and Donna Carmela swept in and through each room, offering a monologue as she went.

'Very spacious ... much larger than these places usually are ... this must be the master bedroom, I suppose, what a view. The bathroom is ... hmm, maybe I won't go in there. The kitchen you would rip out completely as well. And then this whole place could open up more onto the terrace, which is huge. Have you been out there?'

'Yes but I'm not sure how safe it is.'

'It has survived for hundreds of years I am sure it won't

collapse today.' Opening the French doors, Donna Carmela stepped out into the softly falling rain.

'That's exactly what I thought,' said Mimi, following her.

Donna Carmela was standing on the very edge of the terrace, peering down. 'You have land here,' she breathed. 'It would need to be properly tiered but I think that maybe ...'

'I could put in a pool?' finished Mimi.

'It might be tricky, but yes. And imagine how spectacular it would be, with that view across the valley. I didn't expect this at all.'

'So you like the place?'

'It is damp and filthy but the house has good bones. Structurally, things might not be as bad as you might think. Perhaps it is too large for you, though. How many bedrooms are there?'

'Officially three but four if you count that small room I would use as my studio,' said Mimi. 'The others would be ideal for my sons and any friends who wanted to visit. So it's not the size that's the problem, just that I can't envisage the place ever being anything but a dump.'

'I know exactly what you mean,' said Donna Carmela. 'When I first saw my *trullo* it had no doors, no windows, no floors, nothing. It was just a shell of stone. Now it seems impossible that it ever looked that way.'

'Do you think I should actually consider buying this place?'

'First I think we should investigate the garden. Are there steps? Surely there must be.'

Donna Carmela was opening and closing doors, raising dust, exclaiming again at the generous size of the rooms, gasping at the stench coming from the drains. A small, round woman who seemed to take over any space she entered, she was chasing the ghosts away. Mimi could almost feel them leaving. The house was still carpeted by decades of dirt, the smell as musty and there was too much old junk left behind, yet somehow it felt less bleak with Donna Carmela in it, less discouraging.

'Ah, here we are.' She opened what had looked to be a cupboard. 'Let's brave the jungle out there and see where you might put this swimming pool.'

Edward

Standing on the Pincio terrace, looking down across the rooftops and domes, Edward felt slightly dizzy. He hoped it was only jet lag, that he hadn't picked up some bug on the long flight over, because now they were finally in Rome he wanted to make the most of it.

Right up until the last moment he had been concerned Gino might back out of the trip. There were issues with work, furniture that had to be delivered, bills he absolutely had to pay before they got on the plane. In the end, Edward had packed a suitcase for him and it wasn't until it was checked in and they had cleared customs and were in the bar having a pre-flight glass of champagne that he really felt this was happening. They were going to Italy.

Gino still didn't know about the house in Montenello. Instead, Edward had been focusing on all the other things he planned for them to see and do. The rocky coves where they could swim through caves, the restaurants that had been recommended, the history and art, even the roads where he had been told they might be able to open up the red convertible 1960s Fiat he had rented.

Edward knew at some point he would have to admit to Gino that he had an ulterior motive for this trip, particularly as he was growing more enthusiastic about the idea of restoring an old ruin in some forgotten corner of Italy. In his head he had already begun to progress the plan. They could rent out their home in Bondi and spend at least six months away from their ordinary lives. They could take time to tackle the project together, turn a run-down old house into something really special, and escape to other places he had always hoped to visit – Prague, Berlin, Barcelona. Money shouldn't be an issue as he was sure to pick up writing work to supplement the rental income from their Bondi house. But everything depended on Gino. He was the practical one, clever at renovating, skilled with his hands. He spoke the language. And besides, Edward wouldn't want to do something like this without him.

With a last look at the view, they turned and headed along the shady avenues of the Villa Borghese Gardens towards the boating lake. They had only been here a couple of days but Edward thought Gino already seemed a little more Italian. He was wearing new sunglasses and a close-fitting shirt from Dolce & Gabbana. With the olive of his skin he could easily pass for a local.

It was Gino who had wanted to hire one of the rowboats. The idea wasn't especially appealing but lots of other people were out on the small lake, so clearly it was a tradition, and Edward wasn't going to refuse anything he seemed keen on.

It turned out to be pleasant enough sitting in the stern of the wooden boat, fingers trailing into the cool, greenish water as Gino handled the oars and slowly sculled from one side to the other, past umbrella pines and the pillars of a small white temple.

'Mmm, this is nice,' sighed Edward, his face tilted to soak up the warmth of the spring sunshine. 'I'm loving this city.'

'It'll be completely different further south,' Gino warned. 'There are gay clubs here in Rome, there's a bit of a scene.'

Edward opened his eyes. 'You're not telling me you want to go out and discover it?'

'My point is this is a conservative, religious country.' Gino sounded impatient. 'You might not notice it so much in Rome, but when we get to the rural places ...'

'I guess we'll just take things as we find them,' said

Edward. 'I'm not expecting to go clubbing. I think we're a bit past that, don't you?'

Gino's response was an arch look. 'Really, Ed? Speak for yourself.'

He was using one oar to turn the boat, smoothly and expertly. When had he ever rowed before? Edward was mystified. He thought he knew all there was to know about Gino. They had been close since they were boys. Back then they were so different: Gino the quiet one, Edward always in trouble; Gino dark and serious, Edward prone to playing the clown. It was a friendship that shouldn't have worked but they seemed drawn to each other. Whenever Edward thought about the past, Gino was somewhere in the memory.

They shared everything: lunches, toys, homework, adventures, even a couple of girlfriends when they were teenagers. They were in and out of each other's homes on weekends and pretty much always beside each other at school.

When things between them started to shift and deepen, Edward was afraid. He didn't want to be different; he couldn't see why it was happening. It was the only time he ever avoided Gino. It must have been six months, perhaps a little more, and Edward remembered them as the most confused and lonely of his life. He had been angry, mostly with Gino. The only thing that made sense was that all of this was his fault.

Trying to ignore him didn't work. It was like a spotlight was shining on Gino, when he was in a room there was nowhere else to look. And Edward was swamped in feelings he didn't understand, an excitement, a longing that made him want to close his eyes and pretend he wasn't in the world. For a while he kept pushing Gino away, when if anything he wanted him more.

Watching him now, as he manoeuvred their boat past another, Edward could see the boy he used to be. His face had changed, softened and lined; silver now flecked that dark,

dark hair; his body had broadened. But at heart he was still the slight, shy boy who had told Edward he loved him, who had put his arms around him and promised it would all be OK in the end.

For a long time it had been fine, mostly. When Edward looked back on their life together it seemed to be arranged in chapters. There was the secrecy of the very beginning, the growing stronger until they were ready to face friends and family, the determination and pride when they managed it. There were the wild party years that seemed to go on forever but had now blurred in both their memories. And there were those few times they were tempted away from each other, somehow always knowing they would end up back together.

'How long since we went out to a club?' Edward asked now.

'I don't know. Mardi Gras? Wasn't there a party?'

'That was last year.'

'Yeah, you're right, it was.'

'We're old,' Edward said. 'When did that happen?'

'Have you only just noticed?' Gino was clearly amused. 'You're not about to have a big gay midlife crisis are you?'

'Of course not.'

'Anyway, we're not that old. No need to panic yet.'

Edward stared out across the lake, thinking it was different for Gino. He had established himself, was Sydney's top custom furniture designer, according to all the interiors magazines. Hugh Jackman had commissioned one of his layered tallboys. Miranda Kerr had been photographed draped over his iconic curved table for the cover of *Vogue Australia*. What had Edward done in the meantime? Written some interesting articles, too many press releases and lately a lot of website content. It felt like he had been filling in time while he was waiting for something better to happen. Now he was forty-five and still waiting

'I'm not panicking,' he told Gino, although he suspected it wasn't entirely true.

From the lakeside, a man with a loudhailer called a number and beckoned the boat in. Their allotted twenty minutes was finished.

'That went quickly,' said Gino.

'Time does,' replied Edward. 'It goes really quickly. Have you only just noticed?'

Elise

Elise had never seen Richard so angry. He had shouted at her and slammed the front door as he stormed out of the flat. For four hours he had refused to respond to a single text or call. Elise was worried at first, then angry, then worried again. This wasn't like him at all. She hadn't even realised Richard had a temper to lose.

Maybe she ought to have handled things better. She had been cooking dinner, sizzling diced onions and garlic in oil to cheer up a jar of pasta sauce. He had been opening a bottle of supermarket red, since it was Friday night. As he was pouring it into a decanter to breathe (which he reckoned made even the cheapest wine taste better) he mentioned the half-term holiday, suggesting they went camping or headed to the coast.

'I can't, I'll be in Italy that week,' said Elise, stirring the sizzling onions and not quite managing to look up at him.

'What do you mean?' He stopped pouring the wine.

'I've booked my flights and I'm going to see my new house in Montenello.'

'But you can't—'

'Yes, I can. I've emailed the mayor and told him I want it. And I'm really excited now. I can't wait to get over there.'

Richard's eyes widened and all the ruddiness drained from his face. 'We talked about this. We agreed we weren't going ahead.'

'You talked and we didn't agree on anything,' she pointed out. 'If you're not keen then I'll do it on my own.'

'So we're breaking up? That's what you want?' Richard

was chalky pale now. He poured himself a glass of wine and gulped down a mouthful.

'Don't be ridiculous. I didn't say that.'

'You as good as did. Couples discuss things and make joint decisions, Elise. They don't go off and do stuff like this. Not if they want to stay together.'

'Come with me, then. You know it's what I'd prefer.'

He glared at her. 'Are we going to keep going round and round in circles on this.'

'I'm not going in circles; I'm going to Italy. There's a house there and it's mine. I'm doing it, Rich, with you or without you.' Elise wasn't backing down.

That was when he had raised his voice and told her she was being selfish. He downed the rest of his wine and said Elise could do what she liked because he didn't care, swore a bit then walked away. She had assumed he was going to sulk in the bedroom but the loud slam of the front door and the silence that followed signalled things were more serious than that.

Now the onions were congealing in the pan, and Elise was alone on the sofa with the rest of the wine and her phone within reach, feeling guilty and wondering what she might have done differently. Perhaps Richard was bound to feel rejected and hurt however she broke the news. Still, it seemed unreasonable of him. There was no rule that couples had to do everything together, was there?

It was so quiet without the television on or Richard's music blaring. They ought to have been settling down right now with bowls of spaghetti, drinking wine together, talking about the things in their day that had amused or annoyed them. It was the way they had spent so many Friday nights at home.

Elise wondered what was going to happen next. Would Richard come back soon? Walk through the door and hug her, saying he had changed his mind and was coming to

Italy. That was what she was hoping for. Over the years he had always gone along with what she wanted and it was what she expected this time. But as the hours ticked by and the wine decanter emptied, Elise began to realise she had taken a risk.

It was late when she got the text. Richard was out with friends and they were in a pub that had a lock-in. She shouldn't wait up. He didn't refer to their fight at all. But neither did he finish his message with the usual kisses or a heart emoji.

Elise cleared up the half-cooked mess in the kitchen and got ready for bed. She fell asleep straight away, knocked out by the wine, but then woke again at 3 a.m. to find the space beside her still empty.

'Richard?' she called quite loudly, in case he was in the bathroom or dozing on the sofa, but no voice called back in reply. Elise climbed out of bed and checked the flat was empty then stared out of the window. Below she could see the kitchen of the Indian restaurants all lit up. Its staff must be cleaning or cooking up tomorrow's curries. The other windows that lay in Elise's view were curtained and dark. Here people were sleeping while in other parts the city they were still leaving clubs and hailing taxis or buying late-night kebabs. Where was Richard?

In the morning Elise woke to the smell of coffee and burned toast. For a moment she felt almost shy of facing him but then pulled herself together. It wasn't selfish to have big dreams, only a shame that Richard couldn't share them.

'Good morning.' He appeared in the doorway with a mug of coffee in hand.

Elise stared up at him from her pillow, thinking he looked pretty rough. 'Did you just get home? Where did you stay last night?'

'With a mate,' he told her, putting the coffee mug on the bedside table.

'Which mate?'

'No one you know.'

Elise eased herself up tiredly and reached for the coffee. She sat with the mug warming her hands, wondering what to say to him.

It was Richard who spoke first, surprising her with an apology. 'I'm sorry I walked out like that. I was pretty upset though; still am, to be honest. It was big news to take in.'

'This is something I really want to do,' Elise told him. 'It doesn't have to cause such a problem between us.'

'I think it does. It means something has changed. We want different things now. Before this we were always on the same side.'

'I'm still on your side, Richard.'

'But you're aiming for a different future than the one we've been working towards?'

'I suppose I am,' Elise admitted.

'That's why I think the best thing would be for us to take a break right now. Have some time apart to really consider how important we are to each other.'

'Are you dumping me?' Elise couldn't believe what she was hearing. 'Is this real?'

Richard reached to take down the big suitcase from the top of their wardrobe. 'No, I'm giving you some space. I think it's what you need right now.'

'Where will you go?' she asked in a small voice, as he started opening drawers and pulling out socks and sweaters.

'To stay with a mate.'

'The same mate as last night? The one I don't know.'

'That's right.'

A suspicion hit Elise with such force it took her breath away. 'Are you seeing someone else?'

'No, of course not.' He stopped packing and perched beside her on the bed. 'I love you, Elise. You're the one for me; I've always known it. But with this Italy thing I feel like you're leaving me, that our life isn't enough for you any more, and I can't take it. So if I go now then maybe it'll give you the opportunity to think about what you really want. I'm hoping it will be me ... but it's up to you now.'

Richard kissed her and it felt comfortingly familiar. Then he carried on packing. Elise got up and helped, folding his work shirts so they wouldn't crease too badly. She stood at the front door and kissed him one last time before he lugged the heavy suitcase down the stairs because as usual the lift wasn't working.

Elise didn't cry until he had gone. She went back to bed and stayed there for most of the morning. Hunger pangs finally drove her out from beneath the covers. She made some cheese on toast and ate it with a dollop of the tomato relish she and Richard had bottled last summer.

He may have gone but still Richard seemed everywhere. There were photographs of them together in clip frames on the walls, there was the coffee table he had found in a skip and spent a weekend sanding and varnishing. His books were on the shelves mingled with hers and there were things they had collected dotted about everywhere.

Elise picked up a large wooden bowl of shells they added to every time they visited a beach. Limpet shells, periwinkles and dog whelks, they were so fragile and pretty. Every shell represented a happy day they had spent together. Elise thought of how Richard always wrapped them carefully in a towel so they wouldn't crack or chip while he was carrying them home.

With a small sigh she put the bowl back on the window ledge. She supposed she had two choices now. Email the mayor and let him know she was changing her mind after all. Or deal with losing Richard completely.

Montenello

Already, Salvio's home seemed different. First the smell of his mother's fragrance had laced the air then the sound of her favourite music filled it. Soon her possessions were strewn about: reading glasses left here, a scarf draped there, a book on the table, a half-finished crossword on the counter. And now there was the cooking. Every pot that Salvio owned seemed to have been commandeered to simmer sauces, to steam, bake and sizzle.

'There are only two of us, Mamma,' he said, alarmed on arriving home, 'not a whole restaurant to cook for.'

She peered over the top of a tray she was pulling out of the oven. 'We are having some friends over to share a meal. Did I not mention it?'

'Not that I remember.' Salvio had been looking forward to an evening spent together. 'Anyway, what friends? You don't know anyone in this town.'

'I do now,' she told him. 'So you had better set the table for six.'

Augusto arrived first, clutching a bunch of flowers he presented to Donna Carmela with a flourish. There was a fuss about the necessity of arranging them in a water jug because Salvio didn't own a vase and then two more guests arrived, a woman whose round, friendly face seemed vaguely familiar and a stern-looking man he was sure he had never set eyes on. After hasty introductions he was despatched to make everyone an *aperitivo*.

'The English signora will be here soon,' Donna Carmela told him. 'She will have a gin and tonic, not too strong.'

When Mimi arrived it became apparent that his mother had chosen the other guests on the basis they spoke some English. Even so, the conversation stumbled along. They talked about the weather and how it was unusually chilly for the time of year. The new recycling plan didn't interest anyone as much as it did Salvio and there was only mild enthusiasm for a discussion about the history and traditions of the town.

'Wasn't there a curse on Montenello at some point?' asked Mimi as they settled at the dining table and Donna Carmela went to fetch the first course.

Salvio sensed the other people around him had stilled on hearing her words, and there was an odd moment of silence. 'A curse? Whatever gave you that idea?' he asked.

'Someone mentioned it to me in the bar. Old stories, apparently,' said Mimi. 'From long before your time, perhaps.'

Augusto's eyes had widened and his mother's new friends were shifting awkwardly in their seats.

'There are always superstitions in small towns like this. It is part of their charm,' Salvio told her.

'That is exactly what I said,' agreed Donna Carmela, as she set down a long platter covered in arancini. 'No one believes in these curses nowadays. They are forgotten.'

'I suppose I was intrigued because I illustrate children's books and those traditional fairy tales often featured curses,' explained Mimi. 'This is the first time I've come across one in real life.'

Augusto was shaking his head. 'It is all forgotten like Donna Carmela told you,' he said, frostily. 'Best not to mention it.'

Salvio wondered if he had heard a hint of warning in his words. Could there actually be a curse? The last thing he needed right now was yet another thing to deter people from settling in Montenello.

'It is all nonsense though, yes?' he said, quickly.

'Of course,' agreed Augusto, but without his usual breezy confidence.

The food was on the table and the wine glasses filled. This was usually Salvio's favourite moment in any dinner party but tonight was becoming more awkward.

'I have friends who are superstitious,' his mother chatted away as she began to serve the arancini. 'They watch out for the evil eye and won't put a hat down on a bed. I have never had time for any of that myself. Bad things happen or they don't; it is random.'

'Of course,' said Augusto, more vigorously. 'You are very wise, Donna Carmela.'

Salvio added this mysterious curse to his mental list of things he was certain his assistant knew more about than he was saying. Thankfully, the food was a distraction from any more talk of it. Biting into a golden risotto ball filled with melting, stringy mozzarella dredged in crunchy breadcrumbs and piping hot from the deep-fryer, he felt some of the strain begin to leave the evening. A glass or two of wine helped things ease a little further.

'None for me, I'm driving,' said Mimi, covering her glass with her hand.

'What a pity I don't have a second spare room, otherwise you would be welcome to stay the night,' said Salvio. 'Will you be OK getting back to the *trullo* in the dark?'

'Yes, yes,' Mimi reassured him. 'I'm sure I'll be fine. Although I am thinking it would be good to spend some time staying in Montenello. Before I make a decision about buying the house I'd like to get to know the place a little better.'

Salvio might have preferred that Mimi kept a distance for now. There were aspects of this town that didn't reward a closer look. Not only the vacant, run-down buildings but the sense the place was slowly giving up as its inhabitants aged and died. Years ago there had been an annual *festa* with a parade and street stalls and, according to Augusto, on summer evenings there had been music and dancing in the piazza and the young folk had courted each other during the Sunday afternoon *passeggiata*. All of it was only a memory now.

'Unfortunately, there are no hotels open in Montenello,' he told Mimi. 'Possibly there may be someone who will rent out a room to you. Augusto, what do you think?'

'I could ask around, signore. There are many empty rooms, of course, but whether people will be prepared to invite a stranger into their home ...'

Donna Carmela was in the kitchen, putting the final touches to the second course. 'Why don't you stay in the house you're thinking of buying, Mimi?' she called. 'That would make sense, wouldn't it?'

'But it is such a mess,' Salvio objected.

'We could clean it up, borrow furniture, get the power switched on and perhaps have the chimney swept. None of that sounds impossible. And I can help,' Donna Carmela offered. 'I have some free time at the moment.'

Mimi turned to Salvio, her expression keen. 'Would that be OK, do you think? It would give me time to get an architect to look at the place and maybe I could talk to a builder. It might help me make a decision.'

'Don't you have to return home to London soon?' he asked.

'There's no reason why I couldn't extend the trip,' Mimi told him. 'I think it's worthwhile because I still don't have a proper sense of what it would be like to live here.'

'It will be so uncomfortable for you there,' Salvio protested.

'I'll think of it like camping. And I'll stay off the terrace until I'm sure it's safe, don't worry.'

'That is settled then.' Donna Carmela sounded pleased. 'I will come in the morning with rubber gloves and lots of disinfectant and we will tackle that bathroom first. Best to get the worst job over with. And then we can start to think about the furniture.'

'All I'll need is a mattress and some bedding. I don't mind roughing it,' said Mimi.

'I am sure we can do better than that. Salvio, don't you agree?'

The mayor of Montenello sighed. There was no point in trying to argue with his mother. And now her new friends were chiming in, offering their good linen sheets, plates and pans, wondering if a neighbour might have a bed they didn't need, or a cousin a couple of spare chairs.

'We all want to contribute to making your plan a huge success, signore,' the round-faced woman told him, beaming.

Salvio smiled and thanked her for the support. He told Mimi Wilson he would help make the house comfortable in any way he could. Then he agreed with his mother that they should start a list and began jotting down her many suggestions between mouthfuls of lamb spiked with thyme and covered in a salty sharp crust of pecorino cheese. It was the right thing to do.

What he couldn't bear was the idea he might fail at being mayor of Montenello. It was the thought that woke him in the middle of the night and chased away sleep for hours.

And so Salvio would keep on trying to do the right thing, day after day, and hope his plan to save the town succeeded in the end.

Mimi

Mimi wanted the house although she hadn't dared admit it. Even the Silver Divorcees only got a brief message to say she was staying on in Italy and wouldn't make the next evening they had planned. She sent Otis and Ben a couple of photos of the view from its terrace but didn't bother replying to her ex-husband's email at all. She was keeping this excitement to herself.

Every time she visited the place it seemed to have more potential. This morning, arriving early with bags of newly purchased cleaning products she noticed the way bright morning light flooded into the kitchen. It was picking out cobwebs strung like bunting from the ceiling, and an expanse of tired Formica, but Mimi could change all that.

She hadn't expected Donna Carmela to make good on the previous night's promise to help so the knock on the door surprised her. 'I have face masks,' she announced, bustling in, 'and some disinfectant that apparently they use to clean the insides of ambulances. Your bathroom is no match for me.'

'Thank you so much—'

'I called my husband Giovanni and he will pick up the furniture you have been offered. Salvio is making sure you have electricity and gas to cook with. So everything is under control.'

Mimi was grateful to the point of being almost tearful. For so long she had been coping alone and to have someone on her side again felt overwhelming. She tried to thank Donna Carmela but there was no way to express exactly what it meant to have her there, putting on a face mask, and taking up a mop to do battle against the filth and neglect.

It was a long morning and the cleaner the house became, the more dishevelled she and Donna Carmela seemed to look. By the time the bathroom seemed just about acceptable, they were both badly in need of a rest.

Collapsed on the newly scrubbed floor, leaning back against a wall, Mimi felt too exhausted to think about moving but another knock on the door forced her to her feet. This time it was Salvio who had brought lunch and three folding chairs for them to sit on while they ate it.

The day was noticeably warmer so they risked the terrace. Mimi tore into a crusty bread roll filled with slices of velvety cheese and a fiery chilli paste, half listening to Salvio and Donna Carmela whose conversation had drifted from English to Italian, and thinking how much nicer the place felt already.

'Next the kitchen and that will be enough for today,' Donna Carmela broke into her thoughts. 'Tomorrow we will sort the living area and one of the bedrooms. And then once you have furniture—'

'I can stay here for a few nights,' Mimi said, happily.

'Which is perfect for me, too, as there are more guests arriving at the *trullo*,' Donna Carmela admitted.

Mimi was interested when she heard these new arrivals were also planning to look at one of Montenello's abandoned houses. She hoped they were people she could be friends with.

'That was delicious,' Donna Carmela dusted the crumbs from her lap. 'But now it is time to start on that kitchen. You cannot live on *panini* for ever.'

'Actually, I could. I'll only be here for another week or so, surely. Why don't we forget about the kitchen for now?' Mimi really couldn't face it.

'Absolutely not.' Donna Carmela was on her feet. 'It's the

most important room in the house. And besides, with no kitchen how are you going to invite me for dinner?'

As the afternoon lengthened they tackled sticky, dusty surfaces. Side by side they scrubbed nicotine stains from the walls, scoured the sink and the stained hob of an old stove, only baulking when they opened the oven door.

'Oh no, no, no.' Mimi slammed it shut again fast but not before she had glimpsed the desiccated remains of someone's long ago meal.

Donna Carmela's face screwed into a grimace. 'What sort of person leaves a house with food still in the oven; even for a week, never mind forever?'

'Who knows? I keep thinking about who might have lived here and why they went.' Mimi leaned back against the oven door, hoping Donna Carmela wasn't going to insist on them cleaning it. 'Perhaps whoever it was got driven away by this curse I'm not supposed to talk about?'

Donna Carmela laughed. 'I'm certain it was something much less exciting.'

'Montenello doesn't feel very cursed today.' Mimi glanced out of the kitchen window towards the dramatic view of mountains and clear blue sky. 'I hope the people who left found happy lives somewhere. It must have been so sad to go away from home and never come back.'

'And what about you?' Donna Carmela wondered. 'Will this place be your home soon?'

'I hope so. I wasn't sure at first but now I think it may be where I want to be.'

'You will need to buy a new oven then,' Donna Carmela observed. 'But for the time being don't open up that door again.'

Edward

Annoyingly, Edward had been sick. The long flight over, the stress of not being entirely honest with Gino, the change in temperature – whatever caused the dizziness and fever, it hit him hard for a couple of days. While he was stuck in bed, Gino explored alone, coming back to their hotel room with stories of the things he had done. Watching the stray cats that lived amid the ruins of temples in the Torre Argentina, seeing the sunset from a garden filled with orange trees on the Aventine Hill, eating the best pistachio gelato of his life. Edward was sorry to have missed out, but pleased to see him so happy.

'I'll take you to all those places,' Gino promised. 'We have to see that sunset together; it's an absolute must. And the gelato was sublime. Let's stay in Rome for longer, forget about the south.'

'We'll be back here at the end of the trip. There'll be time then,' Edward told him.

'You're so stubborn.'

'Really? I'm stubborn?'

Gino flopped down on the bed beside him. 'Seriously, are you sure you're OK to do a long drive tomorrow? Because I'm happy to stay here for a few more days and then maybe we could head north to Venice or Florence.'

'We're going south, so stop looking for excuses.'

'You really want to see the part of Italy my parents fled from all those years ago?'

'They didn't flee, they emigrated to Australia for a better life; it's not quite the same thing.'

'Whatever you want to call it I'm glad they left.' Gino rolled onto his back and stared up at the ceiling. 'Imagine if they'd stayed and I'd been born there. What sort of time would I have had? I might be married now to some poor woman, have a family. There must be lots of men in those small towns who know they don't fit their lives but haven't the courage to escape them.'

'You'd have found a way out somehow.' Edward said with certainty, resting an arm over Gino's flat belly.

They dozed for half an hour. Edward woke first and slipping quietly out of bed, moved to the window seat where he could watch the life of Rome pass over the cobbles below. Within view was a stone fountain where earlier he had watched a street artist sketching tourist portraits. Now there was a young woman filling her water bottle and a man slowly cycling past. Beyond them a waiter was hanging a dinner menu beside the entrance of a small *osteria* and a well-dressed couple had paused to read the daily specials.

Edward was tired of this; he wanted to be out there with them. The dizziness seemed to have lessened and he couldn't stand to miss out any longer.

'Gino, wake up,' he called. 'I'm going to take a quick shower and then if we hurry we might be able to reach the Aventine Hill in time to see that sunset.'

Edward let Gino take the wheel for the drive south with a pang of regret because he had been looking forward to seeing how the vintage Fiat handled. But he still didn't feel a hundred per cent and, after only a short stretch of *autostrada*, he could tell it had been the right move.

'Are there any road rules at all?' he wondered as the car in front straddled the white line, the driver apparently refusing to commit to either lane. 'This seems like total chaos.'

'It helps if you imagine you're in a video game,' said Gino, cheerfully. 'It's quite fun, actually.'

Edward watched him as he drove. He had been looking at his face in profile from a passenger seat for so many years now. At the curve of his slightly aquiline nose, the tiny creases starting to appear beside his ear, the arch of his brow. He was a good driver, handling a car with just enough care and confidence.

In the early days they'd had an old Triumph Herald, white with a red stripe down the bodywork. It was fond of breaking down at inconvenient moments, still they drove in it together to beaches and barbecues, to ecstasy-fuelled parties where they danced all night and once all the way up the coast to Byron Bay for a holiday.

As soon as they could afford to they swapped it for a Jeep that took them to mountain bike trails through eucalyptus forests, had a rack on the roof for the kayaks and plenty of space for their camping gear. That car had been a constant in their lives while other things had changed. But it started spending more time in the driveway and less with muddied tyres so Gino bought their first Mini Cooper, brand new because they had the money by then, which better suited a quieter, more city-bound life.

Edward missed the Jeep and the adventures they'd had in it. He always loved the moment at the very start of a road trip together, with so much possibility lying ahead.

Now as they sped on south through Italy, the traffic thinned and the mountains grew steeper. Edward glimpsed towns clinging picturesquely to the slopes of some and thought of Montenello. When was he going to confess to Gino, tell him about the house waiting for them there and all his hopes for it? At the very last minute, as Tia had suggested, or would it be better to give him some warning now?

It felt as if things between them had settled a little since arriving in Italy. Gino seemed less preoccupied by work and more energised by being in this new place. And last night, sitting amid the orange trees in an old walled garden as the sky turned pink and gold – it had been as romantic a moment as any they had shared.

'Do you want to stop for lunch? We could get off the *autostrada* and check out one of the hill towns?' Edward suggested as the car sped on.

'I don't think so. Those places look pretty from a distance but you never know how safe they are. If you're hungry we could call in at an Autogrill.'

Edward closed his eyes. If he couldn't get Gino to a hill town for a quick meal how was he going to make Montenello happen?

'I'm not that hungry yet,' he said. 'Let's keep going.'

It was late afternoon when they reached the *trullo* and Edward couldn't wait to escape the tension in the car. He wasn't sure where, but somehow they had taken a wrong turn and become lost in a maze of narrow lanes that according to their satnav didn't exist at all. The road yielded no clues and they circled for a while until at last they spotted one of the signs they were meant to be following.

'Ristorante di Donna Carmela ... hopefully that means we'll get a decent meal there,' said Gino.

Manoeuvring the car round a sharp bend and into the narrow gateway of the *trullo* made for another tricky moment. Edward couldn't hide his concern that its gleaming panels would be scraped, and Gino was affronted. Still, they were here now, at this quirky little house encircled by olive groves.

There was no one to be seen but they found the key beneath a potted geranium as promised and let themselves into the house.

'This is completely adorable,' said Edward, gazing about. 'Don't you love it?'

Gino was staring up at the conical roof and frowning. 'In an earthquake all that limestone would fall on us, you know.'

'What are the chances?' asked Edward. 'At least we found the place. Why don't we see what time the restaurant opens and then we can have a gin and tonic by the pool and enjoy the last of this sunshine.'

It was a disappointment to find a sign on the restaurant door saying it was closed for the evening with no indication of when it might open again. Edward felt put out. He had wanted everything to go perfectly but so far nothing seemed quite right.

'I expect there's a town nearby where we'll find a decent restaurant.'

'If we stray too far we may never find our way back,' Gino said, dubiously. 'We need pointing in the right direction. There's got to be someone around here who can help.'

They found a small, sun-baked man watering a herb garden just beyond the restaurant. He spoke no English and even Gino seemed to struggle to communicate with him. Their conversation went on for a long time, with a lot of head-shaking and arm-waving, and Edward shifting impatiently on his feet and trying to show an interest in the garden.

'He was speaking the local dialect,' Gino explained later, as they turned back towards the *trullo*.

'Did you understand any of it?'

'I think so. His wife Donna Carmela is away, which is why the restaurant is shut. There's another place close by where we can eat pretty well and there hasn't been an earthquake in years apparently. Oh, and it's going to be sunny and much warmer tomorrow; an early summer's day is coming. So we could just laze around here by the pool.'

'Sure.' Edward wanted to keep him happy. 'There are a few things on my must-see list but we don't have to rush to them.'

'Did you actually make a list?' Gino sounded amused. 'It's not like you to be so organised.'

'Did you really ask that old man about earthquakes?'

Gino laughed. 'What do you think? Of course I did. It's entirely like me to be so cautious.'

Elise

Afterwards, it was as if life had made the decision for her. Elise went into work on the Monday right after Richard had left and was called into the office. It seemed like bad news. The teacher she was covering for wanted to come back from her maternity leave early. She ought to have given more notice but the decision had been made to let her resume her old duties and use Elise as a relief teacher for the remainder of her contract.

Elise knew exactly what that meant. Moving from class to class, not having the time to build relationships with her pupils, following the format set by an absent member of staff, dogged by the knowledge she could be doing better. All she wanted was to call Richard and spill everything out. When he didn't pick up, she was angry and upset.

The rest of the week was spent in a fug of despair. By Friday lunchtime, Elise was seriously considering walking away from the job but then confided in another teacher over cups of tea in the staffroom.

'Can they actually do that?' the teacher asked. 'It doesn't sound right to me. What does your contract say?'

Elise returned to the office and demanded another meeting. This time the headmaster was more apologetic. It was a difficult situation, he conceded. The person she was covering for had financial problems and badly needed her job back. He was sure Elise understood and really appreciated her stepping aside.

He handed her a box of tissues when she started crying and promised she would get all the support she needed. Elise felt trapped. Then she remembered what the other teacher had said and mentioned her contract. The headmaster frowned. Surely she wasn't going to be a stickler about that, under the circumstances. Despite feeling shaky, Elise made it clear that yes she was and after a long and fairly fraught discussion, she was offered a far better solution. They were going to pay her out: two months money without any need to work for it. She had won. Elise could hardly believe her luck.

It was almost dizzying. Now she had no boyfriend, no job and soon there would be some more cash in the bank. That evening Elise re-booked an earlier flight to Italy and started to fill a large backpack with essentials. A torch, batteries, a sleeping bag, as well as a couple of pretty dresses, her bikini and an old boiler suit of Richard's to wear when she was cleaning up her new house. She didn't try to contact him again. She would wait and perhaps send a text once she had reached Montenello.

The journey was trickier to plan than expected. An evening of hunting through websites and travel forums revealed that Elise's best option was to catch an express coach from the airport to the nearest large town, Borgo del Colle, and then a smaller local bus to Montenello. It was daunting, given how limited her Italian was, but she was sure she would manage.

On the plane, when she wasn't playing Candy Crush on her phone, Elise lost herself in daydreams. She thought about Montenello with its steep streets and higgledy houses, of summer sunshine, big bowls of pasta and glasses of flinty red wine. Soon she was going to be there, enjoying it all.

In the airport it was exciting to hear Italian voices all around her and bliss to breathe in the bitter roasted smell of coffee. Elise would have loved a quick espresso but instead hurried to catch her bus. She needn't have bothered, as its departure was delayed and, even when it set off, the *autostrada* was choked with traffic and the going was slow. Tired of gazing out the window at the scenery they were creeping past, Elise distracted herself with several more games of Candy Crush.

Inevitably, she missed her connection and had to wait for over an hour for another local bus. Still, that wasn't so bad because the small town she was stuck in seemed pretty and she took lots of photos and played around with filters before posting them on Instagram.

The bus when it arrived was ancient, and its driver in no hurry as they rattled along the winding mountain roads. The day was dimming by the time Elise saw Montenello perched high above, dark and shadowy. Up there the mayor would be waiting to greet her with the keys to her new house. She sent him a quick text saying she wasn't far away.

In their emails they had agreed to meet at the Town Hall, not far from where the bus would drop her off. But she was more than two hours late now and the road seemed to be winding away from the town rather than towards it.

It was dark when Elise found herself standing in the piazza of Montenello, her backpack at her feet and the Town Hall in front of her. There was a heart-sinking moment when she realised it was all closed up for the night. Even so, she tried the door, hammering on it just in case there was someone left inside.

When she got no response, Elise sat on the steps, leaning against her backpack. She couldn't quite believe this. Hadn't she said she was definitely coming? The least the mayor could have done was held on and waited.

Pulling out her phone, she tried to call him, but went straight to his answering message and listened with frustration to his cheerful voice saying something incomprehensible in Italian. She would just have to find a hotel or a B & B to stay in, and then come back in the morning.

Elise started to google but could see nowhere nearby

offering accommodation. The low battery warning flashed on her screen and, regretting all those games of Candy Crush she sped up her search but still found nothing. Giving up before the phone died, she sat on the steps in the dark and tried to decide what to do. She would have to ask around, find someone who could help her. On the far side of the piazza she could see a bar, its windows lit. Picking up her backpack, Elise hefted it onto her shoulders and headed across the cobbles.

The bar was busy and tightly packed with tables. Elise battled to manoeuvre through with her backpack.

'Do you speak English?' she asked the man behind the counter. He only stared at her so Elise raised her voice. 'Excuse me, does anyone here speak any English? I really need some help.'

Her words seemed to have no effect. Half the people in the bar didn't look up, the rest offered the same blank stare the bartender had given her, and one man just glanced at her and then walked out. Elise was starting to panic. Would she have to spend the night outside, sleeping rough? There had been a breeze whipping through the piazza and the idea didn't appeal.

'Excuse me, are you looking for someone who speaks English?'

'Yes,' Elise was so relieved she nearly shouted the word. 'Oh thank goodness.'

The woman was middle-aged and very slender, with cropped fair hair. 'I was in the *trattoria* next door and a local came and fetched me,' she explained. 'He was very insistent.'

'I'm looking for a place to stay,' Elise told her. 'Is there a bed and breakfast nearby? Or a hotel?'

'No, I'm afraid there isn't.'

'In that case I'm not sure what to do.' Elise felt a bit shaky. 'I was meant to be meeting the mayor but got here too late and the Town Hall is closed now and my phone is about to go flat and I don't know if there's another bus back and if there isn't then I'm stuck.'

'You're supposed to be meeting Salvio?' the woman asked.

'Yes that's right, he's selling me a house for one euro.' As she said it Elise feared she sounded deluded. 'It's a scheme he's got going, apparently ... for real.'

'Yes, I know. I'm Mimi Wilson, he's selling one to me as well.'

'Really?' Elise was relieved. 'Do you know where I can find him then? I need to get to my house.'

'You're not planning to stay there tonight? Have you any idea what sort of state it's in?'

'I don't really care,' Elise told her. 'I've got no other options at this point.'

'You're here in Montenello on your own?' Mimi sounded concerned.

'Yes.'

'Look, I'll try to get hold of the mayor and see what he suggests.' Pulling out her phone, she made a call, frowning when there was no answer. 'Why don't you come next door and have some dinner with me? If he doesn't call back then I'll try him again in a little while.'

Elise realised she was hungry. She had eaten nothing but snacks all day and if she was going to be sleeping on the street then at least she could do it on a full stomach.

'OK,' she agreed. 'That would be great.'

It was cosy in the *trattoria* and Elise could smell good things cooking. Wedged beside her backpack at a corner table, she felt her eyelids drooping. She wished she could stay here, warm and safe, listening to the sound of people enjoying themselves, the throaty laugh of the woman at the next table, forks grazing plates, wine glasses clinking, and Mimi Wilson sitting opposite trying to make sense of the menu.

'It's handwritten and all in Italian,' she was explaining.

'I haven't a clue what anything means but fortunately they speak some English here.'

'I just want pasta and a glass of wine,' said Elise. 'Whatever is cheapest will do.'

She was happy to let Mimi take over the ordering, happy with the basket of bread and carafe of wine that was put on the table, and the bowl of food that followed, some sort of thick broth filled with vegetables and broken spaghetti, then cloaked in coarsely grated nutty cheese. Elise spooned in slow, comforting mouthfuls, almost sighing with the pleasure of it.

'You're the first other person I've met who's thinking about buying one of the houses,' Mimi told her.

'I'm not thinking about it; I'm definitely going to do it.' Elise hadn't come this far to walk away with nothing.

'How can you be so sure if you haven't seen it yet?'

'This is my chance to own a house. It doesn't really matter what it's like, at least I'll be on the property ladder.'

Mimi seemed troubled. She started talking in a motherly way about things like budget blow-outs and over-capitalising, but Elise had already been through similar conversations with Richard and wasn't interested in having them again.

'If all that is such an issue then why are you buying one?' she asked.

'It's my divorce present to myself.' Mimi explained. 'I know it's probably crazy but I'm going to do it anyway. This seems like the right time in my life for irresponsible behaviour.'

'Well, I think that's brilliant.' Elise raised her glass. 'We're two independent women renovating houses in Italy, without any men telling us what to do – let's drink to that.'

Mimi smiled, lifting her own wine glass. 'I guess you're right. Here's to us and everything we're going to do.'

'Yes, here's to us,' echoed Elise. 'It's so exciting.'

'It's also scary,' Mimi admitted. 'I've never done anything like this, not on my own.'

Elise stared at her, wondering why she was worrying. Mimi Wilson had a glossy, finished look that spoke of money. Her hair hadn't been tinted over the bath from a packet she had bought at the supermarket. Her French manicure, light merino wrap, soft leather handbag and discreetly elegant jewellery; all of it looked expensive. This woman had plenty of cash to smooth the way, didn't she? Everything would be easier for her.

'Would you mind calling the mayor again?' Elise asked, steeping a crust of bread in the last delicious puddle of broth and worrying that soon she might be out on the street again. 'My phone is almost flat.'

'I could but ...' Mimi's brow creased. 'I think you'd be better coming to stay with me tonight. At least there's a sofa you can sleep on.'

Elise was hesitant. 'Are you sure? I mean we've only just met ...'

'We're two single women renovating half-ruined houses in a small town in Italy. I think we'll be friends soon enough.'

'I guess you're right.'

'We ought to support one another. I have a feeling we're going to need to,' said Mimi. 'And besides, I'm reasonably confident there are no rats at my place. Who knows what might be living at yours.'

Edward

It was a scene from a movie: the olive groves spreading over the red earth; the small pointy-roofed house at their centre; Gino in a lounger beside the pool his body oiled and glistening; a low table loaded with fruit, breads and cheeses that the farmer had brought over earlier; the sky tinted blue and barely a breeze.

Gino had surrendered to laziness. He had not moved in over an hour and might have been asleep, except now and then he murmured something: how good the sun felt on his skin, how nice it was to completely unwind for once, how he could stay there for ever.

Sheltering for shade beneath an olive tree, trying to read the novel he had brought, Edward was unconvinced by this new laid-back version of Gino. It seemed another ploy, a way to delay a visit to his parents' village or whatever it was he thought Edward wanted and therefore had decided he wasn't going to do.

'Shall we make a move this afternoon?' he called. 'Go and explore?'

'Hmm?'

'There's a couple of towns nearby I'd like to take a look at.'

Gino lengthened his body into a stretch then rolled onto his stomach. 'How far away is the beach?'

At home Gino never enjoyed lying around beside pools or on beaches. 'It's a decent drive,' Edward told him. 'And it might not be so warm there. We're very sheltered here, I think.'

'Let's stay here then. It's perfect, isn't it? We may as well enjoy the place.'

Edward reminded himself that they still had plenty of time to sightsee, to taste the local food, to get a sense of southern Italy. Time to be lazy, if that was what Gino really wanted. And time enough to get to Montenello, he was determined to manage that. He had such a clear vision now: the town, the house and the way their future could play out there. It had come together in his mind and he couldn't let it go.

There were other things he hadn't shared with Gino in the past. A couple of brief flings that didn't seem important, work niggles he wouldn't have been interested in, fleeting worries and short-lived dreams. But Edward was aware he had never kept a plan this big from him before.

Gino interrupted his thoughts. 'We'll do it tomorrow, OK?'

'What?' Edward was startled.

'Visit this godforsaken place my parents abandoned years ago for a better life.'

'Your mother would like it if we do.'

'Tell her we went. Google it, get a few details, she'll never know.' Gino rested his face against the pillow he had made from his folded beach towel. 'What else is on that list of yours?

'Lots of places, a whole town of *trulli*, a restaurant in a sea cave, a kayaking tour round the coastline, a lot of baroque architecture.'

There was a muffled groan from Gino. 'Tomorrow, OK? We'll do something tomorrow. I'm happy here today.'

For a while longer Edward stayed in the shade with his book, but he was too restless to focus properly. Giving up, he went alone for a walk. It took him along dusty lanes past small farmlets where barking dogs ran out to greet him, beside fields boxed in by stone walls, lots more olive trees and several *trullo* houses. He wondered about the people who lived here. Could their lives still be so shaped by tradition as Gino believed? It seemed unlikely.

The midday sun was on his neck, burning through the cream he had slathered on much too long ago. Edward turned back but his steps weren't so easy to retrace. The groves of trees, the farmhouses, even the roaming dogs and chickens; all looked at once unfamiliar and the same. Pausing at a crossroads, trying to decide which narrow lane to follow, he regretted not taking better notice of the landmarks.

Then he heard the pooping of a horn and a small car braked urgently beside him, throwing up a cloud of dust. Its bonnet was mottled and every panel dented, but the woman in the driving seat was beautiful, with dark eyes, finely lined skin and long glossy hair shot through with silver.

She called at him in Italian through the open window and he shook his head. 'Sorry, I'm English,' he called back.

She leaned closer. 'You are lost?'

'Possibly a little bit,' he admitted.

'Tell me where it is you are trying to go.'

'I'm staying in a *trullo* house nearby,' Edward told her. 'It's right beside the Ristorante di Donna Carmela.'

'Then you are not lost because I am Donna Carmela and that is my *trullo*.' She smiled at him. 'Get in. I will make some space for you ... one moment.'

Wooden crates were stacked along the back seat, almost to the roof. Edward saw gems of baby artichokes and fronds of fennel. As he climbed in, the crisp green scent of celery rose from a box in the foot-well.

'Are you Edward or Gino?' she asked, speeding off as soon as he closed the door.

'Edward.'

'I'm so sorry not to have been home to welcome you yesterday. But my husband has looked after you, I hope? And the weather is perfect for your holiday. Today it seems like summer is come very early.'

Edward's walk must have taken him further than he realised. They rattled over a lot of ground before Donna Carmela made the tight turn through the high gates and came to a sudden stop.

'Can I help you carry some of this stuff?' asked Edward, gesturing towards the crates of vegetables.

'That's very kind of you. I passed a market and bought far too much.'

'Does that mean your restaurant is open this evening?'

'Not officially, but I will cook and see who wants to eat.'

'Should we book a table?' asked Edward.

'No, no.' Donna Carmela gave a swift shake of her head. 'Just come and I promise you a delicious dinner.'

Gino had pulled his lounger into the shade and covered up the food with a tea towel but, aside from that, the scene Edward found hadn't changed much. Sticky from the walk, he peeled off his clothes and dived into the pool, relishing the cold shock to his skin.

'Come in, it's great,' he called to Gino. 'You can't lie there all day.'

'I wasn't planning to.'

Edward swam the few strokes to the edge of the pool. 'What's on the agenda then?'

'There's champagne chilling and it's probably time we had a glass.'

'And after that?'

'It depends on whether you're still feeling dizzy.'

'Not even slightly,' Edward told him.

'In that case fetch the champagne, we'll drink it in the pool and I'll tell you what I've got in mind.'

It had been years since they had spent an afternoon in bed. When you knew one another's bodies as he and Gino did, there seemed little point. But here, with their warm

154

skin smelling of chlorine and sunscreen, in the half-light of the thick-walled *trullo*, as the sky outside clouded and the temperature dropped, they took their time. Afterwards they drank the rest of the champagne, slept for a couple of hours, then lay tangled beneath the sheets and talked. At last everything seemed perfect.

Edward came close to mentioning the house in Montenello but he couldn't bring himself to risk ruining the moment. Tomorrow would be easier – in the car, perhaps, or while they were discovering some scenic spot or lingering over lunch. Tomorrow he would tell Gino everything, not right now.

Both of them were hungry when they headed over to Donna Carmela's restaurant. They were met by the smell of simmering sauces and charmed by the rustic feel of the place. Usually Gino chafed in restaurants if things weren't done properly. But here with no written menu, and only Donna Carmela to cook and serve, everything was casual. The dishes weren't cleared away promptly, the water glasses not topped up and Gino didn't even remark on it.

They ate spears of steamed asparagus drowning in butter and covered in shavings of piquant Parmesan. Shared a bowl of seafood in a peppery broth and a dish of sweet peas stewed with smoky prosciutto and the hearts of baby lettuce.

'My parents would love this,' said Gino. 'Can you imagine my father?'

'And Tia too,' agreed Edward. 'We should bring them back here. We could rent a big house, plenty of rooms, a pool, of course. It would be a really special thing to do.'

'We've only just arrived and already you're talking about coming back.'

'I love it. And I think you do too.'

'I don't know,' Gino began. 'It's an odd feeling being here. Like when you start watching a film then realise you've seen it before. I've had this sense of déjà vu ever since we arrived.

Just watching the people, the way they are when they talk to each other, always slightly more excitable than they need to be. The smell of the food, the sound of their voices ...'

'It's like constantly being at a Sunday lunch with your family.'

Gino laughed. 'That sounds like a nightmare but this ... I'm not sure if I love it or not, but I do think I'm glad that we're here.'

Donna Carmela interrupted, clearing their plates at last and asking about their food. She wanted to go over every dish in detail and pulled a chair from a nearby table without a word of encouragement in order to join them.

'I open properly for the season next week,' she explained. 'Now is the time to decide on my spring menu.'

'You have an actual menu?' Gino sounded as if he was teasing.

'And a waitress and a kitchen hand. Just like all the other restaurants.'

'That's a shame; I rather liked being fed delicious things by you. It was relaxing.'

'It is the way I prefer it too,' agreed Donna Carmela. 'But some people don't want surprises. They need to know exactly what to expect.'

'We're a bit more adventurous than that,' Edward told her.

'I knew that, of course,' said Donna Carmela. 'Just the fact that you are here, all the way from Australia, to buy an abandoned home in a small Italian hill town. That is not for the faint-hearted, is it?'

Edward froze; Gino only looked confused.

'My son is the mayor of Montenello,' she went on, 'the one who embarked on this whole scheme to sell off the houses for one euro. I hope it works out for him. And I very much hope your place is in better condition than the one I helped to clean. The bathroom, the oven, the garden – what a disaster.'

'You must be us confusing with someone else,' Gino told her. 'We're here for a holiday, not to buy a house.'

'But I'm quite sure that Salvio said ...' Donna Carmela glanced from Gino to Edward then gave a quick shrug. 'I must be mistaken. Ah well. I am glad the weather has improved for you. Summer always arrives very quickly here. Soon it will be too hot but right now it is perfect.'

Scooping up the plates and still murmuring about the weather, she stood and turned for the kitchen. Edward watched her, wishing he could follow.

'That was a bit weird,' said Gino

Edward felt his whole body tense. Heat flooded his face as he tried to manage a reply.

'I said that was weird. Wasn't it? That whole business about us buying an abandoned house in my parents' village?'

Still not quite able to meet Gino's eyes and after several awkward beats of silence, Edward began, 'Not really ... you see, there's something I haven't told you.'

Montenello

Salvio had organised everything, even taking time to personally check the house assigned to the young English girl. Wandering through, he saw that once this had been a very fine home. The reception rooms were spacious with faded friezes and frescoes around the walls and the remains of decorative plasterwork on the ceilings. Eager for a good first impression Salvio had paid a local woman to give the place a thorough clean so although Elise Hartman would still be camping here, at least it wouldn't be too unpleasant.

He had meant to be the one to welcome her to Montenello, however Donna Carmela had undone his plans. It was her last night in town and she had wanted to eat at a hotel up in the mountains, a luxury boutique place in a converted monastery where the chef was famed for his tasting menu. Salvio couldn't let his mother down so had turned to his assistant.

'Of course, of course,' Augusto had said. 'I will be happy to meet the young lady. Leave everything to me.'

Salvio had enjoyed his evening: the drive along the winding roads, course after course of exquisite food, the company of his mother, a couple of glasses of very good wine. He did remember to check his phone but so far into the mountains there was no reception and he could only trust that everything had gone to plan.

It wasn't until Salvio was home again that he had seen the text Elise sent hours earlier to say she was running late and realised he had missed a call from Mimi. By then it had been almost midnight and he was certain both women would be asleep. In the morning he would pay Elise a visit, take some pastries perhaps, see if she needed anything else. His bed was calling him and he was too drowsy to resist it.

The next day had started slowly. Salvio helped his mother retrieve her belongings, which seemed to have found their way into every corner of the house, and packed them into the decrepit car she insisted on driving. Then she had wanted them to drink a coffee together and, even once he got her into the driver's seat, chatted through the open window, saying goodbye to him several times but not making a move to drive away.

'I have to go to work, Mamma.'

'Then go, I'm not stopping you.'

'The English girl, Elise Hartman, arrived last night. I need to check on her.'

'The pretty one with the boyfriend?'

'There's no boyfriend any more. It seems they have split up.'

'Then go, Salvio, go,' she had urged. 'What are you waiting for?'

It only required a small detour to take him past Elise's house and Salvio decided it was worth dropping in sooner rather than later. He knocked on the splintering wooden door but there was no answer and the place looked as it had when he saw it last, with a few of the smaller windows left open to air the rooms. After one final knock, and a call of 'Signora Hartman' that brought no response, he continued on his way.

As he was trying to decide whether to head to Renzo's bar for one more coffee before work, Salvio's phone rang. He dug it from his coat pocket and recognised Elise's number.

'*Buongiorno*,' he said. 'I hope you had a wonderful first night in your new home.'

'Obviously, I didn't,' She sounded irritated. 'How could I? You weren't there to take me there. Didn't you get my text to say I was running late?'

'Signora, I don't understand. My assistant was waiting for you with the keys—'

'No he wasn't.'

'Are you sure?'

'Yes. The whole place was closed up, there was no one around.'

'I don't understand it,' Salvio repeated, wondering what could have happened to Augusto, and feeling a quick surge of irritation followed by concern. 'I am very, very sorry. Where are you now?'

'With Mimi, I stayed with her last night. We're walking up to the bar in a moment to have some breakfast.'

'OK, I will meet you there. I am on my way.'

Salvio hurried up the steep streets towards Renzo's bar. Arriving slightly out of breath, he secured a good table near an open window, and ordered an excessive number of pastries oozing with almond paste and sweet custard.

He spotted them crossing the piazza. They stopped at Francesco Rossi's stall to buy a bag of apples, which gave Salvio time to observe them: two slender, fair-headed women who might have been mother and daughter, one stylishly attractive and the other even prettier than in her photograph. Elise was wearing pale blue jeans and an embroidered top. Her long blonde curls fell softly over her shoulders. She was smiling at something Mimi was saying. Salvio couldn't take his eyes from her.

He stood as they entered the bar, shaking Elise's hand and kissing her lightly on both cheeks. 'I am so sorry,' he said, again. 'My assistant promised he would be there waiting for you. I have no idea why he let us down.'

She was staring at him, uncertainly. 'You are the mayor?'

'Yes, and I am so pleased to meet you at last.'

'I thought you'd be much older.'

'Everyone always does.'

Salvio had to remind himself not to keep staring. It

wasn't easy. Elise was dazzling, a bright light in this small drab room, and certainly he wasn't the only one watching her. With creamy skin and clear eyes, she seemed to glow. Everything about her was compelling, even the way she bit hungrily into a pastry and the powdery sugar dusted her lips.

On the phone earlier she had sounded so cross but now, as Renzo brought over their coffee, she talked cheerfully about how fortunate she was to have met Mimi and how pleased her sofa turned out to be so comfortable.

'I love her house,' Elise enthused. 'I'm even more excited to see mine now. Do you think you'll be able to take me there this morning?'

'Yes, of course, and afterwards I can show you round the rest of the town if you wish.'

'That would be lovely, if you have the time.'

'Absolutely,' said Salvio, thinking of the work piling up, the staff with their endless questions, of Augusto and whatever could have happened to him. 'I am entirely at your disposal.'

'Great, let's go then.' She turned to Mimi. 'Will you come too?'

They finished their coffee, wrapping pastries in paper serviettes to eat as they walked. Leaving the bar, they had to squeeze past a delivery truck parked beside the boarded-up shop next door. Two men were unloading lengths of wood, most of them worn and scarred. The door to the shop lay open and they were carrying them inside. Usually Salvio would have stopped to find out what was going on, but right then he only had time for Elise. He wasn't much interested in anything that might distract him from her.

It was a bright day, though a cool breeze frisked through the streets, ruffling her curls and making her cheeks pink. Pulling a long fringed scarf from her bag, she wound it round her shoulders. Salvio thought she looked even more beautiful.

He was nervous as they approached the house, so badly did he want her to love it. 'This place has been empty for a while, so it feels neglected,' he warned. 'There is something sad about a home no one has loved in a long time. You will need to use your imagination, visualise what it might become.'

Elise didn't seem perturbed by the broken steps and splintered door. She appeared not to notice the musty smell and walked through the shabby, vacant rooms, a look of wonder on her face, commenting on everything.

'The terrace looks in much better shape than yours, Mimi. And don't you think the living area could be lovely? Look at the friezes on the walls; wouldn't it be great to restore them? Oh and there are cupids painted on the ceiling. The bedrooms are all upstairs, yes? So many windows ... I wonder what the view is like from up there.'

Salvio exchanged a look with Mimi. 'She is very enthusiastic,' he said.

'Yes, isn't she.'

'The master bedroom is completely massive.' Elise's voice floated down to them. 'And there's a peep of a view across the mountains. Oh it's amazing; I never imagined anything like this.'

The stairs creaked beneath Salvio's feet as he climbed up to join her.

'I was planning to decorate the whole house in white, Scandi-style.' Her voice rose with excitement. 'But now I'm here, I can see it would be completely wrong. This place needs lots of ochre and old gold, vintage glamour, chandeliers and tasselled satin cushions.'

'It needs rewiring.' Mimi's voice came from behind him. 'And a new roof too, by the look of that ceiling.'

Elise glanced up and frowned. 'Yes, I see what you mean.'

'With old houses like this, once you start working on them you only discover more problems – rot, subsidence, dodgy plumbing,' Mimi continued.

A little of Elise's glow seemed to be fading. 'I know that.'

'There will be lots to do here before you can start hanging chandeliers.'

'I'll help in any way I can,' Salvio put in. 'By far the most important thing is to have a vision. Then little by little you can make it happen.'

Elise stared up at the sagging ceiling. 'Nothing is impossible, right?'

'Exactly,' agreed Salvio. 'It may take time, but you can definitely transform this place.'

She beamed a smile at him. 'It could be a palace.'

'It will be,' Salvio promised.

'I hope so,' added Mimi, who was poking at a soft spot on the wall. 'I think you should stay at my house for now, though. At least I've got some furniture.'

She seemed so determined to be discouraging and Salvio found himself wishing he could be rid of her, then immediately felt uncharitable as surely she was only trying to be helpful.

Still, he was pleased when Elise refused her offer to stay because she was desperate to sleep in her own house. And he had to hide his relief when Mimi announced it was time for her to hurry and meet the architect that Donna Carmela had recommended.

'I don't want to be late. If you change your mind, Elise, then you're very welcome to come over.'

'Thanks, but I really want to be here, getting to know the place.' The two women exchanged a quick hug. 'Thanks so much for looking after me last night. I'll come by later and pick up my backpack. I want to hear what your architect says.'

Elise stood in the doorway to wave goodbye. Looking on, Salvio thought she already seemed at home here. He must make the sale official as quickly as possible: organise a notary, get the contract signed and the deal completed;

he would ask Augusto to sort it out. At the thought of his assistant, he frowned. What could have happened for him to let everyone down like that? Salvio hoped he was OK, that he hadn't been taken ill, had a fall or some other calamity. What other excuse could there be?

He watched Elise. She was pressing one palm flat against the wall and standing still and quiet, as if the building was whispering to her.

'Who lived here?' she asked him. 'Do you think it was a happy house? I suppose if everyone left then it can't have been.'

'I don't know its story. But Augusto might.'

'Your unreliable assistant?'

'I'm so sorry about last night,' he said again. 'I can't apologise enough.'

Elise's fingertips stroked the wall. 'I'm here now, that's the important thing. I'm here, in my own house.'

Mimi

Heading back through the piazza, Mimi raised a hand to the old man who sat day after day amid his few boxes of apples, unconcerned at rarely having a customer. She smiled at Renzo, standing in the doorway of his bar for a few breaths of fresh air, and said a hesitant *buongiorno* to a couple of other people whose faces she half-recognised.

There was no architect waiting yet on her crumbling doorstep, so Mimi filled in time sitting on the sofa, her laptop on her knee, checking for messages. Already it seemed as if they had been sent from a different life. The queries from her agent, the update from her lawyer, the emails about designer sales and supermarket specials, even the selfie that Sinead had sent of the last Silver Divorcees meeting. Three wine glasses raised, three good friends smiling, the blurry background of a restaurant she didn't recognise. Mimi enjoyed those evenings but wasn't particularly sorry to have missed one. This house, this town and all her thoughts of whether she might make a life here, were filling her up. In any moment she might swing from terror to excitement, then back again.

She wished she had some of Elise's attitude, she seemed so definite, so convinced. At that age, Mimi had been settled safely in her husband's shadow. Would she ever have dared to strike out on her own?

Last night Elise had seemed such a lost waif that Mimi felt obliged to look after her. She offered up her sofa, hoping someone would do the same for her kids if they ever needed it. But once installed on that sofa, sipping camomile tea and talking about her plans, Elise had seemed to change. She grew stronger and surer. Then this morning, meeting the mayor and seeing the house she was determined to buy, she had been unstoppable. In the meantime, here was Mimi, still hesitating, hoping this architect would say something to sway her one way or the other.

He was almost an hour late, and unapologetic as he introduced himself. 'Alessandro Ferrario,' he said, holding out a large square hand.

Donna Carmela had warned her that he could be gruff at times, so as he took his time strolling round the house, taking in the bowed ceilings and scuffed walls with his dark, deep-set eyes, rubbing at his silver down of beard from time to time, shaking his head, scribbling the occasional note in a small leather-bound book, Mimi tried not to read too much into the fact he wasn't saying anything.

He finished his tour out on the terrace where he made a clucking sound in the back of his throat as he walked from one end to the other.

'Is it that bad?' Mimi asked.

'That depends.' He looked at her, calmly weighing her up as he had the walls and ceilings. 'Signora, tell me, why do you want this house?'

She could have told Alessandro Ferrario that she was breaking free from a life that was making her unhappy. That she was trying to save herself, not just this decrepit building, and give them both a better future. That the town was drawing her in and the mountains made her heart sing.

'I'm looking for a project,' she said instead.

'Why this house?' His dark eyes held hers.

'It needs me.' No one else did, realised Mimi. Not her sons any more, certainly not her ex-husband, not even her friends. But this house, it needed her badly. 'Can I tell you what I've got in mind for it?'

She saw a glitter in those deep dark eyes. 'Please do.'

For the next half hour she talked him through her dreams. Plans to open up the living area, move the kitchen, extend the bathroom to make space for a spa tub, put in en suites for when Otis and Ben visited, install cupboards for linen and clothes. She wanted to retain a sense of tradition, to replace the cracked ceramic tiles with replicas and source fittings that looked original, but at the same time everything would need to be so much lighter and brighter. Then of course there was the terrace to restore. And did he think a swimming pool was possible?

Alessandro nodded thoughtfully, made more notes with his stub of a pencil, but said nothing at all until she had finished. Then he sighed.

'You will need to spend much more than the house is worth.'

'I'm only paying one euro for it.'

'Still, as an investment, it is not a good idea. It will be a wonderful home in a town where no one wants to live.'

'All that might change if the mayor's plans work.'

'It might ... but I doubt it,' he said, matter-of-factly. 'That is why I asked why do you want this house. If it is to make money, then walk away. Buy a *trullo* or a place near the sea and perhaps you will have an asset. But a ruined house in a cursed mountain town, signora, if it were me—'

'Cursed?' Mimi interrupted. 'Is that actually an issue? I was told that it's just a few silly old stories that no one speaks of any more.'

'They may not speak, but they remember.'

'What is it about then, this curse?'

He waved a hand, as if trying to brush away her words. 'I come from Borgo del Colle. I only know what my nonna told me.'

'So what was that?' Mimi asked, insistently.

He sighed again. 'Local people believed the women here were cursed, that they wouldn't have babies that survived.

167

I suppose there must have been miscarriages and stillbirths, more than normal. Villagers in this part of Italy are superstitious. A curse is how they explained it.'

'Is that why they deserted the town?'

'It may have been a part of it. And there are no young people here now are there? No babies?'

'You think that is a good reason for me not to buy the house?'

'I was talking only about the financial reality. If it were me I would buy this place if I loved it, if Montenello was where I wanted to be, if transforming it would make me happy, but not as a wise investment.'

Mimi felt a stab of anxiety. 'I don't know. My heart is saying one thing and my head another.'

For the first time he half-smiled. His heavy cheeks lifted, his mouth twitched and he said in his deep rumble of a voice. 'I am an architect, signora so I am not qualified to tell you which to choose.'

'My heart seems to be winning.'

'In that case I will tell you how we might save this house and make it beautiful together.'

Walking slowly back through the house, they discussed how each room might be transformed. Mimi put herself in the picture that was forming in her mind, an older and happier version of herself, sitting in the space she had earmarked for her studio, sketching out illustrations. There was a lot to be achieved before then, but she might enjoy working with Alessandro. He seemed calm and kind, and most importantly he understood what she wanted.

'If I do go ahead with the purchase will you draw up some preliminary plans?' she asked.

He nodded. 'And we can talk about the cost estimates and timing, what consents we may need, whether I will manage the project, all of the practical things. But first you have a decision to make.'

Mimi tried to remember when she last decided on anything so important without a husband there to guide her. Glenn had shaped her life so far. No wonder making a significant move without him seemed so difficult.

'I'll let you know soon,' she promised.

'There is no hurry. Take the time you need. I will be waiting,' said Alessandro.

As he left, the architect shook her hand. 'I am sorry to have been late this morning,' he said in his deeply accented English. 'It was a pleasure to meet you. And I think you may be right, this house does need you.'

Mimi had to stop herself calling Salvio straight away. She would let what the architect had said settle in, allow herself to think and dream a little longer before making a commitment. Still, she was so close now and, even though it wasn't hers yet, she had the urge to buy something for the house: a throw, perhaps, or some bright cushions, a plant in a pot. As she thought about it her eyes traced the line of the wall and rested on the cracks in the painted ceramic tiles. Alessandro had mentioned a place in Borgo del Colle where she might find replacements and checking the map, she saw it wasn't too far a drive. A shopping trip might be what she needed.

She was easing the rental car through Montenello's tight streets, doing her best not to scratch it, when she noticed Elise, walking alone and apparently in a daydream. Mimi hooted the horn to attract her attention, braked and opened her window.

'You're not heading over to see me by any chance?' she asked.

'Actually I was,' Elise told her, bending to the window. 'I wanted to grab my backpack. But there's no rush if now isn't a good time.'

'I was just going out to do some shopping. I'm buying myself a little housewarming present.'

'Seriously? Does that mean you've decided to take the place?'

'I think so, almost definitely.'

'Your meeting with the architect must have gone well then?'

As Mimi started to speak, a car drew up behind her, the driver leaning on its horn and flashing its headlights. 'I'm blocking the way, I'd better move,' she said, slightly rattled.

'Why don't I come shopping with you,' Elise suggested. 'Then you can tell me all about it on the way.'

'Oh good idea, jump in.'

Driving across the causeway, she began to talk though her meeting with the architect, but leaving Montenello behind, Elise seemed not to be fully paying attention and Mimi realised she was staring back at the town.

'It's the first time I've seen this view properly,' she explained. 'It was almost dark when I arrived last night so I couldn't get a proper impression. And in the pictures it didn't look so dramatic. I can hardly believe I'm going to live there.'

'Did Salvio say anything to you about a curse?' Mimi wondered. 'Apparently the town is famous for having one.'

'Oh don't,' said Elise. 'A curse?'

'I'm not trying to put you off, honestly. It's just that a few people have mentioned it. And you spent time with Salvio this morning so I thought ...'

'He had to cut things short because he got a phone call. And he only told me good things, definitely nothing about curses. Why? What did you hear?'

When Mimi told her, Elise laughed. 'I don't think I've got anything to worry about. Even if I wanted babies, I'd need a boyfriend first. Mine dumped me, remember?'

Mimi nodded. 'That's right, you mentioned it last night.'

'We're supposed to be taking a break, but you know what that means. So I'm considering myself single.'

'You might meet someone else, you never know.'

'I don't think that's very likely. Every man in Montenello seemed to be about a hundred.'

'Not every man surely,' said Mimi, glancing over in time to see a faint flush stealing over Elise's cheeks.

'Just don't,' was all she said.

Edward

The *trullo* was too small for two people who weren't talking to each other; still, Gino was managing it. Last night they had slept apart and now he was spending his time deliberately shifting from any space Edward entered, not meeting his eyes or showing any sign he had seen him. His anger seemed reasonable enough, but Edward couldn't bear this silent treatment. It was boring and unpleasant.

After Donna Carmela had blurted out about the house in Montenello, Gino held it together until they were on the way back to the *trullo* by torchlight. It should have been perfect – a warm evening, a velvety sky studded by stars, their way lined by the dark shapes of olive trees. Instead Gino's anger had laid waste to the last of the day. How could Edward have tricked him? What had he been thinking? Why was he making these sorts of plans without him?

Edward had let him vent until he couldn't stand it any longer then interrupted, trying to be reasonable. After all, he hadn't actually bought the house, only registered an interest, so they weren't committed to anything. All he was asking was that Gino should take a look. The place might capture their imagination or turn out to be a dump. How could they know without seeing it?

'This is ridiculous,' Gino had snapped. 'You know we'd never fit in here; you're dreaming.' And then there had been the slamming of doors and the beginning of a long silence.

'You're right, dreaming is exactly what I'm doing,' Edward had yelled at the walls before taking off to bed for a sleepless night alone, going over all the things he should have said.

Now there was this awful stalemate. Staring out over the sun-soaked garden, the blue rectangle of water, and the silvered green leaves of the olive trees, Edward almost screamed. The warmth was stealing from the afternoon and the shadows lengthening. He wanted the day back. He had meant for it to be filled with far better things than this.

'I'm making a drink,' he called. 'Do you want one?'

He didn't expect an answer from Gino who was sitting in the last of the sunshine pretending to read the novel Edward had given up on yesterday.

'If you don't say anything I'm going to take that as a yes.'

Edward clinked ice into glasses. He poured in a good measure of gin, topped up with tonic, threw in thin slices of cucumber and took them both outside.

Gino's head was bent over the book. Even the back of his neck looked intractable.

'I made them strong, I think we need it,' said Edward. 'Don't make me drink them both.'

Gino looked up over the top of the reading glasses he had only recently conceded he needed.

'This isn't getting us anywhere.' Edward stood, a glass in each hand. 'So let's have a drink and try and talk about it. And don't tell me there's nothing to say, because there is. I have things to say, even if you don't want to hear them.'

Gino put down his book and took the drink. 'OK then.'

'Have you noticed how it's always me that does this?' said Edward. 'I'm in charge of making up and apologising.'

'Why wouldn't you be?' Gino was hostile. 'You're the one that manipulated me into coming here because you've been planning on secretly buying a house.'

'I've said a hundred times that I'm sorry.'

'I assume you've emailed this mayor now and told him the deal is off?'

'Not yet,' admitted Edward.

'Why are you waiting? You know I'm never going to get

173

involved with this. Are you planning on going ahead alone?'

The thought had crossed Edward's mind once or twice, but he didn't admit it.

'If we did this thing together it could be amazing. Can't you consider that for a moment?' he said instead.

'No.'

Edward sat in the chair beside him, resting his hand close to Gino's but not quite touching it.

'I want this,' he said. 'I can't fully explain to you why, at least not easily, but I need it.'

'You have a dream,' Gino scoffed.

'Yes, actually, I do. Until now it's all been about your dreams – your career, your creativity. I've been along for the ride.'

'You have a career as well.'

'It's not a passion, only a way to make a living, and I need something more.'

'And this has to be it?'

'For a single euro we get a house and the land it's standing on. I mean it's unreal. How can we say no to a deal like that?'

Gino removed his glasses and rubbed his eyes. 'Have you really been feeling so unfulfilled all this time? Is that what's been wrong?'

'I think so.'

'I thought it was me you were bored with.'

'I know, I'm sorry.'

'You're apologising again.'

'Yeah.'

'This dream you have, how do you see it playing out?'

Edward told him, talking until the gin glasses had long been emptied and his mouth was dry. He described the stretch of time they would take back from their ordinary lives. How they would spend it renovating a house together, travelling and having new experiences. Gino listened without interrupting or giving any clue what he might be thinking.

'Let's do this now, have an adventure in our forties and then we can go home, get married and grow old together,' finished Edward.

'Married?' Gino sounded surprised. 'Do you want that?'

'I think we should talk about it now that it's an option; find out if it's what we both want. And I think we should go to Montenello, see the place your family comes from and check out this house while we're there.'

'Even if I don't want to buy it, whether it costs one euro or one million?'

'We can still take a look,' Edward insisted.

'My father has never had a good word to say about Montenello. He always calls it, "that cursed place".'

'When did you start caring so much about your father's opinion? And anyway, your mother doesn't feel the same way. She dreams of the place, remember. So why not go and take some photographs of ourselves there? I think she'd like that.'

Gino groaned. 'If we really have to do this, let's get it over with.'

Edward touched his hand. 'I'm sorry I didn't tell you about the whole thing sooner.'

'Yeah and I'm sorry you felt you couldn't.' Gino's long, slim fingers clasped Edward's palm and squeezed it tight.

Edward kept expecting Gino to change his mind. They had spent an evening edging round each other, both wary of the tensions between them, careful what they said and did. But now they were in the car together, negotiating the narrow gateway and the confusing maze of dirt roads, he was starting to feel hopeful they might at least reach Montenello.

The road climbed into the mountains and Gino slowed the car through its twists and turns. The olive groves and *trullo* houses were left in the valley behind them and the landscape grew more dramatic with densely wooded hillsides and craggy outcrops of rock. Edward had seen pictures of Montenello but rounding a bend and glimpsing it suddenly, looming above them on a high peak, swathed in morning mist, was breathtaking.

'Wow, look at that,' he said.

Gino's eyes flicked away from the road, but only momentarily.

'There's a place just ahead where we can pull over,' Edward told him. 'Let's take some shots from there.'

The air was noticeably cooler and they bundled themselves into jackets and stood at the edge of the road gazing upwards. For a moment neither of them spoke, and Edward tried to guess what Gino was thinking. Was he feeling some connection with the place? It was impossible to know and far too soon to ask.

'Shall I get a photo of you with the town in the background?' he said instead.

'Sure,' Gino agreed, but as he posed for the shots Montenello loomed behind him looking bleak and forbidding. Edward feared this was going to be a short visit.

'Can you imagine your parents leaving this place all those years ago, not realising they'd never come back?' he said, taking one last picture.

'I expect they were happy enough to be escaping the grinding poverty.'

'What made them choose Australia?'

'I don't know. Perhaps it seemed as far away as it was possible to get.'

'Haven't you ever asked them?'

Gino still stood with his back to the town. 'My father told us stories but never cheerful ones. How hungry they were during the war; how hard they had to work; how lucky we were to be growing up in a land of opportunity like Australia, that kind of thing.'

'And your mother?'

'I guess she spoke about family and showed us photographs. But the place itself never seemed important to her, at least not that I remember. Maybe I wasn't paying attention. You know what we were like as kids, so caught up in our own world. What we wanted was to get away from our parents, not find out more about them.'

'True,' said Edward, who hadn't forgotten any important detail of their boyhood together.

'It's strange to think how my parents must have been before my sisters and I came along.' Gino turned his gaze to the mountain and the houses clinging to it above a sheer sheet of rock. 'I suppose that's the last sight my mother ever had of her home town. She'd have been so young, heading into the unknown, full of hope for the future and trusting my father to look after her.'

'And he always has, you can't fault him there.' Edward held up the screen of his phone. 'Can I send one of these shots to Tia?'

Gino wore his usual critical frown at the sight of himself. 'I suppose so,' he agreed. 'Say to tell my mother the place doesn't look like it's changed at all.'

Edward drove the rest of the way so Gino could appreciate the view as they crossed the causeway. He steered carefully up through the crazily narrow streets, trying to find a parking place. The small piazza seemed their best option and from there they walked in a wide loop, up and down steps and through tiny passageways, past a church with barred doors and houses without windows, half lost for most of the time.

'Do you have any idea where your family might have lived?' Edward asked. 'Didn't one of your grandfathers have a bakery here?'

'Yes, but that's long gone. After he died the rest of the

family must have moved away too and the same goes for my father's side. He always says no one is left.'

'What happened to all their houses?'

'I suppose they must have been sold or abandoned. My parents have never mentioned having property here.'

'So there's a chance the place we've been offered once belonged to one of your relatives.'

'It's possible but I very much doubt it; there's no shortage of empty buildings. And where are all the people? Had you wondered about that?'

It was true they had barely seen anyone but as they found themselves circling back to the piazza, Edward saw a small gathering. There was an old man selling fruit from a stall beside a dry fountain and beyond him a cluster of people who seemed to be milling about aimlessly near a statue of Garibaldi.

'What's going on over there?' he wondered. 'Do you think there's any particular reason for them all to be standing around like that?'

They headed over to take a look. Nearby there was a bar and a small *trattoria*, however the building everyone seemed interested in stood between them. It might have been a shop once but there was no awning now and its windows were opaque with dust. As they drew nearer they heard the roar of power tools and there was the sharp smell of fresh sawdust.

'Someone is renovating, working with wood,' said Gino. 'I'm not sure why everyone is finding that so exciting. Clearly not a lot happens here.'

'This could be one of the buildings they've sold off for one euro. If so, it would be great to meet whoever has bought it,' said Edward.

The shop door was half open, but the crowd was hanging back and they stared as Edward passed, with Gino a step or so behind him.

It took a moment to recognise the figure at the circular

saw as a woman. She was wearing headphones and a chunky tool belt, one kerchief over her mouth, another covering her hair, and was busily carving into a large piece of wood.

Edward waited until she had finished then called a loud *buongiorno*.

She turned, pulling the scarf from her face and removing the headphones. 'Hi, can I help you?' she asked in a not entirely friendly tone, her accent sounding American.

'You seem to be attracting a crowd out there. We wondered why.'

'I suppose they're all desperate to know what's going on because this shop has been closed up for so many years. Oh well, they'll find out soon enough.'

'I wondered if this might be one of the places they're selling off,' explained Edward. 'They've offered us a house, you see, and—'

Gino interrupted, asking, 'Is this reclaimed oak? It's beautiful.' He was pointing at a pile of wood stacked against the far wall.'

'That's right,' the young woman told him. 'I'm making a counter and some shelving from it. But no, this building isn't for sale. It belongs to my family and has done for ever.'

'What have you got here exactly? Doors and planks ... but what are these?' Gino was running his fingers over the grain of some old posts, finding the scars and old holes.

For the first time she smiled. 'Ah, they are very special. They're called *briccole* and they are the oak posts you see in the lagoon in Venice. From time to time they are replaced. I was very lucky to get some of the old ones.'

'These marks and perforations, were they made by sea creatures?'

She nodded. 'Shipworms have burrowed in and also the wood has been worn by the movement of water over it.'

'Beautiful.' Gino touched one again, lightly and reverently. 'What will you do with them?'

'I'm not completely sure yet, maybe use them as part of the countertop? I have some ideas. Would you like to see them?'

In a flash, Gino's spectacles were out of his jacket pocket and on his nose. Together they bent over a large sketchpad and Edward realised from the expression on their faces that they were kindred spirits. What he thought of as sticks of old wood, they viewed as treasure. They were murmuring now about the story of the materials and the importance of respecting them. Gino offered a suggestion, hesitantly at first, but soon he had a pencil in his hand. Edward had always loved this, seeing him lost in small details. In the old days he spent time in his workshop just watching him work, but somewhere along the way had got out of the habit.

The woman removed the kerchief from her head to reveal a tangle of messy, dark hair and Edward saw she wasn't quite as young as he had first thought.

'How long have you been a carpenter?' he asked

'Actually, I'm a pastry chef. This is just a hobby.'

'So what are you building the counter for?' To Edward it seemed the obvious question, the one to ask before all that talk of the wood and its history.

'I'm opening a *pasticceria*. It's what this shop always used to be. My nonna made and sold pastries here, and I want to continue the tradition. I'm Cecilia, by the way.'

Edward introduced himself and Gino too, since he was still too absorbed to bother. 'Are you from the States?' he asked.

'No, from Canada,' she replied. 'My family came from Montenello originally, but Toronto is where most of them ended up.'

She was intrigued to hear Gino's grandfather had once been the town's baker. 'If he made the bread here and my nonna made the pastries, surely they must have known each other. If only I could ask but sadly we lost her last year.'

'Gino's grandfather is gone too, but perhaps his mother might recall something,' said Edward. 'We'll have to find out.'

'It seems we're practically family then. How long are you staying for?'

'Actually we're not too sure yet,' admitted Edward, glancing at Gino who was entirely absorbed in his sketching.

It was the mayor's assistant Augusto who took them to view the house. Edward thought him quite a character, about a hundred years old, birdlike, very dapper and overflowing with apologies.

He was sorry the mayor hadn't been free to see them; very sorry he walked so slowly; that a layer of cloud was masking the view across the valley; that he hadn't thought to offer them a coffee and most sorry of all that the house earmarked for them was small and quite run-down. He led them up four stone steps and through a doorway that was overgrown with jasmine and so low both Gino and Edward had to duck to fit beneath it, even apologising about that.

'The people who lived here can't have been very tall,' remarked Edward, looking about. There wasn't much to it. Single-storey with oppressively low ceilings, cramped rooms and windows that meanly let in the light, it was a place where poor people had eked out an existence, not what had been in Edward's mind at all.

'There isn't even any land with it,' he said dismissively. 'What a shame.'

Augusto might have started apologising again, except Gino said, 'My family would have lived in a house very like this. Mamma said they only had two rooms and they all slept together, her sisters, parents and her. Imagine that.'

Augusto interrupted, 'Your family is from the south, yes?'

'Actually from Montenello,' said Gino. 'One of my grandfathers had a bakery here and I think the other worked in a forge.'

181

'From Montenello, but that is wonderful.' Augusto sounded thrilled.

'I guess,' said Gino, far less thrilled.

'Now let me think.' The old man paused, one hand to his forehead as if trying to touch the memories. 'There was a small bakery. It had a wood-fired oven and only produced one kind of bread. I remember the smoky, yeasty smell and the round loaves with their crusts baked brown. The true pane casereccio. My mother used to send me out for a large loaf each week. It was coarse and chewy but after a few days it grew tough and then we soaked it in olive oil so we didn't break our teeth on it. That must have been your grandfather's bread I was eating.'

'Made with his hands,' said Gino, lightly. 'My mother always says it was like no other bread she's ever eaten.'

'It's such a long time ago, but still I recall the taste.' Augusto beamed. 'How exciting that you have come home! When I picked out your application I realised you were Italian but not that you are one of us.'

'None of my family is left here,' Gino told him.

'Are you sure? This is a small place. Go far enough into the past and we are all related.'

'My father's name is Luigi Mancuso, do you remember him? He left when he was young.'

Augusto thought for a moment then shook his head. 'No, no although the memory may come back to me. These days thoughts often appear in my head and take me by surprise.'

'Did you say it was you who picked our application?' Gino asked.

'Of course,' said Augusto. 'The mayor supervised but he is a busy man so I went through all the emails myself. What a job that was. So many people wanted to come and help us revive our town. The decision wasn't easy.'

'So why us?' Gino wondered.

'The process is confidential.' Suddenly Augusto sounded

official. 'I can assure you we gave it a great deal of thought in order to be sure we selected exactly the right people.'

'What a pity the house isn't larger; it's not really an option.' Edward knocked a fist against the wall and there was a dull, solid thud rather than the hollow sound of plaster and paint he was used to at home. 'We're never going to buy something this poky.'

Augusto was standing between them, a little dot of a man, struggling to keep up with the conversation.

'But of course you must buy it. Montenello is your home and you belong here in the mountains with us. Of course, of course.'

Elise

Elise had bought a single ceramic tile during her afternoon shopping with Mimi. It was blue and white, with a pattern of fruit and flowers, and she propped it against the smoothest stretch of wall and took a photograph to post on Instagram.

My very first purchase for my house in Italy #happy #newlife #bellissima

She hoped her friends in Bristol saw it, and some of the teachers at her old school, and most of all Richard, wherever he was. Elise had sent him a text to say she was here and heard nothing in reply so obviously he was sulking. If he saw this place most likely he would be glad to have walked away. It was so vast the thought of trying to tackle any sort of renovation was overwhelming. Even using up all her savings and with the money from her parents, it wouldn't be nearly enough. Elise kept reminding herself she wasn't in a hurry. If she did it bit by bit, taking baby steps, then she was going to get there in the end. In the meantime, her Instagram page would be limited to shots of details – an intact section of stonework above a window, the wooden shutter that seemed most picturesquely worn, a view of the mountain range through one of the few uncracked window panes.

Having been persuaded to sleep twice more on Mimi's sofa (bless her, she seemed so worried), Elise was determined to spend her first night in her own home. She had borrowed some cushions and a rug to make up a bed on the floor. Still, as the daylight faded and the house started to creak and groan it did feel a little creepy. Convinced the wiring was dangerous, Mimi had made her promise not to switch on too many lights at once or leave anything at all plugged in while she was sleeping. In the dull yellow glow of a single bare bulb, Elise scrolled through all her social media feeds, on the off-chance Richard might pop up somewhere, and tried to convince herself she was perfectly fine by herself in this half-abandoned hilltop town that was quite possibly cursed.

And then there were the rats. She hadn't seen any yet but what else could be making that scrabbling sound up in the ceiling?

The best thing would be to eat her planned picnic supper of crusty bread, waxy cheese and green olives, and go to bed early. Elise had always been one of those people who could sleep anywhere so wasn't at all concerned about the hardness of the floor and was sure once she closed her eyes she would drift off in no time. The only trouble was the skittering of claws was right above her head now.

'Go away,' she shouted and her voice sounded small in the huge empty room.

When her phone rang loudly in the silence, Elise was so startled she almost dropped it. Seeing the mayor's name flash up on the screen, she answered it quickly.

'Ciao, Elise, I am just checking everything is OK with you,' he said in his smooth, low voice.

'It's all fine,' she replied, not wanting him to think she was the kind of person who couldn't cope with a few rodents.

'That is excellent news. You will be pleased to hear I found my assistant. He insists he was here waiting for you the other night, so perhaps there has been some sort of mis-understanding.'

'He definitely wasn't.' Elise was indignant. 'The whole place was closed up and I did try knocking. If it hadn't been for Mimi I don't know where I'd have gone.'

She heard Salvio sigh. 'Augusto is old and a little deaf and forgetful too sometimes; that is the only explanation I can think of. Again, I am very sorry and perhaps if you have no plans for this evening I could offer you dinner to make up for it? I was just about to go over to Renzo's bar if you would like to meet there.'

Elise leapt at the offer. 'Yes, dinner would be great. Thank you.'

'*Va bene*, come when you are ready, I will be there.'

It was creased from being in her backpack, still Elise wore one of the dresses she had packed and even dared to switch on another light so she could see well enough to apply make-up. There was no mirror so she had to use her phone but the results looked good enough.

All that time emailing back and forth with the mayor she had assumed he was a much older man. To discover him not only young but also good-looking had disarmed Elise who had entirely forgotten to be angry at how badly she had been let down. She kept finding her thoughts drifting back to him. How old was he? How could he have landed such a senior job? Was there a girlfriend somewhere? Over dinner there might be a chance to find out.

The mountain air was chilly so Elise wrapped herself in her fringed scarf and walked briskly up the narrow streets and steep steps, finding herself in the piazza more by luck than good judgement. A welcoming light shone through the windows of Renzo's bar and the *trattoria*. Hurrying past the building that stood between them Elise heard the whine of a saw. Someone in there was renovating; she felt a rush of excitement: hopefully that would be her soon too.

Salvio was waiting, watching the doorway and he smiled as she walked in. Elise wondered if he knew the effect that smile of his had. Did he look in the mirror and see how it changed his face, the dimple that appeared in his left cheek, the light that sparked in his long-lashed eyes, and understand how infectious it was, how impossible not to smile right back?

He ordered drinks, then asked what she had been up to for the past couple of days and seemed interested as Elise described the trip to Borgo del Colle and how Mimi had bought boxes of tiles, enough to cover whole walls, while she was more cautious and invested in only one, but that it seemed symbolic, the first small move to make the house her own.

'I'm on a tight budget,' admitted Elise. 'I'm surprised that you chose such a big place for me.'

'It was Augusto's idea,' said Salvio. 'Mimi is older and the other couple we have chosen are gay, so he must have assumed you and Richard were the most likely ones to want to have children some day and need the extra space.'

'Gay people have families too,' pointed out Elise.

'True, but perhaps Augusto didn't realise that. He has lived all his life in Montenello and I would be surprised if there have been any gay couples here before.'

Elise thought it interesting that everyone assumed women her age were longing for kids. 'Isn't there some sort of curse? That's what Mimi told me. She said women in this town can't ever have babies.'

'Really?' Salvio's eyes darkened. 'She said that?'

'Yes, she heard it from her architect, apparently. It's the story his grandmother told him. So is it true?' Elise didn't believe in curses but then she hadn't actually seen any children so far on the streets of Montenello.

Salvio looked serious, his brow drawn into a frown. 'To tell you the truth I had heard something of a curse. I was hoping to discourage too much talk of it. These superstitions, people still put weight in them and they are unhelpful. But Mimi, she seems fascinated for some reason.'

'How are they unhelpful?' Elise wondered.

'I am a young mayor and I want to build a better future

for Montenello. My hope is these houses will only be the first to be sold, that more people like you and Mimi will come and reinvigorate the town. If I am successful this will open up the way for many other positive changes.'

'And you're worried a curse will put everyone off?'

'Exactly.'

'Probably Mimi doesn't realise that.'

'She keeps talking about it, asking questions,' Salvio was aggrieved. 'Wouldn't it be a shame if my project failed and all because of some old fairy tale?'

'I'm sure she doesn't mean to create any problems ...'

'And I myself would like to have a family here some day so I don't want to hear of this curse. It is an ugly thing.'

'Mimi will soon be much too busy to bother with curses,' Elise reassured him. 'Once her renovations begin she'll have loads of other things on her mind.'

Salvio perked up. 'You think she is going to take the house then? She definitely wants it?'

'She'll need a wall to put all those tiles on, won't she?'

'That is very true.'

'So all you need is your gay couple to come on board and you're all set for your scheme to be a success.'

Salvio's smile lit his face again. 'I hope so; I hope very much.'

They ate dinner at the *trattoria*, plates of baked cannelloni filled with chicory and creamy ricotta, a dish of crisp fried artichokes, another of baked fennel coated with Parmesan. Elise experienced that same feeling she'd had last time she was there, of somehow being apart from the world, warm, comfortable and well fed. She listened to Salvio talk about his hopes and dreams for Montenello, eating slowly, wanting the meal to last.

'Tell me, what does your partner do?' Elise interrupted. 'Is she living in Montenello?'

'My partner?' Salvio sounded confused. 'Ah no, at this moment I don't have a *fidenzata*. I am still single.'

Elise hoped it wasn't obvious how glad she was to hear it. 'Oh I see, when you talked of wanting a family I just assumed ...'

'Some day in the future, yes. My mother would never forgive me if I didn't. But as I am always telling her, there is no hurry to embark on that stage of my life. And I must meet the right woman, which is no easy thing.'

Elise stared at this handsome man sitting a short stretch of chequered tablecloth away from her. The smooth olive skin, the glossy black hair and the slightly too aquiline nose, he was unlike any guy she knew at home and entirely different to Richard.

'I'm not planning on rushing into anything either,' she told him, 'and don't worry – I'm not even slightly put off by any talk of curses.'

She ordered dessert, a rich and gooey tiramisu, even though sweet things didn't normally interest her. And then there were glasses of liqueur. But finally their table was cleared, and they could find no more reasons to stay.

'I will walk you home,' Salvio offered, once he had settled the bill.

'Thanks, I'm not sure I'd find the place by myself now that it's dark,' Elise admitted. 'I'd hate to have another night facing the prospect of sleeping on the streets.'

Salvio opened the door and stood back to let her pass through. 'I promise I will never let that happen again while you are in Montenello.'

Outside Elise could hear the sound of hammering and there was a light glowing in the cloudy windows of the building next door. Salvio paused for a moment, listening too.

'My assistant Augusto is very concerned this place is being altered without the necessary permissions,' he confided. 'He is upset about it and wants me to intervene. But why would

I create paperwork and special permits that make it difficult to renovate an empty building? Surely that is the opposite of what I am trying to do?'

'So is this the place you're selling to the gay couple?' asked Elise.

'No, with this building a member of the original family decided at the last moment that they wanted to keep it. Augusto has a problem with that for some reason. He is being a little ... frustrating.'

'Will I need lots of permits when I start working on my house?' Elise was concerned.

'My plan is to make life as easy as possible for you,' he assured her. 'So long as any structural changes are safe you are free to do whatever you wish.'

As they walked on over the uneven flagstones, it seemed natural to link arms. Elise felt the warmth of Salvio's body through the wool of his jacket, and the strength of it too.

He knew a better route than the one she had taken earlier and far too quickly they were standing at the foot of the steps that led to her front door.

'I will come in, make sure everything is OK,' he told her.

'I don't have anything to offer you, not even coffee, but thanks, that would be great.'

The front door creaked as she pushed it open and inside was impenetrably dark. Elise felt along the wall until she found the light switch. She heard it click but no glow of soft yellow lit up the hallway.

'Damn,' she said.

'Maybe it is only the bulb, let me see.'

By the torchlight on his phone, Salvio found more switches but none that worked. 'I don't know, it could be a fuse or perhaps the power has gone out altogether,' he said.

Glancing out the window Elise saw none of the other houses were lit. But some of them were empty and others occupied by old people who must have gone to bed ages ago.

Further away, on the corner, a single streetlamp was shining.

'It's hard to know but that's OK, I'll sort it out in the morning,' she told Salvio.

'*Va bene*, tonight you must sleep at my house.'

'No, no—'

'I have a spare room, fresh sheets, a nice bed, it is very comfortable,' Salvio promised.

'Thanks, but I really, really want to spent my first night here, otherwise I feel as though it will never happen.'

'Without power it is impossible,' argued Salvio.

'I have my phone, I'll be fine.'

'I cannot leave you here alone in the dark.'

'Really, I don't mind,' said Elise.

'No, no, if you want to stay then I will keep you company.'

'I'm sleeping on the floor.'

'Ah, yes.' A hint of doubt crept into Salvio's tone but then he rallied. 'That is fine, it will be an adventure.'

Elise couldn't see much of his face in the light from his phone, still she could tell he was smiling.

'OK then.' If she was honest with herself, she was relieved. 'If you really don't mind.'

Salvio rummaged through cupboards until he found some ancient stubs of candles and in their soft flickering light things didn't seem as awkward as they might have. He kept on his shirt and boxer shorts, she wore loose cotton pyjamas, and they bedded down together in the nest she had made on the floor.

'Are you cold?' Salvio asked.

'A little bit,' she told him.

He curled his body closer, touching her just slightly. 'Is that better?'

'Yes, thanks,' was all Elise could manage.

Almost straight away she heard his breathing change and slow. As he started drifting off to sleep he fell in a little closer and Elise felt his weight and warmth against her back.

For a moment she thought of Richard and all their nights sleeping together in the horrible little flat that smelled of lamb rogan josh and chicken korma. This felt like a different life completely.

'Goodnight, Salvio,' she whispered.

He was much too sleepy to reply but his slow, steady breaths touched the back of her neck and his chest rose and fell against her spine.

Montenello

Salvio knew he shouldn't have spent the night with her but didn't regret it. Even waking on the floor, with a crick in his neck and sore shoulders, he had been happy to find Elise so close, her face creased from the cushions, morning sleepy and a little shy with him.

There hadn't been much time to talk because Salvio had to get home to shower and change, then hurry to work. Now, as he went about his usual routine – carefully shaving, running a comb through his short hair, putting on a crisp shirt and a good suit – he wondered how soon he could call her. Perhaps he should offer to make dinner at his place; Elise didn't have a proper kitchen, after all. He wasn't an especially confident cook but there were a couple of dishes Donna Carmela had taught him that he could reliably re-create. Or he might even take her to his mother's restaurant for a long lunch. Yes, more food, wine and conversation: that was what was needed.

He walked to work feeling lighter than he had in a long time. Even the thought of how much Augusto might be planning to complicate the day ahead didn't trouble him as much as it might have.

Salvio wished his assistant would return to being the helpful, reliable presence he had seemed at the beginning. He seemed oddly unsettled by the sudden start of renovations at one of the more unsightly buildings in the piazza, the one they had been hoping to sell until a member of the family who once lived there had claimed it. Augusto appeared to think this person, a young woman apparently, should be filling out applications and waiting for permissions and had started up a panicked searching through the old filing cabinets, pulling out documents, raising dust and muttering. None of it had made sense to Salvio.

'Why don't we go and greet this woman, welcome her to Montenello and ask what she is planning?' he had suggested. 'Surely that would be better than all these unnecessary formalities.'

That had brought a hiss of disapproval from Augusto. 'We are the town's administration. There are rules and regulations we must abide by.'

Salvio had gazed at him, ankle deep in yellowing documents, a frantic light in his eyes as he searched out what he needed. 'Nevertheless, I ought to go over and say hello.'

'That would be inappropriate.' Augusto had been adamant. 'It would send the wrong impression entirely. This person cannot expect the mayor of Montenello to appear when she demands it.'

'No one is demanding anything,' pointed out Salvio, hoping his assistant was planning to tidy away the mess of old documents. 'I think we should be more welcoming.'

'Of course, of course,' Augusto had said, but then all afternoon made sure that Salvio was tied up in unexpected meetings and sudden crises, making it impossible for him to get away. It had been one of those days when he found himself wondering if taking this job had been a mistake. Everything in Montenello happened so slowly and was always more complicated than it needed to be. He would be a saint if it didn't grind him down.

After work was finally finished Salvio might have stopped in to meet whoever was so busy sawing wood and hammering away in the empty building, except by then he couldn't wait to see Elise. Holding off from calling her hadn't been easy. And after such a long, frustrating day he was longing to spend time with someone like her, young and enthusiastic, who knew how to embrace change and make progress.

Now, as he made his walk to work on this bright sunny morning with a crick still in his neck from the night he had spent on the floor with her, Salvio thought of Elise's face and smiled.

In the piazza he stopped for coffee at Renzo's bar as usual. Clustered round the counter, eating their morning pastries from paper serviettes, three men were deep in conversation. Listening in, Salvio realised they were arguing about the building next door.

'It is going to be another *trattoria*,' said one, 'in competition with Assunta and she is furious.'

'No, you are wrong. My wife heard it will be a salon where she can have her hair done every week. She is very excited.'

'In the old days it was a *pasticceria*. Imagine being able to buy rum baba and cannoli fresh every day.'

'Ah, it is years since I have eaten a good rum baba. Let us hope for that.' One of the old men touched his balding scalp. 'I have no need for a salon.'

Salvio checked the building as he left the bar but it was closed up and silent. Later on he would return and see if he could meet whoever had embarked on this renovation, no matter what his assistant thought about it.

At his desk he tackled even the dreariest of his tasks with more vigour than usual. Augusto arrived late again but seemed in a more positive frame of mind. Today he was more concerned with the Australians, particularly Gino's roots in Montenello. He thought that at last he might remember his father but wasn't entirely certain if he had the right person.

'Do you think these Australians are going take the house?' asked Salvio, cutting off this uncharacteristic rambling.

'Of course, they must, of course.'

'Is that what they told you?'

'Not exactly.'

Salvio wished the pair of them hadn't appeared without

any notice and that there had been an opportunity to meet them. 'So what did they say? Have you heard from them at all?'

Augusto sidestepped his questions. 'I have an excellent idea,' he declared. 'We must hold a ceremony in the Town Hall to give our new citizens the keys to their homes and welcome them officially to Montenello.'

'Only Elise has committed herself definitely so far.'

'Still, we must plan if we are to do things properly.'

'Perhaps you do have a point,' said Salvio, realising it might be a good idea to keep Augusto busy planning this ceremony. 'Can I leave the organisation to you?'

'Of course.' He seemed pleased. 'You know, I definitely do recall the father. Luigi Mancuso, a very proud young man so convinced he would find a better future far away from here. And now at last his son is back. Yes, yes a ceremony. I will organise it all.'

Salvio waited until his assistant was deep in a telephone conversation before he got up and left the office. He didn't take his jacket, so Augusto would think he had only popped out for a moment. While it seemed ridiculous, he had been raised to respect his elders and didn't want to make it obvious that he was going against his advice.

The building next to Renzo's bar had been opened up and from inside Salvio heard the scream of metal on wood. Knocking, although there was little hope of being heard, he continued inside. Through the haze of dust he saw three figures, ears muffled and faces swathed in scarves, all intent on what they were doing. The taller of two men looked up and noticed him.

'*Buongiorno*,' shouted Salvio.

The man touched the arm of the woman beside him, and she stopped working the saw.

'*Buongiorno*,' he repeated, with a smile. 'I am Salvio Valentini, the mayor.'

Pulling the kerchief from her face, the woman stared at him distrustfully. 'Yes?'

'I came to introduce myself. We are all intrigued to know what it is you are doing here.'

'Nothing that needs some sort of permit you can charge me thousands of euros for,' she told him.

Salvio seemed to have started out on the wrong foot with this woman but had no idea why.

'I'm not changing the building's use in any way, only restoring what was always here,' she added.

'You mean the *pasticceria*?' Salvio widened his smile, trying to demonstrate that he was friendly. 'With excellent rum baba and Sicilian cannoli?'

She hesitated, as if unsure how to respond to this onslaught. 'Maybe not cannoli, at least not at first,' she said, eventually. 'They are difficult to make.'

'You are really opening a *pasticceria*, the three of you?' asked Salvio.' I think people here will be very pleased.'

'I am the pastry chef.' She seemed to be thawing a little. 'Gino and Edward are helping me build a cabinet that's all.'

The men removed their protective face masks and Salvio was surprised to discover they were his Australian couple who, for some reason, had decided to spend a day helping this woman Cecilia build her shop cabinet. He was confused but didn't want to be seen to be asking too many questions.

'It will be wonderful to have a *pasticceria* here in Montenello,' he said instead.

Gazing around he saw that against one wall there was a trestle table covered in smudged pencil sketches and columns of measurements. Piled along the other was a stack of wood.

'What about the outside of the building?' Salvio asked. 'It needs quite a bit of work too, I think.'

'Unfortunately that will have to wait. I can't afford to do it all at once.'

Salvio risked one more question: 'Who in your family does the place belong to?'

'It was my grandmother's. I have every right to be here.' Cecilia had returned to sounding hostile. 'And it's actually nobody's business.'

'I am not suggesting there is any problem,' Salvio was quick to say. 'I am curious, that is all – everyone here is, I think. Montenello is a small town and no one has opened a new shop for a very long time.'

Cecilia gave him a cool look. 'Everyone can be as curious as they like, it's my place and they will have to wait to see what I do here ... and whether I make cannoli.'

Salvio thought her prickly and rude. Still, determined to be welcoming, he made an offer of coffee but Cecilia gave a shake of her head. She had turned her attention back to the wood and seemed impatient to continue.

'Perhaps an *apertivo* later then,' he suggested, looking over at the Australians. 'I am keen to know what you think of the house we are offering you.'

'Unfortunately, it is too small,' said one.

'We're still thinking about it,' replied the other.

'Let's talk later then,' said Salvio, who'd had enough of being confused by these people. 'Renzo's bar is just next door, and I will be there at six thirty.'

The sound of sawing and hammering followed him out of the door. Outside, lined up on a bench close to the shop, were the three old men who had been eating breakfast beside him earlier. All were staring in his direction.

'Well?' asked one.

'A *pasticceria*,' Salvio told them. 'That's all I know.'

Passing the fruit seller, old Francesco Rossi, he repeated the words. To the man who swept the streets, despite no evidence of him being on the council pay roll, to the woman his mother had invited to dinner, to a group that gossiped over their shopping baskets at this time every morning, Salvio spread the news. 'A *pasticceria*, opening soon I believe. My plans for Montenello are starting to work already.'

Mimi

Mimi couldn't stop shopping. She had been back to Borgo del Colle and spent an entire morning looking at bathrooms and kitchenware. It was a heady feeling knowing she was able to choose whatever she wanted – every last bowl, cup and spoon. Once when she was married she had bought some little plates she liked the look of. They were from a shop in Notting Hill that sold Italian ceramics in bright colours. Mimi thought eating slices of toast and boiled eggs from them would be a cheerful start to her morning. She ought to have remembered that plates were meant to be white, just like glassware only came from Iittala, knives were all Nesmuk and sharpened with a special strop. Glenn was a designer, he cared about objects, form and function, he was the one with the good taste and it extended to every room in the house. Would her ex-husband have even sat on the sofa if it hadn't been an Eames, cooked in a kitchen that wasn't by Bulthaup, turned on a desk lamp if it wasn't exactly the right shape, size and colour? Even the cupboards weren't permitted to have handles; they had to be a seamless and invisible part of any wall. Mimi's little toast plates were much too garish. No piece of artisan bread fresh from their four-slice Dualit would ever find its way onto one.

Buying all those boxes of brightly coloured wall tiles had felt like being set free. Her favourite were covered in a pattern of lemons. She had far too many, some would most likely be passed on to Elise who was on a tight budget and didn't have a hope of being able to renovate a house as large as the one she was buying. Mimi tried not to worry – the girl wasn't her responsibility – but if she could help in small ways then she would in the hope someone would do the same if her boys ever needed it.

Mimi made herself a cup of tea in one of the new mugs. It was definitely garish and she imagined the expression on Glenn's face if he saw it. As she was browsing round the shops she had realised she wasn't really certain what her own taste was. Did she mostly like things plain and simple, or long for interesting shapes and textures? She was still trying to decide.

The one thing she was certain about was what she wanted for the house. It had to be comfortable. A place you could leave out books and magazines rather than returning them to a neat pile, put your teacup down on the table without a coaster. It was to have comfy sofas and too many cushions, and you would be allowed to come inside with your shoes on. Just thinking about it made Mimi happy.

Settling down with her tea and laptop, she knew exactly what she was going to do. First she emailed Otis and Ben to give them the news. Then re-booked her flights and the rental car, extending her visit for yet another week. Next she sent an email to the mayor to confirm she wanted the house and another to the architect wondering how long it might take for him to come up with some initial ideas and costings.

Finally Mimi embarked on an email to her ex-husband. She told him she was ready to put their house on the market, would be happy with whichever estate agent he chose, would move out when he wanted.

'I've bought a place in Italy and I'm going to be spending lots of time here,' she typed. 'Don't worry about the boys; there's plenty of space for when they want to visit. And I'm only ever a flight away if they need me.'

She thought of Glenn reading it, how much he was going to disapprove and how powerless he would feel. For the first time since they were married, Mimi had chosen to do precisely the thing he had advised against.

'My new house is in a small southern Italian town and I'm excited about making my future here. I won't pretend it hasn't been hard since you left me, but I'm beginning to see it might have been for the best after all.'

Mimi reread her words then hesitated, trying to decide how to sign off. 'With love' wasn't right, because it wasn't how she felt, not any more. Since arriving here, somehow the last traces of affection for Glenn had evaporated. She had stopping waking every morning to the thought her life would be better if nothing at all had changed. She felt fine without him.

In the end she settled for 'best wishes', which seemed coolly polite and more suitable for communications with former husbands. Once she had sent the emails, Mimi had the urge to tell someone. She thought about calling one of the Silver Divorcees, perhaps Sinead. But that would mean too many questions and explanations when all she really wanted was to share her excitement.

Instead, she called Donna Carmela's number and after a few rings heard her answer with a crisp 'Pronto.' It was noisy in the background so Mimi assumed she must be in her kitchen.

'I wanted you to be the first to know,' she said. 'I've decided to buy the house.'

'Fantastic!' Donna Carmela shouted down the line. 'I wasn't sure you were going to take it.'

'Also, it looks like I'm going to hire the architect you suggested,' added Mimi.

'You liked him?' She sounded pleased. 'I had a feeling you might.'

'I'm impressed with him.'

'Ah yes, he is very impressive.' There was a smile in Donna Carmela's voice. 'But we must have a celebration. I will talk to Salvio. Surely he will want to organise something.'

'That would be nice. We should invite Elise too. She's definitely going ahead with her purchase.'

'The young English girl, what is she like?'

'Very pretty, extraordinarily beautiful, in fact.'

'And her temperament?'

'She's lovely.'

'In that case I look forward to meeting her, and to toasting both your futures. And congratulations, Mimi. I am sure this is the right thing for you.'

'I feel good about it too.'

Saying goodbye to Donna Carmela with promises to meet soon, Mimi thought about what to do with the evening ahead. She had the urge to take a stroll through her new town. To say *buongiorno* to the old fruit seller in the piazza, and nod a greeting to the people standing about in groups beside the statue of Garibaldi or the fountain that never seemed to be working, then enjoy a drink at the bar. That was how the locals spent their time and she thought the easy rhythm of their lives had a lot to recommend it.

Mimi walked through streets that were gradually starting to become more familiar. She passed a church with a tall bell tower then found a shortcut that led up some steps winding their way behind a row of houses with tiny balconies strung with empty washing lines. As she passed each one she tried to peer into its windows to see if anyone still lived there.

The bar was busy and she spotted the mayor seated at one of the tables. He was with a group of people – two men and a younger woman, all of them dressed in exceptionally dusty clothing – and Mimi didn't like to interrupt so instead she went and ordered an Aperol spritz.

'Signora Wilson.' Salvio had spotted her and was waving to attract her attention. 'Come and join us, please. Let me introduce you to some more new arrivals in Montenello.'

It took Mimi a while to work out the relationships between

these people. Was Cecilia the girlfriend of the shaven-headed Australian or with the darker, quieter one? They were both good-looking but too old for her, really. Then it occurred to Mimi that she had it entirely wrong and it was the men who were a couple.

'Edward and Gino have been looking at one of our abandoned houses,' Salvio explained. 'They're not sure if it's right for them. We've just been discussing why.'

'It's taken me a while to reach a decision,' Mimi told them. 'But this town does seem to grow on you if you spend enough time here.'

Salvio looked at her hopefully. 'A decision?'

'Yes, I sent you an email. I definitely want the house.'

'This is great news. We must celebrate.'

'That's what Donna Carmela said. But perhaps we should wait and see if Edward and Gino are going to be celebrating something too.'

The dark, intense one shrugged. 'Edward thinks the house is too small so I doubt it.'

'Gino didn't want to come to Italy in the first place,' said the other.

They were snippy with each other. Mimi had friends who bickered like that with their partners. She found it exhausting. It was one of the reasons she had mostly gone along with whatever Glenn wanted.

'That's a pity,' she said, turning her attention to Cecilia. The girl had a lovely face but was doing her best to disguise it. Her hair was scraped back roughly, her skin streaked with dust, and Mimi didn't think she had seen her smile yet.

'Are you buying a place here too?' she asked.

'I already own one,' said Cecilia. 'Right next door.'

'Cecilia is opening a *pasticceria* here in Montenello,' Salvio explained.

'First I need to rebuild the shop.' Cecilia rubbed at her eyes and Mimi realised she must be exhausted. 'It's in a much worse state than I thought so I'm very grateful to have had some help today.'

'We'll be back again tomorrow,' Gino promised and his partner Edward gave him a sharp look. 'I'm not going to miss the chance to work with oak posts from the Venetian lagoon.'

'No, of course you're not.'

Mimi would have preferred to escape this tension. She longed to be enjoying her drink in peace up at the bar. If it hadn't been for Salvio, she might have made an excuse and left. But he was trying so hard to make this project work, it seemed important to him. And he was the son of Donna Carmela, a woman who had been very kind. So instead Mimi made an effort, smiling at Cecilia and saying, 'You're a carpenter and a pastry chef, that's very impressive.'

'Not really, I had some good teachers. My father taught me the woodwork and my nonna showed me how to bake her favourite pastries before she died. She could make all the traditional things: little almond paste biscuits, strawberry tarts filled with pistachio cream, cannoli. She learned everything in that building next door when she was still a girl.'

'Cecilia's grandmother was from Montenello,' Salvio explained to Mimi. 'Now she has returned here to carry on the family tradition in her memory. That is beautiful, I think.'

'Oh really, is that your story now?' Cecilia gave him a sharp look. 'I saw the email saying you wanted to sell our building. The rest of the family were happy to let it go. Only I cared that Nonna wouldn't have wanted that.'

'We would never have sold it without your agreement,' swore Salvio.

'Yes, you would. I read the email where you said you were going to. It's why I came so quickly. I am occupying the building now. You can't take it away from me.' Cecilia was fierce.

'Of course not,' Salvio told her, but Mimi noticed he was frowning. 'This email, it came from me?'

'Your name was on it, yes I'm certain.'

'I think there has been a misunderstanding. My assistant Augusto may have overstepped the mark in his eagerness to make our little scheme work. To be clear, I am delighted you have come back. This town needs young people like you or it will die.'

Cecilia's expression was still distrustful. 'Nonna always said they had no choice, that the family had to leave when they did. It was as if they'd been driven out but she never really explained it.'

'Perhaps it was the curse of Montenello that frightened them away,' suggested Mimi. The story seemed such an interesting part of the town's history and she repeated what the architect had told her. 'Apparently it was the reason a lot of people left. Was your grandmother very superstitious?'

Cecilia thought about it. 'Actually, she was. She had some odd ideas. If anyone left a hat on a bed she said it was a sign of death and she thought spilling olive oil brought bad luck. She never mentioned a curse, though.'

Until then Gino had been gazing into the middle distance, apparently deep in thought and not paying much attention to the conversation. Now he seemed interested.

'That's funny because my father has always called Montenello "that cursed place". I assumed it must because he hated it. Are you saying it actually is cursed?'

'Apparently,' said Mimi. 'That's the rumour anyway.'

'Please, please.' Salvio held his hands in the air. 'This town is not cursed. Yes, many families left, but that was not the reason why. How am I ever to rebuild Montenello if everyone keeps saying so? Nobody at all will want to come here.'

'I'm sure it won't really put people off,' Mimi was surprised at how upset the mayor seemed. 'It's just a little bit of local colour.'

'But what if it does? I am working very hard to make this project successful. It isn't easy at all.'

206

'I'm so sorry,' said Mimi, although she was sure if this scheme of the mayor's wasn't successful it wouldn't be because of some old folklore. The problem here was a lack of proper planning. The town had launched into selling off these abandoned properties without considering all the details.

Mimi wasn't used to speaking out. She had plenty of opinions but found life tended to be easier if she didn't voice them. Now, though, it all seemed so obvious she felt it would be wrong to stay silent.

A hot blush spread across her cheeks as she began cautiously, 'I wouldn't normally interfere, and I hope you don't mind me saying so, but I think the biggest issue with your project is a mix up with the way the houses have been assigned.'

'What do you mean?' Salvio sounded defensive.

'The house allocated to Elise is much too big for her. I'm sure it could be wonderful but the roof leaks, all those terracotta roof tiles need replacing and the ceilings are about to collapse. The wiring, the plumbing everything needs attention. Elise may think she can handle it but she's being unrealistic. She doesn't have enough money or expertise. She's going to get into trouble there.'

Everyone was staring at her: Salvio through narrowed eyes, Edward more quizzically, Cecilia coolly, Gino with an expression that was impossible to fathom.

'Elise wants that house,' argued Salvio. 'The decision has been made.'

'I know, but it's not practical. You need to find her something more manageable.'

'She loves it, she told me so.'

Mimi spoke very gently because she didn't want to upset him but how could she not feel protective towards a girl who was only a little older than her sons. 'Just because Elise loves it doesn't make it the best thing for her.'

Salvio gave a soft sigh. All the fight seemed to have gone out of him. 'That is exactly what my mother would tell me.'

Edward spoke then. He said what Mimi had been hoping he would.

'What's this too-big place like? I'd love to take a look at it.'

Edward

Edward had been feeling ridiculously disappointed. He had imagined they would see the house and fall in love, but the opposite had happened. It was an ugly, squat building, without so much as a balcony, and surely the smallest place in the whole town.

Surprisingly, Gino was the one to defend the house – praising it as unpretentious and solid, a good home for someone else – and Edward was the moody one now. Not that Gino seemed to care, or even notice. He was more interested in some old pieces of wood dug out of the silt of Venice's lagoon. So now it seemed they weren't even going to get the proper break they needed, instead they would be spending time helping a stranger and, while Cecilia seemed fine, it was hardly what Edward had been planning on for this holiday.

He was still trying to resign himself to his dream of Italy being over when Mimi Wilson mentioned another house, much too large and dilapidated for the girl who was meant to be buying it, and a last tiny spark had caught.

'What's the place like?' he asked.

'Practically a *palazzo*. Vast and crumbling with faded frescoes on the walls.'

'I'd love to take a look at it.'

'I'll text and see if Elise is there,' she offered, 'although I can't imagine where else she'd be.'

A flush had risen up Mimi's neck. Carefully chic and very slender, she was one of those stylish older women who seem so polished and poised, but Edward noticed that whenever she spoke it was with a slight hesitation, as if she was expecting to be shouted down.

'We could take a walk over that way together,' she was suggesting now, the flush reaching her cheeks. 'Show you round the town, then call in to introduce you to Elise. It's a nice idea for us all to meet, isn't it? We're in the same boat, after all.'

'Absolutely.' Now Edward had heard about this house, he had to see it.

'Shall we go then? So long as everyone has finished.'

Salvio insisted on paying the bill then took the lead, walking them through the narrow streets, past buildings made of stone pocked by time and worn by harsh weather. There was an old hotel with its windows boarded up and a sign pointing the way to a long-gone public telephone. A few of the houses were almost in ruins, their walls scored by deep fissures and weeds sprouting between their terracotta roof tiles. Others looked neglected but Edward heard radios or televisions playing at full volume inside and once he smelled frying onions.

'How many places are empty?' he asked Salvio.

'I have never made a count.'

'But you're only selling three, is that right?'

'It is a beginning. If it works then we may extend the scheme. Perhaps someone will buy the hotel we just passed and reopen it. And all the other things a town needs – a pharmacy, a butcher shop, a place selling gelato – if enough people come all these things will follow.'

'That's your dream?'

'Not a dream, a vision' Salvio corrected him. 'But I need this beginning to be a success. Talk of curses, of houses being wrongly allocated … it is not helpful. It is only creating more complications for me.'

Rounding a corner, Edward spotted a small shrine, a figurine of a Madonna in a cracked glass case surrounded by posies of wilted wildflowers that must have been left as offerings. He glanced over to check if Gino had seen it, knowing it was the kind of religious iconography that made him shudder, and realised he had fallen behind. A stranger was shaking him by the hand, a man with an old face and the finest sprinkling of white hair on his head. He was speaking to Gino who was nodding and smiling. After a few moments they shook hands again, even more energetically, and the old man patted Gino on the shoulder as he walked on, calling after him in Italian.

A similar thing happened a few metres further on, but this time with a woman. Her back was bent and her steps unsteady, still she rushed from her house and they all had to wait while she talked to Gino loudly and rapidly in Italian. To Edward, who didn't understand a word, it sounded like she was scolding him

The third time it was a man who had been sitting on a bench, his walking stick beside him. As they approached he grabbed the stick and started waving it, the folds of his chin trembling and his creased old eyes peering disbelievingly at Gino. 'Luigi Mancuso?' he asked.

'No, no, I'm his son, *suo figlio*.'

The old man insisted on getting to his feet. He held onto Gino, kissed both his cheeks and leaned into his chest. Edward realised there were tears in his eyes and Gino looked quite moved as well, quickly brushing his cheeks with his hand.

Once the man had released him, Edward asked, 'Did all those people know your father?'

'That last one seemed to think I was him. He used to play cards with one of my grandfathers.'

'And the woman?'

'I think she was saying my mother's family should have stayed here. Now she has to ask her niece to bring her bread from the bakery in Borgo del Colle and it isn't as good.'

'How do these people know who your family are?' Edward wondered.

'I think I may be able to guess.' Salvio was smiling. 'My assistant Augusto has been telling everyone you are here. Ever since he learned you come from this town he has been highly excited and word gets round fast. Also, I think you look very like your father, yes?'

'I suppose I do but still I didn't expect such a warm welcome.' Gino seemed dazed.

'People are always leaving Montenello but they don't often return home,' Salvio explained. 'That is why it is so remarkable.'

'I must seem like a ghost from the past walking through their streets.'

'A ghost we are very happy to see,' Salvio told him. 'I am sure you will meet other people who remember your parents. Maybe even some that you are related to.'

'Your assistant said I might,' said Gino, 'although my father has always claimed there is no one left.'

'Almost everyone here seems to be a cousin or a nephew. It is that kind of town. Small and closely knit.'

'But why is all the fuss about me?' wondered Gino. 'No one seems to have recognised Cecilia yet.'

They all looked at her and she gave a wry shrug. 'I don't know. Maybe the mayor's assistant isn't quite so excited to have me here. Perhaps he'd prefer the word not to get out.'

'I don't see why,' said Salvio, frowning as if there were something he couldn't quite fathom. 'Everyone is pleased to have families return to Montenello. It is what we were hoping for.'

Cecilia shrugged again. 'It doesn't matter anyway. I don't care about people fawning over me, just as long as they come and buy my pastries once the shop is open.'

They walked on and Edward was beginning to wonder how much further they would have to go when they came across a very pretty fair-haired girl standing out on the street beside a battered old Vespa that she was wiping free of cobwebs carefully with a cloth.

'Elise, what is this?' Salvio asked her. 'You have bought it?'

'Yes, from the old man three doors down,' the girl explained. 'He never uses it any more but it all works fine. I thought it would get me to Borgo del Colle since the bus seems so unreliable.'

'Have you ever ridden one before?' Salvio sounded anxious. 'The roads here can be dangerous, people drive too fast, there are tight corners and narrow places.'

'I'll be fine.'

'It is such an old Vespa; I could have helped you buy a newer model.'

'That would have been too expensive. He practically gave this one to me.' She looked towards Mimi who was standing with the rest of them. 'It's not that bad, is it?'

'It does look a little rough,' Mimi said in her careful, half-hesitant way. 'Perhaps before you take it on the road Salvio could give you some lessons?'

'That's a very good idea,' agreed Salvio, straight away. 'Then I will feel happier you are safe. But I am forgetting that I need to make some introductions. Elise you haven't met Edward and Gino yet. Or Cecilia.'

There was handshaking and some kissing of cheeks. Elise repeated several times how great it was to have other English-speaking people in Montenello who were looking at doing the same sort of thing as her.

Even from the outside Edward could tell the place Elise had been allocated had once belonged to one of Montenello's more important families. The yellow paint on its walls had faded and the plaster columns around its arched entranceway were scuffed. But all along the upper level were large shuttered doors opening onto wrought-iron balconies and, as Elise invited them inside, Edward gave a long, low whistle at the height of the ceilings. Each new room he entered confirmed his first impression of grandeur He found the remains of frescoes in what must have been the dining area and a broken chandelier on the floor of one of the bedrooms upstairs. It wasn't difficult to imagine what this house must have been like in its day.

'Wow, just wow,' he said to Gino. 'I suppose whoever lived here fell on hard times. Why else would you abandon a place like this?'

'Mmm ...' Gino was staring at the ceiling, distracted by practicalities. 'That needs shoring up pretty urgently. The roof above it must be leaking badly.'

Elise was standing at Gino's shoulder frowning upwards with him. 'Mimi told me not to come up here. She thinks it's really dangerous.'

'Yeah, she's right. If I could borrow some tools and get hold of some timber then Ed and I might be able to make a brace as a temporary measure.'

'Will it be a major job to fix properly?' asked Elise.

'It's hard to tell. You need to get a roofer in, a local who understands the way these houses have been built. Maybe the mayor can recommend someone. But if I were you the first thing I'd do is make the place watertight otherwise it's going to continue to deteriorate quickly.'

She nodded worriedly and her too-wide eyes followed Gino as he moved on to another room. 'It's not quite as bad in here but there's definitely some water damage,' he called back. 'And those stairs aren't in the greatest shape when you look down at them.'

Elise trailed after him, shoulders drooping. The sound of their voices echoed through the empty spaces as they discussed what needed immediate attention and where it might be safe to wait.

'A house like this will be very expensive to maintain even once it's refurbished,' Gino was warning.

'I was planning to rent it out on Airbnb and hoping it might pay for itself eventually,' replied Elise. 'That could work, couldn't it?'

Edward left them to it, heading back downstairs and walking through the reception rooms again, this time more slowly, taking in every detail. He loved this place; it would be a privilege to return it to elegance. The parties you could throw here, the whole house glittering with candles and filled with music. The lavish dinners, course after course served on a magnificently long table Gino would make to measure. This was the house they should have had; the one he had been dreaming of. Not that ugly little peasant's hut.

He found the others downstairs, trying to pull down a shutter in the kitchen. Cecilia was claiming the hinge was so rusty the whole thing could fall off and injure someone but it seemed to be taking a lot of effort for her and Salvio to wrest it from the wall. The mayor was bright red and beads of perspiration had formed on his brow, Cecilia's face was screwed up with determination.

'Careful, careful, yes, nearly there, have you got it?' With a final grunt of effort it broke free, Salvio and Cecilia staggering back.

'Ah teamwork, very good,' said Salvio, panting slightly. 'Shall we take down the other one now too?'

Elise was dismayed when she saw what they were doing. 'I'm sleeping down here. I need those shutters.'

'They'll all have to come off eventually,' Cecilia told her. 'See how rotten this one is.'

Elise seemed not to have heard her. 'I was going to sand and varnish them.'

'They're rotten,' Cecilia repeated impatiently, poking at one with her thumb. 'I wouldn't even bother trying to fix them. Just get new shutters made. How many do you think there are?'

'Loads and loads,' said Elise, despondently. 'Too many.'

Edward felt sorry for her. She had been like an excited child out there, polishing her ancient Vespa. Now all of them were ganging up on her, forcing her to face the realities she had been managing to ignore.

'There's a huge amount of work to be done here,' he said, gently. 'It'll cost you a lot just to make the place reasonably sound.'

'I know that,' she said. 'But I don't have to do everything at once.'

'Didn't I hear you say you wanted to rent it out on Airbnb?'

Elise nodded, her pretty face slumping into a frown.

'For that it will have to be properly refurbished and fitted out.'

'Yes, but ... I'll figure something out. Mimi's place needs a lot of work too. You should see the state of her terrace.'

'That's true,' agreed Mimi. 'The architect warned me I'm going to be investing far more than it's worth.'

'The place we've been offered is far less of a project,' said Edward. 'You should come over and see it some time. We've got the key. The mayor's funny little assistant was determined Gino should keep it.'

'I'd love to see it,' said Mimi, her face pinking again. 'Should we go over there right now before it gets too late.'

'What, all of us?'

'Why not?'

They moved through the streets in a flock and Edward was aware of being watched every step of the way. A priest stared out from the doorway of a church, three old men on white plastic chairs stopped their game of cards, a woman pulling a trolley of shopping paused, open-mouthed.

Only one more person recognised Gino, a man of about his father's age who pumped his hand up and down, shouting hoarsely and excitedly. Edward too thought it odd no one had recognised Cecilia. Surely some of these people

216

remembered the family who owned the *pasticceria*? Why would Augusto not put the word out that she was back in town?

'Are you feeling like a celebrity yet?' he asked Gino.

'It's the strangest thing, quite overwhelming.' He looked pale. 'All these people with their memories of those that have died or disappeared ... I want to tell my parents about it but I think it would make them too sad.'

Both Mimi and Elise exclaimed when they saw the low doorway with the tangle of jasmine growing wild over it. Neither had to duck their heads to fit under and unlike Edward, they didn't appear to think the house was poky or depressing, that the ceilings were too low or the windows mean and small.

'It's adorable, like a hobbit house,' said Elise, who was taking photos with her phone. 'What would you do with it, do you think?'

'You'd keep things very rustic,' Gino told her. 'Use old materials wherever possible so it looked humble and honest. This is a worker's cottage and shouldn't pretend to be anything else.'

Elise peered upwards. 'The ceilings are cracked. What sort of state do you think the roof is in?'

'I'd say lots of the tiles are lifting but since it's small it shouldn't be too big a deal to replace them. And the walls were built to last. See how thick they are.'

Elise seemed to digest that, although she didn't say anything just ran a careful hand over the rough stone.

'You'd leave the walls unfinished,' said Gino, 'no need to worry about plaster and paint. Get tiles for the floor, replace the broken windows, new bathroom, decent kitchen and you'd be pretty much done.'

'Do you think there might be space for a small courtyard garden in that sunny spot at the front beside the steps where all the jasmine is?' asked Elise.

Gino nodded. 'You could have a bench out there; a few plants in pots; a shade cloth even.'

'It could be so lovely when it's finished,' exclaimed Elise.

'Maybe, but we're not taking it,' Edward told her. 'It's not what we're looking for at all. And besides, Gino doesn't want a place in Montenello.'

'Really?' She was surprised. 'Then why did you come here?'

'It was my idea,' admitted Edward. 'I thought we'd see the house and fall in love. But it didn't happen.'

'That's such a shame.'

Edward looked over at Gino. He was staring through a hole where once there must have been a small window. It looked out over a patchwork of rooftops towards the vineyards and olive groves in the valley below. Something down there had interested him but Edward couldn't tell what.'

'Maybe you could get a bigger house,' Elise was saying. 'Would that make a difference?'

'I'm not sure,' Edward said, truthfully. 'It would be up to Gino. And anyway, there aren't any more houses available right now. That's right isn't it, Salvio?'

The mayor nodded. 'Unfortunately that is the case.'

'But there are so many lying empty,' argued Elise.

'It doesn't mean they're for sale.'

As Gino turned towards them, Edward could tell from his face that he had been lost in his own thoughts rather than gazing at anything in particular.

His focus had switched to Elise now. 'You would put in a much bigger window here to make the most of the view,' he told her, 'with a wide enough ledge for pots of herbs or geraniums. And this is where you'd have the kitchen, so you can cook and look out at all that countryside and sky. You might not even need an architect, just someone with decent building skills. I could sketch up a rough plan for you if I had some paper.'

'For me?' Elise sounded confused.

'Only if you want me to, obviously, but I have a few good ideas.'

'For my place?' She was still lost.

'No, for this house.' Gino gave her that calm, steady look he reserved for clients. Countless times Edward had witnessed him talk them round to his way of thinking. How many tallboys, dressers or dining tables were in the homes of people whose views had been ignored entirely and who somehow found themselves happy with what Gino said they wanted?

'Come with me, and I'll explain exactly what I'm thinking,' he said now, and the girl nodded, clearly still uncertain, but too curious not to do as he asked.

Gino talked softly and slowly, painting pictures with words, bringing the girl round to his way of thinking little by little. Once or twice Elise made a suggestion, and he nodded encouragingly, and kept talking, pacing from room to room with her trotting beside him, filling the silence with his brilliant ideas.

This was his real skill, Edward realised, this ability to carry people into his vision and make them want to stay there. Everyone in the room was listening, Elise with rapt attention, Mimi absent-mindedly biting a ragged fingernail, Cecilia and Salvio nodding along with his words. Now and then one would speak.

'What a great idea.'

'Oh yes, that would be perfect.'

Gino finished as he always did, with the practicalities. How long it might take, how much it was likely to cost. His clients always commented on how rigorous he was about that sort of thing.

By the time he stopped talking Elise seemed convinced this was the house for her, this sweet little cottage she could transform for next to nothing. If only it wasn't too late for her to change her mind.

'Would it be possible?' she asked Salvio. 'After all nothing has been signed yet has it? Oh, please say it'll be OK.'

'I can't see why there would be any objection if Edward and Gino don't want the place.' The mayor sounded bemused. 'But are you sure this is the best plan? You are happy to give up the bigger house?'

'It's got twenty rotten wooden shutters,' said Elise. 'Yes, I did count them. Also, the roof has completely fallen in on one side. And there are rats, lots of them.'

Mimi was biting her fingernail. They were all nibbled to the quick, Edward noticed, although she was otherwise so chic and beautifully groomed.

'If you take this one then who will get the larger house?' she wondered.

Edward met Gino's eyes. All the words he wanted to say were stopped by the silence between them. Twenty rotten shutters wouldn't present too much of a problem, they could afford to pay for the roof to be fixed and the frescoes to be repainted, the rats would be no match for them.

'It seems completely obvious, doesn't it?' Elise spoke into the quietness. 'You guys should have it. You want a bigger place and you could make that one amazing.'

Salvio looked keen, Cecilia intrigued and Mimi was smiling, as if this was what she had been hoping for. Only Gino's expression was unreadable, his face smooth, his gaze so steady, not frowning but not smiling either.

'Well?' Edward asked.

'It's what you want, isn't it?' said Gino.

'Yes, of course. I love the house, it's what I was dreaming of. How could I not want it?'

Gino's face didn't change and Edward braced himself for the words that were surely coming. Then Gino did something he hadn't in a long while – surprised him completely.

'If you want this place so much, I want you to have it.'

'Seriously?' Edward couldn't quite believe it. He thought

of Tia and wished she was there to witness this moment. 'Are you sure?'

At that Gino laughed. 'I've never been less sure of anything in my life.'

Elise

Elise didn't think she needed a lesson to ride a Vespa. Surely it wasn't so difficult; all she had to do was twist the throttle to go faster and pull the brake levers to stop. Still, spending a Sunday morning with Salvio as her teacher was no hardship.

They began in the piazza as it was one of the flattest parts of Montenello. Salvio had brought her a helmet and gloves that he insisted she wore. He spent time adjusting the mirrors to exactly the right position, talked her through the controls and how important it was to be smooth with the throttle and gentle on the brakes. Then they did a few laps with Elise riding pillion until she was ready to take over.

Astride the Vespa, Salvio's arms resting round her waist, Elise circled the statue of Garibaldi, the old fountain and the lonely fruit seller. She moved slowly at first, wobbling so much Salvio had to use his feet to steady them as they went, but soon grew more confident and his grip on her waist tightened as they picked up speed and left the piazza.

They circled past the abandoned hotel and the huge old house she was so relieved not to have bought. Just the sight of its scuffed yellow walls, rusted iron balconies and rotten wooden shutters was enough to remind Elise of how overwhelmed she had been by the size of the project. She had already moved her few belongings to the smaller place and slept a night in her makeshift bed on its hard stone floor. There had been no sounds of rats scrabbling and no fear of the ceiling falling in. And the next day she had sat with a cup of tea, looking at the way the morning light shifted through the rooms and thinking about Gino's ideas. If that window was enlarged so the kitchen had a view, if she grew a garden beside the entranceway, if she tiled the floors with terracotta – she would have a home she could live in or rent out. It didn't seem too much work at all.

Elise rode the Vespa across the causeway and onto the main highway. She was careful here as there was more traffic and it moved far faster but she wasn't scared. When they reached the roadside viewpoint overlooking Montenello she pulled over and turned off the ignition. Together, she and Salvio gazed back at the town hugging the hilltop, at its tall church spires, half-ruined tower and clustered houses in shades of gold and burnt sienna.

'I'm trying to find my new place,' said Elise, 'but I can't make it out.'

'Over there somewhere.' Salvio pointed. 'Hidden among the other houses. All you can see from here is rooftops.'

One of his hands was still resting on her hipbone and his body curved against her. If they hadn't been wearing such bulky helmets, Elise might have turned and kissed him. She wondered how his lips would feel, whether he would be surprised at her making the first move, how keenly he might kiss her back.

'I love seeing the town from here,' he was saying. 'It always makes me feel proud to be its mayor. I only hope I can do what is necessary to make it thrive again.'

'It must be such a challenging job.'

'Yes, and frustrating too,' he admitted. 'With the three houses sold and Cecilia opening her *pasticceria* it feels as if I am making a little progress at last. But there is still so much to do and I have no idea how I'll manage most of it.'

Elise hated to hear him so disheartened. She remembered the book about success that Richard had read and found herself quoting from it.

'I think you're meant to have achievable goals along the

way you can build on for long-term success … at least that's what I've been told.'

'It's good advice but I have so many goals and I'm not sure any of them are achievable. I want to have young families living in Montenello, to open a school and maybe even a medical clinic, for there to be a proper market in the piazza instead of a single stall, lots of shops not just a *pasticceria*, I'd like to celebrate a *festa* every year and—'

'They're all big things, just pick some small ones.'

'I can't.'

'OK, I've got something for you. I'd love to see the fountain working properly. It looks sad at the moment and makes the whole piazza seem depressing. I think it would be so lovely with water flowing out of it. That should be an easy thing to manage, surely?'

'In Montenello nothing is ever simple,' said Salvio, wryly. 'But if it will make you happy then I will try to do it.'

'Great, now choose another thing. One that would make you happy.'

Salvio gave it some thought. 'I would like to officiate at a wedding in the Town Hall,' he said, eventually. 'Mayors in most other towns do this all the time but in Montenello it must have been years since anyone got married. It would seem symbolic – a happy occasion, a new beginning.'

'It sounds trickier than fixing the fountain.'

'I'm not so sure.'

Elise hadn't seen this side of Salvio before; up till now he had seemed so self-assured. She was pleased he was confiding in her, had let some of his uncertainty show, and again the urge came to kiss him.

'Shall we head back?' she suggested. 'I'll buy you a coffee to say thanks for the lesson.'

'Actually, I was hoping we could eat lunch together. My mother has a small restaurant in a valley about forty minutes' drive from here. It is a beautiful place and the food is always excellent.'

'Your mother?' To Elise it seemed a bit soon to be introducing her to his family but perhaps that was just what Italian men did.

'Her name is Donna Carmela and I know you will like her.'

It was too far to take the Vespa so they returned to Montenello and exchanged it for Salvio's car, a gleaming white Alfa Romeo Spider he must have spent a lot of time polishing. Behind its wheel he seemed his usual self again, driving a little too fast, steering with one hand and using the other to point out landmarks as they sped past.

Elise noticed how the countryside changed as they left the mountains behind. Field after red-earthed field of olive trees surrounded by drystone walls, smallholdings with carefully tended vegetable plots and a few rows of vines, and the *trullo* houses with their pointed roofs that were so pretty, although Elise much preferred the plainness and simplicity of her own house.

Spotting a sign pointing the way to Donna Carmela's restaurant, she felt an unexpected rush of nervousness. It seemed important to make a good impression. She wanted to be liked by this woman.

Salvio hadn't exaggerated, it was a very beautiful place, an old barn cloaked in bougainvillea that was blooming in shades of scarlet and pink, rustic furniture beneath the olive trees and the smell of something delicious cooking.

'Choose a table while I go and tell my mother we are here,' said Salvio. 'I will only be a moment.'

Elise sat down in a spot set slightly apart from the others, shaded by a wisteria-covered pergola. A few minutes later Salvio returned, clutching two glasses of Prosecco and a menu he handed over to her.

'There is probably no point in you choosing,' he admitted.

'My mother will send out what she thinks we should eat. But if there is anything you very much dislike ...'

'Offal,' said Elise, quickly. 'Especially tripe. Oh, and bone marrow.'

'God yes, me too.' Salvio screwed up his face. 'There is none of that here, I promise. Only good things.'

'Will your mother come out and say hello?'

'Yes, but not until a little later because she is busy cooking. First we eat, then you will meet Donna Carmela.'

A young, dark-haired waitress brought out their meals and Salvio stood to kiss her on both cheeks, chatting for a few moments in Italian, while Elise examined all the dishes she had set out. Seared aubergine glistening with olive oil, crisp fried red peppers, tiny black olives flavoured with garlic and fennel, cured meats and waxy pale cheeses, a basket teetering with crusty bread.

'So much food,' she said to Salvio. 'It looks amazing.'

'This is just the antipasto. There is much more coming.'

Elise loved to eat but would never be able to do justice to this lunch if every course that arrived on the table was such a size. And she didn't want to offend Donna Carmela by leaving too much food.

'Don't panic, we have all afternoon.' Salvio smiled. 'A long Italian lunch, it is a good way to spend a Sunday. And later on there is nothing we need to do except have a lazy time.'

Elise ate tried to eat strategically. She avoided the bread, even though it was warm, crusty and coarse, and tasted a little of everything else. The pasta arrived, handmade orecchiette in a puddle of fennel-spiked ragu and a crumble of salted ricotta, and she couldn't help finishing every last delicious mouthful.

Before the next onslaught of food, Salvio suggested a walk. He showed her the *trullo* house his mother owned and took her through an orchard of fruit trees, introducing her to a small, suntanned man in a wide-brimmed straw hat.

'My stepfather,' he told her, wrinkling his nose a little as if the word wasn't entirely to his taste. 'He farms the land and grows a lot of the food my mother uses in her kitchen.'

The final course was simple, grilled swordfish in a light buttery sauce fresh with lemon and mint. Still, Elise had to dig deep and by the time Donna Carmela arrived, bringing a plate of sweet treats, she knew she had overdone it. Standing to greet Salvio's mother, she wished the waistband of her jeans didn't feel quite so tight.

Donna Carmela was flushed from the kitchen, her cheeks dewy and her skin warm. Embracing Elise, she pulled over a chair so she could join them.

'Try one of these little coconut cakes,' she urged. 'Only a tiny taste, surely I can tempt you.'

Elise couldn't say no. She took a golden orb of cake and nibbled on it, aware as she did so of Donna Carmela watching, her eyes never leaving her face. She wondered if what Salvio's mother was seeing met with her approval.

'That was the best lunch ever,' Elise told her. 'I've eaten some good meals since I got here, but nothing to match it.'

Donna Carmela accepted the compliment with a polite smile. She must be used to hearing how wonderful her food tasted but Elise couldn't think of anything else to say.

'And that pasta dish, so good, I'd love the recipe,' she added.

'Do you cook?' asked Donna Carmela.

'Yes but not like that. I just kind of make meals – what you do is an art.'

Donna Carmela shook her head. 'Food is not art and cooking isn't about being impressive, only about warmth and generosity. A good meal can be simple. A salad in a dressing of olive oil and lemon, fresh bread, ripe tomatoes, good cheese ... you don't even need a kitchen to prepare it.'

'That's handy, because I don't actually have a kitchen at the moment,' she admitted.

'Ah, your house in Montenello.' Donna Carmela leaned forward. 'Tell me everything about it.'

Elise described the place and what she hoped to do, almost envisaging each room as it would be when finished as she spoke about it.

'It's smaller than the house Mimi is taking on?' said Donna Carmela, when she had finished.

'Yes, but that's a good thing because my budget is small too. I'm hoping to do some of the work myself and find a builder for the structural stuff – one who won't charge me a fortune.'

'Let me think about it, I might be able to recommend someone,' offered Donna Carmela. 'I found an architect for Mimi, you know.'

'Yes, I heard. She seems very excited.'

Salvio turned to his mother. 'Who is this architect you have told Mimi to use?' he wanted to know. 'How did you hear about him? Is he any good?'

'Oh yes, he is perfect,' Donna Carmela said, breezily, 'divorced just like her, with grown-up children, quite handsome, a big bear of a man.'

'Yes, but is he a good architect?'

'I am sure he is fine. Mimi is happy with him, isn't she?'

'Mamma, are you matchmaking ... ?'

She laughed, mischievously. 'I had to try.'

'Mimi wants her house renovated, not a new boyfriend.' Salvio's tone was disapproving.

'Why shouldn't she have both?' Donna Carmela plucked a chocolate truffle from the dessert plate and popped it whole into her mouth.

'Have you considered that maybe she isn't looking for love?'

Donna Carmela finished her truffle, running her tongue over her lips to taste the last of its sweetness. 'Everyone needs love, Salvio. Along with food it is one of life's greatest necessities and pleasures.'

'Yes, yes I know.'

'I have taught you nothing if you haven't learned that.'

'Yes, Mamma.'

Elise hadn't expected to like Donna Carmela so much. She had envisioned a matriarch, a protective Italian mother, not this woman with her natural beauty, her eyes dancing with wickedness and her secret plan to help Mimi find a boyfriend.

'Everyone should have companionship,' she was saying to Salvio. 'Yes, we can survive alone, but why would we want to? Life is better with some love in it.'

He was nodding now, his face bearing a resigned expression, and Elise assumed these were things he was used to hearing.

'It would be lovely if Mimi had a romance,' she told Donna Carmela. 'She seems a bit sad to me, maybe even lonely.'

'Mimi is a woman who has lost her confidence thanks to a husband who made her feel she was never good enough.' Donna Carmela said this crisply, adding a warning. 'Be sure not to let that happen to you, Elise. Marry a good man.'

'Mamma?'

'Salvio?'

'Don't you have things to do?'

'Always, *caro*, always.' Donna Carmela stood. 'It has been a pleasure meeting you, Elise. I hope my son brings you back soon. Good luck with your house. Perhaps I will pay you a visit next time I'm in Montenello, whenever that is.'

'You're coming to the ceremony, Mamma,' Salvio reminded her. 'The one Augusto is organising to officially hand over the houses.'

'Ah, the celebration, yes of course. I will see you both soon then.' She looked from Elise to Salvio and smiled. 'You are so good together.'

229

In the car on the way back to Montenello, Salvio tried to apologise. 'She is incorrigible,' he began. 'Always telling everyone who they ought to marry ... particularly me.'

'I loved her, and her restaurant, and our lunch ... everything about today,' said Elise.

It was true, she couldn't remember having such a perfect time. Maybe it was the sunshine, or the fact she wasn't teaching sulky teenage girls all week long, but life here seemed brighter, and Elise felt younger and freer than she had in ages.

'Shall we stop at our favourite view of Montenello?' she suggested as they neared the town. 'The light is so lovely now, sort of golden.'

'Sure, if you like.'

Salvio slowed the car and pulled over, parking to face the town, which did seem scenic in the soft glow of a late afternoon, although Elise wasn't interested in looking at it. Instead she gazed at his profile, his smooth olive skin and dark Italian handsomeness. A first kiss was always such a tricky thing. The pair of them might well fumble into it, teeth clashing and noses colliding and then everything that followed would be awkward. But somehow Elise didn't think so.

'Salvio,' she said, and as he turned to her she leaned in, her lips touching his. She felt a flare of excitement, pushing closer, tasting him, feeling his arms wrap round her, hearing him softly moan. He kissed her back, his fingers slipping beneath her flimsy top, caressing and pressing, sending a shivery feeling over Elise's whole body. They stayed there until the light turned from gold to pink, kissing and touching until they felt dazed by it.

'What now?' Elise asked, resting her head against his chest.

'What would you like? A drink at Renzo's bar?'

'OK, that would be nice, so long as afterwards we can do this some more.'

He touched her once or twice as they made the drive, a hand brushing her knee as he changed gear or his fingers quickly brushing the lengths of her hair. Elise knew what she would say if he asked for more.

They parked in the piazza beside the fountain that he had promised to restore just for her, and then walked to the bar, more self-conscious now and not quite touching. That's when she saw him at a table near the doorway. He was drinking bottled beer and eating peanuts from their shells, cracking them open with his strong fingers. Elise looked at his familiar plain sweet face, at his broad shoulders and wide-barrel chest, at the pale blue eyes that met hers as he gave an uncertain smile.

'Richard?' she asked. 'What are you doing here?'

Montenello

Salvio felt as though he had been given everything he wanted then had it taken away from him moments later. He stared at the young Englishman in the bar, recognising him from his photograph in the same instant Elise said his name.

'Richard? What are you doing here?' she asked.

'It's half-term holiday so I came to check out your house,' he replied. 'Are you pleased to see me?'

Elise murmured something that wasn't quite an answer and sat down. Then Salvio had to offer drinks, and join them until they were finished, making polite chit-chat but all the while wanting to say to this Richard: 'Go back home. She's mine now.'

As Elise began talking about her new house, he imagined the night ahead as it ought to have been, staying lost in his thoughts until he was aware of the conversation changing. She must have asked where Richard was going to stay … and he could only have replied that he was planning to sleep at her place, because now she was shaking her head and saying, 'That won't work. I'm sleeping on the floor and it's really uncomfortable. I don't even have any hot water.'

'That's fine,' said Richard. 'I brought loads of our camping things. I've got the Primus and the Billycan because I thought you'd want them anyway, and my sleeping bag, of course.'

'Right.'

'I'm here for the whole week so I can help you tackle a few projects. I even brought some tools.' Richard patted his backpack. 'This is pretty heavy, so I hope it's not too far to walk.'

Salvio knew he ought to offer them a lift but the thought of it was unbearable. He couldn't have this man in his car, on the red leather seats where he and Elise had been together such a short time ago. Throwing back the last of his drink, he got to his feet. 'I must go. Tomorrow I have a busy day. I will see you soon, Elise.'

She looked over at him, eyes wide, and her expression said everything she couldn't. 'Thank you for lunch.'

'You're welcome.'

Driving away, Salvio knew it was unreasonable for him to feel this jealous. He parked his car and let himself into the house in a kind of a daze, trying not to entertain thoughts of the pair of them spending the night in the nest of cushions and blankets Elise had made on the floor, waking together, her blonde head and his gingery one side by side on the pillow. To blot the vision from his mind Salvio found the bottle of brandy he kept for the coldest winter nights and poured a large glass.

It had all been going so well. Their lunch together, his mother's obvious approval, and then just when he had been thinking how much he wanted to kiss her ...

Salvio gulped down more brandy and it left a fiery trail as he swallowed. He wondered if Elise was quietly pleased to see her boyfriend. Had she been missing him? Did she want him to stay? In his gloomy state he imagined seeing them eating dinner together in Assunta's *trattoria*, constantly bumping into them in the bar, passing them in the piazza as they walked hand in hand. It was a small town; there would be no avoiding them.

In the morning, Salvio woke with a headache and regretted chasing the first glass of brandy with a second and third. Once he had taken some painkillers and drunk a cup of coffee, he dressed for work with his habitual care, ironing his shirt, smoothing his hair, and choosing a light jacket as the day ahead was set to be a warm one. He refused to think

233

about Elise any more. Instead, Salvio decided to tackle the challenge she had set him and have the fountain working again as quickly as possible. His hope was she would notice and know it was for her.

It was the first thing he mentioned to Augusto when he arrived in the office that morning.

'That fountain in the piazza, when did it stop running? Is there something wrong with it?'

The old man didn't reply. He was staring fixedly at his computer with his head turned slightly away from Salvio, and didn't appear to have noticed he had arrived. Perhaps he was becoming very deaf. Salvio made a mental note to talk to him about a hearing aid.

Over the course of the next hour he asked several other people what they knew about the fountain but all he received in return was blank looks. Rummaging through the filing cabinets didn't yield any information either so Salvio put on his jacket, straightened his tie and wandered down to the piazza to inspect it.

This town must have been flourishing when they decided to erect a fountain. It was made of stone with three tiers for water to tumble over prettily. Leaves had collected in its empty basins now and moss was springing from tiny cracks in its scalloped edges but to Salvio there didn't seem to be anything wrong with it, aside from the fact it looked long dry.

Francesco Rossi was watching him curiously. For a change he was selling peaches today, overripe and bruised.

'Have you any idea how long it's been since the fountain worked properly?' asked Salvio.

The old man shrugged. 'I don't remember,' he said, low and gruff.

'Ten years, twenty, thirty?'

'Yes,' Francesco Rossi agreed.

Salvio stifled a sigh. This wasn't getting him anywhere.

Noticing the door to Cecilia's building was ajar, he decided to drop in on her then go back to try Augusto one more time.

As soon as he stepped across the threshold of the *pasticceria* it was obvious to Salvio that Cecilia had been busy. The rough plaster walls had been washed a rich cream, the floors had been covered in a mosaic of painted ceramic tiles, and the stack of wood had disappeared. In its place was a long wooden cabinet like nothing Salvio had ever seen. Whimsical and rustic, its legs were twisting spirals of twigs. It had a tall back inset with shelves, and was covered with sliding glass panels.

'Hello?' Cecilia emerged from a back room and offered him a long, cool stare. 'Can I help you?'

'This place looks wonderful. That cabinet is incredible.'

His admiration was rewarded with a tired smile. 'That's Gino. He is a genius. And Edward spent all weekend painting and tiling the floor, the poor man.'

'When will you open?'

'I'm waiting for the ovens to be delivered and some other equipment I need. And then I'll do some trial bakes and get to know my *pasticceria*. So many things can change the way a pastry turns out – cold weather, rain, humidity, the temperature of my hands, the evenness of the oven. And I've never baked at such a high altitude. So I won't open until I'm completely ready.' She delivered the words with her usual intensity.

'I think your nonna would be very proud of you.' Salvio looked about the room. 'What you have done here in just a short time ... it gives me hope for all the other changes I would like to see.'

He was in a much better mood as he walked back to the Town Hall. At least some things seemed to be going right. And he was looking forward to choosing cakes from her beautiful cabinet. Crisp cookies filled with almond paste, deep-fried shells of dough oozing with ricotta cream, chewy little biscuits covered in pine nuts, yeasty baba drenched in rum. Salvio loved sweet things; he had so many favourites.

Augusto seemed not to have moved at all. He was still staring at his computer screen, his face blank and his fingers not moving on the keyboard.

'I just went and took a look at the fountain and I think ...' Salvio began, then faltered mid-sentence. The old man's eyes were red and his cheeks were glistening with tears.

'Augusto, are you crying? What is wrong?' Moving round the desk, Salvio put a hand on his bony shoulder. 'Tell me what has happened.'

'Nothing, nothing, there is no need to worry.' Augusto's voice was shaky. 'I will be fine in a moment.'

'Are you unwell? Do you need to go home? Has someone upset you? Is there bad news?' Salvio tried to guess why the old man might be tearful but at every suggestion he only shook his head, repeating that he was fine.

Finally, Augusto cleared his throat and said a little more steadily, 'You were asking me about the fountain?'

'Yes, but that is not important now.'

'It was when we had a long drought, no rain all summer and hardly any over winter, the same the next year and the next. The town's water supply was only turned on for a couple of hours a day and everyone had to queue at a standpipe in the piazza and fill their pans and buckets. I suppose no one ever thought to turn it back on again once the drought was over. That was a long time ago, thirty years, maybe more.'

As he spoke, Augusto was drying his cheeks with a hand-kerchief and dabbing at his eyes. 'There is no reason why it shouldn't work,' he continued. 'But I think we should have it examined by a stonemason and a plumber too. It may need some repairs. Leave it to me, I will see to it.'

'You have enough to do,' Salvio tried to argue but the old man was insistent.

'I want to keep busy. And besides, I know exactly who to call. I will have them look at it, get some estimates of what it will cost, see what approvals we need, form a case for any repairs it needs, and having it running again,.'

'Don't worry about any of the formalities, just have it fixed,' Salvio told him. 'I want it to work. I'll pay the bill myself, if necessary.'

'Are you sure?' Augusto sounded dubious.

'We're going to have a new *pasticceria* and a fountain that works, the changes are starting to happen Augusto.' Salvio hoped to cheer him up. 'I think we are going to be successful.'

The old man nodded but said nothing.

'And if there is something wrong; if I can do anything; you must tell me.'

'Of course, of course,' Augusto was still nodding but he turned his face away from Salvio before he could decide if those were traces of tears starting in his eyes again.

Mimi

There were things Mimi would miss about England. The cut-grass smell of Sundays in summer, ploughman's lunches and cloudy beer in pubs, nights out with the Silver Divorcees, and most of all having her sons only a train ride away. But Montenello was her life now. She had such a sense of purpose here. One wall of her house was covered in lists of practical things she needed to do. Buying a car – because she couldn't keep the rental forever and a Vespa wasn't an option – opening an Italian bank account, finding out how to register for healthcare with a local doctor.

Her hair was all wisps and flyaways but she had no idea of the best place for a decent trim. There were no handy nail bars to pop into for a pedicure. It amazed Mimi how many small things she had to consider and new ones occurred to her all the time to be added to the ever-lengthening lists.

This was the day she had been most eager for. In the morning her meeting with the architect, in the afternoon the big step she couldn't turn back from. Mimi ran her hands through her hair and wished she had made time for that overdue trim. She couldn't decide how to dress: casually, because after all she was living in a semi-ruin, or smarter and more professionally.

She had offered to go to the architect's office in Borgo del Colle but he preferred to come to her. Mimi felt strangely fluttery as she prepared for Alessandro's arrival. She told herself she was nervous because she had never done anything like this without Glenn before. The house they had renovated together only required the most cosmetic of changes and her ex-husband had dealt with every detail. At the time Mimi thought she was grateful to be spared the stress. She hadn't chafed against the plain white walls, the undyed alpaca carpets or the honed marble countertops she had to be careful not to stain or scratch. It was a beautiful home, as friends often told her.

But now there was no Glenn with all his commanding certainty. Mimi was the one to make the decisions, examine plans, deal with tradespeople, handle unexpected dramas and pay all the bills. As excited as she felt, it was daunting.

She fiddled with her hair, applying more expensive waxy product to try and restore its shape. She put on the pink and orange Hermès scarf Glenn had always said suited her. She reapplied her lipstick for a third time. She was entirely ready but even so, felt herself startle on hearing Alessandro's knock.

'Good morning,' she called then found she couldn't open the old wooden door. It had poured with rain overnight and perhaps it was swollen as it seemed stuck fast. On one side Mimi tugged while on the other Alessandro leaned his weight against it and pushed. Finally, with a loud creak they managed to get the door open.

'Oh dear,' said Mimi, pink-faced. 'That's not good.'

Alessandro was so broad-shouldered he almost filled the low doorway so it was a moment before Mimi realised he wasn't alone. His companion was a younger man, dressed in tight T-shirt and jeans and wearing lots of gold jewellery.

'These old houses do shift a bit, it might not be a problem, but Vito here will tell us.' Alessandro gestured towards the younger man. 'He is very skilled at this kind of restoration, although I am afraid he speaks no English.'

'He's a builder?' asked Mimi, as Vito strode ahead of her into the house.

'He is the best builder in the area and the one I would prefer on a job like this. While we talk through what I have been working on I thought he could have a good look at the place.'

Mimi glanced at the things she had set out: the two cups for coffee, the small plate of biscuits, the water jug and duo of glasses. It hadn't occurred to her there would be a third person in her house that morning.

'Would he like coffee? I'll fetch another cup.' She still felt fluttery.

'I think what Vito would like is to get underneath that terrace of yours. I have told him of our concerns it's not stable.'

'Yes, of course, tell him to go wherever he likes.'

She spooned coffee into the Moka while the architect laid out a sheaf of floor plans and images. As he talked her through them, she imagined folding linen into the tall storage cupboards along the walls of the spare bedrooms, relaxing in her newly expanded living area, admiring the view through better situated windows, gathering friends for drinks on the refurbished terrace.

'And the swimming pool?' she asked, impressed with how faithfully he had followed her brief.

'It will be expensive,' he warned. 'This site is steep so you will need an engineer and a geologist. And access is difficult, which means smaller machinery to excavate and build the retaining wall – all that inflates the price.'

'But it can be done?'

'If you want it, then I don't see any reason why not.'

'Yes, I do want it, definitely.'

'Then we will make it happen. I am assuming you would prefer me to project manage for you? Lots of the contractors won't speak English.'

'Yes, yes,' Mimi agreed, hastily.

'There are always unexpected setbacks, things that have to be changed as we go along, but this is your house, so we will work closely together to make sure you get the place of your dreams.'

'Thank you.' Mimi smiled at him. There was something reassuring about his size, a gentleness and calm that she hadn't thought to find in an architect.

Vito was back inside now and in an upstairs room. His footsteps sounded surprisingly heavy. There was a banging noise that stopped after a few moments then started up again.

'You will go back home to England while the work is taking place?' asked Alessandro.

'I'm not sure.' Mimi didn't especially want to be there. 'I might go back and forth a bit. How long do you think it is likely to take?'

'Who knows?' Alessandro gave a shrug of his strong, wide shoulders. 'This is Italy, signora. It is impossible to say.'

Vito reappeared and for the next few minutes talked rapidly in Italian, barely pausing for breath. Alessandro nodded a great deal, jotting in the notebook he pulled from his top pocket from time to time.

'*Va bene*,' he said, when the builder ran out of words. 'There is some subsidence and a lot of rot. Vito wants to come back with ladders and get on the roof. But I don't think we are looking at anything we hadn't expected, so if you are happy with these basic designs we will proceed with the costing and contracts.'

'Please,' said Mimi.

'In that case you can expect me to be in touch again before too long.' Alessandro smiled and moved towards the front door, which opened more smoothly this time. 'For now I will say *arrivederci*.'

'Actually, there's a ceremony planned,' Mimi said, as he stepped outside. 'It's to celebrate us purchasing the houses and officially hand over the keys. I wondered if you might like to come. After all, you're going to be a significant part of the whole journey.'

'I would be delighted.'

'Oh good, I'll make sure you get an invitation. And Vito too.'

From the doorway, she watched him and Vito walk towards his dusty Fiat 500. Somehow he squeezed his large frame inside it, raising a hand as he drove away.

The Silver Divorcees would approve of her choice of architect; Jayne might say he was a hunk, but Mimi hadn't expected to find him attractive. Usually she preferred skinny, intense types, not big bears of men who moved and spoke slowly. That was why she had ended up with Glenn and in all their years of marriage she could honestly say she hadn't flirted with anyone else. She wouldn't know how, she always told friends. She wasn't interested.

Staring out at the street, long after Alessandro had driven away, Mimi felt quite encouraged. Surely it was a good thing if she was finding random men attractive? It meant she was coming back to life, recovering herself again. Obviously nothing would happen between them, but she was starting to quite like that fluttery feeling she got whenever they met.

Mimi glanced at the vintage Patek Philippe watch Glenn had strapped onto her wrist for their last wedding anniversary. By then there had been another woman in his life that he was also giving gifts to, although Mimi hadn't realised it until after he had left and a few friends helpfully told her. That had been a hard time, with a sense of betrayal adding to the hurt and rejection already weighing so heavily. Still, she continued to wear the rose-gold watch with its square-cut face because she liked it and it kept good time. Right now it was telling her she needed to get to the Town Hall, to meet the mayor and notary, sign the contract, pay her one euro and make the house her own at last.

In the end it was anti-climactic. Edward and Gino had already been in, Elise was due to follow, and the mayor seemed distracted and harried. As she scrawled her name on the contract, Mimi was glad there was going to be a more formal occasion with all of them present. This was a major milestone for her. She wanted popping champagne corks and clinking glasses, not a quick handshake and a murmured congratulation.

On her way back down the Town Hall's steps, she heard Wagner's *Ride Of The Valkyries* echoing from her handbag. It was the ringtone Glenn had assigned to himself, thinking it was hilarious, and Mimi's phone had been noisy with it a lot in the last few days. Up till now she had steadfastly ignored him but, with the house officially bought and paid for, she felt safe to answer.

'Oh, so you are alive,' Glenn said on hearing her voice. 'I've been getting anxious.'

'Really? There's no need. Everything's fine.'

'You're in Italy.'

'That's right.'

There was a short silence while he waited for more. Then he said, irritably, 'Hello?'

'Yes, I'm still here.'

'Have you spoken to the boys? They're worried about you buying this house. They think you're taking on too much.'

'Do they?' Mimi didn't believe it for a moment. 'That's sweet of them to be so concerned.'

'When are you coming home? There's a lot to be done, you know, if you're serious about us putting our place on the market.'

'I am serious and I'll be there soon.'

'We need to divide up our belongings. Have you thought about what you want? Because there are some things I'm not going to be negotiable on.'

'Keep whatever you like. I'm starting afresh here.' It felt so good to say it. 'Most of our stuff won't look good in my new house anyway.'

'Right.' Glenn sounded deflated. Perhaps he had wanted

a fight over Swedish teak ice buckets and Knoll Diamond chairs.

'I'd like to get everything sorted as quickly as possible, to be in Italy again before my renovations begin,' Mimi told him. 'And I don't want Ben and Otis upset by any of this if we can help it.'

The truth was she didn't want to plunge back into all that old unhappiness either. In Montenello she had forgotten she was a woman abandoned by the man she had thought of as her closest friend. Here she was a different, more confident Mimi, not the one people pitied.

'I'd bank on spending a good few weeks at home,' Glenn was saying. 'You'll want to see the process through, won't you?'

'Maybe,' Mimi wasn't going to try and argue, but there was one thing she did need to say. 'And Glenn, perhaps don't call me out of the blue any more, not unless it's an emergency. Let's stick to text and email. We're separate people now, aren't we? We've got different lives.'

Afterwards she spent a few moments changing his ringtone, just in case. A duck quacking. It made her smile, despite the prospect of having to see him again so soon.

Edward

Edward had been expecting Gino to change his mind. He tried not to become too excited about the palatial old ruin they were meant to be buying, and threw himself into helping with the rush to get Cecilia's shop finished. During the long days of work they were each focused on their separate tasks and couldn't talk much. And in the evening, tired and sore-backed, Edward didn't want to risk a fight, only drink wine and fall into bed early, so he steered clear of trickier conversations.

Once or twice he questioned why they were doing so much for a woman they barely knew but Gino shrugged off the comments.

'I'm interested in the project. Anyway, Cecilia will help us with our place,' he insisted.

'Won't she be busy making pastries?'

'She's a good worker; I'm sure she can do both.'

At last he and Gino had their chance to change out of dust-ruined clothes. They went to the Town Hall, waited while the painfully slow notary read through the paperwork at least three times, then were allowed to sign their names, hand over a token one-euro coin and, Edward almost holding his breath, claim their keys.

He sent a text to Tia straight away, even though in Australia it was the middle of the night. 'We did it ... bought the house ... can you believe it!'

'OMG ...' came the reply. 'Finally news worth waking me for ... call – I want to know everything.'

'Later ... too much to do now,' Edward texted back.

They needed to take another look at the place, come up with an action plan and work out how best to progress it. Now the house belonged to them, Gino didn't want to wait.

'Will we even bother with this ceremony they're planning?' he asked, as they headed over there together.

'We have to,' Edward decided. 'It's important to Salvio. And it might be fun to have a party with the others.'

'We're meant to be flying home the next day,' Gino pointed out. 'And we need to get back. If we're going to spend at least six months here while we renovate then we've got to pack up our stuff and rent out the house. There's work I have to finish, things to sort. I can't just walk away from my business, obviously.'

'No, but I can,' pointed out Edward. 'With a laptop and my phone I can work pretty much anywhere. So why don't you go and deal with everything at home while I make a start here? We've got a big job ahead of us, and as you said, the roof needs to be fixed as fast as possible. We don't want to wait for more water damage, do we?'

Gino glanced at him. 'You trust me to come back then?'

'I think so, yeah.'

There was no missing how Gino was starting to blend in here. He looked so Italian and, even now, walking across the piazza, people nodded and smiled, raising hands in greeting. They were treating him as one of their own, and Edward could see that he liked it.

'You'll be back,' he told him. 'You've never reneged on a contract in your life, have you?'

'That's true,' agreed Gino. 'But I've never done something this rash either. We haven't even talked in any detail about our plans for this house once it's finished. Will we live in it? Rent it out on Airbnb like Elise was going to? Sell it?'

'I guess we can do any of those things. We don't need to decide now.'

'Are you sure?' Gino looked troubled. 'This is not how I usually live my life.'

'Why then?' It was a question Edward had been almost too scared to ask. 'What made you agree to it, sign that piece of paper, do this?'

They paused at foot of the broken steps leading up to their new front door and took in the jaded beauty of the house they had bought. 'You were so unhappy,' Gino said. 'You were set on taking our lives apart one way or another.'

'Perhaps I was,' admitted Edward.

'At least now we've got this place to keep us together. You can't do it without me, can you?'

'Gino, I've never wanted to do anything without you.'

'Really?' He sounded so uncertain.

'I love you, nothing has changed about that – it's everything else I've been struggling with.'

'I want you to be happy,' Gino said softly. 'It's all I've ever wanted. For us to be happy together.'

'Me too,' Edward promised.

Once they had climbed the steps and were through the front door and alone in the quiet of their dusty hallway, they stood chest to chest, breathing the smell of each other's skin, holding on tightly.

'So we're good now?' Gino asked.

'We are, we will be.' In that moment Edward was sure of it.

This time, walking through the house together, Edward saw so many things he had missed previously. How uneven the floors were, how cracked the ceilings even on the lower level. The place was a shell and he realised he didn't know much about what it took to renovate an old house in Italy. Would they need to navigate bureaucracy, apply for planning permissions and obey complex regulations? He remembered Gino's talk of earthquakes and feared there might be rules that meant all the walls would have to be reinforced.

'We're going to need a surveyor,' he said.

'A *geometra*,' replied Gino. 'That's what they're called here. I've been googling while you were sleeping. We'll want one that speaks English if you're planning to make a start without me. Oh, and I've also been looking for somewhere to live because this place won't be habitable.'

Edward had a sudden rush of reality. 'What's all this going to cost us?'

'I've worked on some estimates. I'll show you later. It's not going to be cheap.'

'You think I'm worth it?'

'Yes, obviously,' said Gino.

They spent the whole afternoon at the house, Gino making lists and not saying much, although every now and then he would wonder aloud about having some timber treated or suggest solar panels might be possible. To Edward he seemed in his element, dreaming up ideas, making plans.

'Cecilia will help make the new shutters, she's got all the gear we need.'

'What about the frescoes?' Edward asked. 'Do you think we should just paint over them? It would be much cheaper.'

Gino glanced up from his notebook. 'No, we'll restore them. And we're going need chandeliers in every room, parquet on the floors, gold-framed mirrors, huge rugs ...'

'I think what I need is a drink,' said Edward.

'Surely there are people you can hire to re-paint frescoes.' Gino squinted up at a wall covered in a pastoral scene with rows of vines, terracotta pots spilling over with bright flowers and cupids smiling down benignly from a faded blue sky. 'This one wouldn't work anywhere else, but in Italy it seems to fit perfectly.'

'Just like you do,' observed Edward.

'Hey?' Gino looked at him quizzically.

'You were the one so worried about coming to southern Italy. Look at the way you've been accepted.'

'Not really.' Gino frowned. 'The people here don't know who we are.'

'Are you sure?'

'They see me as my father's son, that's all.'

'They'll get to know who we are and they'll be fine with it.' Edward was confident that was true. 'We were chosen from hundreds of applicants, weren't we? It wouldn't have happened if there was any issue.'

'I hope you're right but even if you're not there's nothing we can do about it now. We're committed to this town and this house.' Gino tapped his notebook against a section of wall and the plasterwork crazed beneath it. 'You'd better be pretty happy about that. Are you?'

'Yes,' said Edward, although the truth was more complicated. This new happiness was a cocktail of excitement and terror, anticipation and doubt. It was a lot like the feeling he'd had seconds before his first bungee jump. 'But can we go and get that drink now?'

The bar was one of the only places in Montenello that ever seemed crowded. Its tables were filled with the same old men playing cards and that evening Edward didn't think there was any space left until he spotted Mimi Wilson, sitting alone, with a glass of Prosecco in her hand.

'Do you mind if we join you?' he asked.

She looked up and smiled. 'That would be lovely. I was just having a quiet drink to celebrate buying the house. I can't quite believe I've done it.'

'Neither can we,' responded Gino. 'I'll get a bottle, shall I?'

While he was at the counter, Elise came in with a man that Edward hadn't seen before. He called her over. 'We're having a few glasses of bubbles. It's celebration time.'

249

'Oh right.' Elise's expression looked strained.

'Everything went OK?' asked Mimi. 'You bought the house?'

'Yes, it's all official.'

'Well, grab a seat then,' Edward urged her. 'You and your friend, and I'll tell Gino we need a couple more glasses.'

'This is Richard.' Elise introduced the stocky, ruddy-faced young man beside her. 'He's my ... my boyfriend from Bristol.'

They borrowed chairs from other tables, and settled down together. Edward saw how Elise turned a shoulder on this boyfriend she had unexpectedly arrived with as she started talking to Mimi. When the Prosecco arrived and was poured she clinked glasses with him but diffidently. Clearly, she wasn't ecstatic to have him here then. Something was wrong.

'When did you arrive in Montenello?' Edward asked Richard.

'A couple of days ago. I came to see how much trouble Elise has got herself into with this house.' Richard gave a broad, friendly grin. 'Bit of a mess, isn't it? I'm trying to convince her to let me rip out all the overgrown jasmine from around the doorway so at least she can get into the place properly.'

Elise had heard him. She glanced over, saying, 'I like the jasmine', before turning back to her conversation.

'I've spent all day trying to borrow a ladder from someone so I can get up on the roof. Can you believe she bought the place without checking it out properly?' Richard said, fondly.

'Yes, because we all did the same thing,' Edward said, as Gino nodded in agreement.

'Seriously?'

'We've seen Elise's place, it looks pretty solid,' added Gino

Elise shot them a grateful look, while Richard seemed shocked. 'So none of you bothered with surveyor's or builder's reports before you signed up?'

'Why? It's a one-euro house, practically a gift,' said Gino. As Edward well knew, he didn't like his judgement being questioned.

'Still, it seems very risky.'

Edward wondered what the story was here. Where had this boyfriend materialised from? Hadn't Elise said several times that she was tackling her renovation alone?

Gino must have been wondering the same thing. 'Are you going to be helping Elise do up her place?' he asked Richard.

'I'm only here for a week and there's not much I can achieve in that time – she hasn't even got any electricity on yet,' Richard said with a shake of his head. 'But I'll come back in my summer holidays so I can help her with a cheap and cheerful makeover – paint everything possible white, plain tiles throughout, kitset kitchen, keep things simple, no fuss. What about you guys, what do you have planned?'

'I'd say pretty much the opposite,' Gino told him.

'Yes,' agreed Edward. 'We're going for the maximum amount of fuss possible.'

'What on earth will you do with the house once you've finished it?' Richard was bewildered. 'You're both Australian, right? You live on the other side of the world.'

'Well, we could do anything, really.' Gino gave an exaggeratedly carefree shrug. 'We might open it up as a bed and breakfast, for instance.'

'That's right,' agreed Edward. 'Or we could rent it out to film companies looking for locations.'

'Or start a rest home; after all there's no shortage of old people.'

'We might even open a pop-up restaurant,' Edward volleyed back.

'Lease it out and renovate another one, buy up half the whole town eventually. The great thing is we can do whatever we want,' said Gino.

'Hell yeah.' Edward raised his glass. 'Let's drink to that.'

Elise

Elise was peering upwards trying to work out where Richard was. He had finally managed to borrow a ladder and was up on the roof out of sight. She hoped he was being careful. The last thing she wanted was for him to fall and get hurt.

'Richard, what are you doing? Can you come down please?'

'Hang on, I'll just be a minute. Oh bugger, never mind.'

'What's happening?' She was getting impatient.

It was at least another five minutes before she heard the sound of scrambling and he reappeared at the top of the ladder. She held it steady at the base while he climbed down.

'So?' she asked, when Richard was back on the ground.

'I was hoping if there were only a few tiles out of place that I could put them back myself, but it's a mess. Also I broke a few while I was moving about.'

'So you made it worse then?'

'A bit ... but you'd have needed to get a roofer in anyway.'

'That's what I was planning to do.' Elise tried not to sound irritable. 'It's why I said there was no need for you to go up there. But still you insisted.'

'I was only trying to help.' He sounded hurt. 'And maybe save you some money.'

'I know that.' She felt guilty. 'But I can afford to pay for a roofer. I've got my half of our savings and the money my parents are giving me. And I want to do things properly.'

Elise hadn't been able to say any of the things she had wanted. Every time she started to try, Richard had cut her off, steering the conversation to some detail about the house, a problem she shouldn't worry about too much as he was sure to be able to help her. In many ways she was grateful to have him there. In the torchlight at night having him close beside her felt reassuring. He was cheerful and funny, and they had been together so long that even the smell of him made her feel safe.

'How are you going to find a roofer? One that speaks enough English and knows what he's doing?' Richard was asking now.

'The mayor said he'd help. He'll come and translate if I need him to. Or there's Gino who you met last night, he speaks Italian too.'

Richard frowned. 'You don't really know these people.'

'They're becoming my friends. We're going to be seeing a lot of each other over the next few months.'

'What are you doing here, Elise?' Richard's tone was disapproving. 'What about your career? Your future? This house, it's just a distraction.'

For a moment Elise entertained the idea he might be right. Perhaps she really was wasting her time.

'And this town,' Richard continued, 'well, it's hardly the Amalfi coast is it? No wonder half the houses are empty.'

He started to work the stiff latches on the ladder so it could be folded down and returned to its owner, the same man who had sold her the Vespa.

'Leave that, I want to take a look at the roof myself.' Elise put her foot on the lowest rung and started upwards before Richard had time to argue, stopping short of actually clambering onto the roof. He had been right; it was a mess. The tiles were higgledy-piggledy as if the whole thing had been shaken, there were weeds growing from the cracks and crevices, and far more broken pieces than she could blame Richard for. She was fortunate it hadn't leaked in the heavy rainstorm a couple of nights earlier.

'You see what I mean?' said Richard, as she descended carefully. 'It's pretty busted up.'

'Yes,' she agreed.

'I've been thinking, you could sell the place. Weren't there lots of other people who applied? Maybe one of them will buy it.'

'But this house is my dream, Richard. I want it. Nothing is going to change my mind.'

'OK then, let's come back here together in the summer holidays.' He sounded resigned. 'You could probably line up some relief teaching this term. When will you be home, exactly?'

'I was planning on giving up the flat, unless you want to live there.'

His face froze into the sullen, closed-down expression she remembered from so many previous fights. 'So you're going to stay in Italy on your own? Not coming back at all?'

'I'd prefer not to.'

'It was a mistake me coming here then, wasn't it?'

'Richard, the thing is …' Elise faltered. 'You walked out on me, remember? You said you wanted a break to consider how important we are to each other.'

'And I did consider it: no one is more important than you, Elise. That's why I'm here. Isn't it obvious?'

'You should have called me, not just turned up.'

'I expected you'd be pleased to see me.'

'I was, I am—'

'No you're not.'

Elise didn't know what to say. She looked at Richard staring at her so intensely, and she thought about all the love there had been, all the times she had felt so happy that they belonged together.

'You've got your new friends here and your new house, you don't need me.' He sounded so bitter. 'It's over, isn't it? That's what you've decided?'

'It's obvious we don't want the same things any more—' she began.

'Don't bother justifying it. If you don't love me, then there's no need to say anything else. I shouldn't have come. I just assumed ...' Richard's voice broke. He was still staring at her but now there were tears in his eyes.

'Oh Rich, I'll always love you, but maybe this is for the best.' She hated to say the words, to hurt him even more. 'You'll see that too, I know you will, once you've thought about it properly.'

Shaking his head, he pressed his eyes closed, tears streaming from them. Elise put her arms around him and held on, feeling his heartbeat against her, the day's growth of stubble on his wet cheeks, the familiarity of his bulky body. She might be making a mistake, throwing away what they had; she may very well regret it. And it was going to be hard to forgive herself for breaking such a good man's heart.

'I'm sorry, Rich. I'm sorry.'

Montenello

Salvio couldn't work out what Augusto was up to. He had been watching through a window and there seemed no logical explanation for the old man's behaviour. At first when he noticed his assistant standing in the middle of the piazza, Salvio assumed he was there to check the fountain. Earlier that morning he had been on the phone to a stonemason and probably wanted to take a few photos to send him.

But Augusto wasn't paying any attention to the fountain. He was standing there, not talking to anyone, not doing anything, as if in a trance. Salvio looked on curiously. Was he hoping the *pasticceria* would open? Did he want to eat a cake? Whatever he was doing, Salvio wished he would get on with it because the ceremony was happening that evening and he wanted to go through the running order with him.

Ten minutes passed, then fifteen. Augusto was still standing there. At last Assunta emerged from the *trattoria* and, taking the old man's arm, led him back inside. Salvio hoped she would give him lunch and that it might revive him. Whatever was going on, it didn't seem right.

It was mid-afternoon when Augusto shuffled back into the office. He seemed fine and wanted to get on with the final preparations for the ceremony. But standing there, looking over his shoulder at his assistant's computer screen as they finalised the running order, Salvio sensed he was growing tearful again.

'Augusto? You must tell me what's wrong.'

'Nothing, nothing,' the old man mumbled into his sleeve.

'Please, this can't go on.'

There was no reply

'I will cancel the ceremony. I will send you home.'

Still nothing.

'I will ... I will ... fire you.' Salvio didn't mean it. 'Unless you explain to me right this moment why you are so distressed.'

'I can't.' Augusto's head was in his hands. 'I am too ashamed.'

'Whatever it is, it can't be that bad.'

'Yes it is.'

'One moment then.' Salvio strode over to his desk and found the bottle of brandy he had brought from home in case he bumped into Elise and her boyfriend and needed a small measure for strength. 'This may help.'

Augusto grasped the glass but his eyes seemed to glaze as he stared at its contents.

'Take one big sip, then tell me,' Salvio ordered.

He raised the glass to his lips and took a tentative taste, then drank more deeply.

'She's my granddaughter,' he blurted out.

'Who is?' Salvio was confused.

'That girl in the *pasticceria*.'

'Cecilia? But how?'

'It is a long story and we have our ceremony to prepare for; this is not the time—'

'I want to hear.' Salvio poured another slug of brandy. 'Tell me, please.'

Augusto stared down at his computer keyboard. 'She was beautiful – not Cecila, her grandmother. Even when we were at school I thought we would marry. But I couldn't wait. In those days we would go to the tower and climb onto the roof, so high it felt as if we were far away and nothing we did counted. We weren't careful enough and she got pregnant. Of course, of course.'

'And you didn't want to marry her any more?'

257

'Oh I did, I loved her and she loved me.' With a shaky hand Augusto raised the brandy glass again. 'But in those days everyone believed Montenello was cursed. There had been miscarriages, stillbirths, women who couldn't conceive. And she was frightened, she believed our baby was in danger, so she wanted us to leave. I refused because I thought the curse was a story only idiots would believe in. I told her so and we fought about it then she threatened to leave without me. I said she should go, I was angry, I said many things I shouldn't have. I was too proud.'

'And she left?' Salvio guessed.

'Her parents took her. They closed up the *pasticceria* and went. So many people were doing the same back then that it hardly seemed remarkable, except to me because I loved her so much and my heart was broken.'

Salvio felt sorry for him. He knew how it felt to have a woman you cared for snatched away.

'Did you try to find her?'

'Of course. I assumed they were in Canada with the rest of their family. But it's a big country and there weren't all these wonderful things we have today – the Internet, Facebook. I didn't even have a telephone in my house, never mind my pocket. So I gave up looking after a while. Still I stayed angry for a long time, with her for leaving me, with myself for letting her go, and especially with the curse and anyone who was ignorant enough to believe in such a thing. I set out to disprove it.'

'But how?'

Augusto set down the empty glass and gave the tiniest of shrugs. 'I made babies.'

'Seriously?'

'Oh yes.'

'But ... who?'

'Assunta is my daughter, Renzo is my son. Their mothers were kind to a heartbroken young man.'

'You never married though?'

Augusto shook his head. 'I was a rascal but charming. There were always women to comfort me but I never loved another like her; she kept my heart.'

Salvio was struggling to come to terms with this new vision of Augusto as a lothario. 'I suppose no one could say Montenello was cursed after that.'

'People like to talk, even Assunta, she thinks it's amusing, and Signora Wilson who finds it romantic, colourful. And in a sense the curse did work. Because it took her away, didn't it? Now this girl is back, and she looks so much like her, and I want to say something but I'm not sure how.'

Salvio didn't know what to advise. He suspected that Cecilia, who could be so severe, might not fall into the arms of her long-lost grandfather.

'That is why you were standing in the piazza for all that time?'

'I was trying to find the courage but it seems I have none.'

'What do the others think?' Salvio wondered. 'Assunta and Renzo? They are related to her too.'

His assistant sighed. 'You know Renzo, he is a closed book, and I couldn't tell you what he thinks of anything. Assunta doesn't understand what I am making such a fuss about. She says I am a silly old man.'

'This is a delicate situation and you're right to tread carefully,' Salvio assured him. 'But Cecilia chose to return here and reopen the *pasticceria*. She must want to connect, find out more about her family.'

'I feel so ashamed,' Augusto repeated. 'She will think only the worst of me, and perhaps I deserve it. From the moment I heard she was coming, it has been tearing at my mind. What would I do, what should I say? It would have been better if she'd stayed away.'

'This is why you've been so distracted lately,' Salvio guessed. 'I was worried when you started forgetting things.'

'You thought I had the dementia? Perhaps I do. My mind feels like it doesn't belong to me. It is too full of shame and sadness, of regrets.' Augusto's eyes brimmed with tears again. 'I lost her and it was my own fault. If only I hadn't argued, if only I had gone along with the foolish superstition ... but we are old now, we've had our lives and it is much too late for us.'

'I think Cecilia's grandmother may have died recently, I'm sure that's what she said. I'm so sorry, Augusto,' Salvio said gently.

The old man looked desolate. 'If only the girl hadn't come and brought the past with her. If only she had stayed away. Every time I see her I will be reminded. What shall I do?'

Salvio wished he knew what to say. He had the urge to call his mother and ask for her advice. Then he realised he didn't need to. Donna Carmela believed in family, in bringing people together, in love.

'We will find a way to resolve this,' he promised. 'Just give me some time to consider the best approach. In the meantime, you must stop upsetting yourself. I need you, Augusto. I can't rebuild this town without you.'

The old man sat a little straighter. 'Of course you can, of course.'

'Well, I don't want to.'

Salvio kept a close eye on him for the rest of the afternoon. Shortly before the ceremony they went together for a final check of the chamber where it was to be held. It was a beautiful room, with vaulted ceilings and marble floors the colour of honey, perfect for the civil weddings he hoped to conduct some day. Augusto had located a large silver ice bucket engraved with Montenello's coat of arms, and several bottles of Prosecco were chilling in it. He had asked Assunta to supply the food and she had promised arancini, as well as lavish amounts of olives, sheep cheese and prosciutto crudo. He had made sure every corner of the room was dusted and gleaming, and had vases filled with flowers to offer a blaze of colour.

'It is perfect, you have done a wonderful job,' Salvio told him.

'Of course, of course,' the old man murmured.

'I never dared to hope we would get this far. And I couldn't have done it without you Augusto, really that is true. I might not have always made it clear how much I appreciate your work, and if so I'm sorry because—'

They were interrupted. The chamber door creaked open and on its threshold was Cecilia, holding a tray wrapped in glossy gold-embossed paper.

'My ovens have arrived and I've been doing some trial bakes,' she said. 'I thought you might like some for your ceremony, just a few pasticcini – pistachio biscuits, chocolate truffles, mini strudel with raisins and pine nuts, small pastry horns filled with hazelnut cream ...'

Both of them stared at her, speechless, and Augusto took a step backwards.

'They'll only go to waste otherwise and it seems a shame.'

Salvio wanted to seize the moment. He looked from Cecilia to Augusto, aware that some well-chosen words might solve their problem right now, but the wrong ones could do irreparable damage. He searched his mind wildly but nothing came.

'Fine.' Cecilia gazed at their two blank faces, sounding offended. 'I'll throw them away then, shall I?'

'No, no,' Salvio held out his hands to take the tray from her. 'We are delighted, pasticcini, how wonderful, and what pretty paper you have wrapped them in.'

Cecilia softened. 'I'm hoping it's similar to the one my nonna used. I don't suppose you remember?' She looked at Augusto, whose skin had paled to alabaster.

Salvio held out a hand to steady the old man. Gripping his bony elbow, he continued staring at Cecilia. There seemed no family resemblance at all, her face was all curves with round cheeks and full lips, while everything about Augusto seemed narrow and sharp. Could she be aware of their connection?

'I am going to stay on for the ceremony. Edward and Gino invited me. I assume that's OK with you.' She tilted her chin at them.

'Of course, of course,' Augusto said faintly.

There was a chiming from the gold ormolu clock on the mantelpiece. It was 6 p.m. precisely and people were about to start filing into the room. Salvio felt the moment slipping away from them.

'It was silver, the paper your nonna used,' Augusto said suddenly. 'And she never put pine nuts into her strudel.'

'Yes she did.' Everything Cecilia said sounded defiant.

'Not when I knew her.'

Salvio thought him poised to tell Cecilia who he was. Augusto certainly seemed as if he wanted to but then he hesitated, and frowning, shook his head.

'Perhaps I am wrong ... it was a long time ago.'

'Exactly.'

Mimi was punctual and accompanied by Donna Carmela, who had closed her restaurant for the evening and dressed up in a pale blue jacket trimmed with feathers. Local dignitaries, town councillors, a burly man Salvio didn't recognise, Edward and Gino, several curious townspeople, even the man he often noticed sweeping the streets: the room was soon humming with conversation.

He glanced at his assistant, pleased to see some of the colour restored to his cheeks, asking quietly and discreetly. 'Are you OK?'

Augusto's eyes were directed towards Cecilia. He raised his phone and took a photograph of the room, one that surely included her in it. 'For Instagram,' he said. 'I will record everything while you greet our guests and make your speech. Don't worry about me.'

'Later, we will sort it all out, later,' Salvio told him.

'Perhaps, perhaps.' Augusto sounded unconvinced.

He moved away, phone in hand and Salvio was drawn into the nearest group of people, lost to handshaking and pleasantries. As the clock struck the half hour his assistant reappeared.

'It is time for your speech now.'

'But Elise isn't here yet.' Salvio had been watching out for her, braced for her appearance at her boyfriend's side, hoping that seeing them together wouldn't distract him from the three pages of closely written notes he had to deliver.

'Keep to the schedule,' Augusto insisted. 'We can't wait.'

'OK,' he agreed, reluctantly.

Salvio took his place at the marble plinth, glancing down at his notes. He sipped some water and cleared his throat as the conversation died away and everyone stared at him expectantly. Skimming their faces, he focused on his mother who was smiling up at him and he began to talk.

'Today marks a new beginning for the town of Montenello, a town with a long and noble history, that I am proud to serve as mayor ...'

Mimi

Mimi wondered how much longer the mayor was planning to go on for. She had tuned out while he was detailing the distant history of the town, something about the Byzantines and Lombards, and now he was describing the beginnings of the scheme to repopulate it, in both Italian and English so no one missed a word. She glanced down at her watch discreetly as, beside her, Donna Carmela shifted from foot to foot.

Salvio began talking about the new citizens he was pleased to welcome. Mimi was flattered to hear herself described as stylish, artistic, warm-hearted and kind. He made a great deal of Gino's roots in the town and of Edward's passion to restore an important part of its heritage, and then talked of Elise as young and with a bright future ahead of her, an asset to the town.

Mimi searched for her distinctive fair head among the many dark ones, but there was no sign of her, not even hiding away near the back. She hoped everything was OK. It would be a shame if she missed the ceremony.

Salvio was looking out for her too, Mimi realised, his eyes sweeping the room as he talked about her skills as a teacher and her plans for the humble but charming home she was going to transform.

It must be nearly time for him to present them with their keys – not the real ones, but beautiful vintage keys that had been framed as a keepsake for each of them. Mimi was planning to hang hers beside the front door of her new home once the wall had been replastered and painted, although she suspected that might be a while away.

Her architect, Alessandro, had come to the ceremony as promised. From where she was standing Mimi could just see his wide-set shoulders and the back of his head. She was hoping to talk to him but he was busy chatting to other people and there hadn't been a moment so far when she had felt able to interrupt one of his conversations.

Now Salvio was telling his guests about the *pasticceria*, encouraging them to try some of the pastries Cecilia had kindly brought along, and from there he moved on to outlining his hopes for Montenello's future.

'I love him but I do wish he would stop talking,' Donna Carmela said through a smile.

Behind them other people were becoming restless. There was a murmur of conversation and the clinking of glasses being topped up. Even Augusto had lost his enthusiasm for taking photographs.

'I have to do something,' Donna Carmela whispered.

And then abruptly Salvio went quiet, his attention drawn to the far side of the room. Mimi turned to see that Elise had been trying to slip in quietly, and was pink-cheeked and mouthing an apology for her lateness.

Salvio glanced back down at his notes, but must have lost his place, as he seemed flustered and there was a drawn-out, awkward empty moment. Mimi sensed Donna Carmela tensing beside her.

It was Augusto who moved to fill the silence. He stepped up to the plinth, saying smoothly. 'And now the mayor and I would like to present each of our new citizens with a symbol of our warm welcome. Signora Wilson, please will you be the first.'

Mimi found herself the centre of attention, shaking the mayor's hand and then Augusto's, receiving the ornate brass key in its frame, stumbling over a few words of thanks, feeling self-conscious and stared at.

It was a relief to return to Donna Carmela's side as

265

Edward and Gino moved forward, casually handsome in crisp linen shirts and dark-dyed jeans. Gino made a short speech in Italian and Edward gave the English version, both doing a much better job than she had, as they talked about the adventure of coming to Montenello and falling in love with the house they had bought.

Finally, Elise took her place beside the mayor. Seeing them together Mimi thought how striking they looked, her so blonde, him very dark and both extraordinarily attractive.

'He is in love with that girl, completely crazy about her, I have never known him like this,' Donna Carmela whispered as the mayor and Elise shook hands. 'I think this time he may have found the right woman.'

'Oh no, but I think she's back with her boyfriend from home,' said Mimi. 'Richard is his name. He was with her in the bar the other evening.'

Encouraged over to the microphone, Elise thanked everyone who had helped her realise the dream of owning a house, making special mention of Salvio and how grateful she was.

'I can't see the boyfriend here now, though.' Mimi checked around the room. 'No, definitely not.'

Donna Carmela was watching through narrowed eyes as her son presented Elise with her symbolic framed key. 'I can't interfere,' she said. 'Oh, what am I talking about, of course I can.'

She launched herself across the room, and Mimi wished she could follow to find out what she said. Instead, looking on from a distance, she noted how vivacious Donna Carmela seemed, holding her son and Elise in conversation, the feathers on her jacket quivering as she tossed her head, laughing and chatting. Mimi wished that she possessed that same social ease. She still didn't quite see how to cover the short expanse of floor separating her from Alessandro and begin a conversation with him.

When Donna Carmela returned she was smiling. 'Good

news, the boyfriend is no more,' she said. 'He left town this afternoon and won't be coming back.'

'I see.'

'However, also bad news, there is some problem with Augusto. It seems again I must interfere.'

This time her body language was different, quieter, more controlled. She formed a huddle with the mayor's assistant, their heads close together, and Mimi saw her nodding as he confided.

'This time things are less straightforward,' she admitted, on her return. 'I need more Prosecco.'

'Me too,' agreed Mimi. 'If you give me your glass I'll get us refills.'

'Fetch our own drinks at a party? Donna Carmela feigned shock. 'Oh no, I don't think so.'

'There don't seem to be any waiters …' Mimi began, but Donna Carmela wasn't interested.

'Alessandro,' she called, holding her Prosecco flute in the air. 'Our glasses seem to be empty.'

The architect looked over, lips shifting into a half smile, and he said gravely. 'Then you do have a problem.'

'Can you help us with it?'

'I will do my very best.' He came for their empty glasses. 'One moment, please.'

Mimi watched as he made slow progress across the crowded room, pausing once or twice as he was caught in conversation.

'Yes, I am still interfering,' Donna Carmela told her. 'Somebody has to.'

It was one of those evenings no one seemed to want to end – even Gino, who had a plane to catch the next day. A group of them had moved from the Town Hall to the bar. Salvio was there, sitting with Elise and deep in conversation. Gino, Edward and Cecilia formed a natural trio. Donna Carmela was at the bar with Assunta, heatedly discussing the best way to make a *pasta al forno*. A couple of the town councillors were ruddy-faced and wine-breathed. Renzo was busy polishing glasses and listening to some lengthy story Augusto was telling him. In the midst of them all, Mimi knew this was one of those times she would want to remember – with new friends, starting out on a new life.

She wished Alessandro hadn't been quite so diligent about keeping her glass filled as she felt heavy-limbed and muzzy headed. The scene was starting to soften at the edges and she had to concentrate on listening to him as he explained why it would be inadvisable to try to hurry the project she was embarking on it.

'It is a mistake to think of Vito as a builder, he is a craftsman, his art is building and it requires talent, inspiration and passion as well as technical skill. People are always so impatient, but to get the best from artisans like him, you must allow them time, so every nail is driven with purpose, every moulding shaped to perfection.'

'But I can't wait to have it finished,' she admitted.

'Try to enjoy the journey; it is full of possibilities.'

Renzo must have dimmed the lights because everything seemed hazier. 'And also full of stress?' asked Mimi.

'For me, perhaps, because things are bound to go wrong, but it is my job to make sure you don't feel it, at least not too much.'

'I have to go home to England,' Mimi told him. 'That's what is stressing me at the moment. I'm worried once I'm there all of this will seem like it wasn't real.'

'I am real, Signora Wilson.' He dropped the lightest of touches on her hand. 'And while you are away I will be working on your plans, making them real too.'

The feeling of his fingers on her skin took Mimi by surprise. She had a sensation that was almost electric, and then it was gone.

'I'll be back as soon as I can,' she told Alessandro, wondering if he had felt the same thing.

'Good,' he said, simply.

Fighting her tiredness, she stayed with him talking away another half an hour. Afterwards Mimi couldn't remember what was said, only how relaxed it had been sitting there listening to his low rumble of a voice. She didn't feel it was important to say anything clever in return, be impressive in any way. There seemed no need at all.

Eventually Alessandro noticed the yawns she was trying to hide. 'You are tired? I will walk you home.'

'I'll be fine on my own.'

'Maybe, but I wouldn't feel fine knowing that you were.'

One of the things Mimi loved about being in the mountains was no matter how warm the day had been the air seemed crisper once the sun had disappeared. Tonight though, in a summery dress, she was unprepared. Alessandro offered his jacket, which was far too big, the sleeves hanging down below her hands and the fabric flapping. He stood back, examining its effect on her appearance, and there was that half smile again. He wore it so often, as if he was quietly finding life amusing, and Mimi thought it one of the most attractive things about him.

She walked on unhurriedly, because who knew how long it would be before she saw this man again. Reaching the house her footsteps slowed further.

'I love your door,' Alessandro told her, looking at the moulded plasterwork around the archway, the rosettes and swirls, and the pineapple carved at the very top. 'I think when it is restored it should set the tone for everything found inside the house – lively, fun, beautiful, like its new owner.'

Mimi had been in the process of taking off his jacket. As it fell from her shoulders, she stopped and stared. It had been a long time since any man had said she was beautiful.

'You know that a relationship between an architect and

client is a very careful balance,' Alessandro continued. 'There has to be trust, respect, understanding, it helps if you like each other.'

She nodded as he helped her off with the jacket, grazing her bare shoulder with his fingers as he did so, sparking that same electric feeling.

'I have a feeling our relationship is going to be a good one,' he said softly.

Edward

Soot-stained fireplaces, watermarked walls, rats' nests in the ceilings. No wonder the *geometra* they had hired shook his head so much at the sight of it all that Edward was genuinely concerned he was going to strain his neck.

There was no way he would try to camp out in the house, as Elise had. They might have shored up the part of ceiling that was most in danger of collapse before Gino flew home to Sydney, but even so he wasn't tempted to rough it. And soon the place would be mantled in plaster dust and wood shavings, noisy with hammers and power tools, and entirely unliveable, at least Edward hoped so.

Because he loved the *trullo*, he had asked to stay on there for the summer, hoping Donna Carmela might do him a deal, but she couldn't give him more than a few extra days as there were new guests arriving. If only the town's hotel wasn't closed and boarded up. There were other places to stay in the valley but everything seemed expensive. Besides Edward knew it would be preferable to be in Montenello, especially once the contractors got to work. He had a feeling the roof would be rebuilt, the bathrooms re-plumbed and the frescoes repainted a whole lot faster with him on the scene.

The person to turn to was surely the mayor's assistant. He had lived here his whole life and seemed to know everyone. Edward and Gino had often bumped into him as they wandered the town and always found him friendly and helpful. But now he seemed elusive. At the Town Hall they said he was taking a day off work. There was no sign of him in the usual places – the *trattoria*, the bar, milling about in the piazza, at the tiny post office or the *salumeria*. And Edward had no idea where he lived.

He would have liked to ask around but Edward was hindered by his lack of Italian. Already he was seeing how difficult it was going to be without Gino here. Considering his options, he ordered a cappuccino, standing at the bar and sipping it, because that was what the locals seemed to do.

The cook from the nearby *trattoria* was beside him, smoking a cigarette and chatting to the bartender.

'Excuse me, do you speak English?' Edward asked her, interrupting.

'Yes.'

'Ah OK, you wouldn't happen to know where Augusto lives, would you?'

'Yes,' she repeated, her tone suspicious. 'You are a friend of the girl next door, the one in the *pasticceria*, is this to do with her?'

'Cecilia? No, why would it be?' Edward was taken aback. 'I was hoping Augusto might be able to help me with something. I need advice.'

'Oh yes.' She still sounded chilly. 'And where is your other friend, the one that comes from Montenello, aren't you always with him?'

'He's had to go home,' replied Edward, wondering why she seemed so mistrusting. Could this be an example of what Gino feared, a quiet resistance to who they were?

'But he is coming back?' she asked.

'Yes, in a few weeks' time, hopefully.'

'Thank God or I think Augusto would have a heart attack.' She rolled her eyes. 'He is so proud of himself for bringing one of Montenello's sons home. This scheme was his idea, you know, not the mayor's at all. He is very forward thinking, eh, Renzo?'

The barman nodded and, reaching for a paper serviette, began scrawling something.

'He is drawing you a map,' the cook told Edward. 'Augusto's place is difficult to find. But you should text him first and say you are on your way. Let me give you his number.'

'Thanks so much,' said Edward, feeling guilty at having misjudged her. 'Actually, I'm looking for accommodation in Montenello. A room I can rent or an apartment, just while the renovation is going on.'

The barman murmured something, speaking fast and low, in what might have been English or Italian. The cook gave a shrug.

'Ask Augusto then, he always likes to help people.'

Edward's text to the mayor's assistant brought a favourable response and so he tried to follow the semi-legible map along a series of lanes twisting steeply down one side of the mountain until, hopelessly lost, he had to send more texts pleading for guidance. He might have given up on the plan to pay a visit in person, except there was something else now he wanted to discuss with Augusto.

Eventually, it became clear that he had already passed the old man's door twice. It was set into the wall of a plain house with ivy climbing over its rough stone all the way to the mossy terracotta roof. Like so many places here it was impossible to tell from the outside whether it was lived in or abandoned.

Inside all was neat and carefully curated. Augusto showed him round its rooms proudly, drawing his attention to the shelves of records alongside the turntable and sleek Bose speakers in his living room. 'I love music. I have the streaming now of course, the Spotify, but I prefer my records,' he said.

Edward agreed with him. 'Gino and I have a record collection at home. We love jazz.'

'Ah yes, I have some Ronny Jordan and Miles Davis, but I prefer rock: Rolling Stones, Fleetwood Mac, Bruce Springsteen.'

They sat together for a while in the small room lined with shelves, talking about music, finding some tastes in common and others that differed. Augusto played him a live recording of Lou Reed from the 1970s, turning up the volume loud, tapping his feet and nodding his head.

'But I haven't offered you a coffee,' he apologised once the track had finished. 'I have so few visitors nowadays I have forgotten what is expected.'

'That's fine, I've just had one at the bar and actually I came to ask for your help.' Edward explained how he was searching for somewhere to live while the renovation was underway, preferably furnished and not a dump because Gino wouldn't stand for that, but it didn't have to be five-star either. 'I was hoping you might be able to make some suggestions.'

'Of course, of course.' Augusto nodded. 'But it will be best to look in the valley, there are plenty of places there. Or if you prefer to be in the mountains there is an *agriturismo* not too long a drive away, a very nice farm where they will also cook your meals. I can email you all the details.'

'I really wanted to stay in Montenello. Would you mind asking round for me? I'm limited by my lack of Italian.'

'You must learn,' said Augusto. 'There are many language courses on the Internet. This is how I improved my English and it is quite good now, yes?'

'It's excellent,' Edward told him. 'And I'll definitely do that but I have to be out of the *trullo* in a few days so my first priority is to find another place to stay.'

'Search in the valley,' Augusto repeated. 'There are some very nice houses with private pools. You and Gino will like them. I can send some suggestions.'

'Thanks, that would be great, and the *agriturismo* too if it's the only option nearby.'

'Is there anything else I can help you with?' Augusto asked, brightly.

'There is something I wanted to ask you about,' Edward admitted. 'I know that it was you who chose our application to buy a house here and I wondered why we stood out. At that point you weren't aware that Gino's family was from Montenello so was it just that he was Italian?'

Augusto shook his head. 'Not really, there were others that applied who had Italian families.'

'What then?'

The old man was thumbing through a through a shelf of records, choosing another track to play. 'The process is confidential, of course. But we are friends now,' he mused, before announcing, 'I chose you for diversity. It is very important nowadays. I wanted a gay couple here. I was hoping also to have more nationalities and cultures but then the mayor made his choice and with the fourth house there was this big problem, so ...'

'Do you think we are the only gay men in this town?' Edward asked him.

'Perhaps ... I couldn't say for sure.' Augusto was still searching through his music collection.

'Had you ever thought that might cause an issue? That there might be people here who won't welcome us?'

'Why?' Now Augusto did look up, sounding genuinely puzzled.

'Religious beliefs, prejudice, old-fashioned ideas they were brought up with, fear of anyone who is different ... there are all sorts of reasons they might prefer us not to be here.'

'If so, those people need to change, move with the times,' said Augusto, resolutely. 'They are being ridiculous.'

'True, but Gino and I—'

'This town has chosen you. We will smooth your path to residency, speed up your applications for building permits and help with whatever you don't understand about our systems and customs. You are welcome.'

'I hope so.' Edward wanted to believe it was true, although it struck him that the old man might be very naïve.

'Has anyone here made you feel as if you are not?'

'No,' he admitted. 'The opposite is true so far.'

'Of course.' Augusto's phone pinged with a text. He squinted at its screen, complaining. 'Mamma mia, why are the words always so small.'

Edward showed him how to enlarge them and Augusto beamed a smile that only widened as he read his message. 'This is excellent news. Renzo must have heard of your accommodation problems. He has offered to rent you his apartment. It is above the bar so can be noisy, but he won't want too much for it.'

'Where will Renzo live if we're there?' wondered Edward.

'He says he will stay with Assunta; she is his half-sister and has a place nearby. So you see, a perfect solution. People here want to help; you are welcome, as I said.'

'If I head back to the bar right now do you he might let me take a look at the place?' Edward was hopeful this might be a solution.

'Of course.' Augusto had another record sleeve in his hand. 'But don't leave straight away. There is time for more music first. I have the Beatles ... Revolution, my favourite.'

Elise

At first Richard's absence felt like a reproach. There was the ladder he had borrowed propped against a wall, the paint missing on the wooden door he had been sanding, the new cuts on the jasmine he insisted on trimming back. Each time Elise's eyes fell on another change that he had made, she felt sorry and sad. Richard was kind, generous, loving: everything you were supposed to want in a man and yet she had thrown all of that away. She couldn't understand herself.

Still, it put her in a better mood knowing there was no one now to tell her how things should be done with this house, with her life. That she didn't have to argue for every choice she made. She began to see it would have been a mistake to try to go on any further with Richard. He was heading in his own direction; this was where she needed to be.

And then there was Salvio. He was a different person – so much bolder, more impressive – but Elise didn't want to rush from one man to another, as much as she liked him. Even if his kisses had left her dazed and holding back from more had been an effort, particularly when he walked her home the evening of the welcome ceremony, arms linked, faces shadowed.

Elise needed to feel like an independent woman, not someone who thought she must always have a man at her side. And so she woke alone every day in her makeshift bed, made her own plans, battled with the power company who were so slow providing her with electricity, found a builder to come and look at her roof, rode her Vespa wherever she went, ate what she wanted, slept when she felt like it.

Today was her birthday and she was taking herself out for lunch. She would sit at a table in the *trattoria*, order a glass of wine and a bowl of something delicious, enjoy the food and her own company.

She liked the small restaurant with its too-close tables and bright ceramics on the walls. She liked the owner Assunta with her comfortably round body and the way she marched from her kitchen to tell you gruffly what she was cooking. And how the wine came in small earthenware carafes, misshapen as a school art project, and the food arrived on orange patterned plates they might have been using since the 1970s.

At first Elise felt self-conscious, sipping on her wine, the only customer with no one seated opposite. She fiddled with her phone, checking Instagram and looking round for podcasts she might enjoy at some point. But then the food arrived and she didn't want to distract herself from a single mouthful. Handmade macaroni in a sweet-sour meaty sauce rich with tomato. She ate appreciatively, soaking up the remains of the sauce with thick slices of coarse bread, finishing her wine as she listened to the hum of talk around her, trying to pick out the few Italian words she was starting to recognise.

She lingered over a coffee, too strong to drink without a little sugar stirred through. There was no point hurrying because everything in Montenello paused at this time of the afternoon. The *salumeria* was closed so she couldn't buy her cheese and prosciutto until later, the roofer wasn't likely to answer his phone, even the shops in Borgo del Colle wouldn't open their doors again for a few hours. Elise had found this annoying at first, never seeming to get her timing right, but she was beginning to ease into it.

With lunch over, she headed out into the bright day. Passing the *pasticceria*, there was the buttery warm-sugar smell of baking and Elise couldn't resist poking her head inside.

'Hello, Cecilia?' she called. 'Are you open?'

The cabinets were empty so it didn't seem likely, but the air was all sweetness. 'Hello?' she called again.

Cecilia appeared, red-cheeked and flour-dusted. 'Oh it's you,' she said. 'What do you want?'

Elise wondered if she knew how curt she sounded. 'I was hoping to buy some cakes. It's my birthday so I'd like to treat myself.'

'No, I'm still experimenting and this morning has been a disaster. My cannoli shells keep breaking because they're so thin but if I make them thicker they're chewy. Perhaps I just won't bother because it's such a hassle but then people like them so ...' Cecilia paused. 'Shit. Sorry, I should have said "happy birthday", shouldn't I?'

'That's OK, I'm not making a big deal of it.'

'I do have some cannoli shells that have survived. I'll fill a couple now and you can tell me what you think.'

Cecilia invited her into the space she had converted into a kitchen. It was filled with ovens and open shelves stacked with equipment, and there were long stretches of gleaming stainless steel.

'Wow,' admired Elise.

'I know, right. Back in her day my nonna wouldn't have had half this stuff. But I want my *pasticceria* to be really special, and she left me some money so this is how I've spent it.'

Elise watched as she filled the crisp shells with creamy, vanilla-laced ricotta, piping in the mixture carefully then dipping each end in crushed pistachios and finishing with a shower of icing sugar.

'They're best eaten straight away, before the shell has time to go soggy.'

Biting in, the cannoli snapping beneath her teeth and her mouth filling with sweetness and cream, Elise sighed with pleasure. 'Oh, that is the best thing ever. You have to serve these, they're too good not to.'

Cecilia tasted one and sighed quietly too, but with resignation rather than enjoyment. 'Yeah, you're right. And I'll need to do smaller ones as well because the idea is to sell miniature cakes by the kilo. I'll just have to keep trying to get them right. If they're not perfect it's not worth bothering.'

'It seems a lot of work,' Elise remarked.

'Try a baba next.' Cecilia was pulling out a tray of golden mushroom-shaped cakes.

Elise tasted the yeasty sponge infused with the sharpness of limoncello.

'Taste one of the rum-soaked ones as well.'

'So good.' Elise licked the sticky syrup from her fingers. 'Did your grandmother know you were going to come here and reopen the family business?'

'No, and she wouldn't have approved; neither does my father. It seems everyone is dead set against me being here.' Cecilia said it with an impatient roll of her eyes. 'Not that I'd ever let them stop me.'

'Why would they want to stop you?' wondered Elise.

'The family left Montenello in a hurry all those years ago; there was some big drama. I used to dream of bringing my nonna back, but the past was the past as far as she was concerned.'

Cecilia produced another sample of her baking – tiny chocolate tarts studded with shards of crystallised orange peel – insisting Elise try one despite being too full already. Then she began clearing up cake crumbs and spilt sugar.

'My nonna was the only one who ever understood me. Now I want to understand her, and opening this *pasticceria* seems the best way. I'm going to walk in her shoes.'

It was the first time Elise had glimpsed any softness in Cecilia. Usually she came across as so focused and entirely unsentimental.

'Let me show you what I'm going to do with the shop,'

she was saying now, leading Elise out of the kitchen again. 'This is the cabinet Gino designed. There's space here for larger pastries, the mini ones in the middle, and then over there I'll have a display of bomboniere – little silk bags and decorative boxes of sugared almonds. I'm going to install an old-fashioned cash register and find someone in the village to come and help serve behind the counter because my Italian is pretty limited.'

Elise was envious. 'You've got it all worked out.'

'It's something I've wanted to do for a long time; I've put a lot of thought into it.'

'I've done the opposite: rushed in without really thinking things through,' Elise said ruefully.

'You must have a plan, though?'

'Not really, I'm just hoping I can give my house a makeover before I run out of money and then I don't know. Probably I'll head home and find another teaching job.'

'Is that what you want?'

'No, I'd prefer to stay here.'

'Then you should do that.' Cecilia told her, uncompromisingly.

'But my career ... I did all that training ... my parents would be so disappointed ...' Elise tailed off.

'It's your life, not theirs. If you want to stay in Italy then start a new career.'

'I suppose I could teach English here,' said Elise. 'I'm sure that's a possibility.'

'You could do all sorts of things.'

Teaching was the safest option; that was mostly why Elise had kept going. It meant money in the bank every month, it meant bills got paid and no one had to worry.

'There have got to be lots of opportunities for tourism in a place like Montenello,' pointed out Cecilia. 'It's undiscovered, authentic, full of character. Just come up with a great idea and get on with it. What's stopping you?'

'You may be right.' Elise looked round at the *pasticceria*, imagining how it would look in a few days' time, the cabinet filled with sweet treats and people crowding in to buy them. 'Thanks ... for the cake and the advice. You've given me something to think about.'

'Any time,' Cecilia told her. 'Oh yeah, and happy birthday.'

Turning for home Elise passed the old fruit seller sitting beside the fountain, still dry despite Salvio's determination to get the water flowing. She thought about him with all his ambition and drive to improve Montenello, thought about Cecilia too, and how she could be more like them.

She would need to dream up an idea, dare to take a risk and work incredibly hard for a while, but other people managed all that. High-strung on sugar, Elise kept thinking. What did this town need that she could give it?

Montenello

Salvio ought to have been pleased. Ever since the welcome ceremony he had been showered in congratulations. Now he was poised to continue finding owners for more of the town's unwanted houses; this was the success he had been hoping for: Montenello's rebirth had truly begun.

Nevertheless, each morning he made the walk to the Town Hall on leaden feet and forced himself through each hour at his desk. He had taken to clicking onto Elise's file on the computer, just to look at her picture. It felt good to rest his eyes on her for a few moments. He tried to focus solely on her face, but Salvio never succeeded in completely filtering out the man beside her. Richard. On that Sunday afternoon before he appeared on the scene, all had been going so well. Since that day something had shifted. Elise was more distantly friendly now; less like the girl who had kissed him.

Idly, Salvio started reading through her application again. She and Richard had described themselves as a young couple keen to take the next step in their lives and become home-owners, writing of their difficulties with property at home so pricey but their determination they would manage it some way or another. There had been so many similar emails at the time. Nothing about this one had stood out, only Elise and the way her eyes seemed to gaze straight from the picture and into his. It was a holiday snap, taken on a beach, and it can't have been warm because she was bundled into the scarf he had seen her wearing once or twice when she first arrived. Perhaps there had been a brisk breeze that day, which was why her cheeks seemed to glow so radiantly and her flaxen hair looked tangled.

Salvio could have kept staring but there was work to get on with. He went to close the file then suddenly realised the significance of the date of birth Elise had given them. It was today, her birthday. He wondered how was she celebrating. Was someone making a fuss, showering her in gifts and treats? Salvio hoped she wasn't alone.

He knew what his mother would say. Sitting in his office staring at her photograph wasn't getting him anywhere. He was the one who ought to be making a fuss.

Salvio looked up from his computer screen. 'Augusto, is there any Prosecco left over from the other night?'

'Of course.'

'I'm going to take a bottle. I've just realised it's Elise Hartman's birthday.'

'And flowers, you must also take flowers. A posy of wildflowers tied with a ribbon, and a note, handwritten.' Augusto sounded very certain.

Salvio stared at him. 'It's just a small gift from me as mayor.'

'But that is what women like, unless they have changed a lot since I was your age, and I doubt it.' Augusto was smiling into the middle distance. 'Flowers you have spent time picking, surprises, personal gestures, not a bottle of Prosecco you happen to have in the fridge.'

'I suppose I had better go and find flowers then.'

'Talk to Assunta, she always grows a few in her garden among the herbs and vegetables. She may be able to help you with ribbon too. Simple but pretty, that is the way. Nothing too impressive.'

Salvio stood at the jasmine-covered doorway, holding the spray of flowers he had managed to gather and bind with a scrap of ribbon. He hoped to charm Elise. To remind her of

284

how it felt in that moment she had leaned across and been the one to kiss him.

He knocked and waited, telling himself he wasn't nervous. Moments later she opened the door, caught by surprise, a little flushed as she took the flowers from him.

'I just realised it's your birthday,' he said, not wanting to admit he had been staring at her application file, and quickly adding 'I'm not sure if you have a vase to put those in.'

She invited him into the house and he noticed she had been busy sanding woodwork and filling cracks in walls. As she arranged the flowers in an empty jar, he peeked into each of the rooms.

'I've found a builder to fix the roof,' she called. 'And I think he's going to widen a couple of the windows for me too. But I'm doing as much as I can myself to try and save money. Richard left me some tools.'

'That was nice of him.' Salvio wasn't interested in talking about her boyfriend. 'And the kitchen and bathroom, what will you do there? Have you any ideas yet?'

'Too many ideas,' Elise admitted. 'There is so much to decide on and everything needs hours of research – taps, light fittings, even the style of power socket. It doesn't help that I have to keep going over to Mimi's place to charge my phone. I'm not sure why it's been so hard to get the power turned on.'

'You still don't have any electricity?' Salvio was dismayed. 'And you're sleeping here alone? You should have told me. I will see what I can do.'

'Would you? Thanks.'

'You must tell me if there's anything you need help with.' Salvio eased the cork from the Prosecco. 'Don't struggle on alone.'

'I'm kind of enjoying it, though. It's a challenge. And I like the fact I get to decide everything myself.

'You're very independent,' murmured Salvio, wishing she wasn't, that she needed him more.

Elise watched as he poured Prosecco into the flutes he had brought along. 'Can I talk to you about an idea I've had?' she asked. 'The more I think about it the more excited I feel.'

'Is it to do with the house?'

'Sort of ... I want to live here rather than rent it out, which means I need to find a way to make a living in Montenello.'

At last here was something to encourage Salvio; she was looking to a future in this town, close to him. 'You could teach, start an English school,' he suggested, enthusiastically. 'Perhaps not here, but in Borgo del Colle.'

'I keep thinking about something we talked about once. You told me you wanted to officiate at a civil wedding, like mayors in other Italian towns.' Elise hesitated for a moment. 'What if I could make it happen?'

Salvio couldn't understand what she meant. There was no one in town showing the slightest sign they meant to get married. 'But how?'

'I was looking online before my phone went flat. Lots of people want to have a wedding in Italy. They go to Tuscany, Venice, Rome, Umbria, all sorts of places, Why not Montenello in that beautiful chamber where we had the welcome ceremony?' She was energised, talking more quickly now. 'Couples would come with lots of guests and stay for up to a week. They'd need a planner, someone to help book accommodation, suggest restaurants and day trips, sort paperwork and every detail of the ceremony. So many friends of mine have married in the last few years so I know what makes a good wedding – I've even helped to organise a couple. Why shouldn't I start up a business?'

Salvio was in favour of any plan that kept Elise here. But he saw straight away this one had other merits. 'Tourism,' he breathed the word.

'Exactly.' She nodded. 'Destination weddings.'

'But this isn't Venice or Rome, it is just a simple town on a mountain. Would they really come?'

'We love it here, why wouldn't other people? As soon as I've recharged my phone, I'm going to do loads more research.'

'Come over to my place.' Salvio was already set on helping her in any way he could. 'We can use my laptop, do this together.'

The walk from her house was a short one and they made it with Prosecco flutes in their hands, feeling giddy although they had barely taken a sip.

They finished the entire bottle in the time spent looking at websites that were promoting the romance of a wedding in a Tuscan castle, on a terrace above Lake Como, inside a frescoed palazzo in Volterra or a cathedral in Amalfi. Salvio wondered how Montenello could compare to any of these settings. For Elise's plan to succeed she would have to offer couple something different. She was going need his help.

'This is the kind of initiative the *comune* should be involved in,' he told her. 'We must work very closely on it. Perhaps we might even be able to find some funding.'

'Really?' She sounded pleased. 'Because the website is going to be so important. Look at this one for dream weddings in Tuscany; the photography is beautiful. I've no clue what it would cost to design something like it but I'm pretty sure I can't afford it.'

Their heads were close, almost touching, and Salvio wished she would look up from the screen. But Elise was too caught up in this new idea.

'When Gino and Edward finish restoring their house it would be perfect for receptions and parties,' she was saying. 'And there are lots of locations for wedding photographs. Imagine the old tower at the top of the hill – so moody and atmospheric. I must get up there for a walk some time. I've never really had a proper look at it.'

'We should go now,' suggested Salvio, wanting to distract her and remembering something Augusto had said about that tower. 'It's such a lovely evening and we can watch the sunset. Don't you need a break?'

'I suppose so,' she agreed.

'We'll talk about your plan some more along the way.'

Together they scaled the steep streets, dreaming up ideas, worrying over practicalities. How would they find the right suppliers? Could Cecilia make wedding cakes? What about flowers, catering and music?

As they reached the tower Elise paused, awed by its ruined beauty. 'What's the history of this place?'

'I'm not sure how old it is, but it must have once been a lookout. From the very top you can view the countryside all around. Would you like to go and see?'

'Isn't it locked?'

'I don't see why it would be.' Salvio tried the door and sure enough it opened with a creak of its rusty hinges. 'We'll go carefully, though. I'm not sure how safe it is.'

He led the way up a spiral staircase, up uneven stone steps that seemed to climb and climb. Reaching an opening, he took Elise's hand and helped her out onto the ramparts. Over the low parapet was the view, as impressive as he had promised.

'Beautiful,' said Elise.

'This is where the young people of Montenello used to come with their lovers, that is what Augusto says. So it has a long history of romance.'

'How perfect.' Still holding onto his hand, she looked towards the distant blue of the hills. 'I love it here.'

Leaning down, Salvio touched his lips to hers, the most tentative of kisses. When she started to respond he felt a tremor run through him. He wanted her so much. And it seemed she wanted him too.

Up there, far above the rest of the world, their bodies met

and they began pulling open clothes, unfastening, unzipping, tearing into each other. Opening his eyes, Salvio saw Elise's face against the sky and for a moment it felt as if they were flying.

'No, stop.' She gasped the words, pulling free of him, turning away, tidying her clothes and smoothing her hair.

Salvio was half-dazed. 'I'm sorry, I thought you wanted—'

'I did, I do ... but it's all happening too fast.' Turning back, Elise reached a hand to his face. 'I really like you, Salvio, but now isn't the right time. I've just come out of a big relationship and there are so many things I want to do – sort my house, start my business. I can't rush into anything else.'

The irony wasn't lost on Salvio. He recalled saying something similar to girlfriends in the past. It pained him now to think about it.

'What if we take things very slowly?'

'I'm not sure I trust us to.' She smiled. 'When Richard was here I realised I need some time by myself. How else will I ever know what I'm capable of, or even what I really want?'

Salvio thought of Augusto. Once he had been up on this tower with a girl he loved and then let her slip away, all these years later still regretting his mistake. Salvio didn't want to be like that. He wouldn't give up so easily.

'Elise, let me have your hand again, please,' he said. 'Just for a moment.'

Clinging tightly to her, he took them closer to the edge, towards a section of the crumbling parapet overlooking the whole of Montenello as it stretched away down the mountainside.

'Impressive, isn't it,' said Salvio. 'I couldn't believe my luck when I was elected as its mayor. It seemed my chance to prove myself, to be a big success.'

'And you have been,' she told him.

'It might seem that way.' Still holding her hand, Salvio

turned his back on the town. 'But now I see that I haven't been successful at any of the things that matter. I don't want to lose you, Elise. So I'm going to keep hoping you change your mind. Will that be OK?'

There was a moment of silence, with only the sound of the wind and the cry of a bird overhead. And then Elise reached up and kissed him lightly on the cheek. 'I think it will be fine.'

Mimi

There was a special gathering of the Silver Divorcees to celebrate her being back. Not at an Italian place this time, because Mimi was craving spice. She was also desperate to escape from the closing down of her old life. Packing things into boxes, deciding what to let go and how much to keep, dealing with Glenn, who for some reason needed to scrutinise every last item and discuss when it was bought and which of them it rightfully belonged to. Even though Mimi told him time and time again he should take whatever he wanted, Glenn had decided things should be fair and equitable. Those were the two words he kept using. If she heard them again Mimi would scream. Actually, she might start screaming anyway. All of this was taking so long when all she wanted was to get on a plane and fly back to Italy.

At least she got to see her friends again. Sinead, Jayne and Dottie were waiting for her in the Indian restaurant, its walls lined with bright silks and the air heady with the scent of curry. They had ordered a creamy dhal, a rich lamb dish laced with cardamom, chicken bright with green chilli and coriander, green beans strewn with a confetti of fresh coconut, soft pillows of naan bread, garlicky prawns. Too much food and wine around a table lit by candles as the conversation and laughter grew louder.

Everyone had news to share. Sinead was considering an eye-lift, Jayne had found a new job with a better salary, Dottie had booked a river cruise. But it was Mimi they wanted to hear about, half in envy, half surprise. They demanded to see photographs of the house and town, and Mimi found herself doing most of the talking.

There were lots of questions. Dottie didn't understand how Mimi would be able to work from Italy. She imagined an illustrator at an easel with paints and was astonished to hear so much was now done on computer. Sinead was worried she might feel too isolated since she didn't speak the language. Jayne wanted to know if there were any men in Montenello with potential.

'That's not what I'm there for,' insisted Mimi.

Jayne was sceptical. 'Surely you want to have some fun?'

Sinead in agreement: 'Yes, you can't stay single for ever.'

Dottie, as always, a little more prim. 'Don't you miss ... intimacy?'

'I've got my renovation to focus on,' Mimi said, defensively. 'The important thing is I've made some friends already. There's a gorgeous gay couple from Sydney and a lovely young girl from Bristol and the mayor's mother is a lot of fun. Oh, and my architect seems great. He's promised things won't get too stressful, that he'll take care of all the problems.'

Jayne groaned. 'Please tell me there will be builders, hot sexy Italian ones who will strip off their shirts and wear tiny shorts when the weather is hot.'

'I've only met one builder so far and I think I'd prefer him with his shirt on.'

'What's the architect like then?' asked Dottie. 'Is he single?'

'Do you know, I think he might be. Not that he's said anything, I just get a feeling.'

They all leapt on that. Why did she think so? What had he said? And what was he like? Sinead demanded to know his name then immediately googled him, finding an old photo of Alessandro with blacker hair and more defined cheekbones.

'Excuse me.' She held up the phone so they could all see the screen. 'Is this not a man with potential?'

'He's my architect,' pointed out Mimi. 'We need to have a professional relationship.'

Even Dottie rolled her eyes at that. Jayne threw a crumpled serviette at her and Sinead's eyes searched her face. 'You like him,' she said. 'Don't you?'

'Well, I—'

'Just let me make sure I've got this right,' interrupted Jayne. 'He's nice-looking, has a good job, is potentially single and wants to take care of all your problems. What's not to like?'

Sinead ordered more wine, overfilling all their glasses, although Mimi tried to refuse because she knew she'd had enough. There was a meeting with the estate agent in the morning and then Glenn was insisting on taking her for lunch and was likely to deliver a lecture.

'You like this Alessandro guy,' Sinead repeated.

'Maybe I do,' conceded Mimi.

'OK, so how are you going to handle things?'

'I'll look at his plans for the house and hopefully get things moving with the refurbishment.'

'Really? Is that all?

'Yes, I think so.' Mimi sipped more wine, even though she hadn't meant to. She thought of Alessandro, so calm in the way he moved through the world, and then Glenn, always twitchy and demanding during all those years of their marriage.

'Who knows though? If I can move to Italy, buy a house and build a swimming pool who knows what else might happen.' Mimi looked at the circle of faces staring back at her. Their expressions were admiring, disbelieving, intrigued.

'Out of all of us I never thought you'd be the one to do something like this,' said Sinead.

'Neither did I,' admitted Mimi, 'never for a moment.'

Mimi had managed all the things she wanted. Spent lots of time with Otis and Ben, spoiling them with lunches and shopping trips. Caught up with friends, packed up personal possessions and whatever Glenn insisted it was only fair she took. Met with the estate agent, signed a lot of documents and lunched with her agent. Finally she had met with her lawyer, who assured her it wouldn't take long to finalise the divorce since both of them were consenting. And now she was dreaming of Italy again.

Glenn was furious; he kept saying she needed to see the process of the house sale through to the finish. Ignoring him, Mimi went ahead and booked her flight. It really wasn't necessary for her to be there. He was bound to want everything done his way and she was pleased to leave him to it.

She said goodbye to England as the plane took off, to a patchwork of green fields and a sludgy blue sky disappearing beneath a cover of cloud. It amazed her how much of her old life seemed to have happened to someone else. Had she really been so unhappy when Glenn walked out? All those tears shed as she contemplated going on without him, how panicked she had been, how lost and lonely. Looking in the mirror it was a jolt at times to see nothing about her had visibly altered, beyond a few more wrinkles and a thicker band of grey showing in her hair. That worried her a little. Was the change only an illusion? It was good that she hadn't stayed in London any longer. She might have returned to being her old sad self again.

Summer had settled in while she was away from Italy. She shrugged off her cardigan the moment the plane landed. Wheeling an overlarge suitcase behind her, she hurried to catch her bus. She couldn't wait to be home again.

Alessandro was there to pick her up in Borgo del Colle. She had heard from him almost every day while she was away. Often he had queries about the house or updates on the plans, but there were times he had texted simply to say hello and ask how Mimi was. When he offered to come and meet her bus, he mentioned a few things they needed to talk through, but seemed in no hurry to get to them now she was here.

Instead, as he drove Alessandro listened while she spoke. Mimi told him about her work and the children's book she was thinking about, not only the illustrations this time, she wanted to try writing. He didn't say much in response, but she watched his profile as he focused on the road ahead, and saw he was paying attention.

'It's Montenello that's inspired me, all the stories of the curse,' she explained. 'I've been thinking about it while I've been away. I almost have the whole thing in my head.'

'Why did you never write stories before?' Alessandro asked.

'I'm not sure. Perhaps I never had an idea that was good enough.' Mimi knew it wasn't true. There were plenty of ideas but until now she had been prepared to let them slip away. 'Or maybe I wasn't very confident.'

'And now you are?'

'If I'm ever going to try it, now is the time.'

As the roads narrowed and grew steeper, they set to discussing the house, running through a few details Mimi needed to decide on. There was some brief talk about using reclaimed stone to restore the walls and the need to reconfigure the upstairs rooms to accommodate another bathroom. But Alessandro seemed more interested in telling her about all the small ways Montenello had changed in the time she had been away.

The *pasticceria* had opened and you had to get there early because the best cakes sold out fast. People were coming from miles around purely for the cannoli, which he could confirm were very good, as he had eaten several. The town seemed fuller, with even more people in the bar and the *trattoria* always busy. There was a rumour someone had bought the hotel and was planning to reopen it, although Alessandro wasn't certain that was true. And the fruit stall in the piazza seemed to have shut down.

'What a shame. That old man sold the most delicious apples, I always bought a few whenever I went past,' said Mimi.

Rounding a corner and seeing Montenello crowning the mountaintop, she couldn't keep the smile from her face. 'It all looks exactly the same from here. I'm so happy to be home.'

'I wondered if you would go back to England and decide this was a mistake,' admitted Alessandro. 'All this time working on your plans I've been concerned you might email to say you were changing your mind.'

'Absolutely not,' she promised.

'Italy feels like home already?'

'It's where I want to be. Does that make it home?'

'I believe it does,' said Alessandro.

He drove over the causeway and through Montenello's tight streets with a sureness Mimi lacked. She promised herself she would buy a car, a small one, and keep driving it until she no longer feared scraping against a wall or skimming past a hands-breadth away from someone's front door. She would do other things: start learning Italian, invite friends over for dinner. Mimi was going to throw herself into this new life of hers. She was ready for all of it.

As the car drew up by her front door, she turned to Alessandro. 'Will you come in?' she asked.

His eyes met hers and there was that brief half smile. 'Do you want me to?'

'Yes,' she said simply.

Alessandro's smile widened, crinkling the fine lines of his face, reaching his eyes. 'Then I would love to,' he told her.

Edward

Edward was convinced Renzo was watching him; he wasn't imagining it. Glancing up while drinking a morning coffee or an *aperitivo* in the bar, he would feel sure Renzo's eyes had been on him only a moment before. And once, while walking across the piazza, Edward had noticed him staring out the window, following his progress.

He was a quiet man, so reticent it had taken Edward a while to realise he understood a fair amount of English. He seemed to spend nearly every waking hour in the bar. His apartment above, the one Edward had rented, was spartan to say the least. There were few books, no pictures on the walls, the bed was bone-punishingly hard and the kitchen barely equipped at all. While it was clean and convenient, Edward found himself living more in the bar below, taking his laptop down and using it as his office.

It wasn't long before he noticed how the place was a part of other people's habits. The same faces could be seen at the same time every day. There was the group of old men with an unspoken right to the far table where they played cards for hours. The cook from the *trattoria* always arrived mid-morning, drank two coffees, smoked three cigarettes, and talked at Renzo the entire time, not seeming to need a response. Most days Elise would appear – Edward often saw her having coffee with the mayor. Augusto came and went and spent a lot of time standing about in the piazza. There were other locals he was starting to recognise, they seemed to accept him as a new part of their daily life, offering a *buongiorno* or *buona sera* as they headed in and out. Most were gruff but friendly; only Renzo seemed curious.

Often there were small kindnesses. Wordlessly, Renzo might set down a plate of biscotti beside Edward's laptop while he was busy with something he was writing. He poured generous glasses of wine, refusing any payment with a shy gesture and shake of his head. Returning to the apartment one afternoon Edward had found a vase of sunflowers only Renzo could have left for him.

Edward found himself curious too. While Renzo was making coffee or clearing tables he did his share of watching. Mainly what he noticed was how much the bartender was trying not to be noticed. Everything about him seemed unremarkable. He spoke to Edward very little: there had only really been that one exchange when they were agreeing on the rent for the apartment and even then it was brief and to the point.

Now, though, there was a reason to talk again because Edward wanted to organise a party. He had been in two minds about it at first, concerned Gino wouldn't approve of the plan. Then he decided to stop worrying. Wasn't it time for them to start celebrating who they were? Wasn't it the reason they had been chosen to come to Montenello in the first place?

There was always a lull in the afternoons, when the card players went home for their naps and the bar tended to quieten. Around then Renzo would lean in his doorway for a while, letting the sun touch his face, staring out at the piazza, deep in his own thoughts. Today Edward interrupted them.

'Renzo, can I ask a favour?' he asked, speaking slowly and clearly to be sure he was understood.

The bartender gave a guarded nod of his head.

'The day after Gino is due back is our anniversary.' In truth, they didn't know the exact date, but had staked out a claim to that one and always marked it with some kind

298

of celebration. 'I expect he'll be really jet-lagged so I just want to have a little afternoon party – Prosecco, cake, a few friends – and I wondered if you'd mind us holding it in the bar?'

Renzo nodded his agreement, his expression unchanging.

'Obviously, we'd want you to supply the Prosecco,' Edward continued. 'And I was hoping if you weren't too busy you might join us for a glass or two.'

Now Renzo's face registered surprise. He looked at Edward, for once making eye contact, if only for a few moments. 'Thank you,' he said in English.

Edward smiled. 'I just need to talk to Cecilia about the cake and we're sorted. She'll be coming, hopefully, and I thought I'd invite the mayor, Mimi, Elise, Augusto and possibly one or two others. Is that OK?'

Edward hadn't expected any more than the restrained nod he received from Renzo. 'Great,' he said. 'I might see about that cake then.'

Since the *pasticceria* had opened there hadn't been much chance to catch up with Cecilia. There was a line out the door some mornings and by mid-afternoon she had closed up, retreating upstairs shattered. Last time Edward was in there, buying some of his favourite rum-soused little sponge cakes, she had admitted to never having worked so hard in her life, and was talking about getting help with the baking. Edward hoped she was going to say yes to a cake for him and Gino.

When he walked in, he had the usual sense of pride at how great the place looked. That extraordinary cabinet Gino had designed, the simple whitewashed walls they had painted together, the abundance of sugary treats. He knew the rooms upstairs were still dingy, and didn't envy Cecilia having to sleep in one, but down here was lovely.

'I'm about to close and don't have any baba left,' Cecilia told him, as brusque as ever.

'Actually, I wanted to ask you about something.'

'Oh God, not you too.' Now she sounded hostile.

'I'm sorry, have I come at a bad time?' Edward was taken aback.

'I know he's my grandfather, OK? And that he wants to talk to me, build bridges, blah, blah. The mayor has told me that, even his mother tried to have a word – as if I didn't know already. The man's name is on my father's birth certificate, I can google, I'm not stupid. Does that answer your question?'

'Erm, sorry?' Edward was hopelessly confused. 'Who are you talking about?'

'Augusto, of course. He's out there right now, look. He used to pretend to be talking to the guy who sold apples. But now he's disappeared and there's Augusto still hanging about and waiting.'

'He's your grandfather?' Edward was struggling to piece things together.

'Is that not what you came to speak to me about?' She bit her lip. 'Shit. Sorry.'

Edward glanced out the window and saw Augusto sitting on a bench beneath the statue of Garibaldi. It was a favourite spot for the older men of Montenello, but usually groups of them gathered there together, and he looked lonely and sad all alone.

'Augusto is your grandfather? But Cecilia, you should talk to him.'

'Why would I want to do that?'

'Because he's family?'

Cecilia narrowed her eyes. 'I keep asking myself why my nonna left this town and never came back. Why she never married, or even had another boyfriend as far as I know. Something bad must have happened here. I think that old man broke her heart.'

'Look, I don't know what he might have done in the past

300

but Augusto's a really nice guy, funny, interesting, kind ...'
Faced down by her sternness, Edward finished weakly. 'He likes rock music.'

'Good for him.' She slammed down a tray and started clearing away leftover cakes.

'I don't really understand.' Edward was losing patience. 'I mean, presumably you came here in the first place because you were looking for your family's connection to Montenello. Well, he's out there wanting to meet you, and you're too angry to go to him?'

Crumbs scattered as Cecilia crammed cakes onto the tray. 'He broke my nonna's heart, I'm sure of it,' she repeated.

'Maybe you should listen to his side of the story. Relationships are complicated; nothing is ever as straightforward as it seems. Trust me, I've been in one for a long time. I've nearly broken Gino's heart and he's given mine a pretty good denting in the past.'

Cecilia sighed. 'That's sort of what the mayor's mother said. She's not one for taking no for answer either.'

'But don't you want to talk to him? Hear what he's got to say? Aren't you wondering?'

'Maybe I am,' she admitted.

'Then what are you waiting for?'

'I've come this far, all the way from Canada. He can cross that bit of the piazza to reach me. It's not too much to expect.'

'Maybe you could give him some sort of sign that you're not going to throw cake at his head when he walks in the door. Because you're kind of scary, you know, Cecilia.'

'I'm not scary, I'm just tired, very tired.' Again she sighed. 'What did you come in here for anyway?'

'It's not important, I can talk to you about it another time.'

'Oh, for God's sake.' She was exasperated.

'I wondered if you'd make a cake for mine and Gino's anniversary, something special,' Edward said hurriedly.

'Yeah sure,' she agreed immediately. 'It's the least I can do after the way you guys helped me. But do you have a picture of the kind of thing you'd like? Because I don't have the time or energy to be creative at the moment but I'm sure I can copy.'

'Thanks, I'll have a look for some ideas.' Edward glanced out of the window to see Augusto was still there. 'What about him? He's very old. There might not be much time for you to get to know him.'

'I know, I know.' Cecilia began wrapping a coconut cake in paper, neatly folding down the edges, pressing them tightly. 'Take this; I'm sure he likes them. Towards the end my nonna started talking. I know all kinds of things about him.'

'OK.' Edward took the small package from her. 'He's a nice guy, I hope she told you that, he's lovely.'

He was aware of being watched again as he left the *pasticceria*. Renzo's eyes were following him as walked over to the old man on the bench and held out Cecilia's offering.

'She asked me to give you this.'

'Really?' As Augusto took the cake, it seemed to Edward he looked frailer and thinner than ever. 'She wishes me to have it?'

He nodded. 'She wants to talk. You should go to her.'

'Now? It will be all right?'

'Yes, I think so.'

Edward stood beside the bench as Augusto made his slow, stiff-hipped way across the stretch of flagstones, waiting for a while after he had gone inside. There were no raised voices, no flying cakes, just two people on either side of a counter hesitantly talking to each other.

Relieved, he made his way back to the bar where Renzo was still leaning in the doorway.

'Thank you,' the bartender said again, holding his gaze a little longer this time. 'Thank you very much.'

Elise

The noise of the sander had been the soundtrack of Elise's week. As she stood in a cloud of dusty air, stripping back the paint from her wooden shutters, she kept reminding herself things could be worse. That decaying mansion with all its many windows – imagine tackling such a huge project alone! She was more than grateful knowing it was Edward and Gino's problem now. Her small place was enough and already she was pouring money into it. New fittings for the bathroom, kitchen cabinets, floor tiles, tins of paint – it was fun doing the shopping, but the bills were mounting.

At least her power had been switched on at last. Her biggest problem now was getting a tradesman to turn up. The builder kept postponing his appointment to inspect her roof, the electrician wasn't answering his phone, the plumber had started work then disappeared for several days, leaving Elise without a shower or washbasin. Yet mystifyingly each time she walked past Edward's and Gino's house, the place was a hive of activity – men up on the roof or rushing in and out with tools in their hands, the sound of grinding, sawing and hammering.

'How are you doing it?' she asked Edward, joining him at his usual table in the bar early one morning. 'Are you paying double time or something?'

'Don't ask me, it's Gino. He's been orchestrating the whole thing from Sydney and I've no idea what he's saying but more people keep arriving and the guy we hired, the *geometra*, seems to be in a state of semi-permanent shock. I don't think he's ever experienced anything like it.'

Elise laughed. 'I wish I had a Gino in my life,' she admitted. 'Even when I managed to get the plumber to turn up he was so easily distracted. He spent fifteen minutes telling me how to make proper Italian coffee – apparently you mix sugar in with the grounds and then pile them into a huge pyramid in the Moka so it's very strong but you only drink a tiny cup, just in case you were wondering.'

'Thanks but I have my own barista here.' Edward nodded towards Renzo.

Elise realised she felt envious. It was all very well being independent, but everyone needed some support. If not for Salvio, she wasn't sure she would be coping. He was the lightness in every day. Most mornings he found time to slip away from work and join her for coffee. In the evenings they might meet again for a drink and several times he had cooked for her – although his repertoire was limited, the dishes Donna Carmela had taught him were always delicious. He never fiddled with his phone or watched TV while she was talking. And she was losing count of all the ways he was helping her.

It was Salvio who made her see she was going to have to do some teaching until she could get her business off the ground. He had even come up with a couple of clients who would pay decent money, cash in hand, to learn English. And he was making good on his promise to try and seek funding from the *comune* so she could develop a website.

But everything took so much time and seemed so difficult. Just researching wedding suppliers and finding out what they offered and charged was a mission. In the evenings, Elise was trying to improve her Italian. Each day was busy and full, and there was so much work ahead of her.

'Has Gino always been so good at getting things done?' she asked Edward as she nibbled at a crunchy sweet biscuit she had taken from a plate on his table.

'Yeah, but the thing you need to know about Gino is that

he's obsessive. He didn't want to come to Italy and buying a house here was the last thing on his mind. Now it's happened and he's like a hunting dog on the scent of his prey: he can't think of anything else. I get calls from him at all hours, I've no idea when he's sleeping, and he bombards me with emails every time he has a new idea, which is all the time.'

Edward sounded fondly exasperated, as if he wouldn't want Gino any other way, even if it did drive him crazy. Elise knew they had been together for a long time. She wondered what it must be like to spend all those years with one person, and if she would ever manage it.

'How did you get him to buy the house if he wasn't keen?' Elise swiped another biscuit. She hadn't been eating properly and realised she was hungry.

'Emotional blackmail, mainly.' Edward pushed the plate towards her. 'Here, have the rest of these. Renzo keeps bringing them over, and they're too hard to resist.'

'But Gino's glad now that he did it?'

'I think he wants to buy up the whole town. He's already wondering about the hotel. He told me to break in and take pictures of the interior.'

'Is he serious? Do you think you actually might buy it?'

'How would I know? I may have started this but I'm not in control any more. Gino's back in a few days' time, and all bets are off.'

'It would be fantastic if you did. The town might be needing some accommodation.'

Elise started to tell him about her plans for a wedding business. He was only the second person she had fully explained the idea to and she watched his face carefully for a reaction.

'It sounds like it could work,' he encouraged her. 'You should talk to Gino, actually. He's good at all that stuff around profit margins. He'll help you do a business plan. I can't promise he's going to provide a hotel for your wedding guests, though. He may just be doing this to torture me.'

'Do you really think so?'

'I'm not sure.' He looked thoughtful. 'It can be hard to live with, you know, this level of focus. But at times it can make life interesting.'

Edward bought her a coffee and another plate of biscuits. 'The breakfast of champions,' he said, watching her eat.

'I don't have anything to cook on,' she admitted. 'Mostly I live on snacks. And I have to wash myself with a bowl of hot water and a flannel. At least I've got a toilet for now.'

'You're not planning to live there the whole time it's being renovated?' He sounded horrified.

'That's the idea.' Elise couldn't afford to throw away money on rent. 'It's not so bad though.'

'There's a spare room in my little apartment above the bar, why don't you come and stay?'

'Oh no, I couldn't—'

'Gino will hardly notice you're there. He'll be so occupied at the house, bossing people around. And the apartment is basic but it's fine.'

'Are you're sure?' As much as anything, Elise thought it would be great to have the company.

'I'll check with Renzo but I'm certain he won't mind. He seems pretty easy-going.'

Almost everybody had someone, Elise realised. The men stood about the piazza in clusters, the women shopped for food together. People sat outside their front doors and talked to their neighbours as they shelled peas for supper. Often Elise saw older couples walking the streets, grey-headed, shoulders stooped, holding on to each other for balance over the uneven flagstones, moving very slowly. No one wanted to be alone.

'Thanks so much, I really appreciate it,' she told him. 'Hopefully it won't be too long. It's not like there's that much work to do at my place, I've just got to get people to turn up.'

'It'll happen eventually,' Edward promised her. 'Don't lose heart, and don't expect to keep pace with Gino. He's phenomenal when he really gets going.'

On her way out of the bar, Elise noticed Mimi sitting at one of the outdoor tables of the *trattoria*. She was having lunch with her architect – again. Elise had spotted them there at least three times before and suspected there might be more going on than discussing renovations. She felt pleased for Mimi who was kind and had seemed a bit lonely.

Elise started to turn for home, to the dust and din of her renovation, but she had been working hard for days now and needed some quiet and empty time. So changing her mind, she walked for a while instead with no real destination in mind. Her feet took her upwards past the crumbling hotel that Gino seemed interested in and on all the way to the tower.

Finding the door still unlocked, Elise couldn't resist going inside. She climbed the winding spiral staircase and carefully out onto the ramparts. It was such a clear day that she could see for miles across the plains and standing there alone, gazing at all that empty space surrounding her, Elise thought about the last time she had been here. She touched her fingers to her lips, remembering Salvio's hot, urgent kisses. Why had she stopped him? Partly because it felt disloyal to want another man so much when Richard was only just gone. Or because of some idea she'd had about proving her independence. But wasn't she doing that now, day after day with a sander and hammer in her hand, with the new directions she was taking, all the big changes and ambitious plans?

Elise turned and looked down over the town. Her eyes searched until she picked out the roofline of the Town Hall, its flags barely fluttering in the light breeze. Salvio would be there right now. She pictured him at his desk, head bent as he frowned over some tricky task, and found herself smiling at the image. He was becoming her very best friend in this new life she was making.

It was true: everyone needed somebody.

Montenello

Salvio had noticed Augusto was taking more and more time away from the office. First there were the hours he had spent lingering in the piazza, hoping to make things right with his granddaughter. It was what had pushed Salvio to approach her in the end and an awkward conversation had ensued, with a prickly Cecilia making it very clear she was aware of the situation and didn't welcome any interference. Still, Salvio could only assume his fumbling attempt to engineer a reconciliation had helped in some way because now it seemed she and Augusto were friends and he was forever popping down to visit the *pasticceria* and returning with offerings she had sent over, broken cannoli shells or yesterday's pistachio cake.

This morning Augusto was missing again. Staring out of the window, Salvio spotted him at the centre of some sort of excitement in the piazza. Francesco Rossi had reappeared but, rather than his sad little stall, he had a flatbed truck loaded with crates of produce. Both he and Augusto were fluttering around, piling up shiny purple-coated aubergines, feathery fennel and green spines of celery. There was a lot of handshaking going on as people came by.

Giving up on the document he had been trying to concentrate on, Salvio decided to find out what was going on. By the time he made it down to the piazza a small queue had formed at the truck to buy produce.

'What do you think?' called Augusto, who was polishing its bonnet proudly as if it were a sports car. 'The latest addition to Montenello: fresh fruit and vegetables every day.'

'I hadn't realised that's what Signore Rossi was planning,' replied Salvio. 'It's great.'

'The truth is we have invested in this together,' Augusto admitted. 'Francesco saw how the town was starting to change. He wanted to be a part of this new exciting era. And I thought it could be a nice little business to keep me going in my retirement.'

Salvio gave him a sharp look. 'What retirement?'

'It is time.' Augusto said. 'Later I am going to give you my formal letter of resignation.'

Salvio had known this day would come eventually but still he tried to object. 'Augusto, I need you.'

'No you don't, not now; you are doing a fine job. You have vision and passion, an exciting future ahead of you. My mind is not as sharp as it was and I don't have so many more years. I want to make the most of my family now.' He glanced towards the *pasticceria*. 'I have a granddaughter to get to know ... and a son in Canada I have never met.'

'Are you sure about this, Augusto?'

The old man nodded.

'I am going to miss you so much.'

'But I will be here very often helping Francesco on the stall. In the mornings I will sell you your apple,' Augusto said, brightly. 'Also, I have another surprise, but not quite now, a little later.'

'Augusto, I will never be able to replace you.'

The old man smiled again. 'Of course, of course.'

For the next few hours Salvio managed to train his attention on work. There was a great deal to do. So many empty houses whose owners needed to be tracked down, and other places too, like the abandoned hotel he had been told was once so beautiful. Salvio wanted to see these buildings restored, to find exactly the right people to take them over. His scheme so far had been a success, but he couldn't afford to falter.

He was so absorbed he almost forgot about the anniversary party, rushing over to the bar at the last moment and finding them all gathered there around a stylish cake, frosted with buttercream and covered with white rosebuds. There was Edward and Gino, Augusto beside them with Cecilia, Mimi who was accompanied by her architect, Donna Carmela dressed in her feathery jacket, even Renzo holding a glass of Prosecco, and Elise, of course, her face shining out among them.

'You made it.' She offered him a glass of Prosecco.

'Only just.' Taking the drink, he kissed her cheek.

Edward made a speech, funny but also moving in places. He talked of Gino as his anchor in life, admitting that he hadn't always appreciated what it meant to be held so steady. Gino was quieter, more restrained, and didn't say much at all, only that he was glad to be back and hoping that some of his sisters, possibly even his parents, might soon follow.

'I thought I belonged in Sydney, but now I realise there's a part of me belongs here too. So I can only thank Edward for dragging me here kicking and screaming.'

Edward raised his glass. 'Here's to the future, you and me, together like always.'

'Together,' Gino repeated, and their glasses clinked. He made to move from the centre of the small circle of friends, but Edward stopped him.

'Before we eat the cake there's one more thing I wanted to say in front of everyone, all our new friends here in Montenello.' Edward hesitated then said more softly. 'Gino, will you marry me?'

Behind his back, Salvio was holding Elise's hand. He squeezed it now and she responded by clasping onto him more tightly while they waited for Gino's reply.

For a moment it seemed as if he was struggling to find the words. His eyes widened and his face paled. 'It's not legal for us here in Italy.'

'Then we do it at home once we've finished the renovation.'

'Do you really want to? Is it so important after all these years?'

'I think it is.'

'Then yes, I'll be your husband, Edward. Nothing would make me happier.'

There were cheers and clapping, someone whistled and Augusto's eyes were brimming. Once his assistant had finished hugging the two men, Salvio did the same to calls of, '*Auguri, auguri*, congratulations.'

'If only the law was different, and I could marry you,' Salvio was regretful. 'I don't suppose you would consider a civil union instead?'

Edward shook his head. 'No, we've waited a long time for this and we're going to do it properly. Beach wedding ceremony, big party, all our friends and family. Hey, Gino?'

'Quiet wedding, intimate lunch,' countered Gino. 'But yes, we'll do it properly.'

No one wanted to cut the cake and spoil it, so Cecilia took the knife. 'Come on, people, cake is for eating, not just looking at. And this one is going to be amazing, because I made it.'

It was rich with dark chocolate and pistachio. Salvio shared his slice with Elise.

'Do you think I should make a speech?' he wondered quietly. 'Would it be appropriate?'

'No,' his mother hissed immediately.

'I'm sorry I missed your last speech at the welcome ceremony,' Elise told him.

'Apparently I was very boring and went on too long.'

'I don't believe you could ever be boring.'

Salvio looked at her. He had been true to his word and taken things slowly but it was getting harder. Twice now they had come so close to being together. All Salvio could hope was that the third time would be the last.

He took in the scene in front of him, this small group of people he and Augusto had brought together, all the love and happiness that had resulted. Surely anything was possible, if you had a dream and tried hard enough to make it happen.

Renzo was at the edge of the group talking to Edward and Gino, Mimi and her architect were standing extremely close, Cecilia was serving cake to his mother, Augusto was by the window looking jittery, Elise still holding Salvio's hand.

Suddenly, Augusto tapped his fork against a glass. 'Everybody, your attention please. You must all come outside. Montenello would like to wish a happy anniversary to our new friends Edward and Gino.'

They gathered in the piazza, milling about, waiting. Augusto seemed even more jittery and there was a moment when Salvio thought nothing was going to happen. Then at last there was a gurgling noise and the fountain came to life, the evening sun catching its jets of water so that they sparkled as they cascaded down over the scalloped edges of its three stone tiers.

Elise gasped. 'You did it.'

'Not me, it was all Augusto's work,' admitted Salvio.

'But you've achieved one of your goals, you've succeeded, so you should feel happy.'

'The fountain is beautiful and I'm pleased to see it working at last.' Salvio took her hand again, this time holding it against his chest rather than hidden behind his back. 'But you, Elise, you are what makes me happy.'

'You make me happy too.'

They stood together hand in hand, listening to the watery music of the fountain, barely aware of the townspeople flocking to the piazza to take a look at it.

'Do you think you might be ready to start rushing things now?' Salvio asked.

'I might be,' Elise agreed. 'Yes, definitely. I am.'

And there in the piazza, with half the town staring and

even his mother close by, they kissed each other, a deep, long kiss that had been well worth waiting for. Hearing people clapping, even a few cheers, Salvio hoped it was in appreciation of the fountain, although it didn't really matter. Nothing was going to stop them now.

Montenello ... one year later

It was a wedding day, the first Montenello had celebrated in many years. The groom looked handsome, the bride lovely in cream lace with a long veil that caught the breeze as the couple walked hand in hand down the steps of the Town Hall towards the fountain where they would pose for wedding pictures.

Salvio didn't think he had ever felt so proud. He knew Elise was nervous; she had been trembling earlier. But no one would guess it to look at her now: hair in a neat chignon, dressed in a pale pink suit, phone in one hand, she was marshalling the newlyweds and their guests for the photographer. Family of the bride, family of the groom, bridesmaids, flower girls – issuing instructions calmly and clearly with every detail of the day considered, confident she had organised a memorable occasion.

Mimi and Alessandro had been delightful first clients. For both it was a second wedding and what mattered most was to have the people they loved celebrating with them. All Alessandro's family was there, a great mob of them. Mimi's sons, smart in their suits and still a little shy with their new stepfather. Her English friends, a group of stylish older women, had instantly bonded with Donna Carmela, and were laughing together, tossing a fragrant confetti of dried flower petals over the couple as the camera clicked, capturing the moment.

As she stepped back to stand beside him, Salvio thought his mother seemed especially pleased with herself. 'Sometimes it is best to interfere in people's lives,' she declared with a smile.

'If you say so, Mamma,' he replied.

A little earlier, while Salvio was leading them through their vows in the wedding chamber, he had noticed that Mimi seemed nervous. Her cheeks pinked and she moved nearer Alessandro, reaching to his hand for reassurance. Now, as the fountain flowed behind them, she was smiling up at her new husband, one arm linked through his, kissing him a little self-consciously at the urging of the photographer, lifting her bouquet of rosebuds over their faces.

When the photographer had finished it would be time for Elise to lead the bridal party to Edward and Gino's house for the reception. The grand old home wasn't yet completely refurbished. There were still doors locked on rooms full of rubble and builder's mess. But the frescoed living areas had been restored and offered the perfect venue for an elegant party.

Gino was already there, fussing to make sure everything looked perfect. Meanwhile, Edward was busy shepherding his sister Tia and his parents who had come to Montenello for the summer. Salvio had seen them several times out and about in the town, lingering in the piazza and bar, eating lunch at the trattoria, the elderly couple looking like strangers and a little shaky at first, then gradually more like they belonged. Today they seemed overwhelmed to have been added to the guest list, but Mimi was too happy not to want to share this day with everyone and half the town had been invited.

As the guest numbers had grown, her modest plans turned more elaborate and Mimi thought of more and more ideas that seemed perfect if only they were possible. A harpist to play at the reception, a band to dance to later, fireworks once the light faded, a breakfast the next day beside her newly finished swimming pool. Alessandro had been pleased to indulge her and now Elise was making it all happen, quietly and efficiently. Salvio caught her eye, smiling encouragingly, and she gave him a quick smile in return.

'It will be your turn very soon,' his mother said, happily. 'I hope so anyway.'

This was the first wedding Elise had planned but there were many more to come. Her success was inspired by all the many older couples she was always seeing around the town. Montenello, the place with the longest marriages in Italy – who wouldn't want to share in a blessing like that? It was a clever marketing ploy. Word had spread and newspapers sent their photographers to take shots of frail husbands and wives arm in arm, sharing lunch in the *trattoria*, drinking coffee in Renzo's bar, making a *passeggiata* on a sunny afternoon. Salvio even found one article describing his town as 'Italy's village of love'.

It might be a while before Elise could take a break from organising other people's weddings and turn her attention to their own, something much smaller and much simpler than this one, with their closest family and friends. They were to be married by Salvio's new assistant, younger and more efficient than Augusto but not nearly as endearing. And afterwards they might hold their reception at Donna Carmela's restaurant, or cram into the small house Elise had transformed with its rustic stone walls and terracotta-flagged floors, and the entranceway covered with jasmine and strung with fairy lights.

For now, Elise was juggling bookings for the summer and the season ahead. Meanwhile, there were four more houses for Salvio to sell off. After much discussion with Augusto – who refused to be involved but couldn't help interfering – they decided to cast the net again and find a fresh set of applicants. Today, even as Salvio was standing in the piazza watching on proudly as Elise rearranged Mimi's veil and smoothed the flyaways of her hair, strangers in far corners of the world would be reading the advertisement.

Live your dream of Italy.

Here is your chance to buy your own home in southern Italy for less than the price of a cup of coffee. The picturesque mountain town of Montenello is selling off some of its historic buildings for just ONE EURO each. The only conditions are that purchasers must renovate their new home within the next three years and that they plan to contribute in a meaningful way to this small and friendly community.

To be considered as a future resident of Montenello contact the town's mayor, Salvio Valentini. Live your dream of Italy for just one euro.

Thank you ...

This is my eleventh novel and mostly I would like to thank whoever invented chocolate because I'm not sure I'd have managed a chapter without it.

But also for help with my ideas and research a big thank you to Maxwell Currie, Lesley and Noel Palmer, Sally Tagg, Sarah Tuck, Massimo Valentini of Puglia Paradise and Flavio Villani.

Thanks as always to everyone at my publishers Orion and Hachette but most especially my editors Clare Hey and Rebecca Saunders, and to Louise Sherwin-Stark, Melanee Winder, Alison Shucksmith, Tania Mackenzie-Cooke, Suzy Maddox-Kane, Sacha Beguely, Alainna Hadjigeorgiou and Jennifer Breslin.

As well as chocolate, also vital for my ongoing sanity is the wisdom of my agent Caroline Sheldon and publishing whizz Kevin Townsend, and the support of my very good friend and fellow writer Stacy Gregg, so thank you to them.

Thanks to all the wonderful booksellers out there – in particular the ones who have organised events for my previous novels - and a final big thanks to you, the readers. I hope this book took you to Italy.

*Two feuding families, two love stories
and a lot of delicious Italian food . . .*

Although settled in London, the Martinellis are a typical Italian family: fighting, eating and loving in equal measure. Now Pieta's sister is getting married and she will make the wedding gown. But she is distracted by a series of mysteries. Why is her father feuding with another Italian family? Why is her mother so troubled? And could the man she's always secretly cared for really be getting married to someone else?

As the wedding draws nearer, Pieta uncovers the secrets that have made her family what it is – and may stand between her and happiness . . .

'*The Italian Wedding*, a feast of food and love, a terrific read.'
Beattiesbookblog

'If your soul needs some nourishing, *The Italian Wedding* is a great pick.'
MiNDFOOD Magazine

'Nicky Pellegrino has crafted a feast not just for the mind but the mouth.'
boomerangbooks.com

'The elements of drama, history, romance and passion are layered, flavoured, tasted and left to simmer, not unlike the Italian recipes which are scattered throughout the book . . . I absolutely loved it!'
Stephanie Zajkowski, tvnz.co.nz

Luca Amore runs a cooking school in the Sicilian mountain town of Favio. He's taught many people how to cook the dishes passed down to him by generations of Amore women. As he readies himself for yet another course he expects it to be much like all the others. He will cook, he will take his clients to visit vineyards and olive groves, they will eat together, become friends, and then, after a fortnight, they will pack up and head home to whatever corner of the globe they came from.

But there is a surprise in store for Luca.

This time there are four women booked in to The Food of Love Cookery School. Each one is at a turning point in her life. Each one is looking for something more than new cooking skills from her time in Sicily. Luca doesn't realise it yet but this group of women is going to change his life. And for Moll, Tricia, Valerie and Poppy, after this journey, nothing will ever be the same.

'Nicky Pellegrino not only knows her Sicilian recipes and cooking traditions, she also keeps an immaculate beat throughout her tale.'
Sainsbury's Magazine

Nicky Pellegrino
Recipe for Life
Under Italian skies, a summer of passion and secrets . . .

Two women, one house – one at the beginning of her life, one nearing the end. Alice is in London, working in the kitchen of a top restaurant and determined to live life fast and to the full. Babetta is living in a lonely house in southern Italy and trying to hang on to the quiet life she has made for herself.

When the two women meet one summer life changes for both of them. This is a novel about what we run from, and the places that make us stop and consider. Drenched in sunshine, it's about friendship and growing up, food and love.

'A slice of pure sunshine'
Good Housekeeping

'An amazing book . . . it's a wonderful and enchanting read . . . one of those books you want to read and reread. It's endearing, entertaining and inspiring.'
Novelicious.com

'The author delivers not only on every sensory front – combining her love and knowledge of food with her passion for the Italian coast – but also with her energetic writing, layering every character with shades of darkness and believable charisma.'
The Australian Women's Weekly

*Imagine swapping your house for a stay in an Italian villa
and falling in love with the owner's life . . .*

Stella has life under control and that's the way she likes it. For 25 years she's been trusted assistant to a legendary fashion designer. But when her boss dies, suddenly everything she loves seems to vanish. Stella is lost – until one day she comes across a house swap website and sees a beautiful old villa in a southern Italian village. Could she really exchange her poky London flat for that?

What was intended as just a break becomes much more as Stella finds herself trying on a stranger's life. Can Stella overcome her grief and find her way into a new future?

'So much to love about this book. I love the way the food makes you salivate for Italy. I love the matrix of complicated women that interfere in each other's lives . . . Reading this felt like a welcome ticket to southern Italy'
STUFF.CO.NZ

'We love this book . . . absolutely delicious, like a warm hug on a sunny afternoon'
HOTBRANDSCOOLPLACES.COM

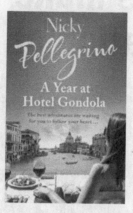

The best adventures are waiting for you to follow your heart . . .

Kat is an adventurer, a food writer who travels the world visiting far-flung places and eating unusual things. Now she is about to embark on her biggest adventure yet – a relationship.

She has fallen in love with an Italian man and is moving to live with him in Venice where she will help him run his small guesthouse, Hotel Gondola. Kat has lined up a book deal and will write about the first year of her new adventure, the food she eats, the recipes she collects, the people she meets, the man she doesn't really know all that well but is going to make a life with.

But as Kat ought to know by now, the thing about adventures is that they never go exactly the way you expect them to . . .

'Nicky Pellegrino goes from strength to strength and A Year at Hotel Gondola shows her skill in full flight . . . If you enjoy intelligent clear-eyed writing – and great recipes – this is the book for you'
NZ Herald

'Warm, engaging and truly delicious'
Rosanna Ley, author of *The Little Theatre by the Sea*

Help us make the next generation of readers

We – both author and publisher – hope you enjoyed this book.
We believe that you can become a reader at any time in your life,
but we'd love your help to give the next generation a head start.

Did you know that 9% of children don't have a book of their
own in their home, rising to 13% in disadvantaged families*?
We'd like to try to change that by asking you to consider the role
you could play in helping to build readers of the future.

We'd love you to think of sharing, borrowing, reading, buying or talking
about a book with a child in your life and spreading the love of reading.
We want to make sure the next generation continue to have access
to books, wherever they come from.

And if you would like to consider donating to charities that help
fund literacy projects, find out more at www.literacytrust.org.uk
and www.booktrust.org.uk.

Thank you.

*As reported by the National Literacy Trust